KOLDIS THE GREEN

BOOK 4 OF THE DRAGONWALL SERIES

MELISSA MITCHELL

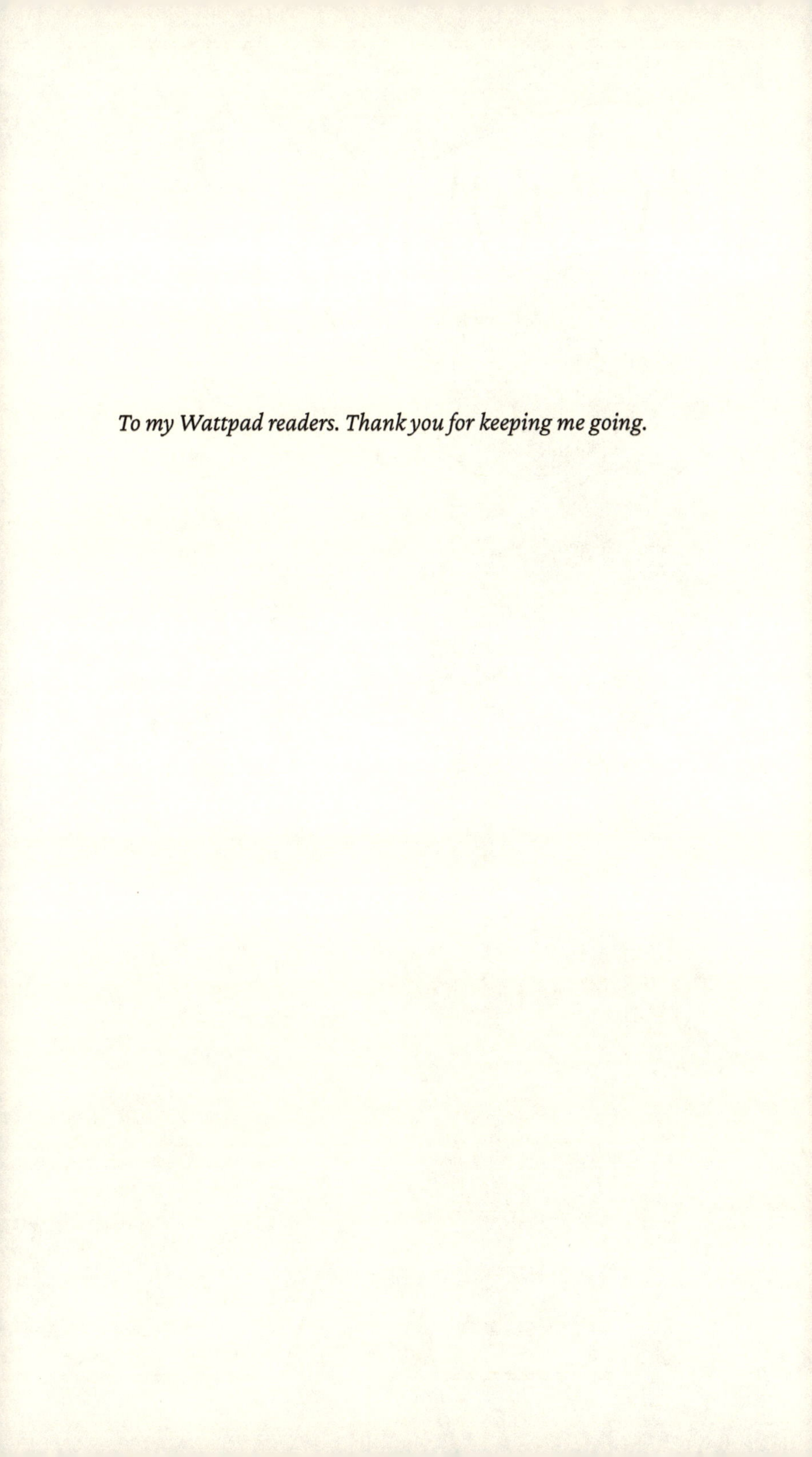

To my Wattpad readers. Thank you for keeping me going.

DRAGONWALL
Dragonfire Sea
Shadowkeep
Beln
Eagle Lake
Mistport
Redport
Squall's End
Three Horned Man
Scattered Islands
Kastali Dun
Bay of Bandu

Gate
Northedge
e Gable
Forest
Kaljah
astle
South Sea

PROLOGUE

The Gable Forest

Isabella parted the forest's foliage and stepped up among the roots of the massive king tree. After days of wandering, calling out in hopes that it would appear, here it was. A familiar sense of awareness washed over her, forcing an involuntary sigh of relief from her chest.

The moment was bittersweet.

She had traveled the forest alone. Klide had gone his own way. Their goodbye hadn't been easy, but he had his own life to live. The capital wasn't the place for a unicorn.

She leaned on her staff, craning her head to see the top of the tree disappear into the mist. It seemed bigger every time she saw it. Massive trunk, thick roots, bulky branches laden with foliage. With hands joined, not even ten people could span its circumference.

She blinked. Her surroundings were different from the last time. Always different. Always changing. The tree did not dwell in her plane of existence, but in one that required a certain mindset to reach. As such, it always appeared in a new location.

"Isabella." The voice was young and old, neither male nor

female, disembodied. It rumbled through her, sending chills over her skin, making her hair stand on end. *"I wondered if you would come."*

"Was there a choice?" A sense of foreboding pooled in her chest.

Vigilance had begged her to stay. Pleaded with her to refrain from this final pilgrimage. He feared more than she, that the king tree would exact vengeance for what she'd done. Despite the young drengr's anger towards her rash actions, he loved her. He would not see so much as a single hair upon her head harmed.

As if sensing her thoughts, the tree spoke again. *"I see you have chosen a new path. One that would take you away from the forest forever."*

"Dragonwall needs me, now more than ever. A monarchy in its infancy is an unstable thing."

"Indeed..." Silence and then— *"You disobeyed me, Isabella. Disobeyed what I asked of you. Do you deny it?"*

"I..." The heat of shame spread through her chest, but it quickly turned into defiance. *"I deny nothing. The dragons will get what they deserve, in time. I have ensured it."*

The roots of the tree rumbled. Several sprang free, only to dive back into the earth, like angry snakes. Like a furious animal pawing at the dirt. *"You have* condemned *them, Sprite Queen. That is not what we agreed upon. That is not what I asked of you."*

"Condemned them?!" A derisive laugh. *"Hardly! They will live long, happy lives. It was their choice to experience humanity. To embrace it. This is what they wanted."*

"And what of future generations?" The roots rumbled and roiled. *"Have you any idea how your treachery has tainted what was meant to bring balance?"* She opened and closed her mouth. *"Humph. I thought not. Long have I waited—since the Awakening, and even before —to bring balance to this world."*

She clenched her fists. Unclenched them. *"I have done exactly that. I brought balance, just as you asked. Dragons are an abomination. You should be praising my efforts, not condemning them. Eventually the beasts will disappear, and their cousins will follow. The world will return to what it was before the Awakening."*

"You mean when Asarlaí walked the earth, hunting your people? No. That was not balance and you know it." Anger emanated from the tree, sizzling through the air.

Isabella glanced about, growing fearful of the massive sentinel for the first time in her life. In all the years she'd ruled, all the times she'd sought its council, the tree had never displayed open emotion.

It did now.

"You disobeyed me," the tree repeated, as if reading her thoughts. *"You are no longer fit to rule your people. You are no longer fit to walk the paths of this forest. This place I created to keep your people safe. You must know. Surely, you must. I would have exiled you, even if you had come back with the intention of staying."*

The audacity shocked her. *"You would dare exile a queen? The birthright is mine! It belongs to me and me alone. A passing of the crown from oldest daughter to oldest daughter. As it has since the dawn of the spriten people."*

"Yes, it is true. The mantle belongs to you. In time, it would go to your oldest daughter. And then her oldest, and her oldest, until the end of time. But how can it be? You have disobeyed me, Isabella. The world will suffer because of what you have done. There must be a price for your disobedience. Balance isn't free."

A price. Balance. Yes, she had suspected as much. Somehow, deep down, she had. Just as Vigilance had warned against her coming. Yet, was that not why she had returned to the forest for the last time? To receive her punishment from the one true authority that governed her existence? To strike balance? To wipe clean the slate?

She sighed, resigned. *"I will hear it then—my price."*

Something of a bitter laugh sounded, rustling the tree's leaves. *"Are you not remorseful for what you have done?"*

"I will not apologize."

"Careful. Your pride will come at great cost, leaving you with nothing."

"Ha! You think it was my pride that urged me to make the choices I did? Who would have saved Dragonwall were it not for me? Who alone

was powerful or creative enough to take a force of nature and twist it into something new? Something better? The drengr would not exist. Everything I did, I did for the sake of saving this world from the Ice Clan. And you say it was my pride?! Bah!"

Another wave of anger rippled out into the air, churning the earth beneath her feet. She staggered backwards, clutching her chest. Pain shot through her. There and gone. A warning without words. It took everything to remain standing.

"Your rule is over, Isabella. You must leave the forest. It is time to lay down your staff."

She clenched her teeth and then—*"Fine!"* She glanced down at the staff in her hand before tossing the beautiful artifact—passed from her mother, and her mother's mother, and so on and so forth —against the tree's roots. Almost instantly, it disappeared, winking out of sight as if it had never been. She stared at the empty space a moment longer, eyes lingering. A profound loss settled over her, as if a part of her had gone missing, and she supposed that it had.

For long years, she had hoped to pass the staff along to her daughter. Yes, she knew she would have a daughter. That was how her bloodline worked. Always a first born daughter to continue ruling. Precious blood passed from one to the next.

She squared her shoulders. *"That is to be my price then? My staff?"*

"Is that what you believe?! ...Ignorant queen!" She jerked, as if slapped. *"You will pay a far greater price than that of a magical heirloom."*

"Then what?"

"I shall not tell you. You do not deserve an answer. But know this, it is not a price that can be paid today or even tomorrow. Perhaps not even a month or a year from now. Nonetheless, it is a price you will pay, Isabella." The words were a promise, filling her with foreboding. Her blood turned to ice. *"A day will come when you will know. And when that day comes...you will scream and weep for what you have lost. And perhaps then—only then—will you understand my wrath over what you have done. Now, be gone from here, and never ever return."*

The roots beneath her feet began to coil and twist. A cry sprang from her chest. She turned on her heel, stumbled, and fled. When she next glanced over her shoulder, the tree was gone.

CHAPTER 1

ARRIVING IN ESTERPINE

Esterpine

Claire held her breath as Esterpine came into view. It was just as she remembered. Beauty without words. Sparkling glass houses. Thick foliage. Vibrant colors. The scent of pine and earth and blossoms. She exhaled, feeling her shoulders relax. It felt like coming home, which both thrilled and terrified her.

The last time she'd been here seemed like an age ago, back when she carried two dragonstones and a message from Cyrus. It was the knowledge of Kane's existence that was so crucial. A greedy sorcerer who planned to bring Dragonwall to its knees. To plunge the kingdom into times similar to the days before dragons existed. Before the Awakening.

She'd traveled into Dragonwall with the sole intention of fulfilling a promise. She'd every intention of going back home afterward, back to her mundane life. She certainly hadn't planned to remain here. Hadn't planned to pit herself against a sorcerer.

Everything had changed, and she'd made another unbreakable promise, much like the first. One that couldn't be broken. Not unless she wanted to face a fate worse than death.

Gods! So much had happened. Now it wasn't just her promise that tied her to this kingdom. It was something much, much deeper. Dragonwall's King. A beast of a drengr known for his terrifying temper and scars. But nothing about King Talon was terrifying or beastly. Not to her. Not anymore. They were mates.

Mates.

That one word still clanged through her when she thought of it. Mates. Even the way it tasted on her tongue sent her stomach swooping.

"If you follow me, Lady Claire, I will take you to your quarters." One of her spriten envoys, Jandar, stopped momentarily, arm outstretched. She hesitated, looking over the scene before her, taking in the outskirts of the city. A city that felt so much a part of her. "The queen has prepared one of the largest suites in the palace for you and your...escorts."

Bodyguards—more like. Because Talon wouldn't dare send her alone. Wouldn't dare risk her safety.

The spriten envoys had met them at the edge of the forest, at Ellia Outpost, to guide them safely to the city. It was said that all outsiders who entered the Gable Forest were condemned to wandering and madness. The forest itself had layers upon layers of protection to keep intruders out. None could travel through its midst and find any of its hidden cities.

No one except her.

That had been the first sign of many that she wasn't simply human. Something more flowed through her veins. Sprite blood. And very likely the same blood as Princess Irelia, Dragonwall's long lost princess.

She glanced at the glass houses beneath the large tree roots before looking back at Jandar. "Can't I stay in one of those—like last time?" Jandar frowned, perhaps uncertain. Perhaps surprised by her hesitance. "Oh, never mind. It's fine. I'm sure what the queen has prepared will be...adequate." Jandar nodded. Behind her, Koldis snickered. She almost elbowed him to shut up.

Koldis was the shield that Talon had chosen to escort her. He had selected one of his prized six (now five, without Cyrus). It was yet another sign of how important she was to him. In fact, she hadn't made a single trip through Dragonwall without the presence of at least one shield, often two or three. That Talon was willing to give up his own protection for her sake both thrilled and worried her.

His shields were meant to keep him safe. He was already short one. Without ample protection, he was in greater danger. But something told her Talon was plenty capable of taking care of himself.

A thought nagged her. Perhaps she needed guards of her own. Something akin to a queen's guard—once she became Dragonwall's queen, of course. Or rather, *if* she became Dragonwall's queen. There was still the big *if*. Part of the reason for coming to Esterpine was to think about Talon's proposal. The thought of never traveling back to her own world, never saying goodbye to her parents and friends, worried the hell out of her. They were probably frantic in her absence. She couldn't bear to think of it.

"This way." Jandar held out an arm, still waiting for her. Hagen and Vaeril, their other two escorts, stepped aside, allowing her and her companions to pass. She led the procession into Esterpine, flanked by Koldis and the twenty pairs sent with them. Hagen, Jandar, and Vaeril kept close.

Her gown fluttered in the breeze. She had decided to wear one of the spriten gowns Talon had gifted her. She'd chosen the light blue one. Both the purple and silver gowns were also tucked in her pack. She had a feeling she would acquire many more whilst here, but she hadn't wanted to come unprepared. In fact, she had everything Talon had gifted her, including the beautiful forest tear she wore around her neck. It thrummed and pulsed, as it had the moment she'd entered the forest. She found her hand frequently going to it, zipping the pendant along its chain, especially now, as her nerves built and built.

The Crystal Palace came into view, towering above them with its tall spires. A rainbow sheen reflected off its walls, casting brilliant light outward. A bout of nausea struck her. Her hand went to her abdomen. She took deep breaths, working to overcome it. Even though this felt like coming home, there was also a wariness deep in her bones. It had struck at random times since entering the forest. As if...not all was well within the ancient trees. As if a dangerous darkness lurked.

She almost snorted. With a disgusting sorcerer like Kane trying to destroy the kingdom, perhaps the forest wasn't as immune as she'd once believed. How could it be?

"Can't say I'm happy to be back here," Koldis muttered, his voice low. This time she *did* elbow him. "What?" he hissed. "You can't honestly be excited about eating plant food for the foreseeable future."

"That's *not* the only thing they eat," she admonished, glancing at their guides. In truth, that was mostly all she'd seen them eat along their trip. But travel food was meant to be simple. She was certain the queen would have something more lavish laid out for them. Or so she hoped, because she had to agree with Koldis: plant food would hardly be sustainable for those drengr who traveled with them. Already, she was ravenous for a good feast.

Queen Jade appeared at the top of the wide palace stairs, as if summoned by Claire's thoughts. Beside her, a sprite with the dark blue hair stood at ease, legs shoulder width apart, hands clasped behind his back. He was the epitome of calm collection. Prince Feowen. She remembered him from before. But where was his sister? The mysterious Princess Taylynn? She glanced about. Other sprites formed a royal greeting party around the queen.

"Welcome home, Lady Claire." Queen Jade descended the remaining steps to meet her, grabbing her shoulders and ceremoniously kissing her left cheek and then her right, as if welcoming home family. Something about the gesture felt...*off.*

"Thank you, Your Majesty. And thank you for so graciously inviting me here to learn. For allowing my escorts to remain comfortably with me."

"Oh! Think nothing of it. You are one of us now, are you not? We would never deprive one of our own from the gifts so graciously given by the king tree. But come, you must be weary. I will show you to your suite." The queen flicked her gaze at their three guides, giving them a subtle nod. A dismissal. All three bowed and retreated, while Queen Jade wrapped an arm around her shoulders and ushered her up the remaining steps and into the Crystal Palace. The place that would be her new home for the foreseeable future.

Hours later, Claire and Koldis made their way down the palace stairs, eager to escape its confines. True to her word, the queen had given everyone comfortable accommodations—as comfortable as could be expected in a structure made of crystal—and excused herself shortly thereafter, granting them the freedom to explore Esterpine and encouraging them to make requests with the palace staff, should they need anything. Of course, the first thing she wanted to do was explore. She hadn't been allowed much time for it during her initial journey. Most of that time was spent recovering from the wound she'd suffered at the hands of the vodar. A wound that still plagued her from time to time, thanks to the permanent effects of the poison. She would always bear a thin, black line on her leg. A reminder.

A buzz of excitement skittered over her skin as she set foot on the plush mossy ground. A whole world awaited in the forests of Esterpine. A world full of possibility.

"Where to first, my queen?" Koldis stood with his arms crossed, watching her. He'd taken to using the pet title whenever possible, but only when they were alone. At first, she'd berated him for it. She was *not* Dragonwall's queen. Not yet, anyway. Still, he insisted on it, took pleasure in it, too, and not simply for the sake of teasing her. Perhaps after so many years without a queen, Talon's shields were genuinely thrilled. Which meant Koldis would go on using the title, if only to remind himself that she was real.

"Let's just walk," she decided. "I want to see everything. Including the unicorns. *Especially* the unicorns."

Koldis snorted.

She faced him, hands on her hips. "In case you've forgotten, unicorns don't exist in my world. I spent an entire lifetime believing they weren't real. So *excuse me* if I want to find one."

"Dragons don't exist in your world either."

"Yeah, well, you've seen one, you've seen them all."

"Oh! Is that how it works?" he scoffed, feigning irritation.

"Yeah. That's how it works." It wasn't. But she knew the words would poke at him. "Besides, unlike dragons, *unicorns* don't talk back."

He opened his mouth, paused, then said, "Fine, point taken."

"See? Come on." She grabbed his arm, looping her elbow through his to drag him along. A grin pulled at her lips, but she kept it hidden.

He allowed her to lead him away, muttering under his breath. Something that sounded a lot like a skewed impression of her saying, *Unicorns don't talk back.* And, *Good gods.*

She ignored him. After nearly a week spent flying by day, camping by night, plus an additional two traveling through the forest, they'd grown quite comfortable together.

Behind them, four of their escorts trailed. While most of the pairs had already been dismissed to do whatever they wished, Koldis insisted on retaining a few. "You're a queen now," he'd said behind closed doors. "It would be best to look as important as your new title suggests."

"Except no one knows about my new title, especially not here."

Koldis had simply shrugged and said, "Regardless, *my queen,* our king would expect it."

So she'd relented.

The two pairs trailing behind them—Aliah, Jorsid, Manir, and Mariam—were already familiar to her. Talon had sent all the same pairs who'd traveled with her into Celenore. She was glad. Though she felt a pang of sadness—and even guilt—when she thought about Hiondel and Lilly. She'd lost them during the fight, lost them because she hadn't acted quickly enough. She wasn't sure the guilt would ever fade. That's why she was here, after all. To master her spriten magic so that no one else died because of her lack of control.

She made her way through the city, still pulling Koldis along. Esterpine was exactly as she remembered. Yet, there was so much more to take in. Especially now that she saw herself in a new light, as sprite kin. This place was *in her blood*. She could feel it in a way that could only be explained by heritage. A connection that ran deep in her bones, to her very soul.

They stuck to the dirt paths, winding between the dwellings, meandering through the city's center. Large communal areas for eating, gathering, and markets were all there. The area for feasting was already abuzz. She lingered, watching as people rushed about. The thrill of attending one, or all of these events, left her body humming with excitement.

Her light blue gown proudly displayed both of her sprite markings with its gauzy, nearly transparent material. Fortunately, the material was thicker over the areas she wasn't interested in exposing. Even with the obvious glowing luminescent swirls, she still felt like an outsider as she passed beneath the watchful eyes of Esterpine's citizens. Some gazed at her with open shock and wide eyes. Others, mild curiosity. A few placed hands over their hearts and bowed deeply; she was almost certain outsiders did not normally receive greetings like this.

"You don't reckon they've seen paintings of their dear old queen Isabella, do you?" Koldis kept his voice low.

"Oh…" She hadn't thought of that. "Do you think that's why some of them look so shellshocked?"

"Well, you *are* a spitting image of her, aren't you?"

"I…yes. Except for my eyes."

"And don't sprites have much longer memories than the average person?" Koldis added.

"I would imagine so." A frown pulled her brows together. She hadn't considered what it might be like for them, seeing her. She'd been stuck in bed most of the last time she was here, except for the feast the night before they'd departed. Now she had sprite markings and an informal opportunity to truly interact with Esterpine's citizens. And if they *had* seen Isabella in paintings, then she could only imagine what her presence might do. While seeing her previously might have been a mere coincidence, with fresh luminescent marks, there could be no ignoring the obvious connection.

They made their way through the city until the dwellings thinned. It was here that Koldis stopped her, growing still. A moment later, she heard rustling and saw the foliage shudder. "I think you're about to get your wish," he mused, sounding bored as he stuffed his hands in the pockets of his trousers.

"A unicorn?" she asked. Hope bubbled in her chest.

"Mmm-hmm." His eyes were trained on the forest's growth. "It seems your presence has created a strong desire for acquaintance."

She frowned, glancing up at him. "I'm sure it's just curious."

"They."

"They?"

"There are four."

"How do you know—?" Her eyes widened, cutting off her question. The foliage parted. Pearlescent horns first, and then heads, followed by snow white bodies. Four sleek unicorns stepped out onto the dirt path looking straight at her, intelligent gazes filled with curiosity. They tossed their heads at the sight of her. One gave a whinny that could only be described as joyful. A smile split her lips.

"The first one you met spread word of your existence, last you were here," Koldis explained. "These are quite eager to meet you. If I'm not mistaken, they began searching for you as soon as you entered the city."

"Right. Says the unicorn whisperer?!" She snorted, lifting a questioning brow at him before taking a tentative step forward. "As if you could possibly know all that."

Koldis frowned, shrugging. "Go say hello. They won't hurt you."

She held his gaze a moment longer, trying to understand his expression before turning back to the sight before her. Further back, she heard her escorts whispering. They hadn't been in the forest before. So they'd never seen a unicorn. Let alone four.

Shrugging off Koldis's claims, she held out her hand. The unicorn in front stepped forward, head lowered, and nuzzled right into her palm. She sighed, suppressing a pleased giggle. She leaned to the side, looking at its body. "It's male," she announced.

"Obviously." As usual, Koldis feigned a lack of interest.

She looked at the other unicorns. Three females. They were all utterly beautiful. She held up her free hand, inviting a second forward. This one eagerly stepped up for pets. She laughed outright, letting the sound of her voice trickle through the trees. Ears pricked, twitching to listen. It was all the invitation they needed. The remaining two came forward, crowding in, each trying to gently nudge the other aside to earn her touch. She rubbed muzzles and heads, cooing, telling them how beautiful they were, laughing.

"You don't need a baby voice to speak with them, you know," Koldis huffed. "They understand normal adult words."

"Oh, quiet, you! Let me have my fun." She shot him a glare and he grinned at the sight of it. "Come on, Koldis, don't just stand there," she added, taunting. "You know you want to."

"Fine." He stepped forward, arm outstretched. One of the females glanced warily at him before looking back at her. "It's okay," she encouraged. "He doesn't bite. I promise. He likes to pretend he's big and scary, but there's a cuddly teddy bear lurking beneath those scales. Go and see."

The female must have understood perfectly, just as Koldis had claimed, because she tossed her head, snorted, then walked right up to him and nuzzled straight into his chest with an angled head to keep from skewering him with her horn. "Oof!" He dropped his hand and laughed, rubbing down the side of her body.

Claire invited the others forward too, until they made a merry party. The unicorns were plenty happy to receive pets. Before she knew it, they were all talking in calm voices, telling the creatures how beautiful they were.

The unicorns grew alert.

"Someone's coming," Koldis warned, and everyone stopped to listen.

"Ah! There you are, my lady." Prince Feowen emerged from the foliage. "I was sent to find you."

"Oh?" She turned. A moment later, a young woman emerged beside the prince. Claire's eyes narrowed. Surprise had her mouth opening. "*You're* not a sprite."

The woman looked just as surprised.

"Indeed, she is not. Lady Claire, may I introduce Jeanine?" Feowen stepped aside.

Jeanine. The name was familiar.

"It's a pleasure to meet you, my lady." Jeanine curtsied. She wore a tunic, vest, pants, boots, and a sword belt.

"Are you a..." A *what,* exactly? She didn't quite know. A soldier?

"She's a refugee, from Kaljah." At his words, Jeanine glared at Feowen. He noticed, and froze. Then a lazy smile pulled at the corners of his lips.

"I can answer for myself, thanks." Jeanine's tone was teasing, but she elbowed him aside and stepped forward. Claire watched with growing curiosity. If she wasn't mistaken, the sprite prince appeared rather fond of this human female, which was entirely unexpected.

"Feowen is correct, my lady. I fled Kaljah during the goblin attacks and brought what was left of my people with me. We have sought refuge here since. The queen and her people have been most gracious. I even had the distinct honor of meeting King Talon when he passed through." Everything clicked into place. Now she remembered where she'd heard the name. "His shield, too. Bedelth? We sparred together, actually. Me and Bedelth."

Koldis barked a laugh. "You and Bedelth?! Good gods. I hope you gave him a run for it."

A smile split Jeanine's lips and she lifted her chin. "Drew blood a couple of times."

Claire's eyes widened, immediately glancing down to the sword again.

"Good." Koldis sounded smug. "Perhaps you'd like to cross swords with another shield? For comparative purposes, of course. I always like a challenge." He winked.

Claire watched Feowen while Koldis spoke. Something passed over the prince's features. There and gone before she could make sense of it. Feowen cleared his throat. "Anyway, I was sent by my mother. A feast in your honor will be held tonight. Already, preparations are underway. The festivities will begin shortly, if you would like to return to the palace and freshen up? I can lead the way." It was now that his eyes flicked to the unicorns and he added in a soothing voice, "*Verah lyessa, mih vynahari.*"

The unicorns flicked their heads and retreated, disappearing almost as quickly as they'd appeared.

Claire's eyes widened. "Did you just...was that sprite language? Will I learn that while I'm here? For magic and...whatnot?"

Feowen held her gaze. "I think you will learn a great many things while you are here, Lady Claire." He glanced down at the mark exposed beneath her shielded breasts. "Now, if you will follow me? Let us return to the palace." He turned without waiting for an answer and disappeared into the foliage. Jeanine caught Claire's gaze and rolled her eyes at Feowen's lack of answer. They shared a secret smile before Jeanine also disappeared. Claire had no choice but to issue a silent command to the others before following.

Her stomach growled. She placed a hand over it to silence it. The time had come to see what Queen Jade considered an *honorable* feast. After the loaded welcome she'd received, something told her Queen Jade was *less* than honored to have her here.

CHAPTER 2
LORD MARQUIN

Esterpine

Claire found herself in the palace garden the morning after the feast. Queen Jade had requested they meet to discuss her training. Koldis trailed after her, along with two pairs, keeping a respectful distance. She hadn't expected a garden in the forest to be much different than the forest itself, but it was. It took her breath away.

Everywhere she looked there was something to gawk at. Fountains gushing with water for birds to frolic, elaborate pots sculpted into the shapes of animals filled with overflowing growth, trees grafted into intricate twisting archways. It was paradise.

The queen appeared, an unfamiliar male beside her. "Lady Claire! Welcome."

"Your Majesty."

The queen took her shoulders and gave her the same greeting as before. "You enjoyed the feast, I hope?"

"I did, thank you. It was perfect."

Much to her delight, there'd been music and dancing and a variety of foods: spiced bread, egg soufflés, vegetable medleys, seasoned potatoes, hard cheeses, custards, fruit pies, cakes, and more. She'd learned more names than she could ever remember. Jeanine had quickly found her, helping her to navigate the rigors of it. By bedtime, she'd all but collapsed into an exhausted, dreamless sleep.

Koldis roused her at dawn, insisting they resume their training. She managed to shrug him off, only to remember she was to meet Queen Jade after breakfast. That had her jumping out of bed and dressing for the day ahead.

"I am glad you enjoyed yourself," Queen Jade said, all smiles. "Now, I wanted to introduce you to Lord Marquin."

"Lady Claire." Lord Marquin bowed. He was half a head taller than she. It was impossible to gauge his age, since sprites were immortal. His skin was flawless, but his golden eyes were old and intelligent. Like most sprites, his features were angular and feline, his chin, the sharpest of all, which made him look inhuman. "It is a pleasure to meet you. I am honored that the queen has selected me for this task."

"Lord Marquin is a dear friend of mine," the queen said by way of explanation. "He has graciously agreed to assist you. Our magic is quite different to that of the drengr, as I am sure you have gleaned." Jade's eyes flicked to her markings.

"Yes, thank you. It is a pleasure to meet you, Lord Marquin. As you say, Your Majesty, I have never felt quite *comfortable* with drengr magic. But sprite magic..." She let the sentence go unfinished. Behind her, Koldis shuffled but said nothing. Thank the gods for that.

"I can assure you, Lord Marquin is accomplished. I can think of none better suited for such a task."

In looking at her new instructor, she believed it. Lord Marquin was dressed conservatively in a pair of knee length pants and a sheer white tunic, which hung loosely about his torso. She saw a plethora of glowing marks through the fabric covering his chest and arms. Badges that spoke of his abilities. She was certain they scrolled over his legs too. And probably in places she'd rather not picture.

"You do me a great honor, my queen." Lord Marquin placed a hand over his heart, offering his queen a respectful bow.

Queen Jade nodded before returning her gaze to Claire. "I will leave the two of you to work out the details of your training. I shall not interfere, but know that you may always come to me for anything at all, Lady Claire." Her tone said more than words could: She expected Claire to trust her, to tell her everything. Which only made her want to do the opposite. "Know that while you are here, you are family."

"I...thank you, Your Majesty." Claire curtsied and watched her go, turning back to Lord Marquin. Sprites were overly formal. More so than the courtiers of Kastali Dun. But she was not ill equipped or ill prepared. Desaree had trained her in court politics. She knew to tread carefully. Words could be weapons in settings such as these, just as smiles and jewels and anything else making a statement. Thus, she'd worn a mask ever since entering the forest—had cemented it into place with each feeling of unexpected unease that plagued her.

"Lord Marquin," she said, offering him a demure smile, "thank you again. I am eager to get started. I defer to your expertise regarding my training."

"Excellent." He eyed her up and down in a way that made her feel all too exposed. "Let us walk." He extended an arm. She took it, disguising her hesitance. Behind her, Koldis cleared his throat. "You may accompany us," Lord Marquin said over his shoulder, giving her shield permission. She bristled but said nothing.

They left the garden in silence. As soon as they began wandering through the city, Lord Marquin spoke again. "Everything in our forest is connected. The lifeblood we call living water spreads through our kingdom like veins, sustaining us, feeding us, preserving our immortality."

"From the king tree?"

"Yes. That is where it originates before flowing out into the world. Sprites, as you know, were not always this way. It is said our people were *Spirit Singers* once, who fled persecution and made a home here, beneath the shade of the tree."

She listened in eager silence as Lord Marquin recounted the history of the king tree and the first sprite. Some of it she already knew, but she listened anyway. Ellia had wandered far and wide, all alone, looking for a place to rest. A place she might call home. When she discovered a small oasis in the middle of a vast open grassland, she took shade beneath its large tree and drank from the water.

Sated, she began to sing a sad, sorrowful song. A song of her nomadic people displaced by the cruel tyranny of the asarlaí. The tree was pleased by her company but saddened by her song. When it asked her why she cried, she told it of her people's struggles. Eager for company, the tree bid her to return with them, to make the oasis their home.

She did, bringing the wandering tribes together. Beneath the tree's shade, they quenched their thirst and laughed, glad for the living water that now flowed through their veins. In joy of finding a new home, they linked hands and began to sing. As they sang, the lonely tree grew and grew and grew. Soon it was a king of a tree, stretching up to greet the heavens. But the tree was still alone, and the people who had settled beneath it did not wish for it to be lonely.

They sang again, and with the tree's help, companions sprouted from the ground, spreading across the land. Channels were cut deeply into the earth where living water extended to quench the thirst of the newly grown but hungry forest. Beneath the shade of its gables, the trees became home. But one tree would always reign supreme. The king tree was pleased by its new family and the people who took shelter beneath its branches. It gave the *Spirit Singers* a new name, welcoming them for all eternity.

"And so we dwell," Lord Marquin said. "But eternity is a long time. When we are ready, so too is our tree, to welcome us with open arms into its bosom where we may at last find peace."

Claire's eyes widened. "So it really is real—the king tree? It's not just a story?" She'd always believed it purely mythological.

"It is real, and when one is ready for death, one wanders into the forest and partakes of its fruit, falling into a soundless but peaceful sleep, to become part of the forest. Reborn in the trees and animals. It is said that all new trees are reincarnations of our people. The animals, flowers, bugs... We are everywhere."

She swallowed and glanced about, suddenly uneasy.

Lord Marquin laughed, a magical, light sound. "Never fear, Lady Claire. Though our forest is a living, breathing thing, I don't think the trees can be expected to speak." She nodded, remembering the sentient intelligence of the forest the first time she'd found her way to Esterpine. "Now..." Lord Marquin led her farther down an overgrown path. They had long since passed out of Esterpine. "Magic is a very personal thing for every sprite. No two marks are the same, though they can be very similar. Yet, for each kind of magic that is learned and then mastered, a mark is gained and evolves. Each mark is hard-earned, as I am sure you understand."

"Indeed, I do." She thought of everything she'd done to earn hers.

"Do you know how our people gain marks?" he asked. She thought at first he might be mocking her, but he appeared genuinely curious.

"They make journeys into the forest where they overcome difficulty and search for inner strength."

Lord Marquin looked pleased. "That is correct. The forest may be home, but it is an untamed thing. We do not have schools like the mages, where one goes and sits in a cramped library to learn diction and...*control*." He spoke the word like it was filthy. "Our magic is learned through experience, borrowed from our environment."

She liked the idea of learning-by-doing. Something nagged at her, though. Something Talon had said. Lord Marquin's explanation was not in agreement with what Princess Taylynn had mentioned to Talon. If she had to learn everything on her own, what was the point of a teacher?

"So I just...go in there for a while,"—she waved an arm towards the dense undergrowth—"and I come out with new abilities."

"If you are lucky." He hesitated. "Before even that, you should become comfortable with the forest. Our children, rare as they are, grow up here. This world flows through their veins before they ever set out on their own."

"And...how long are they gone?"

"Ah. It varies. A day. Five. A month. A year. As long as you wish to spend."

Her stomach flopped. She didn't have a year. But she could do a day. Or five. Or a month...if she had to. Though, the thought of wandering out into the trees for days on end didn't sit well.

"I should also mention," he said, "that these *journeys-of-self* must be done alone." He glanced at Koldis and the others behind her. "Learning stems from need. If you have someone protecting you, there won't be much need."

"That's fair."

"Now, as to the other glaring fact, you do not yet speak our language. That puts you at a disadvantage. Lessons in language and time spent within the forest will help a great deal. I propose that we meet each morning after breakfast to practice speaking our native tongue. It will be an opportunity for us to discuss what you learn from the forest during your...explorations. Afterward, I will release you for the day. I recommend you spend it wandering our paths. Do not go too far—not at first. But spend time outside the city. See what the forest wishes to show you. It has a way of being exactly what we need it to be...if you catch my meaning."

"I do. That sounds...reasonable."

"Good! Then follow me." He led her along a path that opened to a clearing and bid her to sit across from him where they began.

HOURS after she had finished with Lord Marquin—whose first name she'd discovered was Aolis—she ate a hurried meal with Koldis and a handful of her pairs. They ate in the large dining chamber of her apartment suite, which was the second largest in the palace. It seated nearly fifteen. The queen had informed Claire that she would take her breakfast and lunch in here, in the privacy of her quarters, unless otherwise invited to dine with the royal family. Dinners were done in the large clearing outside the palace. She was plenty happy with this arrangement.

With her brain like mush, she contentedly listened to the others talk about all the exploring they'd done that morning. Her pairs seemed at ease in their environment, despite the true nature of where they were. She wasn't sure the drengr and sprites would ever get over their age-old dislike, but at least their hosts remained polite, even if there was a fine line to it. When did politeness turn to disdain? Could sugar be so sweet it burned?

"You will want us with you when you venture out this afternoon?" Koldis asked. It was more of a forceful suggestion than an innocent question. She leaned back in her chair, sighing, contemplating what remained on her plate. She'd stuffed herself with bread, a vegetable medley, and potatoes.

"We would be happy to come along, my lady," Faedrol said, looking up. Beside him, Hannah smiled.

"I suppose you might as well." Though she was tempted to decline. "It isn't as if I'm going to master some monumental ability on my first day trekking through the forest."

"You never know," Koldis said, winking, but she sensed his relief. "Lord Marquin and I agree on one thing, at least."

"Which is?"

"You should better acquaint yourself with the forest before you venture off alone. I'm not sure how safe it is."

"That's the whole point, though, isn't it? That it's not safe?" She frowned. "And besides, it isn't like I'll get lost. Finding my way back is in my blood. *You* on the other hand..." She glanced at the rest of them. "Don't venture out very far alone or someone will need to find you." Nokin and Madeleine shifted uneasily. They'd already gone out that morning and hadn't returned until Faedrol realized they were missing. He told one of the palace attendants who sent a small rescue party after them. Sure enough, they'd wandered outside the city, far enough to get lost.

As they finished their meal, Koldis invited a couple of pairs to join them, then bid farewell to the rest. They set out into the afternoon light, though it was difficult to tell the time of day with the mists and trees blotting out the sky. Claire made a mental note: Ask Prince Feowen to take her up to the treetops and perhaps show her the way, so that she might venture up whenever she felt the need for open sky.

She picked a path she remembered from yesterday, the one that had taken her to the unicorns, and followed it. Koldis kept pace beside her, silent. Contemplative—

"Claire!" Jeanine rushed from an adjacent path, pausing briefly to eye her entourage. They exchanged a friendly greeting, though Jeanine was out of breath, like she'd been in a rush. "Please tell me you're getting out of the city for a little bit? Prince Feowen is driving me mad. I was hoping I might join you?"

She laughed. "He can't be that bad, can he? The prince?"

"You'd be surprised." Jeanine looked as if she wanted to say more, but stopped herself.

"Well, you might as well come along. We probably won't go far."

"No matter, I've got all the paths around Esterpine memorized."

Claire eyed her a moment, impressed. They began walking. This time Koldis took up a position just behind them.

"How do you keep from getting lost?" she wondered. Jeanine frowned, perhaps confused. "Wait...you haven't had any trouble finding your way back to the city?"

"Well...I don't go far. But...no."

"Hmm..." Interesting. She told Jeanine about Nokin and Madeleine, which only made Jeanine frown deeper—as if she'd never considered that getting lost might be possible. "Maybe it has to do with what they are," Claire mused, more to herself. "Being drengr, perhaps the forest sees them as more of a threat."

"Well, I'm certainly no threat," Jeanine said, laughing.

They continued to chat as they walked, discussing everything from Jeanine's village, to her adjustment to Esterpine. She didn't quite have the courage to ask about Prince Feowen, but she was sure it was a story Jeanine would be happy to tell, once they were closer friends.

Around them, the path grew more overgrown, but it never quite disappeared. Perhaps it would've if she'd been anyone else, but the forest knew her. She could sense it. A recognition that hummed beneath her skin. That same awareness she'd felt the last time she'd been here. The same sentient existence.

This time it was stronger. Something in the very air screamed in relief at her presence. As if her arrival had been long awaited and much needed. But why? And what would she find when she learned the answer?

CHAPTER 3
SICKNESS

Koldis followed after Claire and Jeanine. Their chatter was a calm sound at the forefront of his mind. He split his attention between their voices and his surroundings, careful to stay alert. He didn't trust this place. There was something...unwell about it. But he couldn't quite put his finger on it.

Everything around them was teaming with life. Thriving with happiness. Nothing looked amiss. Yet, an undercurrent of fear existed. As if waiting for something. But what?

He'd felt it the moment they entered, days ago. It was the same unease he'd felt months prior, when first venturing here. Only now, it felt worse, like a building pressure, a bubble about to pop. He wasn't sure what it was, but he didn't like it.

"And no one knows where the princess went?" Claire was saying. They were discussing Princess Taylynn, who'd apparently been absent for weeks.

"Not even Feowen," Jeanine said. "I'm told she goes off into the forest whenever she pleases and sometimes Feowen has to go find her."

"To earn more sprite marks?"

"Oh..." Jeanine fell quiet, uncertain. "I'm not sure."

A branch snapped and his shoulders tightened. The others continued like it was nothing. Perhaps it was simply in his nature to be wary. The drengr were not meant to dwell here in the forest. But Talon hadn't mentioned feeling anything like *this*. The other pairs didn't seem uncomfortable, either. Then again, none of them had his particular brand of magic. Just as none of them had magic like Cyrus had.

Cyrus...

Gods, he missed him. It was Cyrus who'd discovered him all those years ago. Seen his potential. Encouraged him to become a shield. Cyrus was the only one who'd known the strange magic that lurked beneath his skin, and kept his secret too, until they'd decided to tell Talon. Because Cyrus was perhaps the only one who might understand what it meant to be...*different*.

It was no wonder he'd lost his head when he saw Cyrus dead, his skin blackened, laying in Claire's arms. No wonder he'd immediately assumed Claire was the culprit. His own queen! What a fool he'd been. But he'd loved Cyrus, deeply—still did. A kind of love words could never describe. Admiration, adoration, brother, friend, all bundled into one feeling. Even the word *love* didn't do it justice. And now Cyrus was simply...gone.

No, not quite gone. Claire sometimes told him of the little snide comments or pieces of advice Cyrus offered. Especially as of late, since they'd taken this journey to Esterpine. And he cherished every word, every tidbit Claire deigned to share. Collected them like the logs of a raft to keep him afloat.

A ball of pressure swelled in his sternum. He faltered but kept moving, rubbing the place with his thumb, keeping his free hand on his sverak. He knew what it meant and had gotten better at ignoring it over the years. Though it was hard to do here in the forest.

His ears pricked right as the forest went silent. They continued walking, making their way down the overgrown path. He strained for sounds of any kind. There was nothing, like an absence had formed, like they'd entered a void.

He glanced over his shoulder. Darcie, Edith, Til, and Verider looked ill at ease. At least he wasn't the only one. *"Stay alert,"* he advised them. *"Something isn't right."*

Ahead, Claire's footsteps faltered. She heard his voice in her head too, though not intentionally. It was simply a product of her impressive abilities—to overhear all telepathic conversations when she wasn't actively blocking. She glanced back at him, brows creased.

"Should we go back?" she asked.

He hesitated. *"I'm sure it's nothing. Jeanine doesn't seem bothered. Just...keep your eyes open."*

He didn't know how deeply her connection with the forest ran, or if she could sense what he sensed.

They moved slower, more cautiously through the undergrowth. Up ahead, he could see an opening in the trees, perhaps a clearing. An area less oppressive than what they currently traveled through. He almost breathed a sigh of relief. *Almost.*

The pressure in his sternum doubled. Alarm coursed through him. He cursed his nerves. Cursed his magic. The forest wouldn't have bothered him half as much if Claire wasn't his responsibility to protect. Talon would *never* forgive him if she came to harm. The king's anger aside, she was his queen. He knew his duty; it was his honor to serve.

"I think there's a break in the trees up ahead." Jeanine's voice carried back to him.

"Have you ever ventured this far?" Claire asked, pushing aside a branch of foliage.

"Not...quite. Or at least, not to this clearing."

His hand shot to his ribcage, rubbing the tender place in the middle. The hairs on the back of his neck stood on end. "Claire, I think we should—"

"Oh!" Claire parted the foliage and stopped short. "Look! It's just—"

He threw a panicked look over his shoulder, signaling to the others, then rushed up behind her, staring into the clearing. "I think we should leave," he said, his voice low, urgent. "Back away, quietly."

"But it's...it's just a stag. *Look.*"

The stag had its back to them, head down, antlers low as it grazed. But there was something very, very wrong with it. As if sensing them, the stag's ears pricked and it lifted its head, swiveling around. Teaming about its antlers, darkness swirled like shadows, where light ought to exist. But it wasn't the stag's antlers that captured his attention. Its dark eyes were surrounded by black veins. Black like poison. The side of its face was...*rotting*. He shuddered, limbs growing heavy.

"Oh my gods!" Claire's panicked whisper broke the silence.

"What in the name...?" Jeanine backed away a step.

The stag's depthless gaze darted between them, assessing. *Enemy!* It thought. *Threat!* It pawed the ground. The pressure in his chest turned painful.

"Claire..." he urged, another warning. He didn't give her time to react. Instead, he grabbed a fistful of her gown and pulled her back.

The stag lowered its head and charged. Claire yelped, her shock finally materializing. He didn't give her the chance to react. He simply acted on instinct, wrapping his arms around her, hauling her out of its path. Just in time. Its antlers caught in the underbrush taking out a swath of low-hanging branches. It charged on, thundering away.

Enemy! Destroy! The thoughts were distinct. Panicked.

"Is it...is it gone?" Claire breathed heavily against his chest.

"I don't think so." He released her, drawing his sverak. The other two drengr did the same. Darcie and Edith drew their bows, nocked arrows, aiming for the unseen enemy. Jeanine removed her kingdom sword. Claire had her spriten dagger in hand. The seven of them backed into the clearing.

Their breathing filled the silence. Everything fell quiet as they listened. There! A thundering crash. They turned as one, towards the location of the sound.

"Jump from its path if it comes again," he advised, herding

everyone into the center of the clearing, to give them the best vantage point. "I'll take care of it."

Another crash. *Enemy!* It was the only warning before the beast burst from the foliage on their right. Everyone spun towards it and jumped from its charging antlers.

He alone stood in its path and lifted his sword to deal the killing blow. The stag's head was low, ready to slam into him. In a split second, he hefted his sverak and side-stepped—

"Stop!"

His blade never reached its target. A flash of blinding white light lit the clearing. He staggered back from the force of it, unseeing. Another pulse of light lit the world before the dim forest returned. The stag lay heaving on the ground, breathing hard, its head at an odd angle to accommodate its antlers. Still alive.

Relief!

The strange thought pounded through him at the same moment as Claire's gasp. He spun, eyes wide. A female stood at the edge of the clearing, arms raised, chest heaving. "You cannot kill him," she announced, a wild look on her face. "You cannot."

He wasn't sure what she meant. Either the stag was immortal, or killing it would be a terrible crime. He didn't care. He didn't care that she was the most beautiful thing he'd ever seen, with bone-white hair woven through with leaves and twigs and flowers and... was that a butterfly? He blinked. Blinked again. She was a wild thing. The sight of her sent heat crawling across his skin, racing straight for his chest, his heart.

He ignored the feeling. Instead, he stalked forward, devouring the distance between them. He stopped a hand's breadth from her, anger coursing through him, and pinned her with his gaze. "That thing almost killed us," he said, his voice turning to a low snarl. "Don't tell me what I cannot do."

"No." The authority in that single word rippled through him. He took a step back. "It is sick. I will heal it and all will be well." She eyed him a moment longer, taking him in, from the tips of his toes all the way to the top of his head. And her expression—like she found him *lacking*—sent irritation coursing through him. When she stepped around him and went to the stag, all he could do was stare, his anger sputtering like a candle flame extinguished.

She knelt beside it, whispering a few words in her native tongue. Words that, for the first time in his long life, he wished he could understand. The stag tried to move, to lift its rotting head, and failed. As if she held it down by some invisible force. Her words became a quiet hum. From her belt, she removed a dagger and sliced open her forearm, breaking the lines of several luminescent markings.

He jerked, took a step forward at the letting of her blood, then forced himself to stop. What did he care if she bled? Claire, however, gasped. She drew his gaze with the sound, standing frozen beside Jeanine, eyes wide, watching.

The spriten female let the blood of her forearm drip onto the stag's rotting jaw. Where her blood landed, the rot sizzled and steamed.

Relief!

The forest around them held its breath. He couldn't pull his eyes away. Fascination gripped him as slowly, the rot subsided, and then disappeared entirely. Even the blackened veins around the stag's eyes began to fade. Next, the dark shadows swirling around its antlers.

Safe. Better! Safe.

The stag's clipped thoughts carried a desperate measure of relief. He blinked, unsure if what he saw was real. He continued to blink as the stag got to its feet and nuzzled the female affectionately.

Safe, it thought again. His brow furrowed.

"Be at peace, great one," the female whispered. "Go."

The stag bounded away, and everyone stared, open mouthed. It was Jeanine who broke the silence. "Princess Taylynn. You're back."

He huffed. Of course! *Of course* this was the princess. No one else would have defied him so thoroughly.

"Jeanine. And Lady Claire." Claire only gaped at her. Taylynn turned, fixing Koldis with her gaze. "And *you*—pompous and controlling—*you* must be one of King Talon's shields."

He sputtered, crossing his arms. "Lord Koldis."

"Right," she said, dismissing him almost as quickly. A flash of extreme annoyance stole over him. He was forced to glare at her back as she turned to Claire. "I apologize that you had to see that. I had hoped to track him and heal him before he got this close to the city."

"What...what *was* that?" Claire managed.

He didn't miss Taylynn's hesitation. "Just as the world thrives, so too does it suffer. Balance is a precarious thing, Lady Claire. Light and dark. Good and bad."

He withheld a snort. It was the worst answer he'd ever heard in his entire existence—a pompous and controlling existence, at that. It was enough to make him roll his eyes at Taylynn's back.

"So that was...evil?" Claire asked. "I didn't think there would be anything like that here." She didn't seem to mind Taylynn's cryptic explanation.

"There should not be. Such is the price." Claire opened her mouth, but Taylynn continued. "It is good to see you again, Lady Claire. Good to see you thriving. I wish we had met here under better circumstances, but there is still much need of me in the forest." Claire frowned. So did he. *Again*?! They had never met...had they? "I will return soon. Until then, be at peace." Taylynn bowed her head and moved away, giving Koldis one final disparaging glance before disappearing into the forest. He gaped at her retreating figure as it disappeared. Was she truly *that* angry at him for almost killing a thing of evil? He huffed. Females...

"Uhm..." Claire stared after the princess. "Did that just happen?"

It was Jeanine who laughed. "Well, I couldn't be less surprised by *any* of that. Feowen will want to know. We'd better return so I can tell him."

"I take it she's always like that?" Claire asked, still staring at the place where Taylynn had disappeared.

"You have no idea."

"I still have so many questions, though." Claire tugged at her braided hair.

"Perhaps Feowen can answer them," Jeanine offered.

Claire nodded. "Yes, I hope so. Plus, I wanted to ask him if he could show me the way into the treetops."

"Oh, *I* can show you that."

And just like that, all was back to normal, as if it had never happened. Claire and Jeanine continued speaking while their pairs sidled close to him. "Some greeting that was, hmm?" Til asked.

This time he *did* snort. "We need to get back to the city. I don't like this one bit. Moreover, I'm not sure how Claire is supposed to make *quests* into the forest when there are things like that lurking about. I'm liking the idea less and less. We should return to Kastali Dun."

"Perhaps Princess Taylynn can teach her how to handle it," Darcie offered. "She seemed to handle the situation just fine."

"Right. By cutting open her forearm and bleeding all over it. What was that, even? Some kind of sprite blood magic? *Gods*!"

Darcie appeared thoughtful as she said, "It was a strange thing indeed. But it worked."

He tsked, annoyed to admit it. Annoyed that the sprite princess didn't give them answers. Annoyed that she'd blatantly insulted him. Annoyed that she'd disappeared as quickly as she'd appeared. Annoyed that she was clearly at ease with what had happened, like it was something she did regularly. But most of all, he was annoyed that he couldn't get the image of her out of his mind.

CHAPTER 4
ARRIVAL IN KASTALI DUN

Dragonfire Sea

Tamara watched the coast sail by from the prow of the *Sea Lion*. True to the king's word, ships had been waiting along Celenore's coast north of The Scattered Islands, ready to take them to Kastali Dun. There, they would be absorbed —albeit temporarily—by Fort Kastali.

At the height of the drengr monarchy, the forts would not have had room, but the drengr race was dying because of what Queen Isabella had done. Dying because each pair could only have one child, unless they were blessed with twins, and that was extremely rare.

The thought of twins had her eyes pricking with tears. Loss followed them like a dark cloud, chasing after their small fleet, and what a sight they were to behold, twelve ships cutting through the water. There wasn't enough space to house both the drengr and all of Fort Squall's staff, so nearly half their forces flew overhead, most often with their riders. When they needed to stop for the night, they either slept on deck under the stars, or flew to the coast and caught up the following day.

The *Sea Lion* cut nearly three weeks off their journey, making it worth her initial sea-sickness.

They were due to arrive in Kastali Dun by nightfall. A nervous excitement had settled over everyone, but none more so than her. She couldn't wait to behold the keep. To see the city on the rise. To look over its vast ports and explore its market. There was a whole world of possibility waiting. It was simply a shame, knowing the price that such a possibility had demanded.

She searched the skies, taking in the small glittering forms high above.

"I'm here, love." Byron sent the thought, knowing she sought him. A projection followed, from high up, accompanied by his joy of flying. A smile tugged at her lips. *"I can come get you, if you'd like?"*

She shook her head. The fort's staff didn't have the luxury of leaving the ships, and if she was to be their leader, she wanted to be here with them.

"You are everything a fort leader should be." There was pride in his voice. He swooped low, circled the ship once, twice, three times, and then retreated back to higher altitudes.

She turned back to the distant landscape. It had taken some getting used to, sharing a mind with Byron, knowing what he felt if she reached for him. She hadn't been exactly sure what to expect after their bonding. But not this, exactly. Less privacy, perhaps? He never barreled into her mind if she didn't want him there. And there were places she could still keep separate from him, if she wished to. But mostly, she enjoyed giving him everything. Except, perhaps, her worry. He had enough of his own.

The ability to share thoughts over great distances made them stronger. As Fort Squall's temporary leaders, strength was something they desperately needed. Soon it would be time for a vote. She wasn't sure what the fort's wing leaders and wing seconds would decide. She certainly had no idea if she was ready to lead. Part of her wanted to make Lord Davi and Lady Emmy proud. To ensure that even after their deaths, their son would take up his mantle. That he would be what they'd hoped. The other part of her

—the weaker part—feared the responsibility. Feared the sacrifices they would make. The road ahead wouldn't be easy.

At midday, she sat with Sophie and a couple of other women from the fort's staff, eating a frugal meal of dried meat, bread, and cheese. Their conversation came easily, especially once the other women had grown more comfortable in her presence. She had Sophie to thank for that. Sophie, with her bubbly personality. Sophie, who was lovely to look at.

"What's the first thing you want to see, Tam?" Sophie asked, pulling her from her thoughts.

"What? Oh. I suppose the market. I hear it's enormous."

"I've heard the same," Jaylin agreed. She was one of the older women who worked in the fort's laundry. "With wares from places like Oshea and other countries that we've never even heard of."

"It sounds spectacular," Sophie said, her voice dreamy. "But the first thing I want to see is the keep. And then the fort. I'm going to touch every dragon I can get my hands on."

"Sophie!" Her eyes went wide. The other women laughed. "You can't just walk up—"

"I know, I know." Sophie sighed. "Be at peace, Tam. I was just kidding. But I wouldn't mind meeting as many of the unmated ones as I can. Sometimes there's a bond realized before the touching part. Like you and Byron, hmm?" Sophie wagged her eyebrows.

Tamara's face heated as the other women began chuckling, pressing her for a repeat of her story. It was well known at this point how she'd met Byron. Of the kiss he'd stolen. She'd been forced to kiss him in exchange for secrecy, despite it being a chaste kiss. She'd hidden her identity and run away from her home in Redport. After all that, she couldn't allow her parents to know where she'd gone. She couldn't allow anyone to know who she was. Little did she know, Byron had already suspected a bond, so he tricked her into a kiss. Everyone knew the story. The whole fort. And they loved it.

She spent more time on the deck that afternoon, watching the southern coast sail by. The Eigaden Peninsula. It sent a thrill of excitement straight through to her bones. When she caught sight of its tip, she could hardly breathe, even if the city on the rise was still too distant to make out.

It was nightfall when she beheld the glittering lights of Kastali Dun. Like a gem beside the sea. Byron left the skies to be with her. She heard his feet hit the deck, but didn't turn. Didn't need to. She couldn't have even if she'd wanted to, because she couldn't take her eyes off of the sight jutting out into the sea.

"It's beautiful, isn't it?" Byron's arms wrapped around her, pulling her back flush against him. He nuzzled her hair and kissed her ear. "I already informed King Talon that we're close," he murmured.

"I know," she said, resorting to the connection they shared between minds.

"I know you know," he teased. *"Thought I'd tell you anyway."* He nipped at her ear. Her toes curled in her slippers. He sensed her arousal, the effect of his actions. Just as she always sensed the effect of her every touch on him. *"Later, love. I promise. After we're settled."* His promise thrilled her.

There had been plenty of opportunity for love-making aboard the ship, tucked away in the captain's quarters. She wondered if this desire ever stopped.

"I hope not," he whispered. "It never did for my parents, or any other bonded pair that I know—"

"Forgive me, Lord Byron. We'll be docking at the port in an hour." The captain sidled up to them. Captain Julian. He'd been shouting orders for the last ten minutes.

"Thank you, Captain. I am eager to see my mate settled."

Tamara all but shivered at his words, which earned a mental growl and a naughty projection from Byron that the captain had no way of sensing as he said, "Understandable, my lord."

Byron and Julian talked for several minutes longer about the docking and unloading procedure, but she hardly listened. A benefit of sharing minds, she supposed. If she wanted to know what they discussed, she could easily slip into Byron's mind later and share the memory as if it were her own. For now, she turned her attention back to the approaching coast. The jewel of the kingdom.

As they neared, sounds drifted out over the water, shouts and merrymaking. *"The many taverns along the port,"* Byron explained silently, still keeping an easy hold of his conversation with Julian. She pinned her eyes on the docks—still a distance away—and thought of all the fun others were having. How the taverns were filled to bursting. She'd never been into a seedy establishment like the ones she expected along the docks.

"I can take you, if you'd like." Byron's voice was low, suggestive. Julian had returned to his crew. She snorted at the suggestion. "No?" Byron feigned surprise. "I suppose you're right. Not really the place for a lady."

"My mother would suffer heart failure if she caught me anywhere near a place like that."

"But your mother need not know. Hmm? We can dress you down and enter inconspicuously. You'd like the music, I think."

"Inconspicuously?" She laughed. Byron would stand out more than she, with his hulking, unmistakable form.

He chuckled. "Yes, that's likely."

Sometimes it was jarring, his ability to answer questions from simple thoughts. Their conversations had become so disjointed. A mix of thoughts, some spoken aloud, some spoken telepathically, and some that were never voiced at all. Outsiders looking in probably suffered immense confusion, watching mated pairs communicate. But she loved it, the ease of it, the ability to leave half her words unspoken and still get her point across. All without trying!

"I love it too," he whispered against her ear.

The docks swept up to meet them. Everything blurred together after that. A rush of activity as deck hands moved about, shouting. They pulled into the harbor, right up to places reserved along the maze of woodwork. She and Byron disembarked, helping where they could, as the fort's staff and dockhands gathered trunks and crates. Carriages were waiting to take everyone, except for those who could fly, to Fort Kastali. It would be an hour-long carriage trip through the city and out of its walls, across the small stretch to the safety of the fort. The wing seconds were assigned to oversee this task while she and Byron and their wing leaders flew to the keep to meet the king.

From the sky, the sight of the city's lights left her breathless. If only it had been daylight. *"I'll take you up again tomorrow, Tam. You'll love it. I promise."*

"Thank you." She was so exhausted, she might not have appreciated it the way she would after a night of rest. As it was, it was nearly midnight, and the night wasn't over yet.

Their small party of pairs was greeted in the lowest courtyard of the keep by the king, his shields, and two ladies. She looked around for Claire and frowned. Reuniting with her had been one of the things she'd most looked forward to.

There were a few familiar faces, like Bedelth, Jovari and Reyr, who greeted his nephew with a heartfelt hug. But there were two other shields she'd never met. One of whom she knew by description alone—Lord Verath. The other was so young she realized he probably wasn't a shield at all, but couldn't understand why he was with them. He was later introduced as Dallin.

Simple pleasantries were exchanged, introductions mostly, even though King Talon had met everyone in her party during his brief stay in Brezen. It was more of a formality, than anything. She was too tired to follow, and too enamored by her surroundings. Her eyes wandered over the looming walls of the keep, over the courtyard, over what she was quite certain to be a decadent garden only a short walk away. Her eyes snagged on it, its torches glittering, beckoning.

"I'll take you there tomorrow, too," Byron said, sensing her distraction. Even as he spoke, he continued his introductions, as if multitasking between two modes of communication was the easiest thing. He managed to introduce every wing leader and be in her head simultaneously. Impressive. She would have stuttered and failed miserably at such a task.

"I've had years of practice, love," was all he said.

"Lady Tamara," King Talon said, drawing her attention back. "Allow me to introduce the ladies in attendance. The kingdom's very own prophetess, Lady Saffra, and also Lady Desaree Kendall." Tamara's eyes widened. She'd heard of both women from Claire. They were her closest friends. "Lady Desaree is Claire's handmaiden." The king continued, glancing at Desaree. There was something in his eyes, something soft behind the wall of stone he presented. Desaree met his gaze offering a curt nod. Tamara immediately admired her for it. Even after days spent in King Talon's company, even after she'd learned of his fondness for Claire, he was still Dragonwall's king. Still intimidating. "I'm afraid Lady Claire is not here, unfortunately," he added, as if sensing her disappointment. It probably showed on her face. She smoothed her scowl. "As I understand it, Claire promised to meet you upon your arrival to the city?"

"I...yes, Your Majesty," she managed. "I was looking forward to her company. Will she return soon?"

"I am afraid not, though I wish it otherwise." There was a hint of longing in his words. Byron shifted beside her and didn't drop her hand. "Hopefully her ladies will suffice. But come, let us not discuss these things out in the open."

Everyone agreed.

The king escorted them through the keep. She was glad Byron held her close. Her gaze swiveled back and forth, never once watching where she stepped. There was too much. This castle was ten times the size of Lord Redwynn's, and still far grander. *"Wait until you see the plumbing,"* Byron said for her only. He sent her a projection of what he meant by it. She gasped. *"I hope you fancy a bath tonight?"* His words, the thoughts he sent along with them, of everything he intended when he meant *bath*, left her shivering in delight.

They walked nearly ten minutes, and by the time they came to a stop, she was hopelessly lost. The hallway was lined with plush carpet and gilded portraits, but she was too dazed to take everything in. Instead, she and the others followed King Talon into his personal tower, where they were led to a council chamber. Byron insisted on standing, offering up a seat to make her comfortable. He stood behind her, a hand on her shoulder. His touch was soothing.

With so many pairs in the room, there weren't enough chairs for all. Most of the males remained standing. And even though it was the middle of the night, what proceeded was a heated discussion of how they would settle in, and when they would begin planning the counter attack on Fort Squall.

It was important enough that no one bothered voicing their complaints, but she knew everyone was fatigued. She couldn't have been the only one struggling to pay attention. Her mind wandered with her gaze, all around the king's chamber. It was luxurious, more so than Fort Squall. Varnished woodwork, chandeliers with hundreds of candles, painted landscapes in gold frames, plush velvet chairs. It was a lot to soak in as the minutes passed.

On the table before them was a map of Fort Squall and its surroundings. Her chest squeezed every time she looked at it. Instead, she retreated into Byron's mind as she often did when she was tired. Let him process everything. She would simply absorb it later. It was a lazy way of doing things, letting him think for her, but she was tired. *So* tired—

"Forgive me, my king—" Byron's voice was jarring. She blinked, retreating from his mind. "—but I believe this would be a good stopping point for the night."

Heat flooded her cheeks as she realized what was happening. He was stopping the meeting for her. She shouldn't have allowed her fatigue to become so apparent.

"I'm not simply stopping for you, love. I'm about to drop. I need sleep and...a bath."

Oh, *gods*! Despite her fatigue, something curled deep in her core that left her skin tingling.

"Of course." King Talon stood. "I got carried away. War does that." The others chuckled. "You have all been assigned accommodations here in the keep, if you will have them. Lord Byron, I think it wise you stay close at hand so that we might continue this tomorrow. And Lady Tamara, I believe Desaree and Saffra would much appreciate your company whilst you are here."

The two women voiced their eagerness. It was only then that she realized they were still present. She was both surprised and impressed that they were trusted enough to remain. It probably had something to do with Lady Claire. She would ask later.

Some of the wing leaders declined the king's generous offer, preferring to go and get settled at the fort. Those who stayed were escorted to individual accommodations, which happened to span the same hall as the king's tower entrance.

She was speechless when the door to her own accommodation closed behind her. Byron whistled into the silence that followed. "I could get used to this," he said, walking through their quarters. He drew back gauzy curtains, revealing a set of glass doors leading out onto a covered balcony. It was lit by the warm glow of torches and brazers. She all but squealed, racing to throw them open. She stepped outside. The sight stole her breath. The covered balcony jutted out over the water, with walls to keep it private from the others, but if she leaned over far enough, she could see them.

"Careful, love," Byron's voice was teasing. "Unless you're hoping I'll have the energy to jump after you."

She turned to him, humming. "While this *is* breathtaking," she said, "I'm told it isn't the most impressive aspect of our accommodations? You said something about...plumbing?" She avoided the word bath. But still, he read her like a book.

A low growl built in his chest, breaking free. He moved faster than she could anticipate, scooping her up in his arms. She screeched, clutching his shoulders. Moments later, she was gasping. The bathing chamber was something of a dream, with a giant pool four times the size of a copper tub, already filled with steaming water. A door at the side of the tiled chamber housed the cleanest toilet she'd ever seen.

"It's magnificent," she whispered, not sure she could form anything beyond those two words. Byron was already stripping off his clothes, which landed in a heap on the floor. She froze, unable to tear her gaze away from his naked body. She traced the deep grooves of his muscles. He moved with ease, with absolute comfort in her presence, stalking towards the bath. She noticed immediately when he turned to meet her, just before stepping up into the bath, exactly how aroused he was. A quick glimpse into his mind showed her everything he planned to do once she joined him in the steaming water. Instead of spoiling the surprise, knowing what he intended, it only increased her anticipation—left her heart racing.

"Quit gawking and join me," he said, grinning, before he sank down into the water. His groan of pleasure broke the silence. She grinned at the sound of his delight. When he popped up from the water and pinned her with his gaze, she knew his patience was at an end. She eagerly shed her clothes, making a pile beside his, and climbed in to join him.

CHAPTER 5
CATS HAVE CLAWS

Dragonfire Sea

Bennett emerged on deck into bright, glaring sunlight. It was one of the rare sunny days during this time of year. He immediately scanned his crew, looking over their activity. Several on duty snapped into action upon seeing him, suspiciously busier than they had been moments before. Those enjoying off-time were scattered about the main deck in clusters, playing dice mostly. He spotted a game of Rue at the foredeck.

His eyes fell on a figure, straight as a rod, standing at the railing. He harrumphed at the sigh of her. No doubt she—

"Afternoon, Captain." Jonah sidled up to him. "I've—"

"How long's she been standing there?"

"Oh." Jonah stopped short, looking in Cat's direction. "Better part of an hour, I think."

Bennett frowned. "Any trouble from the crew?"

"The *crew*?!" Jonah's eyes bulged. "The crew?" he repeated. "Pardon, Captain, but she's the one that gives the trouble, not the crew—" Bennett's eyes narrowed. Jonah cleared his throat. "No. Nothin' more than suspicious looks."

"Good." He gave a nod to dismiss Jonah, though he knew his

first mate had business to discuss. It could wait until later. He strode across the deck and stopped beside the woman who'd become the biggest inconvenience the sea had coughed up.

He'd fought many battles on this deck. Killed assailants who dared to sink the *Lady Faith*. Run every kind of cargo from priceless ice metal to illegal contraband. But something made him hesitate when he stopped beside Cat.

Even from the side she looked...like hell, despite her uncommonly pretty features. Her face was pale. Her hair in disarray. Her clothes wrinkled. But it was more than that. It wasn't the look of someone who'd had a rough past couple of days—and she had, certainly. It was the look of someone who'd had their entire life tipped on end.

She said nothing at his appearance, staring ahead as if he didn't exist. The land was so far away; it was a flat smudge on the horizon. She pretended to watch it.

He chewed on his tongue, eager to say something cutting and harsh. Instead— "You feeling any better?"

"What do you want, Captain?"

There it was—that tone. He'd bet she'd used it often throughout her life. He sighed, praying for patience. "What I *want is* to know if you're feeling better, girl."

She turned to sneer at him. "What do you think, *Captain*? Do I look better?"

Truthfully, no. But he wasn't going to say that. She'd heaved up her guts for the first three days at sea. Refused to come on deck for most of that time, until Jonah convinced her she'd feel better with fresh air. At least she wasn't carting her bucket around anymore.

"Well?"

He shrugged. "Hard to say, which is why I thought to ask."

She snorted. "I do not see how I can be better, so long as I'm stuck on this gods' forsaken—"

"I could toss you over the side, if you like." Now that created a pretty picture. He imagined hauling her up and over the ship, screaming as he tossed her into the sea, and chuckled. "It would do us all a favor, I think."

"I'd like to see you try." Dismissive, she turned to leave. He grabbed her arm, rooting her to the spot. Her face transformed, eyes blazing. She uttered a word and he yelped, pulling back, burned.

Magic.

"You dare?!" he hissed.

"Touch me again and I'll do worse."

He sputtered and watched her go, stunned. She'd used magic—against *him*! She dared, when he was the captain of this vessel. "Prickly as a sea urchin," he muttered. No. On second thought, she was worse. He watched her retreat. She settled herself at the back of the ship, as far as possible from where he stood.

He quickly glanced about, eyes falling on Emmon and Tris, who'd both stopped scrubbing seagull shit off the deck to watch.

"Well?" his eyes narrowed. "I don't pay you to stand around and gawk, do I?"

They quickly returned to their work.

Despite her piss-poor attitude, and against his better judgment, he stalked across the main deck and went straight for her, this time, leaning his lanky frame against the railing. He propped an elbow up to support his weight and faced her. "Let's cut to the chase, shall we, *Cat*? You must be barking mad for wanting to go north. I don't know why I feel the need to talk you out of a stupid idea, but I do. Why don't you let us drop you off in Redport, eh? Or if you must go farther, Kurtcastle?"

"You simply cannot stop yourself, can you?" Her jaw worked. Clenched and unclenched. Her eyes flashed, but she didn't deign to look down at him, leaning against the rail where he might get a better look at her pretty face. Such good looks...wasted.

"I suppose I can't," he admitted. "Not one of my *better* qualities." He flashed her a grin, hoping his efforts might get under her skin—deep under. Hopefully as deep as she burrowed under his. If she hadn't offered to pay so much for her passage...

"*Better* qualities?" She tutted. "I wasn't aware you had any."

"Hmm..." He feigned thoughtfulness. "It seems your window-less room has done nothing for your mood. Not too late to move into my cabin, you know. I promise I don't bite. Not as hard as you, anyway."

"You're disgusting," she hissed. "A scoundrel. A nobody." She snorted, dismissive. "Is this the kind of charm you use on women? I can't imagine a single one taking the bait."

"Hah! I think you forget who you address, girl. Disgusting? Scoundrel? Nobody? Those are all compliments, far as I'm concerned! Besides,"—she opened her mouth but he didn't let her get a word in—"when was the last time you seen a mirror? Hmm? As for my charm, I save that for real women, women who matter."

She blinked. There. That one hit home. A slight pink crept into her cheeks. Otherwise, she gave no sign that his words had come as a blow. He chuckled and added, "If you don't want to tell me why you're going north, fine. I won't try to talk you out of it. I can't say I'll be sad to see you freeze to death in Ice Port."

"Then I don't see what the problem is," she snapped. This time he could sense her anger rising.

He smiled, pleased. "You're right. No problem whatsoever, *Cat*." With that, he left her, glad to have succeeded—even if it was only a small measure of success.

When he walked past Carson at the helm, he almost...*almost* told him to redirect their course, to take them farther from land into choppy waters, if only to enjoy the pleasure of seeing Cat more miserable.

THE FOLLOWING DAY, they reached Scattered Island Bay, cutting through the waters, navigating the bits of land. After a quick knock at his cabin door, a head popped in. "Forgive me, Captain, but is there a reason we're stopping in Tortalia?" Jonah stepped in, shutting the door behind him. "The men are falling over themselves with excitement."

"I suspect they are." Bennett perused his maps, not bothering to look up. He'd marked places along the coast—a total of six infamous ports. The thought left him giddy with delight.

"But...why?"

"Supplies, Jonah. And because none of us likes being at sea for long."

Jonah's jaw dropped. "You cannot be serious, Captain. We've been at sea a mere *four days*. And we have supplies aplenty. Our plan was—"

"I know what our plan *was*, Jonah. Plans change."

Jonah hesitated. Then his eyes narrowed. "We're dropping her off, aren't we, right in the gods' armpit?!"

"Hah! I wish. No. Supplies and a bit of fun for the night."

Jonah moved over to the map then, noticed the pins, and cursed under his breath. "Tell me this isn't what I think it is."

Bennett chuckled. "It isn't what you think it is?" he tried.

"She's not going to like this, Captain. Not one bit."

"No, I dare say she won't." He'd chosen the seediest scoundrel ports along the coast, with Tortalia being one of the worst. None were worse than Bagradas. Oh, she'd be positively seething to set foot in that shit hole. He planned to dock there for two nights. Important business and all that, for all she needed to know.

A fist pounded on his door. He looked up at his first mate and grinned, knowing.

"Right on cue," Jonah announced. "Well, I'll leave you to it, then. Say, you don't mind if I listen outside the door, do you?"

"Be my guest. Now, let her in."

Jonah complied. Cat stormed in, steaming with fury. It practically seeped from her ears. Jonah made himself scarce, closing the door behind him.

Bennett feigned surprise, looking up. "Ah. Cat. Had a change of heart? It's a nice cabin, yes? I can move my trunk if you—"

"Cut the shit, Captain. You never told me we'd be stopping. I paid you to take me to Ice Port. What's the meaning of this?"

"Huh..." He leaned back in his chair, stroked his chin, and looked thoughtful. "Could have sworn I mentioned it when we struck our deal. You want to keep eating, don't ya? We're going to need supplies. Besides, this is Beaky's homeland. Wouldn't miss the chance to let her stretch her wings. She might want to say hi to some of her friends."

Cat sputtered.

As if the damn bird had heard him, her beak tapped on the port window. He chuckled and let her in. Cat screeched at the sight of her, moving across the room, eying the bird with distaste.

"Come now, girl. She doesn't bite as hard as you. Here—" With Beaky on his arm, he moved over to stand by Cat. Her lips were pressed into a thin line. She said nothing, didn't move to stroke Beaky's head. Nothing. "*Well* that's rather rude," he said at last, sending Beaky to her perch.

"I will pay you extra, Captain, to forgo this stop."

"You will, will you? And what about the other stops? Can you pay for those too."

"The other—?"

"There are six, total."

"Six?" she hissed. "Is this some kind of joke?"

"Hardly, but you're welcome to find a new ship captain when we drop anchor in Tortalia. We should be there in the next hour or so."

"Maybe I will," she said, crossing her arms.

He laughed then. "Gods. That will be worth every coin you've paid me, seeing you attempt to broker passage. You know it's naught but pirates that frequent Tortalia, right? Can't wait to see what they make of you!"

"How dare—"

"Oh, I dare. In fact, unless you need to, I suggest you stay on board while we go landside. I'm not interested in makin' sure your *ladyhood* stays intact. I got better things to do."

"What—I—you wouldn't dare!" He ignored her stuttering and shrugged. "I'm going ashore," she decided. "If we stop, I'm not staying on this pile of wood. I can take care of myself quite well. Unless you need another demonstration like yesterday's?"

He shrugged at the reminder, even if it left him uneasy. "No, thank you. Use magic against me again and I will leave you in whatever port we stop at next."

"Fine," she hissed. "But I'm getting off this damned ship as soon as we drop anchor."

He hid his smirk. It was exactly as he'd hoped. It wasn't that he wanted to draw out their trip north. No, he'd sooner be rid of Cat as quickly as possible. But there was something deeply satisfying about inconveniencing her. So much so that he'd extend their journey just to infuriate her.

FOUR HOURS LATER, Bennett found himself deep in drink, sitting around the table in the Braised Duck. Nearly his entire crew had disembarked. Those who'd drawn short straws were stuck on board. But the rest of them converged on Barrel Street. They'd gone from one establishment to another, never staying longer than an hour. This was their third, and arguably the rowdiest; drunks got drunker with each passing hour. Half of his crew had moved on already, but a good handful stayed.

And then there was the matter of Cat.

Upon setting foot in the filthy port island town, she'd immediately changed her tune. She certainly didn't intend to go off and find another ship to carry her north, not when she took one look at what was before her. The clientele in Tortalia left something to be desired. Thiefs , killers, rapists. It was a favorite pirate hideout, ideal for those who wanted to avoid punishment from the crown. A place that spoiled the women who found themselves here, both the willing and unwilling.

Through it all, Cat's expression was priceless—worth every steely he dropped. It came as no surprise that she'd opted to stick with him. Now he'd show her exactly how *disgusting* he truly was. First and foremost, by getting shitting drunk.

"Another round, Sanny! Bring us another round, for the gods' sake." He lifted his tankard, motioning to Sanny behind the bar.

"Another round. Another round!" Beaky was perched in the middle of the table, eating the nuts his crew graciously shelled for her.

"And get Cat here another, too," he added a little louder, noticing her glower. "Drink up, girl. You'll be happier for it."

"Thanks—no." She pushed her tankard away, glaring at him, but he noticed it was empty. She'd had two so far. Yes—he was keeping count, even if he'd lost count of his own. She'd had one here, and one at the Dancing Dog, where they'd been just before this. At the first tavern, she'd been so appalled she refused drink altogether. He supposed this was a good sign that she'd loosened up a bit.

Around them, the tables were full of scoundrels and scum. They were packed close, too, so you could hear the rise and fall of conversations around you. He was particularly entertained by the table beside them. A group of sailors taking bets on how sweet the bonny lass—Cat—would taste. It was the kind of crude talk one could always expect in a place like this. He was certain Cat heard every word, which left him chuckling under his breath. He was certain the rest of their table heard, too. But Cat had already earned a reputation among them, so they'd be just as entertained as he.

"You reckon she tastes like apples or peaches?" one of them asked his mates, slurring. He was a burly man with so much beard, you could hardly see his face.

"I'd say peaches, most like," another answered. This one was younger, hardly any more than fuzz on his jaw. His eyes were already glassy. "The soft orange ones, ya know? Them fancy ones you get down in Eryas and Yicora." He made a crude gesture at his chest. They roared, hands slamming on the table.

Bennett glanced at Cat and noticed her face reddening. How much would she take? Would she suffer in silence or make a stand. He wasn't certain the extent of her magic, but he was certain that any hint of it would scare most of the neighboring table shitless. Tavern fights were common. Normal, even. Expected.

Sanny bustled over with a pitcher, refilling tankards to the last drop. She turned to go just as Bushy Beard, sitting at the rowdy table, snagged her by the waist. Sanny plopped into his lap, laughing. She kissed him on one cheek and then the other, then whacked him over the head with her empty pitcher when he tried to feel her up. Dazed, his eyes went unfocused. Bushy Beard's companions roared at his misfortune. Sanny left, still in good spirits. It took a certain kind of woman to withstand men like this—and handle them, as she did.

He drank deeply, slamming his tankard down.

"Well, since that didn't work out—mayhap I try my luck closer to home," Bushy Beard growled, eyebrows wagging. "I like me some peaches, 'specially them ones in Yicora like you say, Rob."

Rob roared with laughter and turned to their table. "Hey lassie! Mik here reckons you might be sweet enough to eat, eh?"

Cat tutted but ignored the jibe. He knew she was too proud to request Bennett and the rest of their table leave. She'd sit and take the offense, and seethe, but she wouldn't act as if it bothered her. If she hadn't been so outnumbered, perhaps things would have been different. She certainly had no trouble standing up to his own crew.

So...how long?

"What say you, girl? You taste sweet? I bet you do," Mik added.

He noticed the way Cat's fist clenched and unclenched. She kept her gaze forward, glaring directly at Bennett. His table had gone quiet...finally. Jonah sat beside Cat. Emmon and Tris across from her, closest to the adjacent table. Beside him, Thomas, Aaron and Peter watched the adjacent table with narrowed eyes.

"Say, lassie, whatever these old fish are payin' to bed ya tonight, we'll double it. Come on over to our table—"

Emmon and Tris shot to their feet simultaneously. "What did you just say?" Emmon roared.

"Burn me. This won't be good," he muttered, finishing off his tankard. He wouldn't let good ale go to waste in a bar fight. Around the room, faces looked up and did the same, drowning their ale before tankards slammed in succession on tables. Cat's mouth had opened, perhaps shocked at being called a whore. Or perhaps, finally ready with a retort. No words ever left her lips. Thomas, Aaron, and Peter also staggered to their feet, fast as skimmers.

"You heard us." Mik stood, meeting Emmon, eye to eye. "We'll buy your whore off you and pay her double. Though, when she gets done with *me*, she'll be thanking me, probably won't ask for payment at all." He grabbed his crotch in a crude gesture.

The rest of the tavern, already watching, snickered. Emmon's fist slammed into Mik's jaw faster than a blink. Like a bursting bubble, the tavern erupted. Chairs tumbled as tables surged and upended, to join the action. Tris jumped in. Not a second later, Thomas, Aaron, and Peter fell upon the neighboring table. Everyone else in the tavern didn't care who'd said what. It was an excuse to fight. An excuse to blow off steam. A room full of drunks was the perfect recipe for it.

"All right, girl," Bennett growled. "We're leaving." He bounded around the table and took Cat by the arm none too gently, pulling her up and away.

"I can handle myself, Captain."

"I'm sure you can. But don't you dare think of using magic in here. Not now. Let the lads have their fight."

"I have every right to—"

"You think I care about your *rights*?! Let the lads defend your honor. Our time here's up. They'll be fine. Not that you're worried for *their* sake."

Her eyes flashed but she let him drag her out. Jonah was hot on his heels. "On second thought," Jonah said from behind them, "I'd better stay and make sure they don't do anything too stupid."

"Yes, do that," Bennett shot over his shoulder. Tavern fights were nearly always harmless. Black eyes, broken jaws, nothing the local healers couldn't handle. Besides, most towns had a mage of some kind, even if it was a low level one, who could provide tonics and such.

Out in the cold night air, his breathing steadied. Cat ripped her arm away from him, hissing. Beaky soared through the open door a moment later. Blast! He'd forgotten all about her in all the chaos. But Beaky had been in plenty of tavern fights, and poked out plenty of eyes. She could take care of business when she wanted. Oh, yes.

"What now, Captain?" Cat hissed, since he was obviously calling the shots.

He sighed, looking out over the docks, then back along Barrel

Street. He wouldn't mind a soft feathered bed tonight. He'd had every intention of sleeping landside and departing in the morning.

"That depends, Cat. Would you rather sleep on the ship tonight, swaying and sick, or get a room at Marylyn's, up the road there?"

She tutted. "Depends on whether I'll be forced to share one with *you*."

"You got your own gold, don't you?"

Her jaw worked. She hadn't anticipated paying extra coin for stops along the way. No doubt she was rationing whatever she had for her destination—to do the gods only knew what.

The door burst open and his men poured out. Jonah had Peter by the collar. They staggered and stumbled, but they were alive. He looked them over, assessing, proud.

"All right, lads. Rooms at Marylyn's are on me tonight. Let's go." Cat said nothing, following them up the street to a quieter part of the town.

The common room at Marylyn's was a direct opposite to the Braised Duck. And it was blessedly empty. The six of his crew he'd brought along with him collapsed in chairs while he negotiated prices with Marylyn's maid.

"What's the best you've got," he asked her. As it turned out, a single suite with a copper tub was available. And because he was feeling generous, he purchased it for Cat, including the added fee for hot water. She'd want a bath after being at sea for four days. But he didn't tell her this immediately.

With his hands full of keys, he turned to see Cat eying the pathetic scene before them. Thomas was trying to keep his bloody, broken nose from messing up the furniture. Peter looked like he had a broken rib, maybe two the way he was groaning and hunched over. Emmon had a black eye and a finger that didn't look straight.

"Seems they paid a decent price for your honor," he said, sidling up beside her. "And I paid a decent price for you to have a bath and the nicest room here."

Cat's blink was the only show of surprise she offered him. "Will...will they be all right?" she asked instead.

He buried his shock over her concern. "Believe me, they've had worse. The healer won't come cheap, if we can get seen before we depart. But I'll pay it if—"

"I—" She cut him off, then stopped herself. He waited. "I was being trained as a healer back in Kastali Dun. Mage Marcel gave me private lessons."

"Interesting. Does that mean you're offering?"

"I haven't exactly..." She pursed her lips. He wasn't sure what she'd been about to say. "I'll do what I can."

He grunted. "Good. See that you do. I'll leave you to it. That girl over there behind the counter will have your bath done when you're finished." He gave her the key to her lodgings and strode across the room, handing the rest to Jonah, keeping only one for himself. He went to the stairs, taking one final look at his injured crew. He didn't bother telling them what they were in for with Cat. He'd let her deal with the aftermath. "Beaky, you damn bird. Hurry up." Beaky squawked and took off to follow.

When he reached his room, he deposited his things, cracked the window to let in fresh air, and stoked the fire. A few minutes later, his curiosity got the better of him. Cursing under his breath, he stole back downstairs and peaked around the stairwell, just in time to see Cat kneeling over Peter, who moaned about his broken ribs right as she began prodding him.

He studied Cat's expression. Something painful danced behind her eyes. A frown pulled her brows together in deep concentration. Her hands were poised over Peter's middle as she began muttering under her breath. He saw a burst of blue. It wasn't until Peter was grinning like a tomcat while Cat pressed at his healed ribs that he knew she'd been successful. A pleased smile crept over his features —prickly, but useful. Very useful. He'd remember that.

CHAPTER 6

LEARNING THE LANGUAGE

Esterpine

Claire's initial days in Esterpine passed quickly. Each morning she was up early, sparring with Koldis, followed by a rushed breakfast, before meeting Lord Marquin. The time with her spriten teacher was spent wandering the fringes of Esterpine while her afternoons were spent doing more of the same, but without Lord Marquin. At least while she was with him, he improved her knowledge of the spriten language, first by pointing out objects, and then by helping her form full sentences.

As the days rolled by, her progress was impressive. The words, she realized, bore great similarity to the old language, but prettier, more flowing, and more intuitive. When she'd asked Lord Marquin about it—the similarity—he'd sneered. "Our language is exactly as it's meant to be," he had said. "It was the asarlaí who stole it, twisted it for their own means."

She hadn't meant to offend him. Even still, he wasn't anywhere near as bad as her last teacher. Just thinking of Mage Targa left her jaw clenching. She'd take Marquin over Targa any day.

That being said, she was suspicious of him—of anyone favored by the queen—especially because of his excessive politeness. His words were so smooth that it was difficult to decipher the meaning behind them, but she was sure it was there. She often got the impression he was having a laugh at her expense. At each mispronounced sound or incorrect string of words. Even now, as they walked along the city's pathways, hands clasped behind her back, she couldn't help but notice the supreme superiority he radiated.

"That was *almost* perfect, Lady Claire," he said. "Almost, but not quite." There was nothing smug about his words, per se. Yet, she sensed it in his tone, flowing beneath like an undercurrent. She almost snorted, because she was pretty sure she'd said the phrase *exactly* as he'd instructed.

Koldis trailed behind her. He sent a snide remark, saying, *"If he doesn't stop saying* almost *perfect, I'm going to punch him in the face."* He'd kept up a barrage of telepathic insults since the start of her language training. She had to shush him frequently. But it helped her feel better, knowing Koldis was on her side.

"You want to accentuate the '*ui*' on *gui*." Lord Marquin's voice forced her to focus. "*Miella gethlah ohmenel, gui*. Because of the intention behind it. *Gui* means *please*, after all."

"Miella gethlah ohmenel, *gui*." *I would like an apple, please*. She repeated the words, yet again, careful to achieve perfection.

"Heilah, dil." *Good, better*. Lord Marquin nodded, and still, he used that tone. That spriten superiority.

She blinked, trying to hide her frustration. Her annoyance. Were all sprites this egotistical? *Gods, I'm not this bad, am I?* she wondered. After all, she was part sprite.

It is a shame you even question it, came the response. The sound of Cyrus's voice brought a smile, replacing her frown. He'd become easier and easier to converse with as of late. She supposed that was normal, since it had taken her body time to acclimatize to the soul she harbored.

She glanced around, eyes sliding over the lush greenery of the forest. Over the last several days, she'd seen nothing of the darkness first witnessed in the stag. Nothing of Princess Taylynn, either. Everything seemed...normal. They had sought out Prince

Feowen not long after the incident. Even Jeanine hadn't been able to weasel much of an answer from him. "My sister does things in her own way, as she sees fit," was the jist of his response. Though he *did* scowl at the mention of what they'd seen, at the appearance of his sister. "It's best you not concern yourself with the affairs of the forest, Lady Claire, or Princess Taylynn, for that matter. Focus on your training."

Koldis had cleared his throat at that and said, "Isn't being concerned with the forest a big part of Claire's training, Prince Feowen?" Something about the entire encounter had left Koldis on edge. He'd been strange for days, but stranger still after intercepting Princess Taylynn. Muttering, throwing dark glances at every shrub and tree, insisting Claire take a whole host of escorts anytime she wanted to go past the outskirts of the city.

Frankly, it was getting annoying.

But when she remembered the stag, her fear of seeing its rotting face and black eyes, she silenced her complaints. Koldis did have a point, if things like that were stalking the forest, and she was expected to go out alone, she'd have to confront them. That required magic she wasn't much confident in. Sure, she could use her sprite fire, but the thought of setting a fire in the middle of a forest didn't sound like a great idea. She needed to diversify her magic. She needed to gain more marks.

Clearing her throat, she spoke, "Forgive me, Lord Marquin, but we've been going at this for days now. When do you believe I should try my first solo venture into the forest?"

Marquin had been about to launch into a new set of sentences and pronunciations. He paused, face impassive, before saying, "I believe you should possess adequate mastery of our language before you may proceed with confidence."

She opened her mouth, about to speak, when Koldis said from behind them, "She didn't need your language to cast *sprite fire*. She didn't need your language to heal our kind after she defeated the vodar. Can she not *intuit* the words?"

At this, Lord Marquin's brow knitted together. He glanced back at Koldis, but nodded his acknowledgement of Koldis's words. He showed no sign of irritation at the question, though he probably hid it well. "Indeed, Lord Koldis, some things are bred of intuition, but I believe her chances will be better if she knows *and* understands the words she speaks, would you not agree, Lady Claire?" he asked, turning back to her.

She nodded, chewing on the inside of her cheek. So much mystery surrounded the act of learning spriten magic. She felt... lost. Utterly lost. She certainly hadn't anticipated it when she'd insisted on coming here. "I don't have a lot of time, Lord Marquin. Mastering a language could take months, years. I cannot remain here indefinitely."

"I...see."

"Surely you did not think I had come to stay forever."

"I did not. No."

"Then you must understand my impatience," she said.

"Our magic cannot be rushed, Lady Claire. Nor can your journeys into the forest. All things take time. Surely you understand that much."

She sighed. "And when the time comes? When I *am* ready to test myself and gain new abilities? I just...wander off? What do I take with me? Where do I go?" She was desperate to know more. Desperate to uncover the mystery behind these journeys.

He eyed her momentarily. "You take only yourself. I thought I had mentioned that before. The forest will provide."

She almost barked a laugh, her frustration rising. "And what then? Do I gather berries when I'm hungry and hope I don't starve? Sleep on pine straw? Spend my time searching for water? Hope the animals and critters aren't bothered by my presence?"

Hope that I don't encounter more darkness like what I already found? was what she really wanted to say.

"Ah. But you can create your own food, see?"

She frowned back at him. No. She *didn't* see.

"Come." He motioned her forward, where he stopped to kneel beside a bare patch of dirt. She blinked, then followed after. Without checking to see if she was there, he lifted his hand over the ground and began to sing. Some of the words she already knew, like *apple*, since she'd only learned that today. Her eyes widened when a green sprout broke free of the dirt and began to grow. Up, up, up. A quiet gasp broke from her lips.

Lord Marquin continued to sing, his voice beautiful and soothing, a sound she hadn't expected, but shouldn't have been surprised to hear. The sprout widened and a trunk formed, then thickened, and branches sprouted. Years and years of growth squashed into a matter of moments. Soon the tree was as tall as its creator, who stood up. On its leafy branches, blossoms, and then little balls sprouted, growing larger by the second, like time was on fast-forward. They turned a deep red. Apples.

She stared, wide-eyed. Speechless. The forest would provide.

Lord Marquin plucked several apples from the tree. They weren't as large as others she'd eaten, but she suspected that was because the tree wasn't fully mature. "Hungry?" he asked, a proud gleam lighting his eyes. He tossed her an apple before doing the same to everyone who accompanied them.

She bit into hers. Honey sweet, crisp flavor burst over her tongue. She huffed as she chewed and swallowed. "It's..." Quite simply the best apple she'd ever tasted. Though, she wasn't going to admit that to him. An apple bought with the price of Lord Marquin's magic. His markings on his forearm glowed brighter than the others.

"I learned to grow apple trees on one of my many trips into the forest. I was hungry. The forest knew what I wanted." He hesitated, looking at the one he'd just created. His fingers caressed the leaves, an expression of fondness clouding his features. This tender, thoughtful side of him was unexpected. "This one's young, but it has a healthy start. It will grow much bigger in time, all on its own."

"But...how?" She couldn't help the question. Couldn't help her wonder. Her clawing desire to copy his actions and grow her own tree. She didn't even care that he chuckled at her obvious jealousy. "You just created it from...*nothing*? With just the sound of your voice?"

He shrugged. "Yes, and no. To grow, it needed a seed and energy. I gave it both."

"But...I never saw you bury a seed in the dirt."

He laughed. "No need to, Lady Claire. The dirt beneath our feet is teeming with seeds long dormant. The wind carries them and deposits them. I simply coaxed one from the ground. Perhaps it traveled through the soil from somewhere else to reach me, and that took energy too."

She noticed that he did appear winded, especially compared to earlier. His voice sounded tired, not quite as sweet as it had at the start of their lesson. And his eyes looked far older than usual. *How old is he?* she wondered.

As if reading her thoughts he said, "Yes, I think we will end our lessons for today. Feel free to have a few more apples if you'd like."

She'd already finished hers. So had the others. She tossed away the core. An offering for the forest critters. And she knew Lord Marquin was correct about the seeds. The core would wither away in time, and its seeds would return to the earth. There, they would either take root or wait to be called forth again.

Lord Marquin turned to depart. A sudden idea took her. Setting aside her pride, she stepped forward. "Lord Marquin? Do you think—"

He stopped, slowly turning back. "Yes?"

"Do you think perhaps at the end of our lessons, you might show me more magic like that?" His eyes widened marginally, almost imperceptibly. "Nothing...crazy," she amended. "Just small things. I might better understand, if I see what spriten magic is capable of."

"Hmm." He appeared to consider this, then a smile broke free of his lips, the first she'd seen. "Very well, Lady Claire. If you feel it will help."

"I think it will."

"I must caution you, though. Every sprite's magic is different. I do not expect you to do things as I can, or even in the same way." And just when she thought she'd broken through his frustrating *sprite-ness*, there was that calm superiority again. But she didn't care, not if it helped her better understand.

She nodded, relieved. "Shalaya, Kenya." *Thank you, revered teacher.* She'd added *ya* to the spriten common word for *to teach*, as a term of absolute respect and reverence, hoping it would impress him.

"Heilah. Litaya danah." *Good. See you tomorrow.* This time, he bowed before departing, though she noticed he didn't say, *You're welcome.*

Koldis sidled up beside her, staring at the place where he'd disappeared into the forest. "Please tell me I'm not the only one who can't stand him."

She snorted. "He's not *that* bad. You just have to stroke his ego a bit."

"There's no room for ego here," he said.

"Why is that?" She turned to him, smiling, teasing. "Because yours is so large it takes up the entire forest?"

"Ha! Right." He gave her braid a playful tug. "Now, I don't know about *you* but I'm not keen for a lunch of apples. At least back at the palace, I can get some bread and cheese."

"Yes, yes. We'd better return." Behind her, the others grumbled their agreement. Their change in diet was taking its toll in the form of easy irritation. She wondered how long her drengr companions could go without meat before it became too much.

They started back. Koldis was silent a beat before speaking. "What was with all the questions about going into the forest, hmm?"

"I..." She sighed, considering. "I get the impression that Queen Jade isn't in a hurry to teach me their magic. No—" She shook her head, frowning, reconsidering. "That's not right. Because there's no *teaching* involved, it seems. Better that I say, Queen Jade is in no hurry for me to *learn* sprite magic."

"Indeed."

"You picked up on it too?" She turned to better regard him.

"I did." He rubbed the back of his neck. "I understand the need to learn their language. And you should. It's part of your lineage.

But their magic? The way I understand it, and from what I've seen when you use it, it's intuitive. You can create their green fire easily enough. You know all the words, even if you don't exactly understand—"

"I understand them perfectly."

"Oh *gods,* woman. You know what I meant. You understand them *now*. But only because those were the first words you asked Aolis Marquin to translate." Koldis never used Lord Marquin's title when he wasn't around. It was clear he absolutely despised her teacher.

"True. You're right."

"Look, Claire, if you're going to journey into the forest, might as well get going with it. I don't want to be here forever."

"Says the guy who doesn't want me going in alone." She arched an eyebrow at him.

He sighed. "I don't. Talon would—"

"—kill you, if anything happened to me. Yes, I know. But he needs to understand, and so do you. The only way I'm going to learn, is by going on these quest-things."

"I don't like it."

"Neither do I. Not after seeing what else lurks in the forest. And knowing next to nothing about it. I suppose I can take a knife with me and slit my arm open. Bleed on whatever darkness threatens me. See if my blood does the same thing as Tay—"

"No. You're not bleeding on anything."

"I was only teasing." She bumped his shoulder with hers.

LATER THAT AFTERNOON, she found herself alone in the forest. A feat she was proud of, and only because she'd used her position of command against Koldis. He was argumentative when she forced him to stay behind. "I don't plan to go far," she'd reassured him. Not that her reassurances had helped.

"When I said you should get going," he'd groused, "I didn't mean *today*."

"Well, I need a feel for being alone."

"Not at the expense of your *life*, Claire. What if it's too soon?" Koldis was entirely indecisive. She knew he was eager to leave, even after only a few days in Esterpine, but also afraid for her.

"I'll be fine, Koldis. Stay here."

"No."

"You will stay. I command it." She was already on her way to the door when she'd said it. When she'd used a tone that brokered no further argument. A tone that had made Koldis's eyes widen.

"I'm liking the idea of you being queen less and less," he'd darkly muttered.

"I heard that," she'd called over her shoulder, opening the door.

"I intended you to," he'd then shot back, just as she closed it behind her.

Even now, she smiled at the anger that disguised his concern. She really didn't plan on going far. Truth be told, she just wanted time alone, time away from everyone. Koldis never allowed her to venture off by herself. Her only moments of peace were in her bed chamber. And how much peace could be found in the crystal palace, anyway?

She sighed and came to a full stop, stretching her arms out, spinning around, watching the canopy turn into a blur above her. Laughter fell from her lips. This place was truly joyous, even if there was something sinister lurking. It was beautiful, and magical, and *green*. So much green.

Now, what she really needed was a peaceful place to sit and think. The days had begun to press in around her, a blur of activity. She wanted some time to digest everything, to think about the words she was learning, to practice speaking without someone who chided her for every mispronunciation.

"You wouldn't happen to have the perfect place, would you?" she asked the forest, almost jokingly. Though she couldn't help but wonder how deeply the king tree listened and watched from wherever it hid.

She continued wandering until she heard the sounds of metal on metal, a musical sound, purer than that of normal swordplay.

She followed it, curious, and came to a small clearing not twenty minutes from the city. There she found Jeanine and Feowen, sparring. Her eyes widened and she watched silently, until Feowen laughed and stopped, turning to where she stood hidden.

"You can join us, if you'd like."

"Oh." She stepped from the foliage, greeting them. "I didn't mean to pry. I just heard…"

"No matter." His gaze flicked over her. "Have a seat." He motioned to a grassy spot beside where she stood. Jeanine was breathing hard, sweat beading on her brow, sword in hand. Truthfully, she found herself curious. After all, Jeanine was human. Moreover, she and Koldis visited the sparring grounds so early, she hadn't had the opportunity to watch any of the sprites wield their famed weapons. How would Feowen compare?

"Only if you don't mind?" she asked Jeanine, knowing she usually didn't prefer an audience when Jovari and Koldis were beating her to a pulp.

"Not at all." Jeanine rolled her neck and shoulders, taking a few steps from Feowen to ready herself. It wasn't exactly the quiet place Claire had asked for, but maybe the forest knew her better than she realized. Or maybe the forest was trying to guide her to something else. To these two.

<h1 style="text-align:center">CHAPTER 7
PASSING TIME</h1>

Esterpine

Claire sealed her letter to Talon and passed it along to a palace attendant. A week had sailed by in a blink, and with it, a deepening sense of pressure. While she was no closer to gaining any new forms of sprite magic, she was feeling more confident in the language. That had to count for something... right? She could form simple sentences with a decent lilting accent. She could communicate in a basic manner. She could roughly understand the words spoken around her. She even conversed with the residents of the city at every opportunity, immersing herself.

Sure, she stumbled plenty, asked for clarification frequently, and forgot words. But she was learning. This language was in her blood. She was meant to know it. Her body, mind, and soul knew that. Especially because just like her first time visiting the forest, there were words that often popped into her head that she didn't remember learning.

"Letter for Talon?" Koldis asked, grinning as she shut the door to their suite.

His bedchamber was on the opposite side of the living area, across from hers. There were two other bedrooms besides theirs, afforded to the wing leader and wing second pairs that traveled with them. All other pairs had their own accommodations down the hall. Most of the pairs still passed through the suite throughout the day. It had become something of a hub for their companions. Besides the large dining room, the living space boasted two separate sofa arrangements and a small library, replete with plush arm chairs. Everything was centered around a six foot crystalline fireplace taking up the middle of the room. One benefit of crystal was its transparency. The fireplace need not sit against a wall to see the everlasting green fire burning within. A fire that never died.

"Are you feeling better?" she asked, ignoring his question. He looked rested, at least.

"Yes, but you didn't answer," he said, wandering across the room to where she stood.

She sighed. "Yes, if you must know. It was a letter for Talon. I figured it was time to give him an update on my progress, let him know how things were going with my training." She'd drafted a short note to him the day after arriving in Esterpine, just to inform him that she was safe, but the one today had taken a full page.

Koldis snorted. "Riiight. An update." His eyes danced. "Dear Talon. I miss you sooo much. I can't stop thinking ab—*arahhh!*" She punched him in the stomach. Hard. He keeled over. "Gods! When did you get so strong?"

"I have a good teacher." She grinned.

"Why did I ever think teaching you to punch like that was a good idea?" He groaned, rubbing his abdomen.

"Beats me," she said, eying him. "Oh, quit being such a cry baby. You're like a soccer player. I barely put any *oomph* behind it."

"A...*what* player?"

"A soccer player."

He tilted his head. "Is that a kind of...musician or something?"

She burst into laughter. "Soccer isn't an instrument, idiot."

"Well, how am I supposed to know?"

She thought about explaining it to him, the American version of football. "It's a little like mallets," she said. "Except instead of hitting the ball with a mallet, you kick it. And it's a softer ball. And bigger."

"Well," he said, hands on his hips now, "mallet players aren't complainers. Besides, do you even know how to play mallets?"

She shrugged. "I've watched some of the children at the keep."

"And do they strike you as cry babies?"

She grinned. "Nope." Truth be told, mallet players were pretty rough, ramming each other with their shoulders and battering one another with their mallets when no one was looking. But Koldis was missing the point. She sighed and went to her desk, putting away her writing things. They had the suite to themselves, for now.

It was Song Day, the sprite's version of Sunday. Every week's end was spent gathering in song and blessing. They broke into groups with their friends and family, and went out into the forest around the city, singing and giving thanks to the king tree for blessing them with an abundance of food and life. It was a bit ritualistic, but she loved it. The music alone was beguiling and ethereal, filling the trees with hundreds of voices.

She'd joined a small group of them that morning, invited by the queen herself. The queen led them through the trees, singing. Much to her delight, she'd understood many of the words. They spoke of gratitude and love. Of peace. Of all the things she felt here. She'd eagerly lifted her voice to sing along, melding with all the others.

Afterward came the Peace Hour, where sprites were encouraged to break away and wander alone, to speak their prayers in the forest, to be carried to the king tree on the breath of the wind. Thousands of whispers had drifted through the trees, sending goosebumps across her skin as she sat alone against the trunk of a tree, legs crossed, in quiet reflection. Not far from her, she'd heard Koldis muttering under his breath and had to tell him to shut it.

The entire experience was humbling. She loved the connection her people shared with the forest. Loved the respect they had for it.

The rest of the day was meant as free time, to gather and enjoy the company of friends. There would be lunch and dinner both served in the communal dining area—the giant area where they'd had their feast the first night. Usually only dinner was served there, and often a humble affair. Today, musicians would bring out their instruments. There would be dancing and fellowship. She was told that artists often brought their wares to display, or perform poems and other acts of showmanship.

She'd returned to the palace after their Peace Hour with the sole intention of writing to Talon, while Koldis trailed after her. The other pairs had already been dismissed. With her mornings taken up by Lord Marquin, her afternoons spent wandering, and her evenings gathered for the evening meal, she'd had little time alone in her chambers.

The moment they'd strode in and shut the door, Koldis groaned and said, "Gods, I need to rest my eyeballs after all that bleating." He'd crossed the main chamber. "When do we need to head over to the clearing?"

"Soon," she'd said, listening. Her ears had already discerned the faint sound of music. "They've started. But we can take some time for ourselves."

"Good. I need peace and quiet." He pinched the bridge of his nose.

She'd eyed him then, concerned. "Koldis—"

"I'm fine, Claire." He'd said nothing more before disappearing behind the door of his bedchamber for what she assumed was a nap. The walls of the sleeping chambers were thick and textured, diffusing the light and making it impossible to see through, so she had no idea if he'd indeed slept.

He'd been behaving strangely. Not so much the frequent pokes he made at spriten culture, which really didn't bother her. It was part of his personality to joke, and he didn't truly mean it. But she wasn't convinced that his short temper and brooding was due to a lack of meat. She'd taken to asking him if he was okay—frequently. And that was starting to annoy him.

"Shall we head over to the clearing," he asked, massaging his abdomen one last time where she'd punched him. "I'm famished."

"I suppose we'd better." She looked him over again, deciding he seemed well enough, and they set out. There was something he wasn't telling her, and she wasn't sure what to do about it.

～

THE AFTERNOON WAS A JOYOUS AFFAIR. She ate her fill, especially enjoying the peach and strawberry flavored wines the sprites uncorked for the occasion. With the feasting in full swing, she reveled in everyone's company, drifting first from her traveling companions, to the villagers of Kaljah, to various sprites she'd met over the past week. Greetings of "Javah!" rang out wherever she went. The people were growing used to her, accepting her, welcoming her.

Jeanine, much to her surprise, stayed beside her the entire time. Even Koldis had finally taken a seat with his companions to enjoy the entertainment, perhaps deciding she was safe enough to be left unattended. She was happy to leave him behind and escape his frequent scowling.

"Javah mih elam." *Greetings, my student.* Lord Marquin appeared beside her at one point, bowing politely. "Mekvelli an barah nin an morviah sinahaya." *May the peace of the forest be upon you.* It was a popular phrase of honor and respect. She was almost surprised to hear him use it.

She tilted her head and answered, "Edah sinahaya, kenya." *And upon you, Teacher.*

Her words pleased him. "You are learning quickly," he said. "The queen will be...surprised."

"Misaphi en heilah kenya." *I have a good teacher.* Lord Marquin smiled at this. Always one for flattery. She didn't allow herself to wonder why the queen would be surprised, but tucked that bit away for later.

They exchanged a few more pleasantries, speaking of the artists who had performed songs and poetry. Lord Marquin even had the audacity to quiz her on some of the words the artists had used. She was patient, answering each of his questions respectfully, all while Jeanine stood beside her.

She'd become more tolerant of her teacher as of late, especially since he'd been true to his word. Following each of their language lessons, he'd shown her snippets of his magic. Nothing as spectacular as growing an apple tree, but each informative in its own way.

She'd discovered the day after the apple tree that while sprites enjoyed showing off, they did not often give away all their secrets. Their magic was akin to their identity, a secret identity at that. They wore their luminescent tattoos like a language that could be read entirely, if one was well versed. Marks for certain elements like fire, air, earth, and water, had similarities across all bodies, but the dots and accents around them indicated the flavor the magic had taken.

For example, during one lesson, Lord Marquin had used the air around them to dampen sound, blocking out the chattering birds. Mastery of the element allowed for many different devices, he had explained. Not just blocking sound, but also creating gusts of wind, snuffing out fire, suffocating a person. He'd said the last with disdain; sprites were a peaceful people who did not condone killing living things but in the most necessary of circumstances. After all, they didn't even hunt meat in their own forest. It further explained why they were reluctant to join Dragonwall's conflicts.

Lord Marquin had even gone so far as to show her the mark he'd earned for his mastery of air. Unceremoniously, he'd pulled off his sheer tunic, showing off his muscled chest. On his left pectoral there was a triangle shape with swirls curving off the top and bottom points. Around it were dots and bars that decorated the triangle, and other swirls that led away from it, some joining with other shapes. "As I gain more abilities with air," he had said, "see these here?" He outlined the marks with his fingers. "More paths are carved across my skin."

"Like earning additional badges," she'd mused.

"Yes... I suppose so."

Their lessons had become far more beneficial.

Lord Marquin wasn't so bad, at least not as awful as Koldis

made him out to be. Even from across the clearing, she noticed Koldis's eyes glaring at him as he greeted her. He appeared oblivious. Whether or not he truly was, she couldn't be sure. She supposed she knew why Koldis disliked him so much, though she hated to think of it. Koldis saw Aolis Marquin as a threat to Talon. The drengr were territorial. *Quite* territorial.

But Koldis had nothing to worry over.

For every bit of increased flaunting Lord Marquin did with his magic, for every match of flattery she offered the sprite lord, she only thought of how much she missed her mate. What Koldis didn't know was that her thoughts frequently turned to Talon. To what he might be doing, to whether or not he thought of her as often as she thought of him, to how he fared in Kastali Dun. But mostly, she thought of how badly she wanted to return so that she might give him her final answer.

CHAPTER 8
MOVING ON

Kastali Dun

Saffra laughed, the full-bodied sound of it rolling off her chest. It was the first time in days, weeks even, that she'd felt so light. Watching Desaree struggle with a bow in hand, trying to follow a string of directions. Jocelyn's eyes danced too, but she held herself together better. It was clear that Desaree didn't mind their reaction to her half-hearted attempts.

They'd gone to the practice grounds to soak up the afternoon sun. It was the warmest part of the day, and still a late autumn chill tinged the air. Two weeks had passed in Claire's absence. All of them did their best to keep busy. Archery lessons, for one. It was a great way to get out of the keep, and with Lady Tamara's arrival, she was the perfect addition to their group—when she could join them.

"Perhaps you ought to help her with her form," Jocelyn suggested, her voice thick with mirth. "Desaree, let Saffra help you again."

Saffra stifled her laughter, doing her best to put on a straight face before stepping in. She pulled Desaree's bow arm up and into position—

"Forgive me, ladies. I hope I am not intruding."

Time seemed to stop. She sucked in a breath. She would never forget the sound of that voice. But…why was he here?

"Lady Saffra, I had hoped to say hello."

She whirled, almost trembling, as her hands clenched into fists. "Commander Daxton. How…how are you?" Her voice wavered.

Daxton could have picked any time to speak with her, but he'd interrupted while she had companions. The decision was not lost on her. Was he such a coward that he would not face her alone? "I am as well as can be expected, my lady. But tell me…are you…are you well?"

Her heart hammered in her chest. This man, this man she'd loved for years, was finally asking about her wellbeing. It was the first words he'd spoken to her since he'd admitted to remembering nothing. Desaree and Jocelyn suddenly appeared very busy with Desaree's bow, stepping away to give them a measure of privacy.

"I am managing, Commander. Thank you."

He nodded, clasping his hands behind his back. His muscular body wasn't what it once was. Time spent abed healing from the vodar poison had given him a leaner appearance. But he was still familiar. Still loved.

Daxton was quiet for a moment, then—"I wished to apologize."

She scowled. "For what?"

"For all that has happened. I…" He shifted his weight. "I feel responsible for whatever hurt I have caused you. I understand that it was, perhaps, out of my control, but I know that I have caused hurt and that…upsets me."

"You really cannot remember? None of it?"

His brows pulled together. "I remember Marcel hiring me to be your archery tutor long years past," he offered. "I remember going away to fight with our armies. I remember…" He unclasped his hands to rub the back of his neck. "That's really about it, truly. I do not remember returning. Or being promoted to commander. I certainly do not remember…" He gestured between the two of them.

"Our betrothal," she finished. His expression was pinched. "You truly feel nothing for me now? As if...as if there was never anything between us?"

He opened his mouth then frowned. "Forgive me, Lady Saffra. I am sorry."

Heat erupted across her skin. It blindsided her, the anger. The fury. After all this time, waiting for him. And for what? To be told that everything between them had never existed? It was just a dream?

She slapped him. Hard. Right across the cheek. The sound split the air, rising above the clamor of sparring around the field. Daxton's eyes widened. He took a step back, placing a hand over his cheek. Behind her, Desaree and Jocelyn gasped, stepping up beside her, to defend her, if necessary. Never was she more glad to have such fierce friends.

"Forgive me," Daxton said again. "Forgive me." He bowed and spun away, leaving her to stare at his retreating back. She trembled, hardly noticing when Jocelyn took hold of her arm, comforting her.

Her narrowed gaze followed Daxton across the sparring grounds. She noticed Bedelth then, standing with arms crossed over his broad chest. Watching. She could just make out his flashing eyes. His face held storm clouds, but the expression wasn't directed at her. It was focused entirely on Daxton's retreating figure.

"Come, my lady," Jocelyn urged. "Let us go inside. I think a nice cup of tea will help." She said nothing, allowing her handmaiden to lead her away, heartbroken, and fully unable to process what had just happened.

~

THE FOLLOWING DAY, Desaree and Jocelyn made a declaration. The only way to improve Saffra's bad mood was shopping. "Let's spend a frivolous amount of money and charge it all to the king's account!" Desaree said, gleefully. It was unlike her to be so rebellious.

The suggestion did bring a smile to Saffra's lips. "I have enough money of my own, thank you, but I appreciate the offer. Let's do it." Her heart might not have been in it, but they *had* promised Lady Tamara a tour of Kastali Dun's famed seaside market.

This was how they found themselves arm in arm, walking in a procession through the city. King Talon had sent a cluster of guards, as was no surprise to any of them. He'd never expressed such concern in the past. *Never*. But now that they were Claire's dearest friends, things had changed. Perhaps the king had become a little *too* protective, but they would be safer this way.

The world slipped by around her, entire buildings and streets, without much thought. She walked with one foot in reality and the other buried deep within her mind. She heard the happy chatter between Desaree, Jocelyn, and Tamara, heard their thoughts on each of the shops they passed, but only with a mild awareness.

Everything was a blur.

Had Daxton told the truth yesterday? Did he truly remember nothing? Years of a carefully constructed romance between them and...nothing? Why had he bothered to speak with her, if only to cause her further upset? Was it because he knew she was holding out hope for him? Hope that his mind would return? Surely there was still that possibility. But maybe he didn't care anymore. Maybe he was no longer interested in holding her heart.

Fresh anger coursed through her at the idea of him giving up so easily. That was not the man she thought him to be. She hadn't meant to strike him. Hadn't meant to make a scene. But...he'd deserved it. Plus, it'd felt so damned good!

Her cheeks heated. She felt a measure of shame for losing control. It was untoward for someone of her status. She was an example to the king's people. She was the king's prophetess, for the love of gods. How many had noticed? Surely Bedelth had witnessed her childishness—

"Saffra? Are you listening?" Jocelyn nudged her. They had already arrived at the market.

"What? Oh." She eyed the coin purse Jocelyn handled.

"I said, isn't this craftsmanship exquisite?" The booth owner, a middle-aged female with bronze skin and dark hair, flushed under the praise.

"Oh... Yes. It's beautiful," she found herself saying. "How...how much?"

The woman gave a price, but she barely heard. She had the presence of mind to nod at Jocelyn, approving the purchase. Jocelyn quickly exchanged coins and they were on to the next diversion.

They moved from booth to booth. With winter all but upon them, gloves and scarves were a popular item today. They also lingered over the jewelry stalls. Desaree wanted a new hairnet and pair of matching earrings. Jocelyn wanted a new bracelet. Tamara found a pair of cufflinks that would look divine on Byron's tunic sleeves.

It was a blur. She did her best to keep her mind from wandering, but it was a genuine challenge. She was relieved when the hours passed and they finally made their way back to the castle. Relieved that she could be alone to wallow.

"We will leave you to rest," Jocelyn said, seeing her to her room. "Shall we return to escort you to dinner?"

She hesitated. The thought of taking her meal in the great hall with the other courtiers twisted her insides. "No, that won't be necessary. I will ring for dinner when I'm hungry."

Jocelyn opened her mouth to argue, then nodded. "Very well, my lady."

At long last, she found herself alone. It left her feeling overly guilty, allowing her bad mood to seep into everything. She knew she wasn't the best company, that her friends worried for her, but what was she to do? How long did it take one to recover from a broken heart? From the melancholy of loss?

She tried to read out on her balcony, but it was no use. Perhaps a nap? But that didn't work either. She worked on a puzzle, but that only gave her mind more time to think of what might never be. She was *so* angry at herself, at Daxton, at the world, that she screamed and swept the puzzle off the table where the pieces scattered across the floor—

A knock sounded.

Her heart stopped. She blinked. The anger dissipated, popping like a bubble. She looked between the door and the scattered puzzle pieces. If she stayed silent, no one would know she was here. It wasn't Jocelyn—she knew that much. Jocelyn would have simply swept into the room without waiting.

But the knock came again— "Lady Saffra, I'm coming in." The door opened before she had time to insist otherwise.

Bedelth stood there, looking at her. His expression changed, eyes softening. He shut the door and strode across the room, stopping short when his foot landed on a puzzle piece. "What...?" He looked around and saw her mess. "Saffra..."

She said nothing. Couldn't think of anything but her embarrassment.

Bedelth didn't wait for her to speak. Instead, he got on his hands and knees and began sweeping pieces up. She stood motionless, watching King Talon's shield reduced to clean-up duty. His broad shoulders were hunched as he moved.

She tried to work her mouth, to speak, but nothing came out.

When he stood at last, dumping the pieces into the small box on the table, he said, "I have dinner coming. I would like you to eat with me."

"I—"

"Before you protest, I ordered one of your favorites: toasted cheese sandwiches and tomato soup. Oh, and peach cobbler. The cookery made it especially for you. You would not refuse their efforts, would you?"

The air whooshed from her chest. She all but fell into a chair. Bedelth took the adjacent seat, leaning back to regard her. "I heard your ladies talking of the wonderful afternoon you all had at the market today. Did you buy anything?"

Her annoyance evaporated, replaced by immense relief. He wasn't going to jump straight to questioning her about what had happened yesterday with Dax. Even if he had seen it.

"A coin purse?" She opened and closed her hands. "A scarf. A pair of gloves. A hairnet… I think?"

He smiled. "You think? Gods, woman. Sounds like Jocelyn could have spent your entire savings and you wouldn't have noticed."

"Can you blame me?" A smile pulled at the corners of her lips, but she wouldn't give it to him.

"No. Hardly. But I'm glad you went with them. Lady Tamara needed the excursion."

Had she? Saffra had been so wrapped up that she hadn't considered what the excursion might mean to the young fort leader.

"Plans have been tedious," Bedelth said by way of explanation. "I feel for the poor girl, still so young, but thrust into the arms of responsibility. It's a wonder she hasn't crumbled under the pressure."

"Claire spoke highly of her," she mused.

"I can see why. The two were nearly inseparable during our time in Brezen."

She exhaled. "I miss her."

"We all do." He fiddled with a lone puzzle piece that hadn't made it back into the box. "You should see King Talon. His moods have darkened. He snaps at everyone's ideas like they're the worst ideas in the world."

"I take it battle preparations aren't going well?"

No one expected her to attend, but she had been present for a few of the war council meetings. She understood how taxing they were. How exhausting. Which was partly why she avoided them when she could.

"It's hard to make progress when we're cornered—"

A knock cut him off as a servant announced their food. She made to stand but Bedelth beat her to it. "Stay. I'll get it."

She glanced at the table, quickly shuffling away the rest of the puzzle, setting the box on the floor. Bedelth returned with a large tray. She smelled the toasted cheese sandwiches before he set the tray before them and began removing platter covers. She watched him in silence, suddenly grateful for his steady presence.

He was attentive as he placed the food, the glasses of water, and the dessert. She took the first bite, dunking the corner of her sandwich into the tomato soup. It was heaven on her tongue. She almost groaned.

They ate in companionable silence for several minutes until Bedelth said, "I can get wine, if you'd prefer."

She considered, swallowing. "I've probably had enough to drink for a lifetime. Water is fine." She was well aware that she'd spent plenty of evenings alone, drinking several glasses to pull her mind from its thoughts. But if Daxton had no plans to fix things between them...

All those things Bedelth had said, about Dax being a human, about Dax aging when she wouldn't for years to come. There were so many counts against them. It would have been one thing if their love rang true. If they had something to fight for. She'd seen the look in Daxton's eyes. The regret. There was no passion there. None whatsoever. It was all the answer she needed. It was time to move on. She was done waiting for him.

CHAPTER 9
PLEDGED SUPPORT

Kastali Dun

Talon glared across his desk at Reyr. They sat in his study, their goblets of wine mostly untouched on the mahogany desktop. The days were getting shorter and darkness had long since fallen, but he kept the glass doors leading out to the covered balcony open, letting the crisp air flutter the curtains. It was more humid than normal, signaling the approach of yet another storm. Winter would bring days of rain, which also meant days of being sequestered indoors.

"Look, if you'd just think about this rationally, my king, and stop being so temperamental—"

"I am *not* temperamental," he snarled. Reyr lifted an eyebrow—case in point. He exhaled, running a hand through the tangled tufts of his hair, massaging his temples, the bridge of his nose.

"Talon, if the dock master's—"

"*If.*"

"Would you let me finish?!" Reyr snapped. "Gods. *If* his records are correct, then the last time this happened was during Tristan and Lena's reign. Oshea attacked in full force. An entire fleet of ships and nets and dragon lances converged on the Bay of Bandu, hoping to use Kastali Dun as a point of conquest for Dragonwall."

"They were unsuccessful, obviously," Talon drawled. "And those records are what, forty thousand years old? They've probably become unreadable by now, easily misinterpreted. This is *Oshea*, Reyr. They're so far across the sea that sometimes I struggle to believe the country even exists."

Reyr shook his head, his lips pressed in a thin line. "You forget that we preserve parchment with magic. The records can be trusted." His voice was flat. "You cannot deny this, Talon. You cannot deny the implication. The possibility of what is coming. I know with Claire gone..."

"Don't." Talon's eyes narrowed. "Just...don't."

Reyr's expression softened. "You forget that I know exactly what it is like to have a mate. To be separated."

Talon's heart tightened, then. Painfully. At the reminder of what Reyr had lost. And with that reminder came a deep, intense fear. Because he could also suffer the same loss...some day. Nothing between him and Claire was promised. Reyr's past was evidence of that.

He blew out a breath, staring at Reyr. "Is it supposed to hurt this much? That...feeling? It's like something is gripping my ribs and trying to rip them out."

"It hurts." Reyr nodded. "Badly, if memory serves."

"Why?" It angered him, the pain. It kept him on edge. Did Claire feel it too? The unease? The tug? He hadn't felt this way when he'd been in the forest. Not like he did now, and at that time, they'd still been mates. He voiced these concerns, revealing his vulnerability.

"It's the magic of the forest," Reyr said, offering a theory. "The many barriers erected to keep the sprites safe. Think about it. She is cut off from you entirely. It's the same reason we couldn't communicate with anyone outside whilst we were there. Remember? It is its own bubble."

Talon grumbled. It made sense. "Claire said she couldn't eat while I was away," he recalled. He seemed to be struggling with food, too. "She said she lost her appetite in my absence. That something felt wrong the whole time I was gone."

Reyr rubbed at the stubble along his jaw. "It would seem that she bore the brunt of your departure the last time, and now you bear it this time."

"And knowing now what she is to me, how much I love her, hasn't made that burden any easier."

"Neither has the knowledge of Oshea, my king."

He snorted. *My king.* Reyr often did that—called him *my king* to be soothing. Talon had picked up on it over the years. He wasn't sure if it helped or simply reminded him of exactly what he was. Of the burdens he carried.

He leaned back in his chair, finally picking up his goblet, swirling the contents within. "Do you think Oshea has struck a deal with Kane?" His voice was low, afraid to put into words this deep fear. That Kane had done far better than any of them could have imagined, working with so many other countries to weaken them, to bring them to their knees.

Reyr's eyes closed briefly. "It wouldn't be so outlandish, would it? Kane strikes Dragonwall with goblin hordes in the east, turns our focus there. Then with his personal force at Fort Squall. Then he follows it up by sending a tertiary force to our capital from Oshea? If he can't have the dragonstones, why should that stop him from conquering us?"

"Our race is already dwindling. What need has he for the stones if he manages to kill us?"

"Exactly." Reyr picked up his goblet too, and drank deeply. When he set it down, he stared long at Talon. "I miss her too," he said at last, quietly. "She makes things better around here. Happier. She'll make a good queen."

That admission did something to Talon, pulled on something in his chest. Perhaps it was best if Reyr left him to brood. He considered dismissing him—

"Your Majesty? I think you'll want to see this." Bedelth.

His brow furrowed. *"What is it?"* he asked, broadcasting the question broadly enough to encompass Reyr's mind. Reyr sat forward to listen, alert.

"You'd better just come and see." Bedelth sent them the location. Something of surprise laced his words, sending a thrill of excitement through them. *"I've also summoned Verath and Jovari."*

They wasted no time in traveling through the keep to the aviary —a place he rarely visited. In fact, he couldn't remember the last time he'd been here. It looked much the same as he remembered, though. When they arrived, the others were already there. So was the caretaker, along with a man who looked like a farmer, trembling, his wide eyes darting about.

Everyone stood gathered around a stone table in the center of the room.

The aviary housed the keep's birds of prey. Hawks, falcons, owls. He'd never bothered much with the sport, but the nobles loved it. Elaborate cages designed for a comfortable life lined the walls of the circular tower. Most of the birds slept for the night, but there was a plethora of empty spaces vacated for the aviary's owls.

"Want to tell me what's going on?" he said, looking at Bedelth. Impatience laced his words.

"Yes, Your Majesty, though you may not believe it. I was summoned half an hour ago by the guards. We found this fellow arguing at the gate, trying to gain entry into the keep."

"In the middle of the night?" Talon's eyes narrowed.

"Forgive me," the man mumbled, looking at the ground. His quivering voice was hardly audible.

A caw answered.

Talon looked at the stone table in the center of the room. A raven, feathers blacker than black. It hopped from foot to foot, rustling its feathers. It was uneasy. One of its wings was askew, like it had been caught in a windstorm. He noted the metal cuff around its left ankle, and then the small tube lying beside it. The caretaker was attempting to get food and water into the bird. The raven wasn't sure what to make of the man's attention.

"It would seem," Bedelth continued, "that this bird landed in Roden's garden yesterday." *Roden...?* The farmer. He glanced back at the trembling man. "Roden lives half-a-day's ride from Kastali Dun. Is that correct?" Bedelth asked.

"Yes. Yes, mi-milord." Roden was sweating, even in the chill of the aviary.

The flutter of wings sounded. It distracted them momentarily as an owl returned through one of the many arched windows, a fat rat caught in its beak. The tail dangled limply. The owl paid them no mind, flapping over to its cage. Master Keet rushed over and opened the door for it, allowing the owl to settle down with its prize.

Talon glanced back at the raven, considering. "Is this what I think it is?" he asked.

"I would say so, my king." Bedelth handed him the tube. "Only dwargs use ravens. Hearty birds. Good for flying through the mountains."

"And you mean to tell me it flew all the way across Dragonwall to reach us?" Talon had never, in all his life, received word from the dwargs. His father had, apparently, once, but he'd not been alive at the time, so he'd never actually seen the raven that sent the letter. Dwargs didn't much communicate with the drengr, unless the Drengr went north to request the forging of new sveraks and such. It certainly wasn't a deal done through messenger birds.

"It would seem, judging by the state of the bird, that it has flown a long way," Reyr said, voicing his thoughts as he reached out and stroked the bird's back. It was busy pecking at the food, still holding its wing out at an odd angle. "Looks like it's been through a lot. It's a wonder it made it here."

"Indeed, my Lord Reyr, most impressive." Master Keet looked at them. "I reckon I can fix its wing up while it's here. Shouldn't be too hard. If not, I'll get the mages involved."

"Yes. See that you do," Talon said, glancing at the tube. His fingers fiddled with it, but he dare not open it here. He glanced up at the farmer before looking back at Bedelth. "Can we trust him?"

"Hard to say," Bedelth answered. "Perhaps we should question him further. This could be a message planted to distract us from something else." Like an attack from Oshea. The words went unsaid.

"Mercy. *Please*." The farmer groaned, flinching away. "I swear all I said was true. Ask my wife. We can go there now, if it please, Majesty."

Talon didn't have the patience for this, especially not in the middle of the night. "That won't be necessary. Jovari, see that he's given a comfortable chamber for the night."

"I'd rather not trouble no one..." Roden spoke to the ground, still afraid to so much as look upon his king.

"See that he is watched," Talon added. "Until we read the contents of this message I'm not quite sure what to make of any of this."

The tube did not appear tampered with. But he wasn't sure about Roden. Kane's nasks could be anywhere, anyone. He'd been fooled once before, and he would dare not let it happen again.

Congregated around his fireplace with his shields, he unfurled the note. Roden had been seen to, given a comfortable room on the fourth floor of the north wing, with guards posted outside his door. If indeed the man had acted out of goodwill, he would be rewarded. But if this was some ploy...

"Well? What does it say?" Reyr sounded impatient.

He read the note, blinking with disbelief. Then he read it again, but said nothing. His head began spinning, mind turning over and over. "I think it's best if you read it yourself." He passed it to Reyr, who passed it to the others, in turn. They remained quiet until it was read by everyone, even Dallin, who Verath had brought along. It seemed he'd taken Dallin's training quite seriously. Dallin shadowed him in all things now, sworn to secrecy by pain of death, since he'd not yet taken any oath. Talon still wasn't sure if he should admit someone so young into the prestigious position, yet, there had been no other offers. And there should always be six—

"Can we trust it?" Reyr asked, returning the note to Talon.

"This could be the difference between defeating Kane or losing Dragonwall," Jovari said.

"Perhaps it's the sign we've been waiting for, to move against Fort Squall," Bedelth added.

Verath and Dallin remained quiet. He wondered what Claire would make of it. What she'd say, knowing that dwargs were pledging themselves to this fight. He almost snorted at the thought. Claire had never even seen a dwarg.

"The dwargs are much like the sprites," he said at last. "They do not often involve themselves in our politics. Even if they are more a part of this kingdom than our tree-loving occupants."

"Can we trust what Lord Dubrael says, though?" Bedelth asked. "And what he says about Lord Averaen? Was the fort leader truly there?"

"That's a good question," Talon mused. "How fortunate that we have his own flesh and blood in our midst."

All eyes fell on Dallin. "Uhm..." Dallin cleared his throat. "That...I mean to say..." His eyes darted between them, clearly unused to being put on the spot.

"You said Lord Averaen was away, did you not?" Verath spoke for the first time. Dallin seemed to relax at the address, more accustomed to Verath than the others.

"That's correct. He left on a secret mission, decided upon between himself and Lord Davi of Fort Squall." Talon's eyes darted to Reyr at the mention of his twin. Reyr's face was stone. "There were maps found deep in the library of Fort Edge," Dallin continued, "old maps of the mountains. Of the strongholds once held by the Ice Clan. It was his intention to scout Shadowkeep. To determine where Kane might be hiding."

"Interesting..." Talon leaned back, eying the words on Lord Dubrael's scrap of parchment again. "I wonder if Averaen was successful. And what, in turn, took him to the hall of this Lord Dubrael. How did he end up in dwargish hands?" He fell silent for several beats. "I don't think Lord Dubrael would lie. I don't think he would claim that Averaen turned him to our cause if Averaen had not been there. Yet...I am still wary."

"There is one piece that fits," Reyr said. All eyes turned to him in question. "Mikkin. I admit I was most surprised to hear mention of him, and shocked that his travels took him to the same place as Lord Averaen. You remember, do you not, my king? Mikkin was the fellow I spoke with after reentering Dragonwall. He's the survivor from Bellnesse. I never would have imagined..." His voice trailed off.

"Strange," Jovari mused, "how things work out. I remember you speaking of him after you rejoined us. Strange how the fates twine us together."

"So we place our trust in this Mikkin fellow, sent along to the other clans?" Talon asked. "Hope that their small band might convince others to stand beside our cause?"

"If he succeeds, it would be a point in our favor," Reyr said. "We will need help regaining Fort Squall."

Verath snorted. "I'd call it a miracle. But we'll need more than just the dwargs. We still haven't decided how we'll handle the city's occupants. How we will protect them from dragon fire when we face Kane's wild dragons in battle. Dwargish armor is immune. At least we can outfit our armies with it. But the city...?"

Nods of agreement rippled around the sitting area.

"Let that be a challenge we face tomorrow," Talon decided. "We will want to inform Lord Byron and Lady Tamara of this, come the morning. It will certainly change how we plan our attack going forward. For now, it is late. I've kept you long enough."

"What of the farmer?" Bedelth asked, bringing the discussion full circle.

"Harmless, I think," Talon decided. "It was good of him to bring the bird. Courageous even. Most would have disregarded it or taken the message and discarded it."

"Thank the gods he didn't," Jovari mumbled.

"As important as this is, it's a miracle it made it here," Bedelth mused.

"Indeed. He will be rewarded, I think. I would like to speak with him in the morning. Jovari, arrange a breakfast for the two of us, here I think. Then we will see him home."

"Of course, Your Majesty." Jovari stood, as did the others. He dismissed them, but Reyr lingered.

"What is it?" he asked, failing to disguise how tired he sounded.

"If we go north, as badly as I want to, we must face the possibility that Oshea could attack while we're gone, while Kastali Dun is undefended. And what if Claire returns here while we're gone. Alone and undefended?"

Talon sighed. He'd already thought of that. And it didn't sit well.

THE FOLLOWING DAY WAS TEDIOUS. Painful, even. Breakfast with the farmer, who still couldn't bear to look upon him, let alone form a single sentence in his presence. Meetings with Fort Squall's wing leaders and wing seconds about the dwargs. Gathering of his lower council to hear how pirate raids and ongoing goblin attacks were still affecting trade.

The only thing that made the day better was the letter that arrived later that afternoon. The moment it found his hands, he felt Claire's presence lingering over the parchment. He barked commands to the servants in his tower that he was not to be disturbed for any circumstances whatsoever, by pain of death, if necessary. They'd balked at that. But it got the point across. "Even if the castle comes down around us," he'd added, descending to his study where he barricaded himself within.

He sat at his desk and stared at the letter, unopened, for several long minutes. His heart raced, nervousness more than anything. Gods above! Over a letter. He snorted and broke the seal.

Dear T,

Today is a Song Day, so I have some time to

write. I hope you haven't been concerned by my silence. I assure you, my days have been filled with tedium. I've been assigned a teacher and we work together each morning. I'll keep the details from this letter. Anyway, he's rather...interesting. Lord Marquin. Did you meet him while you were here?

I get along with him better than Koldis does. Speaking of. Koldis has been acting strange. Moody, even. I'm not quite sure why. I'm certain there's something he isn't telling me. Is there something I should know?

So much has happened. I met a few unicorns the first day. And then we found something in the forest the day after that. I can't say more here, but it was unsettling. Since then, things have been calmer, but I'm worried. Something isn't right. Koldis threatened to bring me straight back to Kastali Dun.

He won't. It's too important that I stay. I will be careful.

How are plans coming along? How are Desaree, Jocelyn, and Saffra? Will they write to me too, if you agree to send their letters? Has Lady Tamara reached Kastali Dun? I wish I was there to show her around. Are your shields behaving? What of Dallin? I feel as if there is so much I'm missing.

I miss you all terribly. But I miss you, especially. How many kisses will I owe you when I return? One for each day of my absence? And what interest rate will you charge? I'll pay it, whatever *it is.*

Please do not worry about me. I am well. That is all for now. Give my love to everyone. Tell Reyr that he'd better be taking good care of you in my absence. Or else...

All my love,

C

TALON SIGHED, folding the sheet of parchment. His eyes were unfocused, his mind turning over each of her words. Some of what she'd said made him smile. But some of it left a bad feeling in the pit of his stomach. He thought of Koldis and guilt burned in his chest. He'd hardly considered it when pairing Koldis up for this mission. The decision had been purely based on fitment. Koldis and Claire had a unique bond and got along well together. She was comfortable with him, much to his surprise.

Gods! What must Koldis be going through, surrounded by wildlife in the forest? He hadn't thought about how deeply it might affect him. As benign as his ability might be, stuck in closed spaces would pose a trial. Perhaps that was a misstep on his part.

No wonder he'd voiced concern about going.

"Reyr, I need you."

"I'll come at once."

He had time to unfold and reread the letter before Reyr's steps sounded on the staircase. "Yes, my king?"

"Sit," he snapped.

Reyr complied, looking at him from across the desk. His eyes fell to the parchment in Talon's hands and widened. "Is that...?"

A smile came to Talon's lips. "It is. Here." He handed it to Reyr, well aware that his shield would want to read Claire's words, especially her well wishes and the words specific to him.

He watched Reyr's expression while he read, his smile deepening. He felt lighter than he had in days. With just a few words, she had managed to lift his mood.

Reyr snorted, clearly having reached the last bit. "Or else *what,* exactly?" he muttered, but a grin took up residence on his features.

"Or else suffer her wrath."

Reyr chuckled before turning serious. "What is this thing she mentions? Something isn't right?"

"That's what I would like to know," he mused.

"You saw nothing amiss while you were there?"

Talon barked a laugh. "Being in those damn trees sets me on edge. How should I know? Nothing ever feels right in a place like that." Reyr nodded. "But yes, I want to know what she saw. What frightened Koldis enough that he threatened to return her? Koldis isn't easily spooked. None of us are."

"She doesn't know of Koldis's abilities," Reyr added. "I suppose with the time they're spending together, the truth will come out."

He sighed. "I never thought to mention it. Truthfully, I didn't even consider it when I assigned him to this task."

"You aren't the only one. The thought slipped my mind, too. He could have said something."

"He certainly voiced his concern, in the way of disagreeing with their food. I'm sure there was more to it than that, but..."

"But what?"

Talon hesitated. "He wanted to go with her. He wouldn't have jeopardized that by reminding us. He cares for her."

"We all do," Reyr said. "She's our queen. Your mate. Our instinct to protect her is nearly as strong as it is to protect you."

Talon was glad of it. It meant keeping her alive and safe. But unease needled its way beneath his skin. What was happening in the forest? What made her worried in a place that should have been a safe haven? Perhaps only time would tell. For now, it was entirely out of his control. He would simply have to trust her.

CHAPTER 10
CALLING WATER

Claire flipped through the pages of a leather-bound journal in her lap, admiring the hand drawn charcoal sketches. Each showed a different flower with exquisite shading and detail. Beside each flower was a description detailing scent, size, color, and more. Everything was written in the sprite language. *Ednuar*. Reading *Ednuar* was much harder than speaking it. But she considered it an opportunity to improve her knowledge of the forest's flowers as well as its language.

She brushed her finger over a daffodil, shaded by a deft hand. It didn't look quite like the daffodils she was familiar with, but close enough. *Zahreh*. She whispered the word aloud.

Koldis sat in an armchair opposite her. He was reading too, a book on the history of spriten weaponry. She stole glances at him, noticing the way his brow furrowed, the little frown that had taken up residence on his face, pulling at the corner of his full lips.

"It can't be that boring, can it?" Her tone was teasing. He glanced up and threw her a glower. Answer enough, she supposed. She sighed and shut the journal, wrapping its leather ties around it. Koldis pretended not to notice, and flipped to another page. "I think tomorrow is the day," she said, studying him for a reaction. She'd been waiting to bridge this subject, wary of what he might say.

"Day for what?" he said, keeping his voice level without looking up.

"I'm ready, Koldis. It's been two weeks. My use of *Ednuar* has advanced. I'm ready to try my first solo venture into the forest." He shut his book then, and looked at her. "Well? Isn't this the part where you tell me all the reasons why I shouldn't? Why it's too dangerous?"

He exhaled. "How long do you wish to be gone, my queen?"

Her eyes narrowed. She shifted to better face him. "A day or two? Long enough to be alone, short enough that I don't starve if I can't summon my own food."

Koldis regarded her. "I suppose it's time. As much as I hate the idea of you confronting whatever darkness is lurking—"

"We haven't seen anything since that first time."

"I know, and that's what worries me. It's there. I know it's there because I've sensed it... It's there."

"Sensed it?" she hedged.

"It's...not important."

"No, I think it's very important. You've been acting weird. Something's bothering you, and I have a feeling it's more than just the stag we encountered."

He leaned back. "I'd prefer we not talk about it." His fingers traced the surface of the book in his hands, sliding over the text stamped onto the cover.

"Should I be worried?" She didn't want to force him into a discussion he'd rather avoid, but it depended on how important this *thing* was, whatever he was hiding.

"No. I don't see why you should. It does not concern you. Take your trip into the forest. But no more than two days. Any longer and I will come looking."

She snorted. "And get lost in the process."

"I'll drag Feowen along."

"Fine, fine." She exhaled, relieved. He wasn't going to fight her.

Probably because he understood that the sooner she accomplished what she set out to, the sooner they might leave. She wasn't so sure it would be that simple. But one could only hope.

~

THE FOLLOWING day she set out with very little fanfare, just a few simple goodbyes and a word of caution from Koldis to *be careful*. She stayed alert and never lost her path. The forest created paths intentionally, leading its occupants where it pleased, so she allowed it to guide her.

It was easy to lose track of time in a place like this. She didn't think about her thirst until she was really, really thirsty. Only then did she keep her ears pricked for the sound of trickling water. The forest's creeks and rivers were its lifeblood. Like all arteries and veins, it would have many, and she just needed to find one.

She hadn't brought a single thing with her. No weapons. No food or water. Just the clothes on her back—a green tunic and beige pants—and soft boots on her feet. Though, she would have felt safer carrying her spriten dagger.

She began swallowing, trying to moisten her parched mouth. When that didn't work, a light sheen of sweat beaded her forehead. She stopped to breathe, planting her hands on her hips. All around her, insects chirruped and birds broke out into song. There was plenty of noise, but there wasn't a single sound that hinted at water. Her mood darkened.

I doubt the forest would hurt you intentionally, Cyrus said, and she almost snorted, because she still recalled the rot consuming half of the stag's face only weeks ago. *I do not believe that was part of the forest,* he reasoned. *It was something else.*

That was what worried her. Was it Kane? Was it his evil seeping into the purest place in Dragonwall?

There was no use in thinking about it now. She needed to find water or she'd collapse. She groaned, interrupting the forest. Everything fell silent, then, a moment later, the birds burst into song again. Gods, she was *thirsty*.

She contemplated the foliage, considered striking out on her own, then decided against it. Better to stick to the path. Eventually, it widened. She found a log and plopped down—just for a short rest. Despite winter approaching, she was warm. She took slow, deep breaths. When she had the energy for it, she looked up through the canopy of the trees. There was no real way to tell how late it was. She'd left around mid-morning, so it was sure to be mid afternoon.

"I can't learn magic if I'm so thirsty all I think about is water," she muttered, failing to hide her irritation. This had to be a test. Only, she hadn't expected it to happen so soon.

The word for water was *llayah*. Marquin always sang his magic, weaving words together to indicate his intent. Usually, it was some witty form of sprite poetry, the prettier the better.

She didn't have anything witty, so she opened her mouth and tried a few phrases to create water. Her voice was raspy, but she forced herself through. Nothing happened.

A breeze blew, rustling one of the ferns along the path. She received the message loud and clear. Her jaw clenched and she shot to her feet. "Fine. You want me to follow your stupid path? Fine!"

If desperation was a requirement for magic, well, she was feeling pretty desperate. Her feet were heavy, her steps slow. How long did it take a person to die of thirst?

You're not going to die of thirst, Cyrus said, almost bemused. *It hasn't even been a full day yet. You can go several, at least.*

She counted the hours in her head. She'd gone at least seven *hours* and that was bad enough. Traipsing through the forest only made her thirstier.

Just as the light began to disappear, she heard it, the faint trickle that hinted at water. A near sob escaped her chest as she rushed forward, following the sound. Up ahead, she found a creek bed, but when she sank to her knees along its bank, her eyes blurred with tears of frustration. There was no water. It was dry.

"I don't...I don't understand," she cried, hoping the king tree would hear her. "Why would you do this?!"

It felt like the meanest trick in the world. She began digging at the pebbles and sand, hoping that maybe, somewhere underneath, there'd be water. Only, there was nothing.

Her mind must have tricked her, made her hear water when there was none. Like a mirage in the desert.

"I don't understand," she repeated through her tears. Shouldn't all the creeks in the forest bear water? Why was it empty?

Call it, Cyrus said. *Call the water.* She'd done that earlier, and nothing had happened. *Yes, but perhaps you weren't meant to, then.*

Maybe he was right, and this was the true test. An idea took hold. The water lived somewhere. It simply needed to be coaxed, invited forth. She plunged her hands into the hole she'd made in the creek bed. It was cool and grainy against her skin. She closed her eyes and let herself feel it—let herself sense her surroundings. Then she cataloged the words she wanted, the things she wanted to say to invite it forward, rather than simply create it, like she'd tried earlier.

"Stalle, eskh ayah seldah. Amah yaa. Hafa payst. Akis jaan." *Come forth, from your fountain. Give life. Quench thirst. Flow free.* These words felt right. She repeated them again, surer this time. And again, letting the sound of her voice conquer her mind, her thoughts, until there was nothing.

This bed deserved water. Deserved life. And the forest intended for her to bring it.

The ground rumbled then, gentle, but she felt it in each place she made contact. She heard the trickling, faint at first, growing louder. Her voice didn't falter. She continued singing, eyes closed, letting her ears fill in the world around her. Behind her eyelids, a whitish glow appeared. She didn't question it, couldn't question it. Her thoughts were still too blank, too focused.

She jerked as wetness washed over her skin, filling in around her sunken hands, loosening the sand and pebbles. She kept singing. The water rushed and surged, trickling, gurgling, filling in the dry places in want of its presence. As it did, she felt the song flowing to an end. She felt the need deep within her to pull her voice down from its crescendo into something calmer. The water rose to her forearms, then elbows. Her words tapered off, the last note of her voice drawn out and faded away like a tendril of smoke in the air.

She opened her eyes and smiled. Her heart surged with pride. There was water at last.

Well done, said a voice. She sucked in a breath. It was there and gone so quickly she thought she'd imagined it.

The king tree, Cyrus said in answer.

She blinked, stunned, at the sight of the babbling creek. A searing pain flared along her back, over her spine. She gasped, trying to twist, to rub the burning spot with her hands. She knew what she'd find if she could see it. Another mark to document the magic she'd done.

She plunged her hands into the babbling creek and began gulping down water, all but choking. Gods, it tasted good. Pure, clean, crisp. A laugh escaped her lips. She rolled over onto her back, breath heaving, and stared up at the canopy above. She felt lighter, fuller, richer. Better than she'd felt in days.

SHE WOKE TO BIRDS CHIRPING. The forest was alive and teaming with life. Shades of green and brown wove across the tapestry above her. She blinked, bringing it into focus.

Her stomach grumbled, hungry. She groaned and rolled over. She'd found a place not far from the creek after quenching her thirst. She'd been too tired to search for food in the fading darkness.

Yawning, she got to her feet. Her muscles ached. There hadn't been any comfortable way to sleep. She'd found a mossy place that was softer than some of the others. Still, her back and neck twinged as she moved.

Her stomach grumbled again. The path was nearby, the same one she'd stumbled along as darkness had set in. If yesterday was anything to go from, she decided to let the forest choose for her, resuming her walk back the way she'd come.

She found her creek, babbling away. "Quite a happy thing, aren't you?" She laughed as she sank to her knees, drinking deeply.

A full belly of water sated her hunger, but not for long. Time began to stretch as hours passed. Her stomach continued its protest. She kept her eyes peeled for berries. The journal she'd read had mentioned quite a few species. Far more than the usual blueberries, blackberries, and raspberries she was used to. At this point, she'd welcome anything.

She didn't try to grow anything, knowing the magic would be too complex. She wasn't quite ready for that. Besides, she'd probably need to be a lot hungrier.

If she made good time, she'd be back in Esterpine by nightfall. She could go that long without food. Until then, she tortured herself with all the things she missed since coming to Dragonwall. Big juicy hamburgers, pizza, pasta... Oh, gods! There was just so much.

Maybe after she returned to Kastali Dun, she'd drag Talon to the cookery. She was a decent cook, and there were so many foods she wanted him to try.

She snorted at the thought of Talon, cooking.

More time passed. With every step, she was closer to Esterpine. Closer to completing her first successful venture into the forest. She couldn't help but feel a little proud of herself, and she couldn't wait to see her new mark—

She stopped, blinking. When had everything gone so silent? Nothing moved. She didn't see a single bird. The hairs on the back of her neck stood on end.

Something isn't right, Cyrus said.

She hadn't deviated from the path, but nothing around her looked familiar. Was the forest taking her a different way back? Her heart thudded. She wiped her sweaty palms on her pants. She shouldn't have let her guard down.

She crept forward on silent feet, listening. When nothing happened, she hastened her pace, following the path. Every shadow seemed to reach for her, or maybe it was her imagination—

An inhuman screech split the silence.

She froze. Dread kept her rooted in place. It seeped up from the forest floor and into her soft boots, up her legs and body, coming to rest deep in her chest. Her breathing heightened. Every fiber in her being screamed at her to run. To go back! Turn around! She looked behind her. Her eyes widened. The forest was entirely closed off. The path—gone.

"No..." She barely whispered.

Another screech sounded. Her instincts screamed again. She surged forward at a sprint. Shadows sprang up around her, teeming and writhing. Black vines crawled along beside her, like what she's seen on the stag, coating everything, covering the trees. The trees thinned and she came to a stop, blinking, but not quite believing what she was seeing. It was a clearing, but only because some of the trees around her had fallen, creating an open void. Everything inside was...*rotting*. She couldn't move, couldn't take her eyes off the sight. From healthy green to sickly shadowed. Her boots crunched. The ground was charred, as if burned. Pine needles and leaves, crisped. On the trees, the leaves dripped with an oily substance.

The clearing shuddered, heaving a huge rattling breath like it was...*alive*. But it was also dying, fighting a battle, and losing.

Claws scraped against her back and down her scalp. She whimpered and stumbled forward, trying to get away. Her feet didn't go far. They'd become sluggish, caught in the tarry substance below her boots.

A sob broke from her chest.

"Koldis!" She dropped her mental barrier and called to him, desperate. *"Koldis, the darkness! It's here!"*

"Claire? What's wrong? Where are you?"

"It's here. It's trying to get me."

"Tell me where you are!" There was panic in his voice, at not being able to help her.

There was no way to describe how to reach this place. She could barely form words to describe what she was seeing. She sent him projections, images all jumbled up in her fear.

"Get out of there," he commanded. *"Whatever it is, run. I'm coming to find you."*

She was too terrified to form a response. She lifted one foot and then the other. Wading across the clearing felt like trudging through molasses. Her breathing came in gasps between her sobs. This was *not* what she'd expected when she set out to learn sprite magic. Not this—never this.

Something slashed her arm. The skin broke and blood seeped into her tunic. Writhing branches drenched in shadow reached for her. She heard screaming. Was it her own? She couldn't tell. It sounded...pained. The trees, she realized. They were sick, and calling to her. The forest needed her, but she didn't understand why.

"Claire!" A voice cleared the mental fog in her mind. "Run!"

She blinked. Taylynn raced in from the opposite side of the clearing, a dagger in hand. "It wants *you, not* me. Go! Back to Esterpine."

Claire gasped, trying to breathe, trying to calm her sobs. "I—"

Another screech rattled the trees, angrier this time, perhaps at the thought of her getting away. Vines shot up from the surrounding undergrowth, teaming with black. In a blink, they twisted around her legs, her arms, pinning her in place. Pain erupted in the places where they touched her skin.

She choked on a scream. Koldis was shouting in her mind, but she didn't hear what he was saying. She couldn't think. Another scream ripped free of her chest. Taylynn shot forward, dagger flashing. Her voice lifted in song, but she was too frantic to hear, to listen to the magic. Only a few stanzas and the vines retreated, but only just. Blood dripped from Taylynn's arm.

Claire fell to her knees, gasping. She couldn't get enough air in. The world was spinning around her.

"You must go, Claire," Taylynn shouted. "I will be right behind you. Go, now. Back to Esterpine. The forest is not safe here. Go!"

She didn't need telling again. She shot to her feet, stumbling forward. Just before she left, she glanced once more over her shoulder, at the haze of white light surrounding Taylynn's body, casting her in a glow that almost hid her from view. Then she fled.

CHAPTER II
BLOOD LINES

Esterpine

Koldis settled into the role of commander, keeping close contact as he stationed pairs around the outskirts of Esterpine. They were waiting for Claire to appear. His heart raced as images poured in. Shadows. Trees covered in rot. Vines twisting and claiming everything they touched.

Claire's fear leached into her projections.

He was about to storm the palace and demand that Queen Jade go out and retrieve her when—

"Lord Koldis! She's here!" Nokin and Madeleine's telepathic shout pulled him to the northern side of Esterpine. He sprinted, his breaths coming in short bursts. Sprites watched him streak past wearing quizzical expressions. Did they have any idea of what transpired outside their precious city? Any idea of the threat.

He reached the city's edge, panting. A glint of golden hair sent relief coursing through him. She was alive. Safe.

"Claire! I'm here," he said, striding towards her. She spotted him. A sob erupted from her chest as she ran forward and launched herself at him. He folded her into his arms, holding her tight.

105

"I'm fine," she sobbed. "I'm...fine. I'm... I'll be fine. I'm fine." She repeated the words, breathless and gasping. "I'll be fine."

"I know," he murmured, stroking her hair.

He held her there for the gods only knew how long, resting his chin on her head. Her breathing grew steadier and her trembling subsided. Only then did he glance down and notice her hair, infested with leaves and twigs. Dirt streaked her clothes. Despite the tension, he almost laughed, seeing her like this. A wild thing. Untamed. A true queen.

He spotted blood on her clothes, not enough to be lethal. He grasped her shoulders, looking down at her. "Tell me what happened."

"I...it was the forest, but I'm okay. Really. I shouldn't have panicked like that. I just...I wasn't prepared for it." Her face turned a darker shade of red.

"You have nothing to be ashamed of. I would have reacted similarly, believe me. It's this...this place. Something isn't right. Something—" A commotion sounded. He looked up, only to narrow his eyes on the figure that emerged. "You?! What is the meaning of this?"

"I do not answer to you, Lord Koldis," Taylynn said.

"Well, I want answers anyway! Look at her. *Look* at her." He didn't mean to, but he turned Claire at the shoulders so that Taylynn would see her—see what the forest had done.

Claire pulled out of his grasp. "I'm *fine*, Koldis, really. Taylynn saved—"

"I don't care if she saved the whole damn forest," he hissed. "You could have died."

"She wouldn't have," Taylynn simply said. "Now, step aside, Lord Koldis. I have business with my mother."

"No. I want answers."

Taylynn sighed, as if resigned. "Then you will have them. I will meet you in the palace shortly. See to your queen first."

Koldis tensed, glancing around to be sure none of the others had heard. How did she know?

"Her wound requires tending," Taylynn continued. "And I'm

sure she'd appreciate a bath and something to eat. Take her somewhere she can rest. I will visit you then. You'll have your answers, or as much as I can give you."

"Fine," he snapped, stepping aside, only to watch her disappear down the path toward the palace.

Taylynn was true to her word. She came while Claire was tucked away in her bedroom suite, taking a bath. In true sprite fashion, she swept into the room. Her clothes were different. She'd changed into a gauzy gown of silver. He couldn't help his eyes as they roved over her figure, taking in her markings.

She went to the fireplace in the middle of the room and whispered to it. The flames crackled and grew to a roar. The space was suddenly warmer and more inviting. He noticed her back then, the luminescent tattoo shimmering through the fabric. A giant tree. His gaze narrowed, but as she moved, he couldn't get a better look at it.

"How is she?" Taylynn asked, turning to face him. It was disarming, the way her eyes pinned him.

"How do you think? She nearly had her life sucked out of her by some godsdamned blackness."

Taylynn exhaled, paying him a look. Her lips pressed into a thin line. "Claire is stronger than you think. Give her more credit. She isn't a weak, fragile bird. She will not break."

"And you know this *how*? Based on all the time you've spent with her?" His mind raced back to something she'd said before. Something about seeing Claire *again*—

Taylynn barked a laugh. "Believe me, *my lord*, I have seen far more than you might imagine. I know who Claire is—who she truly is."

"Oh? And who is she." A door opened, but he didn't take his eyes off Taylynn.

The princess looked contemplative. "Only blood will tell."

"Is that what Talon was referring to?" Claire appeared beside them. "The blood thing? He mentioned something about tracing my lineage. A way to prove that I really have sprite blood."

Taylynn opened her mouth then paused. "You don't need a blood test to tell you that, Lady Claire." She pointed at a mark shimmering through the gauzy fabric of Claire's tunic. "But yes, there is a way to trace your blood. It is well known to our people, as we use it to keep track of all of our lineage. A family tree of sorts."

"I'd like to see mine."

"Are you certain?" Taylynn asked, hesitant. "Some knowledge is better left undiscovered for what it might do. Not to you, but to those around you. Especially when it reveals answers of *your* lineage."

"I think it's pretty obvious who I descended from," Claire said, crossing her arms. "But having a confirmation would give me... closure."

Taylynn nodded. "I understand. Perhaps it is time. Come."

"Oh." Claire's eyes widened. "Right...right now?"

"Wait a moment—" Koldis held up a hand. "We are here to talk about what happened in the forest. Do not try to distract us from that."

"What happened in the forest was unnatural," Taylynn snapped, showing irritation for the first time. "You wanted answers, fine. I cannot tell you much. A sickness has taken root here. A sickness that should not exist. Evil has found a foothold in the purest of places. It always finds a way in."

"Evil only enters if it is allowed in," he countered, attempting to hide his surprise.

"Yes, exactly."

"What—what caused it then?" Claire asked. "What let it in? Kane?"

Taylynn blinked. "I cannot answer with certainty," she said at last. "I have done my best over the years to reverse its effects, but these past few months it has spiraled out of control. There are ways to cleanse it—"

"Like with your blood," Claire hedged.

"Like with my blood. I am royal. I hold dominion over this place, so I do what I can. But…"

"But what?" Koldis demanded. He was losing patience.

"But like I said, it is getting worse. Especially ever since Claire arrived. Something drives it. I have my theories, but only so."

"Well, I for one would like to hear those theories," he said, glaring.

"That's unfortunate, my lord, as I will not give them. I will not speak about things which I am uncertain of."

"It's Kane," Claire whispered, convinced. "He's growing more desperate."

"That may be," Taylynn said. "Or it may not be. Now, would you like to trace your blood?"

"I…yes."

"Good, then come along."

A muscle ticked along Koldis's jaw. He wanted nothing more than to drag Taylynn over to a chair and tie her to it. Demand that she give him more answers. He was certain whatever theories she harbored had merit. The fact that she wouldn't tell him only irked him further. But, what could he do? He released a slow exhale, calming his nerves, and followed the two women from the room.

"WE CALL IT A *BLOOD STONE*," Taylynn explained, bringing them to stand before a giant crystal protruding from the forest floor. They were near the market. The sprites who passed stopped to watch, curiosity written in their expressions. The stone was taller than Koldis by a hand or two. Its front face was flat and broad, but the back was rough, as if someone had chiseled it from a crystal boulder. Three stairs were cut into its side, but they didn't continue all the way to its top. Most remarkable were the grainlines of green quartz running through it.

"It's…wow. It's beautiful," Claire said. She walked towards it and stopped, lifting her hand and hesitating. "Can I?"

"Of course."

Claire laid her palm on the stone and her eyes closed. She hummed. "It feels alive."

"That is because it is—in a sense. The forest flows through it."

Claire's hand dropped. She walked around the Blood Stone's wide perimeter, eying it with caution, perhaps understanding more about its power than he would. To him, it was just a lifeless crystal, appreciated for beauty and nothing more.

"And it will show me who I'm descended from?" Claire asked.

"It will. Are you ready to know? There is still time to change your mind."

"No—I mean, yes. I am ready. I want to do this."

The small crowd gathering began to whisper. He glanced around. It grew to more than twenty.

"What is the meaning of this?" A voice brought silence with it.

He turned.

"Ah. Mother." Taylynn smiled. "I wondered if you would join us."

Queen Jade stood proud in her sweeping gown and dainty silver circlet. Lord Marquin stood beside her, a single step back. He wore a curious expression in direct contrast to Queen Jade's. Prince Feowen appeared a moment later and went to stand beside his sister. Koldis didn't miss the obvious alliance there. Jeanine slipped in with the small crowd.

"Why have you brought her here?" Jade asked again.

"She wishes to know her lineage, Mother. She has a right to demand it, as do all sprites."

Spots of red appeared on the queen's cheeks. "Of course." But she didn't look as if she wished to permit it.

"May we continue?" Taylynn asked. He didn't miss the underlying tone in the princess's voice, that she would proceed no matter what the queen said. Jade's eyes flicked to the growing crowd. Perhaps she knew she'd been cornered, that it would reflect poorly upon her if she denied Claire this right before an audience.

"Please, proceed," the queen said.

Taylynn nodded. "Very well. Claire—" She took a dagger from her jeweled belt and handed it to Claire, whose eyes widened. "It isn't called the Blood Stone for nothing. You climb the steps there and give it your blood. Best to make a large gash and squeeze your hand into a fist. It should be a generous amount. That is all."

"Oh..." Claire glanced between the awaiting dagger in Taylynn's outstretched hand and the Blood Stone. She nodded and retrieved the dagger.

Koldis took a step. *Are you sure about this?* he silently asked.

Claire's head tilted, listening. *"I'm sure, Koldis. I've wanted answers for a long time. Part of my identity is missing and I intend to find it."*

He nodded and stepped back, giving her space. This he could understand. He'd felt something similar when his brand of magic had first appeared. He'd been young then. Gods...so young. Nearly two hundred years had passed since then. But he'd felt it, felt the thoughts and emotions of other animals. At the time, it had felt like part of his identity was missing. It wasn't until meeting Cyrus, learning that some of the drengr were simply born different from others, with abilities that weren't typical, that he finally under-stood. He wasn't a freak. He wasn't abnormal. He was merely unique.

Claire blew out a breath. She climbed the steps before dragging the dagger over her open palm. A hiss escaped her lips before she closed her hand around the wound, dripping blood onto the top of the stone. The patter of each drop sounded louder than normal, as if amplified. She watched with wide eyes, as if she couldn't believe what she was doing.

"That ought to be enough," Taylynn's voice broke her trance.

She returned to his side, keeping her hand in a fist. He was acutely aware of her presence beside him, the smell of her blood dripping onto the mossy ground, but didn't pull his eyes from the stone. He couldn't. He watched in fascination as its top turned blood red. Lines of Claire's lifeblood raced down the flat front surface, thin as spiderwebs. Words began to appear at the top. No, not words...*names*. Names written in her blood. First one name, and then another. Beneath each name, a new line raced downward to form the next, and another, and another. A cascading family tree took form. When the racing lines reached the middle, they slowed.

He watched, transfixed. A final line shot from a name, lengthening into a long streak that sped towards the bottom of the stone. Only then did a final name appear.

He stepped forward at the same time as Taylynn and Claire. A gasp fell from Claire's lips. He spotted it at the same time she did. Her name was at the very bottom, connected by the abnormally long line that remained strangely empty all the way up to Princess Irelia, as if everyone in between was of no consequence and remained unnamed. Above Irelia's name, Queen Isabella. Beside Isabella's was Queen Ametrine, her sister. Below Ametrine, Jade, with names for her children, Taylynn and Feowen. His eyes continued to trace up the names and lines above Claire's. He wasn't sure if he was breathing properly. He'd shared the same hunch as Claire and the others ever since she'd voiced it. But seeing proof was entirely different.

Above Queen Isabella's name there were more—first daughters. All the way up to a single name. "It can't be," he whispered. Ellia. *The* Ellia. The woman responsible for bringing the wandering tribes of Spirit Singers together. *The First Sprite.*

Collective gasps and whispers rang out around them. The crowd had gathered close to look. When he glanced behind him, it was to see Queen Jade's face, as hard as the stone of her namesake. There was no hiding it now. The entire city was about to know Claire's deepest secret. She was sprite royalty. She had a particular line of royal blood entitling her to sit on the spriten throne, if she wished for it. He was well aware of sprite customs. First daughters always inherited. That gave her more claim to the throne than even Taylynn, and certainly more than Jade. It didn't matter that her line had been diluted during its time in her home world. Blood was strengthened through the use of magic. If Claire worked hard enough, her blood could be strengthened to levels higher than any sprite in existence.

"Why is the line blank for so long?" Claire broke the spell that had fallen around them. "Where is my mother's name? My grand-mothers?"

"Your mother and her mother, and the many mothers before them are not part of our world," Taylynn said. "They are not here. They may carry your blood, but it has not been awoken. The Blood Stone only works for sprites."

Koldis's gaze traced the long line. How many generations did it encompass? How many generations of firstborn daughters had lived and died before Claire?

"It seems we are cousins, in a way," Feowen announced, stepping forward with a grin. He warmly took Claire's shoulders and pulled her into a hug. She huffed, pulling away wearing a sheepish smile. "Oh. Sorry about that." He took her wounded hand and hummed a tune. The gash closed up without his having spoken a single word.

Koldis felt his eyes narrow. He was strangely reminded of the magic Claire had shown once before, while humming. He knew enough about the difficulties of healing to be impressed.

"A first daughter has returned to us!" The shouted statement grounded him. He glanced around to see who had spoken. Excitement rippled through the crowd. It had grown in number over the past few minutes. Strangely enough, Queen Jade had disappeared. He was too shocked by what happened next to question it. Everyone around them went down on one knee.

Claire's gasp was the only thing that broke the silence. "No. You must be...I mean. I am not..."

"You are our queen—by right—if you wish it." Taylynn said, smiling. She too had gone down on one knee. He was the only one left standing next to Claire.

A frown pulled at his lips. Taylynn had known. That damn sprite princess had known all along. That much was obvious in her expression. His irritation rose, but he kept it firmly in check.

Taylynn came to her feet.

Claire took a step back, towards the blood stone. The words and blood had already begun to fade, all but disappearing to leave a clean crystal surface broken only by the grainlines of green quartz. "I'm not your queen," she whispered.

"But you are our heir, technically, if you wish it."

"But I—"

Taylynn laughed. "Come now, Lady Claire. You do not need to decide here and now. They are simply paying you the respect you deserve." Taylynn hesitated, glancing around. "You may rise, all of you. Please leave us. I wish for a word alone with Claire."

The sprites around them rose and scurried away. All but Lord Marquin, who wore a look of humbled respect. "Your Highness," he said, bowing to Claire and Taylynn before disappearing.

"Why...why did he call me that?" Claire demanded, clearly at odds with what was happening.

"Because," Taylynn said, "until and unless my mother steps down, you are technically the heir to the throne. Otherwise he'd have addressed you as *Your Majesty*."

Claire opened and closed her mouth. "I have a stronger claim than Queen Jade?"

"You may depose her, if you wish." The look on Taylynn's face made clear she wished for nothing more. He realized then, how deeply flawed Taylynn's relationship with her mother must be. There was certainly something going on—something he was eager to discover.

"I...I would never do that. I don't want..." Claire shook her head and fell silent.

"Lady Claire, I knew this would be a lot to take in. That was why I wanted to make sure you were truly ready. You need not worry or act. My mother is queen. That will not change unless you wish for it. Now, there are other matters I wish to discuss with you. That of your training. While I *respect* my mother's methods, and Lord Marquin's abilities, I have something different in mind. Will you humor me?"

"I...yes." Claire looked eager to be discussing anything other than the boulder dropped on her.

"Good. Then come. There is someone I very much wish for you to meet." Taylynn wrapped an arm loosely around Claire's shoulders and led her away, leaving Koldis to stand beside Prince Feowen and Jeanine.

"Well," the prince said, "I suppose we should follow. I can only imagine what my sister has in mind next."

"She knew," he said, looking at Feowen with accusation. "Did you?"

Feowen lifted his hands. "Hardly. Trust me, I wondered why Claire looked so similar to Queen Isabella. But without proof? I can't say that I'm surprised though. My sister...she has a way about her. I believe she..." He fell silent.

"Believe she *what*?" Koldis hissed. "Claire is my charge. I am sworn to protect her."

"My sister would never hurt her. She is our blood."

"Still, I would have you tell me, since Taylynn seems so intent on..."

Intent on what, precisely?

"Taylynn is unlike anyone I know," Feowen said, resigned. "Come, let us follow before we lose sight of them." He kept pace beside the prince while Feowen spoke. Jeanine stayed a few paces behind to give them space.

"I don't simply say this because she's my older sister," Feowen said. "She's touched by the forest in a way I've never seen before. It is said that those who first walked this world were often in communication with our king tree, long before its line of contact narrowed to the rightful queen of each generation. Taylynn knows things, sees things...meddles. And I'm almost certain she has left the protection of the forest for the world beyond many times. Not for short periods, either."

"So you're telling me that she's up to something." It did not sit well with him. What could she be doing? Planning? Did it have anything to do with the darkness spreading? He didn't trust her as far as he could throw her.

"I do not think anything she does is harmful," Feowen explained, as if reading his thoughts. "I truly believe that whatever she's involved in is for the greater good. I just..." Feowen rubbed the back of his neck. "I worry about her sometimes. There, I have said more than I intended to. Please do not ask more from me, Lord Koldis."

"I...thank you, Prince Feowen. I appreciate your honesty."

Ahead of them, Taylynn had stopped. She turned to them. "I must ask you not to follow us. What I wish to show Claire is for her and her alone."

"You cannot be serious." Koldis clenched his jaw. "Like hell am I going to let you simply lead her away." He gestured towards the forest.

"She will be quite safe. Unfortunately, I made him a promise and I cannot break it."

"Him, who? What is going on? Where Claire goes, I go."

"Koldis—" Claire opened her mouth.

"No, Claire—"

"Koldis," Claire hissed, more firmly this time. "Stay here. I will be fine." Her command stung. He clenched his fists.

Feowen squeezed his shoulder. "She'll be fine. Come. Let's get some fresh air."

Koldis hesitated, unwilling to let Claire out of his sight, too aware that he'd only gotten her back hours ago. Gotten her back from whatever darkness lurked in the depths of the forest.

Taylynn's expression softened. "I promise on my life, Lord Koldis. No harm will come to her. If it does, I will submit myself to your mercy."

He opened and closed his mouth, unprepared for Taylynn's words. "Fine," he said. "I will hold you to it."

Taylynn nodded.

He watched until they disappeared down a path, leaving him with Feowen and Jeanine. "Come," Feowen said. "Let's show you the open sky. Nothing calms a drengr's nerves faster, eh? Or so I'm told." He let out a grunt and complied, following the sprite prince in the opposite direction, away from his queen.

CHAPTER 12

AN ANCIENT SPRITE

Esterpine

Claire gazed in open shock at the sprite before her, failing to conceal her expression. "You...you're *old*." And...there went her manners.

His hair was white and thinned, his skin wrinkled. He looked positively *ancient*. But sprites didn't age, did they? She'd never seen one.

He gave a bark of laughter, not bothering to look up from the easel where he was painting. She saw part of his work, a unicorn black as midnight, almost iridescent like Talon's scales. Its eyes looked so real, they seemed to watch her, even at an angle.

"Forgive me, *Kenya*," Princess Taylynn threw her an appalled glare. "She is not familiar with our customs—"

"Nonsense! She speaks the truth." He waved a paintbrush in dismissal. Taylynn bowed her head. He looked up then, his eyes falling on Taylynn's figure. "I wondered when you would bring her to me, *Elam*."

"I have been...away."

"Yes." He harrumphed, set his brush down, wiped his hands, and turned to better see them both. "You weren't exaggerating," he said at last. Claire felt the weight of his scrutiny heavy on her. "She looks nearly identical, does she not? I see now why you chose her."

Claire opened her mouth but couldn't find the words.

"I had hoped—"

"I know exactly what you had hoped, *girl*," he grumbled. "Be gone. I will speak with her alone."

"Of course, *Kenya*." Taylynn bowed. She did not appear offended in the slightest. Was this old sprite her *teacher*? They spoke as if it were the case. Taylynn addressed him with deference, using the same honored title Claire used with Lord Marquin.

Now alone, the ancient sprite turned his weighty attention entirely upon her. "Sit, girl. Sit. It tires me to see you standing. These old bones aren't what they once were, as you so obviously pointed out."

"I...I'm sorry. I never meant offense."

"And you gave none. Now, *sit*."

She'd never fallen into a chair so quickly. She watched him, unsure of what to do. Who was he? Why had Taylynn brought her here? The day already felt unusually long. Racing through the forest, fighting for her life. Confirmation of who she was and who she'd descended from. And now this?

"I know why she brought you to me." He scowled, accentuating his wrinkles. "Training, I'm sure. She's mentioned it before, but I never agreed to it."

"I...training?" She blinked. "Lord Marquin—"

"Lord Marquin? *Lord Marquin*?! That stuffy—?" He took a deep breath. "I am sure the queen's favorite has been *superb* in his instruction. Oh, yes." He scoffed, leaning back. "Lord *Marquin* hasn't walked the forest long enough to know the way things used to be. Well now—" He stopped abruptly and wiped his hands, then said, "I suppose I should introduce myself, since our facilitator has run off."

"You sent her away—"

"Yes, yes. I know. Gods above, give me patience."

A grin spread across her face. He was completely unexpected and she liked him already.

"You may call me Pelwynn," he said. "Unless I agree to become your tutor, in which case, *Kenya* until you earn the privilege of my name."

She opened her mouth—

"And yes, I already know who you are, Claire Evans. Taylynn told me about you years ago."

She sputtered. "Years...*years* ago? But, that's...that's..."

"Not possible?"

She stared at him. This was too much. Today was too much.

"Let me guess, you have questions?"

A strangled laugh fell from her lips. "Who *are* you?"

"Someone who would see his past wrongs righted. Someone who has spent far too long among the trees waiting for the opportunity to fix things." She gaped at him. He must have seen her disbelief for what it was. "I knew her, you know? Isabella. That's why I look so old. Sprites don't age, as I'm sure your instructor has probably—hopefully?—informed you. We are immortal. Entirely immortal. Even the drengr age and die."

"Then...then how are you... Why are you...?"

"Because I fight it, girl! I fight it every goddamned day."

She swallowed. "The call of the king tree?"

He didn't answer, but that was answer enough. His eyes had gone unfocused, perhaps reliving the long years of his life. She let his words sink in—truly sink in. "But you must be at least fifty thousand years old. How?!"

"Are you daft?"

All the air left her chest. "But you said..."

"I know what I said. That I'm immortal. So I don't see why you're so shocked. I've resisted the urge to scamper off into the forest and die. And every day that I resist, a small part of my body dies. See me? I'm dying. But I'm not dying in the same way that I would be if I ate the fruit."

Her eyes widened. "You...you're giving up reincarnation."

"Among other things, yes. But not for long. I will find the tree before my death comes. Not long now."

"What are you waiting for?" she asked, hoping he'd elaborate on the *righting past wrongs* thing. Was this too private a question?

"You, among other things. Taylynn, mostly. After I trained her..." He shook his head. "Perhaps I've already waited long enough. Taylynn isn't the only one who speaks with the tree, you know."

"But I thought—"

"Forget everything you ever *thought.* Everything you know about us, girl, unless you hear it from me or Taylynn. Young sprites have forgotten many of our ways, thanks to the disruption of Isabella's—" He cleared his throat. "*Choices.* It always comes down to choice. No, plenty of sprites communed with the tree once upon a time. Now, it only seems to speak to the queen and her descendants. But I hear it still, oh yes. I hear it..." He fell silent, thoughtful.

She watched him, mouth open, hardly sure what to make of this. "So you...you really knew her? What was she like? Why did she—?"

"Good gods! When I said you'd have questions, I didn't mean ask them all at once!"

"I take it the crankiness comes with old age?" She crossed her arms and lifted an eyebrow.

He burst into wheezing laughter. "Among other things." He stretched. His joints cracked like an old tree. Then he sighed with relief. "That's better. Now—"

"My training."

"Yes, yes."

Her eagerness was getting the better of her. This was exactly what she needed, what she had hoped to find in coming here. Someone who would tell her things without sugar coating them, someone who wasn't stuffy and proper and polite. Someone who could train her the way she needed to be trained.

"I haven't committed to anything," he said, as if reading her thoughts. "I see by the look on your face, all moonstruck and such, you think I'm going to solve all your problems. *Varti yifah!*"

Her eyes widened. Jeanine had taught her that one, certainly not a proper stuffy lord like Lord Marquin. It was a curse. The sprites equivalent of *gods above,* but a bit more derogatory. Polite sprites didn't use it. She'd only heard it spoken among a few.

She cleared her throat. "You said you knew about me years ago. How?"

"Ah. That's not my business. You'll have to ask Taylynn about it. But yes, I did."

A sinking suspicion filled the pit of her stomach. "All of this—" She waved a hand. "I was meant to come here, wasn't I? To Dragonwall? Cyrus was meant to fall into my cornfield. All of it."

"Meddlesome girl!" he hissed. Her eyes widened. "No, no. Gods. Not you. The other one."

"Taylynn?" she asked. He barked a laugh. Her eyes widened as the truth sank in. "She's responsible for it, isn't she? For me? For this?"

"You'll have to take that up with her, as I said—"

Someone pounded on the door. Somehow she knew it was Taylynn. Dust fell from the ceiling. Claire took a moment to look around. They were beneath the roots of a giant tree. But rather than glass, the walls were made of wood and shelves covered every spare inch of his cluttered cottage. Nicknacks and books and small paintings. Everywhere she looked, there was something to stare at.

"*Kenya?*" Taylynn called. "May I enter now? Are you finished?"

"*Varti yifah*! Never a moment of peace from you young ones. Yes," he shouted. "By all means, be quick about it."

Taylynn walked in and looked between them. "I hope you've survived his temper."

"Barely," Claire said, eying Taylynn with growing curiosity.

"Well?" Taylynn snapped, looking at Pelwyn. "Will you help her?"

Pelwyn sighed, slouching back into his chair. "I suppose I have no choice, do I?"

"You wanted to exonerate yourself. This seems a good way."

"Training you was—"

"She is more important than I will ever be, *Kenya*." Taylynn pinned Pelwyn with her gaze. "We both know it. It would be point-less for you to argue it. I know the tree has already spoken to you on this matter. Do not deny it."

Claire gazed between them, open-mouthed. "Uhm. I think I'm missing a lot."

"Fine. I'll train her," Pelwyn snapped back. "But that's it. After that, I'm going to find it."

Taylynn gave a curt nod. "I will leave you to it, then. Claire? Learn all you can while you are with him. Your time here is limited. Things are happening—" She stopped herself, snapping her mouth shut. "I am needed elsewhere. I will leave you both." At that, she slipped from the little cottage and disappeared.

"Uhm. Does she always do that?"

Pelwyn barked a laugh. "You get used to her."

Would she? She hoped that Taylynn wouldn't disappear entirely. She had questions. Questions that Pelwyn was obviously reluctant to answer.

"So, I guess I should call you *Kenya* then?"

"If you want me to teach you." He waited for her to contradict him. She didn't. "Good. We won't do much here. Outside. Come." He stood faster than she would have expected for an old man, and strode from his cottage. "I live outside the city of Esterpine for a reason. I've fallen out of memory for most. Maybe all. I don't think even Jade knows I'm here."

She gathered his meaning well enough. "Why *are* you here?" she asked, hoping to get a straight answer this time.

He sighed, leading her to a small area behind his cottage. A garden. She gasped, delighted. It was a smaller version of what she'd seen outside of the palace. "Ah, yes. I delight in growing things," he explained. "Perhaps too much so."

He took a seat on the only bench in the garden and motioned for her to sit on the ground facing him. "I am here because a long time ago, Isabella and I were inseparable. I was so...angry when Vigilance came to her. So jealous. She cared for him, you know. You've heard the stories, I'm sure? I could see it then, and didn't trust it, didn't like it. We said some things…" He shook his head and sighed. "I can't fix the past. But I will regret the role I played in all that happened."

She frowned.

"The drengr," he said by way of explanation. "The humanity she gifted them. Her tricks. I knew exactly what her orders were from the tree and I did nothing to stop her. Some might even say I encouraged her."

"So you blame yourself," she said. He didn't respond. She sat cross-legged, looking up at him. "Kenya, ana luth aikah kihar, nih ayas." *Teacher, it was her choice, not yours.*

Pelwyn lifted an eyebrow, suddenly amused. "Do not think that your mastery of our tongue will work on me, *Elam*."

At this, she giggled. At least he wasn't calling her *girl* now. Even still, it was worth a shot.

"Now, let us begin. Are you ready?" She nodded. "Good. All life is connected. A subtle energy flows through everything. I'm sure you have felt it. For some, it manifests as tingles across the skin, or a feeling in the pit of your stomach. But it is there. All magic does is simply manipulate that energy. For the drengr, their crude, almost vile manipulation is an abomination of what the world intended. They stole it from us, you know. But that is a story for another time. Drengr magic—mage magic—which came from the asarlaí, seeks to control." She knew this already, but didn't dare interrupt. "Sprites have a different way of doing things. We were once *Spirit Singers*. Aolis told you this, I'm sure? Good. Our magic comes from song, or so many today believe. But no, it is deeper than that. Have you ever made something happen without muttering a single word?" Her eyes widened. "Yes? I thought so. Those deeply in tune with themselves don't need to say a thing. The world around us knows what we want."

She licked her lips. "And how…how do I do that?"

"Well, that's what I'm going to teach you, isn't it?"

A thrill sent her blood coursing through her. "Why didn't Lord Marquin tell me any of this."

"Because that groveling bat is too young. Most of them are. Most have forgotten how things were when Isabella walked the forest. The way things were before...before her downfall."

Her eyebrows drew together. "Her downfall?"

"Another story for another time. You want to learn or not?"

"Oh. Yes. Please, *Kenya*. Continue."

"Thank you." He gave her a long look. "To be in tune with yourself and your surroundings, you must possess a certain awareness. Focus is key. I know that sounds..."

"Obvious?"

A wicked grin tugged at his lips. "You'll see how obvious it seems once you try it."

"Whenever I've done anything of note, like sprite fire—"

"*Lac alnar ellohdar,*" he said.

"What does that mean? I understand fire, but the other words."

"*Lac alnar.* There isn't a direct translation. Of being immortal, or eternal. Eternal flame."

"Lac alnar ellohdar," she repeated. *Eternal flames.* The hair on her arms stood on end.

"Feel that?" he asked. "Yes, I thought so. That is what comes with awareness. The subtle change in the air just by saying and thinking of the thing you conjured. You could probably summon them without singing a word if you tried. Singing is for novices."

Novices?! She thought back to the night she'd vanquished the vodar—

Pelwyn opened his hand and she gasped. Green flames danced in his palm. This was also the same fire that burned eternally in her fireplace.

"But..." She blinked. "You didn't even say a word."

"Exactly. Now, would you like to learn?"

She nodded. "Neem gui, Kenya. Shalaya." *Yes please, Teacher. Thank you.*

"Good. See the *asymyn* there? Pluck one of its blossoms."

"The jasmine?"

"*Varti yifah, Elam!*" He pinched the bridge of his nose.

"All right, all right." She jumped up to comply, handing him the blossom. He held it in his palm as she took a seat.

"Commit this blossom to memory. You see it in your mind, no?"

"I see it."

"Good. Now close your eyes. Empty your mind. Picture just the *asymyn*. Nothing else. Your mind should be completely clear. Do you know how it smells? How it felt on your fingers? You can think of that too. Just that. Only that which pertains to this flower. Good. Yes, let your shoulders relax. Take deep inhales. Hold for three seconds, then release."

He began guiding her through a meditative breathing exercise. But surely it couldn't be *that* easy. She did as he asked, picturing nothing more than the blossom. Hopefully Koldis wouldn't be wondering where she was—

"No!" he snapped. She jerked, opening her eyes. "You are not thinking only of the blossom, are you?"

"I was!" she insisted.

"No, you weren't."

"Well, I suppose I got distracted." By Koldis, but she didn't say that out loud.

"I know. I can tell. Remember, I am in tune with my surroundings. And when you tap into the energy around you by emptying your mind, I can see it—feel it. Don't think you can slip past me. Now, try again. The blossom."

They spent the next hour practicing. She did her best to focus on the blossom and only the blossom, but stray thoughts wormed their way in. Pelwyn was the breakthrough she had hoped for. She needed a miracle if she was going to master sprite magic and strike a balance within her. She didn't have months or even years. Every day was a day longer for Kane. She had to do this.

Even if it seemed that focusing on a single blossom felt completely useless.

Eventually, Pelwyn grew impatient. "When you come back tomorrow, you will picture the flower in your mind clearly enough to create a duplicate in my palm." She gaped at him, not quite understanding. "I'll know if you don't practice. Now, off with you. These old bones are tired."

She took the blossom and bid him a respectful goodbye.

Her walk back to Esterpine gave her time to practice, but it was hard to empty her mind and think only of the blossom. She tripped on a root and swore, then gave up entirely.

"What's that?" Koldis asked when she shut the door to their suite. He was sitting on the sofa with another book in hand, probably the same one on weaponry and warfare or whatever it was he often read.

"A flower," she said, holding it up. "You like it?"

He snorted. "You going to tell me who Taylynn took you to see? I doubt she took you off to hunt for flowers."

"My new teacher," she answered.

He opened his mouth—

"We're going to train in secret," she added. "The queen doesn't know about him. So I'll spend my mornings with Lord Marquin and my afternoons with—" She stopped herself just short of saying his name. "Anyway, you need not worry. It's quite safe."

He exhaled, slumping back into the sofa. "Fine. Whatever. Feowen took me into the trees while you were busy, to look at the sky."

"Oh, good. Feeling any better?"

He shrugged. "Maybe if I don't have to deal with that sprite princess anymore I'll be better."

"Hah!" She couldn't help her laugh.

"Where'd she run off to, anyway? Never mind, I don't care. I'm more interested in this mysterious teacher of yours. What happened?"

She told him all she could and swore him to secrecy.

"Sounds like I'm not the only one who can't stand Lord Marquin. But even better, he sounds far older and wiser than Princess Taylynn. No wonder she disappeared during your training."

"She probably just slipped off into the forest again, you know, to do whatever it is she does."

"Well, good," he said, frowning. "And good riddance, too."

"Gods. You really don't like her."

"Understatement," he amended. "I can't stand her."

"Then why do you go all gushy-eyed whenever you look at her?" She wagged her eyebrows. Koldis sputtered, gaping at her. He muttered something about females and quickly returned to his book.

CHAPTER 13

LEARNING FOCUS

Esterpine

Claire's shoulders drooped.

"As usual, you're too distracted." Pelwynn's open palm remained empty. The jasmine blossom he'd given her had long since wilted, so they'd collected another. That one had wilted, too. And a third. Now she was staring at a fourth. Three days had passed since their initial exercise. She hadn't succeeded at what he'd expected her to do on their first day back.

"I don't understand why I can't just sing a few words," she grumbled. She knew exactly which words she'd use, too. She'd practiced in secret the night before, after hours of frustration. Just a few words hummed to a lilting tune and she'd summoned a perfect blossom replica in her hands. There was no mark to accompany the action, probably because it was meant to be something simple.

"Singing a few words is not the point, *Elam*." Pelwyn's eyebrows lowered. "The point is to hone your focus. Without words," he added.

"Taylynn still sings plenty of her magic. I saw her—"

"And you will too, but not yet."

She opened her mouth to protest—

"How many times have you tried singing something into existence, only to fail?" He arched an eyebrow.

She'd already told him about her water summoning experience, how she'd quenched the dry riverbed the day she earned another mark. The day she ran straight into a sick part of the forest. She'd told him about that too, and noticed the frown that had formed on his features. But like Taylynn, he didn't formulate much of an explanation on the matter.

She'd also told Koldis all about her water mark. An upside down triangle with a line that connected it to a hollow circle, with two lines that cut straight through the connector, all sprinkled with dots like confetti. It took up a solid three inches in length along her spine.

Pelwynn slumped against the garden bench. "You will never conjure magic on the first try, *Elam*. Not when your focus is lacking. You got lucky with the creek because you were thirsty and desperate. Even then, it wasn't your first try that day, was it? Is that how you wish to learn? To wait until desperation drives you?" She shook her head. That was absolutely *not* what she wanted. "To be as Isabella once was, as Taylynn is now, you must tap into the energy all around you, at will. Your mind must learn to focus. You must see and feel magic's energy."

"The white glow?"

"Exactly."

She was getting better at spotting it. Pelwyn had done several exercises where he'd instructed her to focus her mind on the blossom—because it was the simplest thing to focus on. Then he would do magic for her. She'd seen him access the energy, seen it warp and flow around him like light. But it was hard to maintain focus with her eyes open, watching him. Most times her worrisome thoughts wormed their way in, dispelling anything that might have been close to success.

"Perhaps we should try another approach," Pelwyn said at last, a deep scowl adding to his lined face. She couldn't help but notice the disappointment in his voice. Taylynn had said she was important, but was she? If she couldn't even complete a simple exercise when Pelwynn expected it.

"Here, come with me." He led her back into his cottage and began shuffling around. She wasn't sure how he managed to locate anything with all the clutter. He was a pack rat. She was certain some of his things dated back as far as he did. Fifty thousand years of accumulation.

"Ah, here it is." He opened a long, narrow case, revealing an unstrung bow. This wasn't just any bow, it was covered limb to limb in sprite markings. She didn't notice them until he picked it up and they began to glow. He ran his hands over it, reverent.

"Here—" He thrust it at her then shuffled around a bit more. She gasped at the sight of a quiver. It wasn't large enough to hold more than ten arrows, each fletched with beautiful reddish gold feathers the color of flames. "Ah, yes," Pelwynn said. "Feathers from the *yirnik*. It took me sixty years to find one and befriend it enough for ten arrows."

"*Yirnik?*"

He opened his mouth, then hesitated. He set the quiver on the table and began shuffling around again until he produced a canvas.

"Oh…" Her eyes widened. "But…phoenixes aren't real, are they?"

"Is that what you call them?"

She swallowed. "In my world, they're not actually real. You have them here?" She couldn't take her eyes from the painting. The detail of the fiery feathers, the plume of its tail, it's intelligent beady eyes…it looked so real. The backdrop was blurred, making the bird stand out even more.

"There aren't many in the forest, but it's the only place in the world you'll find them."

She blinked, unable to look away until Pelwynn stuffed the painting back where it had come from. Even then, she gazed at the place where it disappeared.

"*Yirniks* are smart, *Elam*. They are beautiful for a reason. Their survival depends upon it. They bewitch all who look upon them. Unless your mind is strong enough. Unless you have *focus*."

She didn't miss the way he emphasized the word, taking a jab at her lack thereof. She cleared her throat. "So, it just gave you its feathers?"

"After following it around for nearly sixty years, I befriended it. One day it broke its wing and I healed it. In return, it answered my request with these. It visits me occasionally, though I haven't seen it for some time."

She shook her head, not quite believing. "And you've never used them, all this time?"

"Oh, I've used them plenty. Mostly in the war."

Her eyebrows pulled together. "The war? But I thought the sprites—"

"*Varti yifah!* The war against dragons. Against Rage. Now, take these. Let's go."

In the clearing behind Pelwynn's cottage, he positioned her to face a straw dummy she hadn't noticed before. "You want me to... to shoot it? *How* is this—"

"I want you to listen and *focus!* Now, you have some experience with a bow, yes? Good. Show me what you can do first, and then I'll explain exactly *how* this is going to help you."

She strung the bow the way Saffra had taught her, taking an arrow, nocking it. She hadn't practiced much with traditional bows, but she remembered enough. Taking aim, she let the arrow fly.

"*Varti yifah!*" Pelwyn swore. Her arrow missed the dummy by quite a lot, burying itself into a tree instead. Pelwyn stalked over to it, cursing under his breath. "Kill any of my trees, *Elam*, and I won't be happy. He yanked the arrow from the tree and muttered something over the hole. She was so busy watching him heal the tree that she didn't see where the arrow had gone. He came back empty handed. "That was rather pathetic, no?"

She shrugged, trying to ignore the sting of his words. "I never said I was any good."

"True, but this exercise will be all the more important because of it. Perhaps we should have started here instead of the blossom. Never mind. Take another arrow."

She reached down to the quiver and froze. Her eyes widened. "The arrow!" There were ten again. "Did you replace it? I didn't see..." She trailed off. Pelwynn was grinning. "The phoenix feathers!" she breathed.

"Why do you think I wanted feathers from a *yirnik*?"

"So...the arrows never run out? They're magical?"

"They do not run out. Can you imagine how quickly they'd be stolen if someone discovered what these feathers could do? No, after it is removed, or after a short period of time, it disappears and reappears here."

"Can't someone just steal the quiver?"

"It can only be gifted or lent. Otherwise the arrows and quiver disappear entirely and come right back to me. Take an arrow." She took another and prepared to nock it. "This time, let's try something different. Perhaps you warrant more...extreme measures. Instead of thinking only of the blossom, I want you to do two things. Keep the blossom in the back of your mind where all the noise lives. The place where all those stray thoughts you like to think about spring to mind. Then pick a point on the dummy, its head, and I want you to put that at the front of your mind the same way you've been doing with the blossom. Only, better this time, because clearly you weren't doing a good job of it before."

"You want me to duplicate the dummy's head?"

"*Varti yifah, Elam!*" Pelwyn rubbed his forehead, muttering. "What I *want is* for you to *strike* its head with the arrow. Gods, give me patience."

She ignored his tirade. "And focusing will improve my aim?" She didn't believe it for a second. Maybe if she practiced long enough she'd hit the target where she wanted. She failed to see how staring at something hard enough would bring success.

"Magic will improve your aim, mainly by sending the arrow exactly where you've focused. Think of it as a failsafe way of hitting your target. Here, give me that." He snatched the bow and arrow. "Watch closely."

He took aim up at the canopy of trees. When he released, the arrow shot up briefly before changing direction. It went straight into the dummy's forehead. She gaped at the target.

Now. *Now* she understood.

He handed her the bow. "Go on. Do as I have said. Picture it in the front of your mind and the blossom in the back of your mind. Nothing else. Not what you had for breakfast. Not singing. Not what you're going to do when you leave this forest. Just the dummy's head. How it looks, the shape, the way the straw protrudes where my arrow landed, its angles. Picture it and release."

She did as he said, then released and swore. The arrow still shot wide. Pelwynn grumbled. Once again, he marched over to heal the tree. He removed the arrow and tossed it away. This time she paid attention as it disappeared into thin air, only to reappear right back in the quiver. He did the same with his perfectly aimed arrow still protruding from the dummy's forehead.

She tried again. And again. And again.

She tried until Pelywnn told her to retrieve her own gods-damned arrows before stalking back into his cottage. She spent the remainder of the afternoon practicing—the dummy's head in the front of her mind, the blossom at the back of her mind—until she was certain her arm would fall off. Twice she managed to hit the neck and chest. But she knew that was luck. It wasn't what was supposed to happen.

She knew why she was failing. She couldn't seem to do what he asked. Ever since the first failure when she couldn't recreate the blossom—after Pelwyn confidently claimed she would—she couldn't stop thinking of the pressure. Everything was hinging on this. She was here with the sprites because she had been so sure this was where she would conquer her magic. But now that she was here, she had to do what she'd set out to, and that pressure was stifling.

That night, she dreamt of dummies and arrows and jasmine blossoms. She dreamt of the *yirnik*, watching it fly through the trees. She dreamt of the black rot finding the bird, attacking and decaying it. She woke sweating just as morning light spilled into the crystal palace. But something stood out from her dreams. A deep need. A need only she could satisfy. She was a part of this forest the way Isabella had been. The way all of her foremothers had been. It needed her now, now more than ever. The *yirnik* needed her. The unicorns needed her. The stags. The trees. The sprites. But...why? Because she was the one destined to defeat Kane? Because of her stupid unbreakable promise?

Perhaps if she mastered her magic, she might finally discover the answer to that question. It very likely had something to do with finding the balance, just as Saffra's vision had hinted. And something to do with discovering the quarterstaff covered in sprite markings.

There was nothing for it—she'd just have to learn to live with the pressure. To accept it. To accept the worming thoughts that constantly plagued her. Accept them and move past them.

That day, she breezed through Lord Marquin's lessons, absent-mindedly for most of it, giving only enough focus to adequately pronounce the words and phrases he took her through. If he noticed her distraction, he made no mention of it. He'd gotten more formal with her since the revelation of her blood. He now bowed frequently, and called her 'Your Highness.' She didn't bother correcting him.

When she arrived at Pelwyn's cottage, she went straight for the bow, holding out her hand without a single word. He offered it, abandoning his painting to follow her out to the clearing. Her arm was so sore she could barely lift it, but it was less sore than it had been that morning. Her body healed at a much faster rate than it used to. Without her magic, she probably wouldn't have been able to lift her arm for a week.

She stretched, popping her neck, rolling her shoulders, and planting her feet. In the front of her mind, she saw the dummy's head. In the back of her mind, she saw the jasmine blossom. She saw its white petals, the pistils in its center. She imagined it's cloyingly sweet smell, and let the thoughts of that smell envelop her. There was still doubt in her mind. Still pressure. She accepted that. She might fail, sure. But she would try again if she did. If she failed then, she would keep trying. She would move past whatever barriers were in her path.

Letting go of her worries, she nocked an arrow. She kept her stance relaxed. She didn't bother aiming at the dummy's head. In fact, she kept her bow a little lower, aiming at its abdomen.

Her mind remained focused. Dummy's forehead. Jasmine. Forehead. Jasmine. That's what she allowed to fill it. And failure? She swept it aside, acknowledging it and letting it go.

Then she exhaled and released. The arrow shot through the air and landed.

A cry fell from her lips. Her hands dropped to her sides. Beside her, Pelwyn was beaming.

The arrow had struck the dummy's forehead dead center.

"*Heilah, Elam. Nuah ano!* I will leave you to practice. When you can make that happen every time, no matter what you shoot at, come and find me."

He left her and she continued. Her excitement was short-lived. Perhaps it was the overwhelming elation at succeeding that left her mind jittery, or simply beginner's luck. She only managed to hit the dummy's head a total of five times out of thirty. But it was something. And her aim had improved enough that all her stray arrows landed elsewhere on the dummy, and not in Pelwynn's trees. That was progress...right?

When she retreated for the evening, Pelwynn wasn't within his cottage so she left the bow and arrows on the table and scribbled a little note. She returned to Esterpine and told Koldis of her success.

The smile pulling at the corners of his lips was gratifying. "Just think of what a good rider you'll make after all this," he teased. "Mastering the bow is one of the first parts of training." She gathered his meaning. She wouldn't just be a queen if she accepted Talon for a mate. She'd be his rider.

CHAPTER 14
NEGOTIATIONS

Oshea

Kane walked the length of cages one last time, examining his cauldron of bats. His lips pulled tight, bearing his teeth in semblance of a smile. They were giant, monstrous things with furry bodies and leathery wings. Each had grown to nearly the size of a wild dragon and frightening enough to make a man spill his bowels.

They didn't breathe fire like dragons, but they were strong and ruthless in their own right. Even now, blood and gore stained their maws from their last feeding. He congratulated himself for finding them and raising them so successfully within Shadowkeep.

The ship rocked beneath his feet and he hesitated, widening his stance. Several bats chirped and clicked, using their pinions to climb the bars of their cages to steady themselves. Like most monsters, they would be beautiful in their destruction. Beautiful and deadly. And hungry.

"You will have more food soon, my beauties," he cooed. "I'm told our hosts have been collecting hundreds of slaves, just for you. How does that sound? More blood than you'll know what to do with. And when you fly into battle, you will stain Kastali Dun red." He stuck his hand through the bars of the nearest cage. The bat within eyed his hand then nuzzled it with his giant, furry head.

He chuckled. It was hard to avoid attachments to creatures of the macabre sort. Their inherent nature was so...alluring. But he'd been careful not to bond to these, not even allowing himself to name them, though he'd been tempted to call the one beside him Carver, for the way it liked to carve its food and paint the walls of its old cavernous home red.

"My lord?"A voice called below.

"What is it?" He gave the bat a final caress and withdrew.

"We are safely docked," the ship's captain said. "There is a contingent of politicians and soldiers waiting to greet you."

"Excellent." He strode through the hold. "Take care when you unload our precious cargo this time, Waylis. Not a single one harmed, you understand?"

Waylis turned a shade of red, but nodded. He'd carelessly lost two of his crew when loading the creatures, and in anger, had tried to fight to free his men. In vain, the two careless crew members were quick meals, even though the bats had suffered wing injuries on account of Waylis's actions. They'd only just healed.

The bright light that greeted him left him squinting. Everyone in his path scattered, bare feet slapping against the deck in an effort to scurry out of his way.

He inhaled. *Notna.* The sounds of the port city rose up to greet him tenfold. City bells, shouts as cargo was unloaded, the call of gulls overhead. The air stank of fish and filth. He took in the sight of the numerous ships scattered across the bay while Notna rose up before him.

There was a group waiting to greet him near the dock's entrance. He spotted the bat master he'd previously met, here to oversee the offloading of his precious cargo. Three cloaked figures stood within the group, cowls pulled around their faces. If he looked into the shadows, he'd see red eyes, skin pulled tight, thinned with age. Dragonwall's asarlaí had never truly gone away when the dragons had hunted them. While many had died, many had also fled across the Dragonfire Sea. Now Oshea flourished, and flourished in a way he hoped Dragonwall would.

He sighed, making his way across the deck, keeping his gaze pinned on the party waiting for him. Whether or not they were pleased, he couldn't say. Regardless, now the real negotiations would begin.

∼

"TELL ME AGAIN, Lord Kane, why should we aid you in this plight?" The emperor narrowed his eyes. He was sitting atop a cushion on top of his dais. "Our last attempt to capture Dragonwall's capital city went largely awry. History reports many ships were lost." Emperor Yanna's accent was heavy, as were all the others when speaking the common tongue.

"And if we *do* succeed," barked Yanna's advisor, Lord Xieanne, "then we insist you cede the southern Dragondoms to us. Specifically, those within Eigaden. The city of Kastali Dun." Lord Xieanne held the emperor's ear more than most. The emperor lifted a hand to quiet him.

Kane exhaled, not allowing their petty attitudes to garner irritation. "Kastali Dun is mine, Lord Xieanne. In claiming it, I conquer Dragonwall. I cannot cede any of Dragonwall's lands to you until then. However, it would make better sense for Oshea to hold the western coast and some of its Dragondoms there, Celenore and Galadhal in particular. Those are minor details that can be worked out behind closed doors." He hesitated, glancing around the large hall. Bystanders, nobility mostly, watched intently. "As for your doubt, Emperor, let me assuage your fears. I am well familiar with history, familiar with Oshea's attempt to capture Kastali Dun in the past. Even with the help of your asarlaí, you were unsuccessful. But things have changed. The number of drengr has dwindled. Dragonwall's borders are under frequent attack. Moreover, I have successfully laid claim to one of the four forts. The others will fall just as easily, as the drengr will not risk their people to dragon fire. Trust me when I say, King Talon's efforts are focused elsewhere. He will be plotting to reclaim Fort Squall. Though, you've allowed your pirates to take certain...*liberties* with Dragonwall's shores. I would suggest halting such behavior to avoid drawing increased attention to the cities along the southern and western coastline. Until, that is, you launch a full scale attack. I should certainly hope the combined forces of our battle bats, with the strength of the asarlaí and your navy would pose no true obstacle."

"We cannot recall our pirates. Our need for slaves grows," Lord Xieanne drawled. "Especially if we are to increase our navy enough to carry battle bats and armies enough to conquer the Eigaden Peninsula."

"Have you not slaves enough in your own lands?" He threw an arm wide. Oshea certainly had lands aplenty. It extended far to the west, its territories rumored to be as large as Dragonwall, perhaps larger. There were four main cities, and it was known that Notna was merely the emperor's autumn home. He didn't have but one capital city, he had four.

Kane had never charted much farther than Oshea's largest port cities, Notna included. His attention had always been on Dragonwall. Perhaps that ought to change whilst he was here.

Lord Xieanne's face turned a deep shade of red. "You would dare—"

The emperor held up a hand, halting Lord Xieanne's words. "We will consider your request, Lord Kane. Your offer is tempting. My forefathers have longed to see Dragonwall under the umbrella of our great nation. Even if it is but a few of its great Dragondoms. I have much to discuss with my advisors. I will summon you when I am ready." He gave a flick of his wrist.

Clenching his teeth, Kane offered a respectful bow and swept from the throne room.

～

THE ATRIUM's colloquium table was filled, every seat accounted for. It was a round table. Like they were equals. The thought was appalling.

Above the table, a glass dome with thousands of small panes glittered like gems, letting the cerulean sky with its puffy white clouds play host to the evening's entrance, as stars began to flick into existence. It was a sight. He'd never seen something so staggering. So marvelous. But he expected many engineering marvels to come, when Dragonwall once again played host to vast numbers of skilled magical talent. Talent beyond the mere mockery of the mages. Talent that wasn't afraid to use its resources the way resources ought to be used. Dragonwall's lack of forward progress had always irked him.

Kane sat with his long lost brothers, asarlaí who headed up *The Black Tower*. Those powerful enough to earn a position here, one they *so graciously* granted him in gifting him a seat. The honor was lost on him.

While they were fully extinct in Dragonwall—and had been since the Second Age—asarlaí thrived here. However, they no longer called themselves such, which was a mockery in and of itself. Here they were known as *Wielders of The Black Tower* and this was their university. Wielders were esteemed in Oshea. Revered. Respected. They were not feared, as they were in Dragonwall. Some said the colloquium held more power than the emperor himself. Kane fully believed it, though he despised their obvious weakness, that they were powerful enough to rule but chose to be diplomatic about it. Chose to let a puppet dictate to Oshea's people when they ought to be running the Oshean Empire.

"...a new university will benefit Dragonwall in more ways than one," Lord Cai was saying. He snapped his focus back to the matter at hand. "But I cannot see why we should want to change what already works. Emperor Yanna does a fine job and will send plenty of advisors into Dragonwall in his stead."

He almost snorted. As if he wanted or needed additional Oshean advisors mucking about.

"Wielders are better suited to focus on the expansion of the university and replenishing what was once our homeland."

"You call it your homeland," he said, no longer able to keep quiet, "yet you forsake your true title. You would not be wielders in

Dragonwall." He was trying and failing miserably at feigning patience. "And I will rule Dragonwall just fine without the need for additional advisors. You will have my permission to start whatever schools you deem fit. I'll even let you keep your...new title. Dragonwall will be mine whether Oshea steps in or not. But if the emperor agrees to help, he will have several choice dragondoms to add to his ever growing...collection."

"A few dragondoms is nothing compared to his vast holding. Why, then, should we bother?" Lord Cai snapped, eying the other wielder lords. "What's in it for us beyond the promise of more universities and a foothold to return to our homeland."

"The university land itself will be yours. It will function independently of the monarchy I plan to establish. You will have plenty of freedom. Freedom I'm not certain your precious emperor gives you unless you manipulate him into it."

Knowing glances shot around the table.

"There was a time in Dragonwall's history, long before it was called such, that asarlaí ruled their own territories, each in their own right, in whatever way they saw fit. While I don't plan to plunge us into those days long past, I admire the progression I have witnessed here in Oshea."

"You would allow slavery then?"

He lifted a shoulder. "I don't see why not. It works well enough here."

The others nodded, satisfied. He was well aware that slaves kept their precious university running. Slaves were the backbone of Oshea's empire. Slaves were the reason Oshea was forced to expand its borders regularly. Its own people supported the notion. Better to take foreigners than feel the whip on their own backs.

"Very well, Lord Kane. You have given us much to think over. We will reconvene tomorrow to further discuss plans to invade."

"You will bring the emperor to our cause then?" he asked, just to be sure.

"Oh yes," Lord Cai acknowledged. "He follows where we lead."

"Excellent. Until tomorrow then." He stood. Chairs scraped in his wake as he strode from the room, careful not to let the others see the broad smile that stretched across his face.

CHAPTER 15

THE GREAT STONE ROAD

Northern Barrier Range

Mikkin inhaled and noticed the change in the air. It was fresher, lighter, less damp. His heart thumped in anticipation. Daylight. It was the first true light in nearly a month. Or had it been longer? Perhaps two? It was impossible to tell without the sun and moon. With the time he'd spent first in Shadowkeep's cells, then in Safuil, followed by their time on the Great Stone Road and its subsequent cities, he'd given up.

"Best to keep the cloth down over your eyes at first," Fik warned, his voice echoing down the tunnel to the rest of them.

Beside him, Berbik cleared his throat. "We dwargs don't much care for the light. But it is a nice treat now and again. Fik will want to take advantage of the ravens to send a message to Lord Dubrael."

Fik and Gro had become something of friends to Berbik, Mikkin, Jamie, and Unka. Their other companions had grown closer too. Bul and Moz weren't much for talking. They communicated in strings of grunts when they didn't wish to be bothered with speech. They mostly took to scowling, but they were smarter than they let on, and quite skilled with blades. He was sure they

144

had come along as guards, more than anything. Most impressive was when they'd singlehandedly disarmed Kisteg's patrols. It felt like weeks ago, now, when they'd first arrived on the outskirts of the dwargen city that came after Safuil.

Kisteg's guards had mistaken them for intruders and had charged without warning. Bul and Moz made quick work of the lot before the rest of them pulled their own weapons free. It was all a misunderstanding. One quickly cleared up through a few rushed conversions, but it certainly impressed him.

Net and Bur were the diplomats of the group. They talked plenty when warranted, and their smooth speech was much like what Mikken expected a politician's to be. They were the ones that did most of the work in each great lord's hall, working to convince each dwarg lord to rally to King Talon's cause. Despite their skill at persuasion, they'd had less luck than they'd hoped.

Kisteg being Safuil's neighbor, had close ties and was willing to pledge. Unfortunately, the two cities that followed hadn't been so eager to risk open support. Fauthiel and Tulian both refused. The setback had done little to lift his mood. But there was still Yberg, and then Proaloth, before they came to the coast. Their journey would end at Ice Port.

The torches dimmed as light began to filter into the tunnel. His legs burned something awful with the mix between stairs and upward inclines. His breathing wasn't the only sound permeating the tunnel. Everyone's breath came in short bursts. Beside him, Jamie was gasping.

"Thank the gods!" he managed to growl as light brightened around them. Even with the covering his eyes watered. He kept them narrowed as the tunnel flattened, the air turned fresher and he felt wind. Blessed wind on his skin.

They spilled out of a doorway carved into the side of the mountain and onto a wide stone platform. His eyes adjusted and he removed the covering. A gasp fell from his lips. No longer was the world around him dark and fuzzy. He saw the height of their platform clearly, and the smaller peaks stretched out before him. Those gave way to hills, and beyond that, the grassy plains of Vestur to the south. "Well, that's a sight that takes getting used to," he muttered, almost trembling with relief.

Beside him, Unka had doubled over and was cursing under his breath in some form of goblin gibberish. He almost laughed, laughed because he was so happy to be out of the dark oppressive tunnels they'd been subjected to for weeks.

Jamie collapsed onto his knees but remained otherwise silent. The other dwargs were speaking rapidly in Dwargish; he didn't bother trying to make out any of their words, though he had picked up more of their language over the past few weeks.

"I fear I'll never get you back underground after witnessing it, Master Mikkin," Fik joked. "But it is truly grand. We can stay a while, if you like, but then we best be getting on our way. I'll see to the ravens."

He nodded and took a seat on one of the stone benches placed around the perimeter. This was as good a place as any to have a bite to eat. He intended to soak it all in.

Berbik came to stand beside him and began talking about the dwarg's method of communication. The ravens in question were kept on the mountainside in outposts like this. Carved into the side of the mountain behind him was an aviary where Fik trudged over to introduce himself to the keepers. He planned to send a message to Sky Fall, the mountain outpost above Safuil, where Lord Averaen and his team had been escorted to exit the underground tunnels. From Sky Fall, messages would be taken below. They intended to inform Lord Dubrael of their progress.

This outpost here was Hawk Eye. It was one of the only dwargish sky doorways between here and the coast. There would be one other, Bird's Nest, before their journey ended. He'd been looking forward to this excursion for days. It was well worth the four hour climb.

Jamie and Unka took seats near him as they tucked in to more of the same—dried meat and water. Fortunately, when they arrived in Yberg, a feast could be expected. If there was one thing he'd learned about dwargs, it was their love of drink and feasts.

RETURNING to the Great Stone Road brought melancholy. He tried not to be bothered, thinking of all the food they'd soon have. He also tried to occupy himself with conversation. Unka never strayed far from his side, especially after the cold welcome he'd received from the dwargs.

"Tell me of your home, Unka. Of Pavv. You miss it, no?"

Unka gave a grunt. "Much desert there. Lots of sun. Unka like to return, yes."

"You have family?" Jamie asked.

"Family. Yes. Three wives. Twelve...how say, *kosh*."

"Children?" Mikkin said at the same time as Jamie blurted, "Three wives?!"

In the torchlight, Unka's eyes darted between them. From behind, there came several grunts from the dwargs, including Berbik. Multiple wives wasn't a custom in Dragonwall.

"Children, yes. *Kosh*. Twelve children. Goblin families big."

"But...don't your wives get...I don't know..." Jamie fiddled with his tunic. "How do they get along? I can't imagine my father taking another woman. My mother would go after him with a rolling pin, or worse."

A bark of laughter burst from Mikkin's lips at the thought of Mary going after Tynen with a rolling pin, chasing him around their cottage.

Unka grunted again. "All goblins have many wives. I take three. Plenty. Good friend Grog have eight."

Jamie swore aloud. "*Eight*? Gods above!"

"Unka warned Grog. Hands full. Many...*kosh*. Never peace."

Mikkin laughed again. "I would imagine that you wish to return to your *kosh* and your wives when this is all over?"

"Return, yes. But considered traitor?"

"Because you've helped us?" Mikkin asked. Unka didn't respond. "I suppose so, but if we can bring about an end to this war, I don't think anyone will fault you. I'm sure we can work out some kind of story to bode well in your favor."

"Kane promised new land, land to expand."

"Pavv isn't enough?" Jamie asked.

"Many children. More goblin land," Unka answered.

Mikkin mulled this over. If the goblins killed off enough of their numbers warring in the east, population control would kick in. But he kept this to himself, instead letting Jamie and a few of the dwargs keep up the conversation as they continued to question Unka about his different culture. He couldn't deny he'd somewhat warmed up to Unka in the time they'd spent together. Knowing the little urchin had a family back home did help.

THEY REACHED Yberg a day and a half later. As they walked towards the city, the underground road widened. The glow baskets increased in frequency, and the steady sound of mining vibrated up through their feet. He had come to recognize this with each city they visited. The sounds of industry and productivity as dwargs pulled ice metal, gems, and other precious minerals from the ground to sell in Ice Port.

A contingent of dwarg soldiers met them and spoke with Net and Bur in animated speech. One of the guards clapped Bur on the shoulder. "Bur's cousin lives here in Yberg," Berbik explained, keeping his voice low. "He's well liked among this clan."

Mikkin hummed. "Perhaps that will bode well for us, no?"

"Let us hope."

They were taken to Yberg's great hall to meet its lord. Lord Umdod. He had dark hair, and like all dwargs, plenty of it, decorated with beads in all sorts of colors. His beard was down to his knees, and much of his hair was streaked with white.

"Some say he's nearly two hundred," Berbik uttered, speaking out of the corner of his mouth while Than, Net, and Bur took their places up near the front of the group.

"How old do Dwargs live?" Jamie asked in a hushed whisper.

"If we're lucky, three hundred is a fine age."

Jamie all but choked in surprise while their group offered

respectful bows. Lord Umdod focused his attention briefly on Than, Net, and Bur, speaking rapidly in Dwargish. He then turned to the rest of them, switching to the common tongue. "Tonight we feast, tomorrow I will turn my attentions to the matter you have brought before me." He stood then, lifting his arms, smiling.

They weren't alone in the hall. There were other dwargs scattered about, both males and females. The hall looked much the same as the others they'd visited. Much the same as Lord Dubrael's hall in Safuil. Stone columns spanned its interior, expertly carved from the rock beneath the mountains. Flaming braziers cast dancing orange light throughout the room. The large chair sitting upon the dais was carved to perfection.

Two dwargs approached. When one began hugging Bur and speaking animatedly, he knew this must be Bur's cousin. Bur introduced him to their party as Jagnon, or Jag for short. It was a warm greeting.

"I will show you to your accommodations," Jag said, his voice rumbling with pleasure, thick with his accent. "You will be staying in my house whilst you are here. My family will give you a warm welcome."

They were ushered from the hall and taken through a series of corridors to a large entry chamber. "Welcome to my home." Jag spread his arms wide as several children rushed forward, squealing with glee. They threw themselves upon Bur, babbling in Dwargish with excitement as Jag's cousin swept them up into hugs. Mikkin couldn't help his sad smile at the display. It was the same way his sons would have greeted him.

Another male appeared in the opposite doorway wiping his hands on an apron, brow furrowed as he took in the new guests. "Ah! This is my husband, Azoul," Jag said by way of introduction, eyes sparkling with warmth. "But you may call him Az."

"Az and Jag foster many children in Yberg," Bur explained, hoisting one of them up on his shoulders, much to the child's delight. "Those who have lost parents to sickness, or to mishaps below in the mines. But come, I will show you to your sleeping accommodations." It was clear that Bur was as comfortable in his cousin's home as his own.

Mikkin was eager for a bath, so he couldn't help his delighted smile as Bur led him and the others to their own individual rooms, each with bathing chambers. "Because they foster so many children, they've been given one of the largest dwellings in Yberg. My room is just down the hall."

Jamie cleared his throat. "How...how large is this home?"

Bur laughed. "There are—" He hesitated, as if doing a mental calculation. "—twenty seven sleeping rooms."

Jamie's eyes went wide.

Mikkin hid his snicker as he ducked into his room and shut the door behind him, shedding his belongings. It was grander than he might have expected, had he not already spent several nights in each respective dwarg city along the Great Stone Road. Dwargs were proud of their mining prowess. They liked to decorate their dwellings with the fruits of their labor. His room was furnished with a bed, table and chairs, a writing desk, a number of glow lamps, and several large decorative gems the size of dragon eggs. Or at least, he imagined dragon eggs to be of a similar large size. He went to examine one, a deep ruby red—a small boulder. It was beside the bed with its top sheared off. A side table, he realized, tracing his finger over the cloudy surface.

He let out a soft laugh picturing Unka in the room next door. The little goblin was no doubt wrapped around one of these giant gems, arms and legs, clutching it for dear life. He'd probably never get the creature out of his room for dinner. But...no matter.

He shed his clothes and padded into the bathing chamber. This room *did* impress him. It was all stone like the last, but much of it was carved: a bathing pool, pit toilet, and stone table with a mirror. Here, gems were everywhere, pressed into the stone, making the room glitter with color. He gazed, transfixed. Clearly Az and Jag were wealthier than some of the others. None of the places he'd stayed at had boasted bathing chambers quite this lavish. He made a mental note to check Unka's room before they departed in a few days, just to make sure the little urchin didn't pop some of the gems out to take with him. A grunt slipped from his lips at the thought.

Drawing a bath, he couldn't help his groan when he sank into the hot water. He didn't bother marveling at the ingenuity of it. Dwargs had surprised him at every turn since making their acquaintance. No doubt, some hot underground spring fed these bathing tubs and he was glad of it.

Hours later, they were led back to the great hall where tables had been placed. Roaring fires and platters of food had him all but rushing forward with his party to feast. Lord Umdod gave them a place of honor at his table. That was one thing he'd quickly learned. The dwargs treated their guests like their own family and never hesitated to offer up the best.

The most common course that night was roasted mountain trout, stuffed with earthy herbs that grew well underground in limited light. Much to his surprise, the dwargs of Yberg had a vast underwater lake fed by several mountain rivers and the trout had made a home beneath their city. The flaky white meat was complemented nicely by roasted potatoes and—not surprising whatsoever—mushrooms. But these were done differently than some of the mushroom dishes he'd had before. They were sautéed in goat's butter. There was goat meat too—considered a special treat, as the mountain goats were not butchered for food until they reached old age. Food was never wasted in places like this.

Lord Umdod was pleased to have their company. He told stories of his people and asked them questions out of curiosity, especially Mikkin and Jamie. He even treated Unka with a politeness that surprised Mikkin, given that the past two lords had all but ignored the goblin. Lord Umdod seemed to respect the little creature for switching loyalties, or at least, to regard him in higher standing.

All too soon, talk turned to that of the impending war in Dragonwall. Although their diplomats, Than, Net, and Bur, were supposed to speak of these matters the day following, it seemed Lord Umdod was eager to begin the discussions now. They were happy to oblige, and as the drink flowed more freely, so too did their tongues, outlining all the issues Dragonwall would face if Kane came to power.

As they talked, Lord Umdod's scowl deepened and his good mood darkened until he was all but sputtering with rage. "The absolute gall!" he roared at one point, when they elaborated on Kane's involvement in taking Fort Squall. Mikkin took this as a good sign, even if the vast quantity of drink Umdod had consumed was likely fueling the dwarg lord's passion.

"I will stand with Safuil and Kisteg in this," Lord Umdod said at last. "Even though my neighbors have refused, let none say that Yberg is cowardly. I will join in the efforts to see this sorcerer defeated."

At that, his party of dwargs lifted their tankards and roared with delight. Mikkin and Jamie shared a silent exchange, nodding with relief. He couldn't help the sigh that left his chest, or the way his shoulders sagged. All too soon, dessert—a golden sweet bread drenched in syrup—was brought forth. Its scent was heavenly. With the good news, he allowed himself to eat into a stupor, glad that they'd had some more success, after all.

CHAPTER 16
ELEMENTAL PILLARS

Esterpine

Claire spent the next three days after her first success using Pelwynn's bow. On the third day, her ability to focus had progressed enough to hit the target every time. She didn't miss, even if she aimed at the tree canopy just as Pelwynn had. Moreover, she was no longer sore from pulling the weight of it.

She burst into Pelwynn's cottage that afternoon, a smile on her face. "I've done it," she proclaimed. "I can hit the target every time, *Kenya*."

"Hmm..." Pelwynn's brows lowered. "We shall see how well you have done. Leave it here and follow me."

She frowned. "But, don't you want to see?"

"I do. Leave it and follow me," he repeated, leading her back to the garden.

She exhaled when she realized what he intended. Blossom in one hand, an open palm face up with the other, he took a seat at his garden bench. She plopped down cross-legged on the ground before him. "Let's test your focus, *Elam*. Create a blossom in my open palm."

She frowned. Was it really going to be that easy? Even if she had succeeded with the bow?

"I would explain the mechanics of it again," he added, "but something tells me you have learned a bit more about yourself in the process of working with the bow?"

He was right. Working with the bow had given her two things to focus on and helped her exercise her mind. Trying to think of only one thing was too difficult for her wandering thoughts. By putting the blossom in the back of her mind and the dummy's head at the front, she'd succeeded. Except...how was she supposed to do that now, when she wasn't firing an arrow at a target?

She closed her eyes and pictured the blossom, pictured everything about it. Its white color, the petals and pistils, the smell, the soft feeling of plucking it from its vine. She thought through each of those things. Something told her that wasn't enough.

She opened a single eye just a crack, peaking at Pelwynn's expectant palm. Still nothing. Inhaling deeply, she tried again. This time, she did something differently, she thought of two blossoms. One she kept suspended in the front of her mind, rotating as if floating in mid air. The other more detailed picture went to the back of her mind as she cataloged its characteristics.

A bark of pleasure made her jump. Her eyes flew open and her jaw dropped. "I—I did it?"

Pelwynn snorted. "Well, I certainly didn't do it *for* you."

She leaned forward, touching the blossoms just to be sure. "How do I know which one is which?"

"You don't. Each is as real as the other, a perfect duplicate." He closed his fists around them and when he opened his hands, they were both gone. "Now, two."

"What?" She stopped short.

"Create two."

"But—"

"Just do it, *Elam*. Remake them."

So she focused on his empty palms, keeping her eyes open, something she hadn't yet done for the distraction it posed. This time, she held the one blossom in the back of her mind, but split the forefront into two blossoms, each revolving above Pelywnn's open palm. Her mental picture became the image of what her eyes beheld. She blinked, taking note of the white glow that emanated from her to Pelwynn's palms, like streams of energy connecting her to the world around her, and the world around her to the blossoms.

She slumped down, not quite believing. Pelwynn smiled. He closed his fists and the blossoms disappeared. *"Nuah ano, Elam.* Now your real training begins."

~

LATER THAT EVENING, she returned to find Koldis grinning. "What's got *you* in such a happy mood?"

His eyes darted to the writing desk. "There might be a certain letter that arrived while you were out."

"Talon?" she cried. Her heart leapt when Koldis nodded. She all but squealed, rushing over. Her success with the flowers was forgotten. There it was, a thick envelope this time, sitting innocently, waiting to be torn open. She plopped down and went to open it, then hesitated. Any minute, some of the other pairs would pop into her suite as they were wont to do, and she had no intention of being interrupted.

She jumped back up. "I'm not to be bothered," she told Koldis. "Not until it's time for dinner. Oh, *gods*! Stop grinning at me like that."

He shrugged, but the grin didn't disappear. Like he could assume everything Talon had written and was amused by it. Her cheeks flushed and she retreated to her bedroom, slamming the door behind her.

Comfortable on her bed, she broke the seal. There were two individually sealed letters. She grabbed Talon's first.

Dear C,
I believe Reyr has taken your threat personally. He

hovers. It has become a nuisance, but I cannot fault him. He worries for me in your absence. Apparently I'm moodier than usual. Surely this can come as no surprise.

Things here have been tense. Plans aren't going as smoothly as I had hoped, but I cannot say more of that here. However, I will say we've had a stroke of good fortune borne on raven wings. I wish I could tell you more. Admittedly, I was quite surprised to learn of it.

Lord Marquin...the name sounds familiar. I believe I met him. Pompous fellow, if I recall, often trailing after the queen.

Yes, Lady Tamara arrived safely. Desaree, Jocelyn, and Saffra have made it their personal duty to care for her in your absence. They have shown her around the keep and have taken her to the market. You will be pleased to find the enclosed letter they requested I send on their behalf—

SHE PAUSED and glanced down at the other letter, fingering the seal. A castle turret was the backdrop with an elegant *S* at the forefront. Saffra's seal. A thrill shot through her. She set it aside and returned to Talon's letter.

Dallin's training goes well. Our shields are fine. They are coping in your absence. I believe they miss you as much as I do. Well, perhaps not quite as much. No one misses you more than I. I feel your absence keenly.

My appetite has been nonexistent. I went hunting yesterday and couldn't stomach more than a single grazer. Even that was difficult to choke down. Like the meat had lost its flavor.

As for Koldis, my mistake. I believe I know the reason for his mood. I dare not write it in this letter. Even if I could, it is his secret to tell when he is ready. I would not rob him of that. Be patient with him. But know that it is nothing dangerous.

Which brings me to my next concern. I worry for you. What of this unsettling thing you mentioned? I trust your judgment, that you will keep yourself safe. Be careful!

As for your kisses, one for every day of your absence—at minimum. That's at least fourteen (at my time of writing this), without any incurred interest. But since you insisted on one-hundred-percent previously, I feel it is only fair to enact the same rate, don't you?

I look forward to your next letter, but more so, your return. Come back to me.

Love,

T

P.S. I hope you are enjoying their food.

SHE LAUGHED OUTRIGHT, reading the letter twice over before tearing open Saffra's. She was pleased to find that it was from Saffra, Desaree, and Jocelyn. Pleased that they had sat together penning it. They told her of all the gossip she'd missed, how they'd shown Tamara around. What they'd purchased at the market. And more besides, including Saffra's encounter with a certain commander, which saddened her to hear of. But most of it was happy news, and she found herself smiling throughout.

She hugged the letters to her chest. It was like having a little piece of comfort and familiarity. The idea thrilled and scared her. Kastali Dun had become something of a home in her time within Dragonwall. As much as she loved the forest, she had always intended to return. Home was where Talon was, and she felt the distant tug of him in her chest, now more than ever.

She wanted him in her arms. Wanted his lips. Wanted everything. All of him. Even if it meant accepting the additional responsibilities he carried. Perhaps beside him, he wouldn't feel so burdened. Perhaps she could lighten his load. That alone reassured her—

Koldis pounded on the door. "You going to starve yourself tonight, my queen? I, for one, would like to eat."

"Fine. I'm coming." She sighed and tucked the letters away. She would answer them later.

~

THE DAYS FOLLOWING her success with the blossoms blurred together. Sparring first thing in the morning with Koldis. Lessons with Lord Marquin. Her use of the *Ednuar* was growing stronger. It was her lessons with Pelwynn that made the difference. The day after summoning the blossoms, he'd taken the time to explain the fundamentals behind sprite magic, something Lord Marquin had clearly failed to do. Albiet due to a lack of understanding of the true nature of it, something that had been lost in time.

"Our magic—in case you had not realized—centers around elemental pillars," Pelwyn had explained. "*Vahlim eamtylla.*"

Her thoughts had clicked into place the moment he said it. "Earth, air, fire, and water?" she'd asked.

"Correct."

The more she saw of sprite magic, the more intuitive this had become. She'd done fire magic—*lac alnar ellohdar.* She'd managed to summon water in the forest. But also air magic against Caterina.

Not to mention the aided healing with just the humming of her voice. The blossoms she'd conjured, as it turned out, fell neatly into the earth category, just like healing did. Everything she'd done fell within one of the vahlim eamtylla. *Elemental pillars.* Lord Marquin's demonstrations confirmed this, too. Though he often resorted to air magic—his favorite.

Knowing the theory behind the *vahlim eamtylla* was one thing. Working with this kind of magic was another. It was different from mage magic, which was harsh and commanding. Mage magic— which had descended from the asarlaí—didn't bow to the elements. It didn't care about them. It simply existed selfishly. With mage magic, she could speak a command and meet her needs. Her limit depended on her knowledge of the old language and the energy of her body.

Not so with *vahlim eamtylla.* It relied on the energy of the world, an invisible substance that took on the form of a white glow when she worked with it. An invisible force only seen by those in tune with it. "Most sprites can't see it," Pelwynn explained. "Not unless they're trained as I am training you. The sprites you've met in Esterpine, those following Queen Jade's rule, their magic was acquired through desperation, through need. Yours will be acquired through focus, through mindfulness, through respect for the nature of the world, respect for the *vahlim eamtylla.*"

Perhaps Pelwynn thought too highly of her. After all, he had believed she'd summon a blossom the day after she'd met him. Instead, it had taken nearly a week. And much of the other magical workings he guided her through were just as difficult, despite mastering her focus with the blossom.

Pelwynn was relentless. He led her through the elements she had the most experience with first. Fire, earth, and water. Instead of singing, like she'd done when defeating the vodar or conjuring the creek, he had her practicing first with just her mind. This kind of mental focus could do simple things, like summoning a flame in the palm of your hand, or creating a miniature cloud of mist that rained water when it got too heavy, or making blossoms appear. After that, he had her use simple phrases, sung in a sing-song voice to manipulate these elements. That had been a true challenge, especially when it came to the *lac alnar ellohdar*. She certainly didn't want to burn anything she wasn't supposed to.

"She's learning quickly," Taylynn mentioned one day, startling them out of a practice session. Five days had passed since Pelwynn had declared their real training to begin. Taylynn hadn't been seen since the day she'd taken her to Pelwyn. "What are her elemental strengths thus far," she asked, studying them.

"Fire, earth, and water," she answered, breaking her focus on the vines she'd conjured from the soil in Pelwynn's garden. She stared at them a moment longer, watching them twist up along a trellis before letting her mind truly relax. Taylynn looked the same as always, wild like the forest.

"Nuah ano," Taylynn praised. *Well done.* "Edah jad helloh lame-nah." *And new bright markings.*

Claire nodded. She'd acquired several. It wasn't easy to count them because they'd become continuations of the ones she already had, extending and swirling around her abdomen, back, shoulder, and spine. The one on her shoulder had sent a tendril up her neck that ended in a small spiral below her earlobe. She was rather fond of it, peaking out beneath her clothes. But she'd started wearing a scarf to keep it from Lord Marquin's attention.

"I'm going to take her out into the forest the day after tomorrow, *Kenya,*" Taylynn announced, rather unceremoniously. "We will be gone for several days. I think it is time for her to see more of her world."

Pelwynn sighed, but didn't argue. She glanced between them, her heart picking up speed. She'd been hesitant about going back out into the forest since coming into contact with the darkness lurking there. But if Taylynn was with her, maybe she could.

"Yes, you will be quite safe," Taylynn said, as if reading her mind. "You need not let the others know I will be with you, except perhaps a select few, like that pompous drengr that trails you like a puppy. I don't want my mother to know." She hesitated. "Announce to Lord Marquin that you are taking another journey to work on your mastery. It will help explain the new marks you've acquired. I assume that's why you're hiding them?"

She nodded. She'd had no way to explain to Lord Marquin why new marks were appearing after so many of her lessons with Pelwynn, and she certainly hadn't gone out into the forest for days at a time to earn them. "Won't he be suspicious when he sees me return with so many?"

Taylynn lifted a shoulder. "You are Isabella's heir. Everyone knows this. They will not be surprised to see your skin."

"Koldis isn't going to like it—not after what happened last time. Even if you're with me."

"Well then, shall we return together so I might explain to him the importance of it?"

A slow smile crept across her face as she thought of Koldis's impending reaction. "Yes, I think you'd better speak with him." If Taylynn caught her true meaning, she gave no sign of it. They bid Pelwynn farewell and set out for Esterpine. She couldn't wait to see Koldis's face when Taylynn appeared.

CHAPTER 17

TAUNTING TAYLYNN

Koldis shut his book when he saw the foggy shadows of movement outside the suite's sitting room. "Thank the gods," he growled as Claire emerged. "If I have to read another—what is *she* doing here?" He was immediately on his feet, eying the sprite princess who'd swept in like the tide.

"She is here to explain that I'm going into the forest. The day after tomorrow," Claire said, glaring at him, daring him to protest.

"Is that so?" His eyes narrowed, turning to the sprite princess. Taylynn met his gaze unflinchingly. There were few who had the gall. Most would have withered beneath the stare he paid her.

"Lord Koldis," she said by way of greeting. He almost shuddered at the sound of her musical voice. "Claire needs a way to explain the number of marks increasingly present on her skin. She will accompany me on a week-long journey. Everyone here will believe she is merely taking a routine solo trip into the forest, as is expected for learning our magic. She cannot hide from the task forever."

A whole week? His chest tightened. He wasn't sure what emotion it was, exactly. Likely worry and concern. He glanced between the two women before him, driven to argue Taylynn's point, but...her theory was valid. And as much as he wanted to protect his queen, he couldn't stifle her growth.

"There is something you aren't telling us," he said.

"That is between myself and Lady Claire."

He clenched his jaw and glanced at Claire. *I don't trust her.* There were so many useful reasons he appreciated Claire's ability to use her mind. He was certain—knowing Taylynn—that Claire had no idea why Taylynn was dragging her into the forest.

Claire—gods be cursed—answered him out loud and said, "I trust her, Koldis. I assume she has a good—"

"Yes, I have a good reason. One I shall explain once we set out."

"I see," he mused. "So...this isn't a typical pilgrimage where she will learn new magic."

"Correct," Taylynn confirmed.

"Excellent." A smile curved his lips. "Then you will have no qualms about my accompaniment—to make sure things do not get out of hand."

Taylynn opened her mouth—

"I think that'll be fine," Claire said, looking between them, "since this isn't a solo venture. We can have our pairs cover for your absence." Claire's expression—he recognized it immediately. The slight curve of her lips and the sparkle in her eyes. She was up to something.

Yet, he couldn't help the smug satisfaction at hearing her words, nor the satisfaction that came with watching Taylynn's face dart through several emotions before she nodded. "Very well. But do not slow us down, *Drengr.*"

He held up his hands. "Wouldn't dream of it, *Sprite.*"

Taylynn didn't linger. In fact, she dismissed herself almost immediately. He caught himself watching the door through which she'd disappeared and averted his gaze.

"Is there a reason you insist on being so aggressive when she's around?" Claire snapped, drawing his focus straight to her.

"I don't know what you speak of."

Claire tutted. "*Riiiight.* I could feel the heat sizzling off you. Off both of you. Just so you know, the only reason I'm allowing you to come is to fulfill my own curiosity."

He frowned. "Curiosity, my que—?"

"Curiosity to see what's going on between you and her. I want to see it unfold."

He arched an eyebrow. "And here I thought you agreed because I am your guar—"

"Get real, Koldis."

He huffed. "Nothing is *unfolding*, Claire. Hate to disappoint you."

But he couldn't help the wary feeling building in his chest. Was she right? *Was* there something more than the age-old-animosity between them? Claire crossed her arms and glared at him, as if reading his mind. "Cut that out," he snapped before turning on his heel and retreating to his room.

Inside, he began pacing. Were he normal, he would have simply disappeared into the city to be alone. But he knew exactly what that meant. He'd have to subject himself to the thoughts and emotions of the animals he crossed paths with. He didn't need to know how much fear an insignificant squirrel felt upon smelling him. He didn't need the reminder of his predatory nature. He rejoiced in his dragon, but the animals he encountered made sure to remind him that *they* didn't.

"Koldis?" Claire knocked at his door. "I'm coming in." He opened his mouth to protest but she waltzed in. Her eyes swept over him, calculating. He should have told her. He should have explained why he was so irritable. It was ridiculous that he didn't. But part of him wasn't ready to hear her tell him he was overreacting, that he was making a bigger deal about this than he should have. He was her guard. He didn't need her thinking him weak.

"You know, I'm here if you want to talk about it."

He swallowed, taking a deep breath. "I know," he said at last. "I think...I just need a walk and some fresh air." No, that was absolutely *not* what he needed.

She looked as if she wanted to say more, but stopped herself, nodding instead.

So he swept past her and out of the room.

❧

THE CITY WAS BUSTLING. The hour leading up to the evening meal was always the busiest. Sprites rushed about as they finished their final tasks before retiring for the day.

He set out on a path that took him to the edge of the city, but not too far that he couldn't find his way back. It was only as the dwellings thinned that he realized this was the same path that had led to the sick stag.

A frightened squeak jolted him from his brooding. *Hunter. Beast. Flee!* A rustle followed as a rabbit darted across his path and into the undergrowth on the opposite side. He snorted. As if he'd ever want something as insignificant as a rabbit. More frightened thoughts followed this one. Animal thoughts weren't as coherent as some might think. They were often jumbled and ruled by emotion more than words, yet, somehow his mind managed to put into words the feelings encompassed in each of their desperate inklings. Smaller creatures often didn't have much in the way of words, simply broadcasting pure emotion. Larger animals were more coherent.

He continued onward, well aware of every creature and the disdain they regarded him with. Most chose to stay hidden, hoping to wait out his passing. He pushed their fear away, trying to clear his mind. It was an effort, one easier said than done.

Pets, yes. Itch there. So goooood. The next thoughts he encountered were refreshing. They weren't filled with fright, but rather, joy and love. He hesitated, knowing that if he continued on this path he'd find unicorns milling about.

Love you. Safe with you. Their overflowing emotion hit him square in the chest, pushing deep. It was different from how his chest often felt when encountering large animals. Still, he rubbed his hand over his sternum. He should have stopped, turned around and gone back. But instead, he continued until the unicorns came into view.

Six of them circled around a lone figure in a flowing spriten gown. She was laughing, her head thrown back, delicate fingers rubbing muzzles and scratching ears. The smile on her lips left his heart thudding. He stood, transfixed as Princess Taylynn leaned forward and kissed one of the creatures on the nose, rubbing her own against it in a gentle caress. The gesture was so open, so vulnerable.

A flush washed over him. This felt like a private moment, like something he shouldn't be allowed to witness. Overly aware of his intrusion, knowing that were he to back away, she'd spot him anyway, he cleared his throat.

"Yes, yes," she said, not bothering to glance in his direction. He expected exasperation in those words, but her happiness was fixed. "I know you're there, Lord Koldis. Come. Come and greet them."

New pets? Several of the unicorns glanced in his direction.

He hesitated. The last thing he would ever do was let this sprite know how much she grated his scales. So he stepped forward, donning an air of confidence, and began petting the nearest unicorn.

Ahh, pets. Ears. Pet ears. The unicorn tilted its head, better exposing its ears. He knew what it wanted without it needing the extra effort. Still, he lifted his hand and began rubbing the base of its ears and down its neck.

No, ears. Ears. Despite his rubbing, the unicorn continued to angle its head, clearly displeased.

"Here—" Suddenly Taylynn was beside him, her body angled towards his, so close he could all but feel the heat radiating off her. "Lya likes her ears scratched in a *particular* way. Like this—"

He froze. Taylynn took his left hand without permission, weaving her fingers through his to control his thumb and forefinger, stroking not the base of Lya's ears as he'd been doing, but the inside. All the while, Taylynn's smile was radiant, as if she could single handedly light the world with the brightness of it. He didn't dare move a muscle, overly aware of her proximity, nearly flush against his side. Up close, he all but dwarfed her. She was shorter than Claire, and only came to the middle of his chest.

He dared not meet her eyes, instead turning his upon the unicorn.

Yessss. Pets. Lya radiated pleasure—momentarily distracting him from Taylynn's presence. The unicorn even let out a gentle humming sound. A bark of laughter fell from his lips, unbidden. But it was quickly followed by the realization of what was happening here.

He stepped away, extracting his hand from Taylynn's. He didn't miss the smug curl at the corner of her lips. Almost as if—

"You are always so easy to fluster, *Drengr*," she murmured.

He crossed his arms, immediately on edge. "Why are you taking Claire into the forest?" The question shattered the calm that had settled around them.

Taylynn's expression changed. Her smile slipped away. She whispered a few words to the unicorns that sent them plodding off before turning back to him. "I'm taking her to find answers."

"Answers..." Something in her answer was familiar

"Saffra delivered my message, I trust?"

Things clicked into place. His lips pressed into a thin line. "You're taking her to find the staff, then?"

Taylynn frowned. "The staff?"

A chuckle fell from his lips. "Forgive me, Your Highness, but confusion isn't your strong suit." Something of pleasure trickled through him at seeing her usual shell crumble away. It lent an air of imperfection to her otherwise spotless facade.

Taylynn immediately schooled her features. "Claire has a great deal of work to do if she is to master her magic."

"You didn't answer my question. The staff?"

"Within the forest, she will find a weapon—"

"The staff."

"Yes, yes, you keep mentioning it and I have no—" Her eyes widened a measure. The surprise was there and gone in a flash. "Isabella's Staff," she whispered, almost too quiet to be heard.

He clicked his tongue. "Well, well, well. Isn't this a funny turn of events? And here I thought you knew everything."

"I do," she snapped, hugging her waist. "Usually." She dropped her arms and began to pace, forehead furrowed. He watched her, his eyes never leaving her figure. Her gown was sheer, not so different from the ones she often donned while she was in Esterpine. He found it interesting that those times he'd seen her in the wild, she dressed more like a huntress. But here, she looked every bit the princess her title warranted. He couldn't help the way his eyes fell upon her features, appreciating the sight of her more than he should have.

She halted, turning to him. "I was told of a weapon, but certainly not...wait a moment, how do *you* know of the staff?"

"Oh, this is *great*." He allowed a smug smile to take up residence on his face, sure it would irk her. "How does it feel? Hmm? Someone else holding the cards?"

She took several steps towards him until her chest was all but flush to his. He took a single step back to break the contact, failing to hide his surprise. Somehow, despite only reaching his chest, it was as if she were looking down her nose at him, making him feel... insignificant. His temper flared. "This isn't the time for games, *my lord*. You think all that is happening within Dragonwall is something to take lightly? Leave your insufferable pride behind. Tell me what you know of it."

"Hmm. Interesting." This time he reclaimed that single step, making up the remaining distance between them. Now her chest *was* truly flush to him. He ignored the warmth where their bodies connected. "You know, I think I'll keep it to myself, Your Highness. My queen's business—though it involves all of Dragonwall—is still hers. Besides—" His smile widened. "I'm sure there will be plenty of time to ask her about it while we travel together."

He didn't miss the flush of irritation that colored her cheeks or the glitter that filled her ancient eyes. He was playing with fire. After all, she was thousands of years older than him.

Her shoulders dropped. "It was Saffra," she decided. "Of course. I see it now..." This close, he could see each of the little creases that appeared between Taylynn's brows as they drew together. "Good. Yes, very good. It is as I hoped, then. Her powers are strengthening. The water helped more than I could have predicted."

It was his turn to frown. "Why do I get the impression that your manipulations have extended to our prophetess." He hadn't forgotten Prince Feowen's words.

A huff of air left her nose. "Because they have," she snapped. "But as you so clearly laid out, this is my business and therefore none of yours."

"Ah. So we *are* going to play that game. Very well then, Princess. I feel validated, then, in refusing to reveal all that Lady Saffra has seen."

"Of course you do," she scoffed. "You drengr are all the same."

Instead of feeling insulted, the heat of satisfaction filled his veins. She was easier to rile than he'd first expected, given the way her breathing heightened and her chest rose and fell against him. Still, he dared not back down.

"We are. So you can hardly fault me for keeping silent."

"Fine," she hissed, taking several steps back. "Keep your secrets, *Drengr*. I shall know soon enough."

She turned on her heel and disappeared. He stared after her, annoyed by the yawning hole her departure created in his chest.

CLAIRE JUMPED TO HER FEET, all but shrieking, "Wait...*what*?! You're sure?"

He had only just returned to collect her for dinner, but couldn't help relaying everything that had just happened. Or...nearly everything. He kept his own emotions out of it. She didn't need to know that. It would only fuel her suspicions that something was unfolding between them.

"You heard correctly, my queen."

"You mean *the* staff. The one Saffra saw me wielding in my vision. The one Taylynn spoke of in her message—"

"Not so fast. We only *assumed* she spoke of it. Her message mentioned a weapon. She never said what that weapon was."

"Yes but—"

"Yes, *but*." He mimicked. "I think we can safely assume it's the staff, given that Saffra saw you wielding both the staff and Cyrus's sverak against Kane. And after her reaction…"

"She really didn't know?"

"It would seem not."

Claire's brow furrowed. She plopped back down on the sofa instead of walking towards the door, which was what they'd been in the process of doing as he'd told her. "Isabella's staff," she murmured, sighing. "I knew the staff was important but I didn't realize it belonged to Isabella. How am I supposed to find it now? It probably isn't even here. Didn't Isabella move to Kastali Dun? She would've taken something that valuable with her. How am I supposed to…?"

"Patience, my queen." He held up his hands. "I am sure we will find answers soon enough. Likely on this journey Taylynn plans to drag us on. She was quite explicit that you would find answers. If the king tree gave her this message—assuming it is all knowing, not that I can believe that, but I'm just a lowly *drengr,* so what do I know—then clearly the staff is here and you're meant to find it."

"Koldis! Stop." She got to her feet, scowling. "For the record, you're not just a lowly drengr. You're a shield. Don't let her get under your skin. And, maybe you're right. I'm just overwhelmed, is all."

"Hmm…" He lifted an eyebrow to acknowledge this. She wasn't yet queen in name, but she certainly bore the brunt of the weight already. He didn't envy her. Besides, he was still angry with her for making that dangerous promise, even if his king had already scolded her for it.

"Safe to say, Taylynn isn't as all knowing as I'd come to believe," Claire mused. "I'm not sure if that's a good thing or a bad thing."

"It matters not. You know what you have to do. Master your magic, learn to live with both sides of yourself. Find the staff. You've already got Cyrus's sverak. Now, let us go to dinner before we're so late we make a scene."

Claire barked a laugh, striding towards the door. "We couldn't have that, now could we?"

"I'm not so sure," he argued. "Something tells me you enjoy making scenes. In all the time I've known you, I've never been disappointed in that regard."

"I don't know." She hesitated, chewing on her lower lip. "You strike me as one for scenes, too. If I recall, it was *your* sverak so dramatically poised at my throat when we first met."

He faltered and heat flushed his skin. It was a memory he often tried to forget. "Yes, and I am sorry for that. Sorrier than I can put into words. I beg you, forgive me." His voice came out quieter than he intended. The shame of what he'd done, of how he'd first behaved, was an emotion he wished to be rid of. Drawing a weapon against his own queen, for the sake of the gods, he was lucky he still lived.

She grinned, her smile dazzling. "Consider it done, Koldis. But only on one condition." He lifted his eyebrows. "That you behave yourself on our adventure with Taylynn. Do that and I'll forget all about it."

He sighed. "Very well, my queen. Your wish is my command." He even went as far as to bow deeply, which earned a laugh and a hard smack on his back.

"Come along, then. No scenes, remember." And with that, she was through the door, disappearing into the hallway beyond.

<h1 style="text-align:center">CHAPTER 18
BAGRADAS</h1>

Dragonfire Sea

Bennett lowered his spyglass at the roar of delight that split the air. He turned away from the distant coast sailing by, looking toward the packed bodies in the middle of the deck. It wasn't the usual frivolity he allowed, but he'd made an exception with the hopes of seeing Cat get a black eye, or perhaps a broken nose. He wasn't sure if her healing magic only worked for others, or if she'd be able to heal herself. But even if it was only temporary, it would certainly be satisfying.

New wagers were placed as shouts echoed around the group.

Cat stood in the middle of a mass of bodies, fists bandaged and raised, facing off against Emmon. They circled, eyes locked. He didn't miss the red blossoming across Emmon's cheekbone. So… she'd managed to land a punch already. Interesting.

Ever since Tortalia, a new dynamic had taken form on board the *Lady Faith*, and it was ever changing. The crew still wasn't keen on Cat, but word of her healing six of them had circulated. She still clawed and hissed at everyone she encountered, but the crew was less afraid of hissing back.

They'd even taken to quietly approaching her with requests to heal this and that. Yesterday, he'd spotted Reza requesting she heal the rope burns he'd acquired working the sails. As far as he knew, she'd agreed to each request. But no one broadcasted this; none of the crew wanted to admit they'd turned to her. He couldn't help but admit that for all her inconvenience, she'd suddenly become more...convenient. He'd never considered hiring a mage to sail with them, had never heard such a thing done, but...it certainly made him wonder.

The dynamic continued to change with her aboard. Especially when she'd strode right up to Emmon in sight of all, and asked him to teach her how to throw a punch. Things had truly taken a turn for the interesting. She stood now, in a pair of breeches, tunic, and belt she'd acquired on their latest port stop. Her long hair was tied back in a low bun at the base of her neck. She'd deposited the tricorn she'd taken to wearing next to the stairs leading up to the poop.

Another roar rose up from the group as Cat's fist shot for Emmon's stomach. This time, he dodged, landing a punch of his own to Cat's abdomen. She doubled over, hissing as everyone around them roared and coins were exchanged.

Bennett chuckled.

They continued back and forth like this. He took the stairs two-at-a-time to stand beside Jonah, manning the helm. "Quite the she-cat, eh, Captain?" Bennett hummed in answer, keeping his eyes on the pair, but said nothing. "Least now she'll be able to defend herself better when we stop in Bagradas, assuming...?"

"Yes, we continue as planned, Jonah."

"Right. As you wish. But...two days?"

He shrugged. "Why not? I haven't had a chance to catch up with Aspen in quite a while. Like to see what she's been up to."

Aspen had been the first true captain he'd known. Most of what he knew he'd picked up from her. He'd thought her a man when he first boarded *The Bellona*. She certainly looked and acted the part. A necessity when dealing with sailors, he supposed.

Why Aspen had decided to settle in a shit hole like Bagradas was beyond him, but it was there she'd established a bed and breakfast with a tavern on the ground floor. One of the rowdiest taverns in existence. Perhaps it was a good thing Cat was learning to land a good punch.

Speaking of...he couldn't help but chuckle as Cat managed to land another, right on Emmon's jaw. Before he could recover, she stomped hard on his foot, then—

"Ouch! That won't end well," Jonah cut in as Emmon groaned and doubled over, clutching his jewels. The crew roared with delight and more coins were exchanged. Cat drew herself up, hands on her hips, shoulders proudly drawn back. He saw then that her nose was bleeding. A smirk spread across his face, but it slid off almost immediately when her eyes flashed in his direction, latching onto him.

She didn't see Emmon until it was too late. He lunged and they both tumbled to the deck, a mess of fists and feet. He suspected that cornered like this, the she-cat was using her claws now.

He sighed. "I'll handle the helm. Go break them up. Get them back to work. Land's coming quick."

Jonah gave him a salute and descended to the main deck, roaring at the crew to gain their attention. Those closest to the pair rolling around on the ground didn't immediately stand at attention. Others had to step in and pry Cat and Emmon apart. Soon enough the fun was over and Jonah was ordering the crew back to their positions.

They'd be landside in a few hours and he was eager to disembark. Bagradas was another port town set on a pair of islands near the mouth of Stormy Bay. He didn't plan on going any further than that; he'd heard too many rumors about the dragons controlling Squall's End to get any closer.

He sighed, thinking of the fort leader, Lord Davi, of their meeting together not so long ago. How things had changed. It turned out the ice metal hadn't solved all their problems, and that was a damn shame.

A figure climbed the stairs, heading directly for him. He

blinked, keeping his attention on the helm, navigating the *Lady Faith*.

"I see you're set on stopping in Bagradas," Cat tisked, taking up a wide stance beside him. It was hard to believe, but the past week had seen a change in her. Gone was the green girl who wobbled about the deck. With her tricorn in place, she almost... *almost* passed as a crewman. Except her curves were far too generous for anyone to miss if they looked for more than a second.

"We would reach Ice Port faster if—"

"Come now, kitty cat, I—"

"I told you not to call me that," she snarled, rounding on him.

He chuckled, keeping his gaze forward. "I'll call you what I want. This's my ship, remember. And I wouldn't miss Bagradas for the world. But you needn't worry. Now that you can throw a punch or two, you'll be fine taking care of yourself. Make sure you carry the knife Jonah gave you. But I wouldn't recommend pulling it on anyone unless it's truly necessary. No one will take kindly to a weapon when fists will do."

"Why are you doing this?"

"Doing what?"

"Stopping in the worst ports," she snapped. "Don't play me for a fool, *Captain*. I've spoken to the crew. They—"

"Have you now? They actually spoke to you? Amazing. Have they truly managed to get over their dislike of you? Perhaps I should ask what their secret—"

"Believe it or not, Captain, I'm quite capable of getting what I want."

"Oh." A laugh rumbled in his chest. "Of that I have no doubt. My order stands. We drop anchor in two hours." Though he kept his face forward, he was keenly aware of the way she crossed her arms and glared at him. "Look, girl, the whole reason we stop in places like this is so the crew can have a spot of fun. I told you this wasn't a passenger vessel. Go enjoy yourself. You need not stay glued to me when we embark. I'm sure you can find ways to entertain—"

"Oh, believe me. I plan to stay plastered," she said through clenched teeth. "I wouldn't dare deprive you of my company."

"Ah. So you *are* playing along. Fine. I'll be visiting my old captain while we're here. If you can stand her company, I suppose that's punishment enough."

He spared a glance in time to notice her blink. "Your old captain? Shouldn't someone old enough to be your captain be dead?"

He snorted. "Not sure how old I look to you, but no."

"And how old *are* you?" she asked. He didn't miss the genuine curiosity in her voice.

"I'd tell you were it any of your business."

"Oh, that's rich. How unsurprising. Shall I take a guess then? Forty-five? Perhaps verging on fifty."

He opened and closed his mouth, then clenched his jaw. She was doing it on purpose—he knew she was. And he shouldn't have fallen for the bait, but—"I'm thirty-seven, *kitty cat*."

"Ugh! Call me that again. Go on. Say. It. Again."

He turned to her then, fully facing her. "Use so much as a single measure of magic against me and I will throw you off this ship. I don't imagine kitty cats are great swimmers, but I'm willing to test the theory." He took a step towards her and her eyes widened—a reaction he wasn't expecting. It stopped him short. She quickly schooled her features. He wanted so, *so* badly to take a fistful of the front of her tunic and drag her to the edge of the ship, maybe even dangle her over it to prove he wasn't joking.

Her throat bobbed. She eyed him a final time then turned on her heel and left him fuming on the poop. He returned his attention to the helm, but couldn't help his gaze. It followed her as she made her way across the deck when it should have been tracking their progress.

"Shall I, Captain?" Jonah appeared beside him to take over. "Don't let her get under your skin. That's the trick," his first mate added.

He nodded and stepped aside, clasping his hands behind his

back. His eyes didn't leave Cat's figure. "I need a damn drink, Jonah. Sooner rather than later."

UNFORTUNATELY, it was later by the time he found himself strolling the filthy streets of Bagradas, heading up from the Pits to the Cliffs. Both small districts were aptly named. The Cliffs were considered swanky by the filthiest standards in a place like this. While someone like Cat would be disgusted to know people in these parts considered the Cliffs swanky, it was the most expensive area to live in Bagradas. The view of the port was quite spectacular.

Beaky cawed above him, swooping and bobbing with delight as she surveyed the island town. Those of his crew that were lucky enough to get the first shifts landside had mostly gone their separate ways. But a small contingent was as eager as he to reach the *Crowded Clam*. Houses and shops—if they could be called such, given the constant state of disarray most buildings in Bagradas suffered from—lined the streets leading up to the Cliffs.

His progress was followed by exasperated *tuts*. He didn't bother turning around, but a smile did spread across his lips. Cat had stayed in her new choice of attire. Smart girl. She wasn't keen for more *fruit* jokes, he supposed. The others following in his wake were the same contingent that often did, sans Jonah and Peter, who'd both drawn short straws. Rules were rules. He was glad he hadn't. Most times he lucked out.

"That's the Crowded Clam?" he heard Cat scoff. "I expected..." He didn't bother to find out *what* she expected, and didn't care either.

These buildings, like all the others, lined narrow streets and were stacked high. Each level was wider than the one beneath, until the upper levels jutted out over the lower, hanging over the streets and casting them into shadow. The only benefit to the ones on the Cliffs was they occupied one side of the street with nothing on the other, lending to spectacular views.

A weathered wooden sign hung above the door with an open

clam and pearls spilling out of it. There were other inns along this street, but none as tall as Aspen's *Crowded Clam*. He could hear the roar of noise coming from the open door even in the middle of the day.

"After you, Captain," Emmon said when the others had stopped behind him.

"Yes," Cat said sweetly, voice riddled with sarcasm, "after you."

"Beaky!" he shouted, looking up at the bird. "Find me later, eh?"

"*Find later! Find later!*" That was all Beaky needed to turn on her wing-tip and take off to do...whatever she often did when they were landside. Probably irritate the local birds and forage in the copse of trees just outside of town.

He shot a grin over his shoulder at Cat then strode through the open door. The sound tripled, the light dimmed, and the stink of old drink and unbathed bodies hit him as soon as he stepped inside. It took a moment for some of the regulars to look up from their drinks, but as soon as he was noticed, several roars and lifted tankards greeted him.

"Bless my boots, we've got a scoundrel in our midst!"

He chuckled. Now *that* was a voice he'd recognize anywhere after years of shouted orders.

"Aspen! Good to see you too!" he called across the crowded tavern. She stood behind the bar, overseeing the maids and lads as they served drinks. He strode over, leaving the rest of his crew behind.

Aspen came out from the bar and hugged him. She'd aged a fair bit since he'd last seen her. The wrinkles and tanned skin he was used to, but her close-cropped hair was entirely white now. She'd always been androgynous, but old age made her sex even harder to discern.

"And who's this? A new crew member? You finally took my advice and brought on a female? Never thought I'd see the day," Aspen said, turning to Cat, who must have followed him. He scowled, annoyed to be sharing Aspen's attention with someone so insignificant.

Despite Cat's having pulled her tricorn low over her forehead, there was still no mistaking her curves or the expression of distaste plastered across her face. "So, you're Aspen," she said, not quite a question.

"I am indeed, girl." Aspen eyed her warily. "Prickly, this one," she said to Bennett. "I like her already."

He snorted. "You'd like her less if she graced your deck. And I'd drown myself before ever letting her serve on my crew."

"Then—"

"We're taking her north," he said at the same time as Cat said, "I'd never be caught dead serving in his crew."

He huffed and opened his mouth again—

"How about a round of drinks—on me." Aspen didn't wait to hear whatever else he'd planned to say, turning to the lad left standing behind the bar. She barked orders and led Bennett to the only unoccupied table in the corner. He knew it well. Aspen kept it empty at all times for her own personal business. It was here she entertained favored clientele and cut smuggling deals.

"Tell your lads they can join us, if they please," she said. He motioned to the others with a flick of his head. Emmon urged them forward. There wasn't anywhere else for them to sit anyway. He slid into the booth beside Aspen, none too pleased that Cat made it a point to slide in beside him. He'd have preferred Emmon or Tris.

Not a moment too soon, serving maids bustled over with trays of tankards. He kept his own tied to his belt.

"And some food, too," Aspen added, holding one of the maid's gazes.

"New help?" he asked. "Where's Ferra?"

Aspen snorted. "Don't get me started on her. Ran off with a sailor, like the rest of them."

"Never thought she'd leave, if I'm bein' honest," he said, chuckling. Ferra had always been a favorite. Not quite like Colleen in Kastali Dun, but he'd taken her to bed a few times.

"They always do. Now, you want to tell me why it's been months since you last paid me a visit?" Her scolding tone wasn't lost on him.

He shrugged. "Been busy. Had a couple jobs that needed my attention."

"Like that one?" she asked, flicking her eyes toward Cat.

"Something like that," he grunted, lifting his tankard. "To you, Aspen." The rest of his crew lifted theirs and toasted the *Crowded Clam's* owner. They'd been politely waiting for him to take the first drink. Aspen nodded but left hers untouched.

He drank deep.

"Where you heading? Not north, I hope."

"Unfortunately for me, that's exactly the way I'm headed." He couldn't help but glance at Cat. She'd not bothered to touch her tankard or even toast, but kept her hands locked around it as if it were a warm cup of tea. She certainly wouldn't find any of that in a place like this.

"How far north," Aspen said, cutting into his thoughts.

He sighed. "Far north as north goes, I'm afraid."

Aspen shook her head. "I'd reconsider, were I you, boy."

He couldn't help his smile. *Boy.* If only.

"And where's that cheeky bird of yours, anyway?"

"Beaky's off doing what she wants," he said. "And why should I reconsider? Way I heard it, only real trouble is inside the bay here. How's things been in light of Fort Squall? No trouble, I hope?"

"Oh no you don't," she scolded.

He leaned back, eying her. "You never were one to let a subject drop. Well, if you must know, I tried convincing this one to reconsider,"—he elbowed Cat hard enough that she grunted and turned her eyes like daggers upon him—"but I'm afraid she won't take a lick of advice."

"You should reconsider," Aspen said in answer to his initial question, "because there've been rumors coming my way, and none too good. Word is, Oshean ships, whole fleets of them, been seen docking in Ice Port. Just the other day, I heard of some questionable cargo being loaded a few weeks back."

"Questionable?" He lifted an eyebrow. "That's saying something coming from you."

She laughed. "Questionable, yes. Scores of beasts—unnatural

beasts—loaded into cages. Word is, the port doesn't belong to the dwargs anymore. Not truly."

"Hmm...interesting. Hear that, Cat? Perhaps now you'll reconsider, eh? Doesn't sound like much of a place for a lady."

"I appreciate your advice, captain"—at this she elbowed him back, just as hard— "but I'll take my chances. I have business up north and I will see it settled."

"What possible business could you have with the dwargs, eh, girl? You ought to take your captain's advice."

"He's not my captain," Cat seethed, finally lifting her tankard and drinking it to the last drop.

Tris's eyes went wide as he watched her. Then he clapped her on the back and roared with delight. "See here! She's not just learning to throw a punch. She's going to be drinking like the rest o' us too! Lady indeed!"

Cat tutted but said nothing. Bennett eyed her, wondering what kind of business she could possibly have up north. He still hadn't put the pieces together, not for lack of trying. "Heard anything else?" he asked Aspen, hoping to prepare himself for the remainder of their journey as best as he could.

"Plenty," she said. "Wasn't just beasts they loaded up and sailed off with. Some say they've seen a strange, hooded man in the streets. A sorcerer. Perhaps even the same that was seen with them wild dragons in Squall's end."

Cat sat up straighter. "Did they see him boarding the Oshean vessels, or is he still there?"

"What's it to you, girl?" Aspen asked. Cat shrugged then turned her interest back to her empty tankard.

"Her question is valid, Aspen. I certainly don't want to encounter any sorcerers rumored or otherwise walking the streets while I'm there. I'll feel better knowing whoever it was is off in Oshea at this point." Not that he planned to stay in the freezing north. He'd dump Cat on the nearest iceberg and turn right back around. Probably wouldn't even let his crew disembark.

Aspen shrugged. "Hard to say. They're all rumors, anyway." Her conversation turned to other gossip as she began telling him everything she'd heard about various old crew members who'd moved on. Some had taken up positions of captain and first mate on their own vessels. She always did have a fair share of gossip.

He politely inquired here and there, keeping her talking. But he couldn't help his wandering thoughts. What would he find in the north? And what, for the love of the gods, was Cat up to?

CHAPTER 19

A POISONOUS SOLUTION

Kastali Dun

Talon studied the small group he'd gathered together in his war room—his closest friends and allies. Only those he trusted above all others. Were these simpler matters, they'd have sat by the fire in the sitting room. But no, these were matters of war.

The strategy behind retaking Squall's End had eluded him for weeks. He couldn't count on his lower council to understand the deepest level of dragon affairs. Besides, the majority were occupied with the ongoing goblin issues in the east. He hoped those of his inner circle would offer fresh insight, possibly even a solution.

"What did our spies have to say?" Verath asked, hands clasped behind him. Dallin and Jovari stood beside him, eying the map. He'd debated including Dallin, but Verath had vouched for the young drengr. Bedelth stood across the table beside Saffra. Next to her, Desaree and Jocelyn shifted uneasily. They weren't used to taking part in matters like these. Byron, Tamara, and Reyr were at the head of the table.

"The dragons honor the agreement," Byron answered.

"Then, the people of Squall's End are unharmed?" Verath looked skeptical.

"It would seem so. The dragons haven't bothered the city, though they guard it like a precious jewel. No one enters or leaves."

"Surely that many dragons are unnecessary," Bedelth mused.

"Indeed," Byron scoffed. "They trade duties. Most occupy themselves in leisure." As he spoke, his thumb casually rubbed the back of Tamara's hand. Talon looked away. "They sun themselves in the fields around the city, taking whatever food they please, with no appreciation for the value of livestock. The fort has been mostly destroyed."

"But the people," Saffra interjected. "How long can they go on like that, caged?"

"A city like Squall's End can withstand a siege for several years," Talon explained. "I believe Lord Rhal is a competent lord. He will have had supplies set aside for times like these."

"And their water supply?" Saffra asked.

He looked at Byron and Reyr in question.

Reyr shrugged. "There are wells. Aqueducts too, that feed the city from Plymlet Lake."

Talon nodded. "That should be enough water to—"

"Is that the same lake the dragons use?" Saffra asked. "I assume they don't drink sea water."

Talon's gaze snapped to hers. His voice was measured as he said, "Why do you ask, Lady Saffra?"

Saffra held his gaze before turning to Byron, ignoring his question entirely. It did little to calm his ire. "Well, Byron?" she asked again. "Is it?"

"I believe so, my lady." Byron cleared his throat. "From what our spies tell us, they've made nests along its shores."

"And the next nearest freshwater lake?" she probed.

Talon's brows together. What did it matter—?

"Not close enough to suit them," Reyr answered. "Gretter Lake, I believe, is a half day's flight." Byron nodded to confirm this.

"Then the dragons get their water from a single source," Saffra concluded.

Talon's irritation vanished. He hid his surprise as he looked at Saffra then shook his head. "You brilliant *brilliant* woman."

She shrugged, but a hint of a smile pulled up the corners of her lips.

Bedelth looked between them, his eyes narrowed. "Forgive me, my king, but perhaps the rest of us are missing something?"

Talon's gaze remained locked on Saffra's, silent communication rushing between them with just a single look. He knew exactly where her mind was. He cleared his throat. "Lady Saffra may have changed the tide of this war."

"How so?" several voices rang out at once.

"If the dragons are drinking from a single source—"

"Poison?!" Reyr said, shaking his head. Talon clenched his jaw. That was the *second* interruption today. "But of course. We should have considered it sooner."

"Poison? But..." Desaree's eyes went wide. It was the first time she'd spoken. "You would...you would resort to something so... so..."

"So *what* Lady Desaree?" Talon lifted a brow.

"So *vile*," she whispered, looking at Saffra, hoping the seer might've meant something else—that the rest of them had simply misinterpreted Saffra's questions.

Saffra's face was a mask of calm. She didn't look at Desaree as she spoke, keeping her voice low. "These are times of war. Our people need us. For too long our war council has deliberated with no obvious solution. There is no way to protect the people of Squall's End if we attempt to reclaim it."

"Saffra's right," Bedelth said. "The order was clear. We were to retreat and leave Squall's End to the dragons. In exchange, its people remain unharmed. The moment we lift so much as a claw, the moment Kane's dragons suspect we've moved against them, they will burn the city to the ground."

Desaree's throat bobbed. Her eyes flicked to Verath's. Their gazes held, perhaps exchanging some silent message. Talon turned away. Gods, everywhere he looked were tangled webs. Desaree and Verath. Byron and Tamara. And if he wasn't mistaken,

Bedelth and Saffra. He hadn't missed the way Bedelth gravitated towards her.

Claire should be here—she should be here for this.

A throat cleared. Bedelth's. "What do you propose, Saffra?"

"I'm not quite sure," she mused. "Our mages have experience crafting many useful concoctions, but I cannot say which would be best."

"Why not something that brings instant death," Dallin offered, speaking for the first time. "They drink it, it kills them. We move in and liberate the city."

"It's not that easy," Talon mused, thinking it over. "That lake also feeds the city's aqueducts, remember. We cannot harm the people."

"Then how do you propose we poison the dragons?" Dallin asked, confused.

"It would have to be something non-lethal," he answered. "Something that won't kill them, but will allow us to move in and strike. Something like dragon's bane."

"We must also assume they will not drink from the lake at the same time," Saffra added. "Which means that whatever we use cannot act too quickly. Otherwise, they will catch on."

Talon ran a hand through his hair and bent over the map spread across the table, studying the geography around Squall's End. The lake was there. A small body of water less than a two hour flight. He went through a list of poisons and concoctions in his mind. His knowledge of the craft was far from complete. But...he did know someone who had a vast amount of experience.

"Collier." He stood, straightening the lapels of his coat. The poison maker was still in the dungeons. They'd intended to use him in court, but then Caterina had disappeared. Still, they'd kept him chained and alive. A man with his knowledge could prove useful—like now.

"You would trust *Collier* with something like this?" Saffra's brow furrowed.

"Hardly. Collier need not know what we intend, but he is well versed in poisons. Unless you know of a poison that will suit our needs? Something with delayed effects that will go unnoticed for a day or two?" Saffra didn't answer. "Thought not. Verath will pay him a visit later." To Verath, he added, "Keep the details to an absolute minimum."

"Of course, my king."

"And Lady Saffra?"

"Yes?" She lifted her brows in curiosity.

"We must keep this knowledge restricted. Only those here now. You know what that means, yes?"

"None of our mages," she said, sighing. "You ask a great deal of me, King Talon."

"Saffra's right," Reyr mused. "Regardless of what we learn from Collier, the amount of poison required to saturate a lake the size of Plymlet..."

"Saffra will have help, I'm sure." He looked at the other ladies in the room, offering them a pointed look.

Tamara squared her shoulders. "I will do all that I can, Lady Saffra. Use me as you will."

"We will help, too," Desaree and Jocelyn chorused.

"We will need a safe location," Verath mused. "If we keep this from our mages, it cannot very well happen out in the open. For what we require, a large space with plenty of storage to bottle everything up."

"I can think of at least *one* large space unbeknownst to anyone beyond this room," Saffra said, a fierce gleam in her eyes.

"The cave beneath the keep," Talon said, reading her mind.

"Exactly." Saffra looked pleased.

"Which leaves us to work out the remainder of the plan, should we succeed here. Specifically, how will we transport that much poison across Dragonwall without notice?"

"It need not be decided at this very moment," Reyr said, voice low. He placed a hand on Talon's arm. Much as Talon was reluctant to admit it, Reyr's steady presence calmed him.

"I agree," Jovari said. He'd been mostly quiet during this meeting. "We will think on it. Short of sneaking a group of us into the north ahead of our full force, that might be our only option."

"Let us see to Collier first," Verath decided.

Talon sighed. Reyr hadn't removed his hand from his arm. "Very well, thank you. You are all dismissed."

Everyone filed out except Reyr. His shield stayed a few minutes longer, studying him. He'd dropped his hand and stood with his arms crossed. "If this plan comes together, you know what it would mean?"

"That we will finally be ready to move against the dragons. That we will depart sooner rather than later." Reyr nodded. "I should get word to Claire. Let her know...somehow. Our intentions..."

"A letter like that could be intercepted, Talon. We're taking great pains to keep this plan secret."

"I can't very well say nothing. What if she returns while we're gone?"

"There's no telling when she will return. But we can't very well travel in the dead of winter. There is time yet."

"Still. When the time does come, if she has not yet returned..." He shook his head. "I'd rather not leave any of you here for something like this. And I certainly can't have her return to find us gone, even if Koldis is with her." It was rare that Kastali Dun was left to its human court—it hadn't been done since Talon's father took his shields and went north to fight the Kalds. Talon always left at least one or two shields in his absence, but he would feel safer having his brothers beside him for something like this. He sighed and said, "What do you recommend?"

"A messenger. Me. I will go when the time comes. Let us finalize our plans first," he added. When Talon didn't speak, Reyr continued. "I will go and speak with her—check on her. I can go west from Esterpine and rendezvous with our main force before the battle."

Talon chewed on the inside of his cheek. If anyone went to Claire, it ought to be him. And yet...

"You are our king," Reyr said, reading his mind. "You must remain with our forces."

"I want her in my arms again, Reyr."

Reyr reached over and squeezed his shoulder. "I know. Believe me, I know." With that, Reyr took his leave.

As if summoned by his own melancholy, a thick envelope arrived later that afternoon. He'd been so deep in thought, sitting at his desk, staring out through the fluttering curtains, that when one of his tower servants set the stack of new correspondences before him, he merely thanked the man without truly realizing. He inhaled and nearly jumped from his seat. Her scent—even after traveling halfway across the kingdom—still lingered. A hint of chamomile and florals, elderflower if he wasn't mistaken. Smells he remembered from his time in Esterpine. A fragrance that had always clung to her even before he'd known who she was. He should have put the pieces together sooner. He should have recognized her for a sprite the moment he laid eyes on her.

He tore the envelope open. As suspected, it was thick because she'd answered the girls' letter, too. He pushed the one addressed to them aside, taking his. He lifted the parchment to his nose and inhaled. His eyelids fluttered shut. He could envision her smiling, the glitter of mischief in her eyes, a sharp retort ready to spring from her lips. A chuckle rumbled in his chest and he broke the seal, unfolding the parchment.

Dear T,

Your letter was most welcome! Thank you. And thank you for prompting my friends to write as well. I miss you more than ever. There will be many kisses, I promise, but not because I enjoy delaying my return. Hopefully that will do wonders for your temperamental appetite and mood. I cannot imagine the others enjoying your snappish attitude—they probably can't see past it as I can.

So much has happened, much of which I dare not reveal. I will try to be circumspect. Firstly, the thing we suspected about me is true. My roots were confirmed in the most unique and unexpected way. I can't say the confirmation has brought me peace. If anything, it has disrupted the way of things here. I fear it won't be good. But for now, I have closure and a few answers.

Most importantly, I had the pleasure of making the strangest acquaintance. You wouldn't believe me if I told you. I wouldn't in a million years have predicted this turn of events. I am learning things about myself and my abilities that I began to fear I wouldn't discover. It is exactly as I hoped when I first departed the capital. Still, I have a long way to go. On a brighter note, wait until you see how well I handle a bow!

I cannot say when I will return. I am glad the others are doing well in my absence. Glad that Desa-ree, Jocelyn, and Saffra have taken to Lady Tamara. As for Koldis, I shall not pester him, but I would worry less if he were open with me. Speaking of Koldis, you should see how he behaves around a certain someone. I wish you were here to speculate about it with me. I suppose I must settle for sharing these secrets with you upon my return.

Give everyone my love, especially Reyr. I am certain he worries in my absence almost as much as you do. I shall enclose a separate letter for my ladies, and I trust you won't be nosy and read it. I plan to fill it with all sorts of pining and forlorn thoughts about you—thoughts that only us females share with each other behind closed doors. You need not know the number of times your name is mentioned. I'm serious—don't open it.

All my love,

C

P.s. If I find that you've opened it, I will void all kisses when I return.

HE SNORTED and tossed the letter aside, picking up the other. He ran it beneath his nose, inhaling deep. She'd said those things on purpose, just to drive him mad. Just to leave him wondering what thoughts she might have of him. After her taunting, how could he *not* open it?

He huffed, tossing it back on the desk. Instead, he read his letter several times over. She was in good spirits, at least. He could tell from her tone of writing. It did little for his curiosity, though.

The sprites had confirmed her lineage and suspicions. Which meant she had originated from the long lost princess. To think, the blood of a royal princess passed out of this world and into hers, only to return as his mate. Everything had come full circle. It was a great deal to digest, but even greater to accept.

He turned over the second thing she'd mentioned. A strange acquaintance? He was certain she didn't mean Jeanine. She probably hadn't meant Princess Taylynn, either. Although the sprite princess was certainly odd. No, it had to be someone else. But who?

"Reyr?"

"My king?"

"I've got a letter from Claire, if you have a mind to read it."

Reyr didn't bother responding. Not five minutes later, his footfalls sounded on the stairs before he burst into the room. "Verath questioned Collier," he said, out of breath. "Successfully, I might add. I was already on my way to tell you."

"What did you find?"

"The letter—" Reyr said, ignoring Talon's question. He held out his hand, as if he were entitled to Claire's words.

A flash of possessive jealousy rushed through him, there and gone. He scowled at the emotion. Claire was his. Only his. He forced his dragon to calm, pushing its raw emotions down. Then he lifted the letter and sighed. "Tell me what Collier said and then you may read it."

Reyr eyed him a moment longer before collapsing into the chair. "There isn't a single brew or poison with the exact effects we are looking for. However, there is a possibility we might combine two separate concoctions to get what we want."

"I shouldn't have hoped for an easy solution."

"Well, it might be. We will have to test the effects once we make it. Klizite. Do you know it?"

He was silent for a moment. Of course he knew it. "That's not a poison. It's a popular stimulant—or was, before my father outlawed its use."

"Indeed. Rightfully so."

Klizite was potent. It entered the blood and gave its host a high that lasted a couple of days before wearing off. Those under the influence were known to accomplish great works of art and industry, with soaring productivity as they suddenly felt better than they could remember ever feeling. Sicknesses and diseases were forgotten, even if just briefly. Within a short period, the entire world felt obtainable. Unfortunately, like all drugs, the effects were fleeting. Those under the influence were merely pulling from themselves, overspending. Once klizite left the body, the result was almost paralyzing. After that, it took days and even weeks to return to normal.

He leaned back in his chair. "How will getting a horde of dragons high help our cause?"

"See here, klizite—and this was something I didn't know—delays the effects of feelings, emotions, pain—"

"And poison. Of course."

Reyr grinned.

"Hmm." He fell silent. "So, we mix klizite with something like dragon's bane and for a few days, our enemy will feel at its best, giving them enough time to drink their fill before the effects of the dragon's bane take hold."

"At which point, they will lose their ability to breathe fire along with some of their other draconic abilities." Reyr was smiling wide. "But...they will still be brutes and will still require our strength to bring them down, unless the effects are paralyzing enough. In which case, even easier."

"At the least, it would give us a significant advantage. Without immunity to flame, we can simply burn them." Dragon's bane suppressed all abilities that were draconic in nature. A dragon's ability to breathe and withstand fire was first and foremost its most powerful ability.

"I'd say an advantage like that will guarantee victory."

"And our confidence that this combination of concoctions will work?"

Reyr lifted a shoulder. "Collier seemed to think it would" His eyes fell to the letter still clutched in Talon's hand.

Talon glanced down at it, unable to withhold it a moment longer. "She mentioned you, you know. Here—" He handed it over, deep in thought. Saffra would need to get started immediately. The concoction would require testing, likely on one of them, since they could trust no one outside their group. A plan like this—the fewer involved the better.

"What do you think she's talking about? Who did she meet?"

"Hmm?" Talon looked up. "Oh. I cannot say. I was hoping you might have some ideas on that."

They spent the remainder of the afternoon speculating and planning. Not just over some of the mysteries in Claire's letter, but over what needed to be done with the dragons. With Claire's letter and a potential solution for reclaiming the fort, he felt lighter than he had in weeks.

CHAPTER 20

BREWING POISON

Kastali Dun

Desaree traversed the dimly lit passages, her basket brimming with food from the cookery. One of the king's shields had installed sparsely placed torches along the path leading from Claire's chambers down into the cavern. With how frequently they were coming and going, often by themselves, having a non magical light source was a great help. It had been for her and Jocelyn's benefit mostly, since Tamara was learning magic and the rest of them could easily summon light.

Jocelyn was with Saffra, so she'd volunteered to bring them a hearty meal. Just before heading back down she'd found Jovari, lounging with a book in Claire's sitting room. "What? I'm guarding the entrance," he'd argued when she was about to snap at him for being idle. They'd been working their fingers to the bone, slicing, chopping, and stirring the brews that would become the king's greatest weapon. Both were complicated. Klizite was especially time consuming, given that it took several days of stirring and simmering before the liquid ran clear—the indication that it was ready for consumption.

They'd been using Claire's chambers to come and go, since the king saw to a great deal of business within his tower. Talon insisted that a shield remain on hand both in the caves and in Claire's chambers. They couldn't risk anyone stumbling upon what they were doing. Not even the guards standing outside Claire's door could be trusted, so they'd been given new duties.

"Gods! There you are. I'm so famished I could faint." Jocelyn steered her from the cave's entrance to the makeshift workstation they'd set up. Pieces of furniture had been moved here, but only once Saffra had explained how consuming the project would be, that she'd have to keep an eye on her klizite brew throughout the night. The second Bedelth had heard this, he'd gone on a quest to acquire a midsized dining table with chairs, two cots, and a number of small sofas. Combined with the work tables used for their ingredients, it looked like an underground camp, especially considering the large cauldrons over each fire pit. For now, only two, but if this worked, they had plans to expand and implement as many fires and cauldrons as could be fit into the vast cave, scattered around the cave formations and the mysterious structure at its center.

They still hadn't figured out how to open the small mausoleum.

Fortunately, the cave was vast. It was roomy and airy enough that the smoke didn't choke them. Plenty of sea breeze found its way in through holes in the cliff rock, so the smoke rose and eventually found its way out.

She allowed Jocelyn to steer her over to the table where they'd been taking their meals.

"I've got it, Des." Verath's voice sent pleased shivers through her.

"And when did *you* get here?" she asked, handing him the basket. He was dressed in his usual garb, a sleeveless vest that laced up both sides putting his chest on display, billowing long-sleeved undershirt, tight pants that showed off every muscle in his legs, and knee-high boots of soft brown hide.

"Twenty minutes ago?" he answered, tilting his head. "I sent Bedelth on his way. Dallin and I figured we'd give him some time in the daylight. He's supposed to be helping some of the new recruits on the practice grounds later this afternoon."

"Hmm…" She glanced over at Saffra, who was vigorously stirring one of the cauldrons wearing a frown. If the expression hadn't taken up permanent residence on her face, she'd have worried that something had gone wrong with the recipe.

Verath followed her gaze. "She says it should be done any minute now."

"And thank the gods for that," Desaree muttered. Saffra hadn't given them a moment of rest.

"We can thank the gods when we know it's turned out properly," Saffra chided, having overheard her complaints. Saffra gave the concoction a final stir and muttered something, flicking her hand towards the fire. It winked out. Desaree stared, opened her mouth, then closed it. Seeing magic at work was always a jolting experience. Perhaps she'd never be desensitized to it.

Despite Verath's having laid out the food, they gravitated towards the cauldron to look inside. She felt the heat of Verath's body just behind hers. He peered over her shoulder. Without thinking, she leaned back into him and his arm snaked out, wrapping around her waist, pulling her flush against him. It sent a jolt straight down her legs that left her toes curling.

"There's not much to see," Saffra mused, ladling out a trickle of the liquid to show that it was indeed clear. It steamed as it fell back into the cauldron. "We'll need to let it cool—naturally, of course. I would use magic but I do not want to interfere until I'm certain it came out right. I have the dragon's bane ready. You're sure Collier said it was one part to two, Verath?"

"Absolutely positive." The lack of amusement in his voice was expected. Saffra had already made this clarification at least five times.

"Come, let us eat," Jocelyn said, drawing their attention away. "Lady Tamara promised to join us this afternoon. I will send word to the others that we are ready to test it."

As she turned away, Verath took her hand and steered her over to a chair, which he pulled out for her. She glanced up at him shyly as he moved away to take the one beside her. Jocelyn and Saffra lingered by the cauldron a moment longer before joining them.

"No Dallin?" she asked. The young drengr had been all but attached at Verath's hip.

"I gave him some time off," he said, spearing a slice of chicken with his fork.

"Thank the gods. The poor thing needs it after being stuck with *you* all day." As much as she loved him, she wasn't sure she could put up with his company and brooding all day, every day. Dallin had already shown more patience than she could. Verath harrumphed but took her teasing in stride.

It was a rushed meal. Mostly because none of them wanted to prolong Saffra's grumbles about whether she had truly added the correct amount of sun moss or kikifrass. The sooner they brought the others to the cave to witness their success, the sooner they could take a break and see if it worked.

And of course...none of them had agreed on who the test subject ought to be.

Nearly two hours later, Jocelyn had everyone gathered. The king, Byron and Tamara, Dallin, and the other shields. Saffra had combined a glass vial, two parts to one as advised, but only after checking a seventh time with Verath before corking it. The vial was passed around and examined.

"We won't know exactly how much is needed for a grown drengr, so I was generous," she explained. "I assume it will be the same amount as for a dragon. Once we know, we will still need to determine how much we'll need to add to the lake water."

"And Collier was sure it could be mixed with water? It won't be diluted?" King Talon asked, his arms crossed.

"It can be mixed with water. Any other substance, specifically those with shared ingredients, will disrupt the balance of either the dragon's bane or the klizite."

"A freshwater lake should be all right then," the king mused, running a hand through his hair. It was already incredibly mussed up, almost enough that Desaree felt the urge to take a comb to it, if only to make him more presentable for Claire's sake. Gods! She missed Claire.

Instead, she glanced at Verath. Their eyes met and he winked at her. Her cheeks flushed and she looked away. They hadn't seen each other for a few nights. She'd chosen to sleep in the cave with Saffra, mostly because Bedelth had offered to do so himself. She'd immediately sensed Saffra's alarm and stepped in. Not only was it altogether improper, given that Saffra and Bedelth weren't *together*, but Saffra wasn't ready for any kind of relationship so soon after Daxton.

The vial made its final pass to King Talon. He held it up against the torchlight and eyed it. "Hmm...on the bright side, at least I'll be rather productive for a few days before the effects kick in," he muttered, mostly to himself. "Think of all the correspondences I'll get answered."

It took several silent moments before a number of protests broke out. Verath strode right across the circle they'd formed and snatched the vial from the king's grip. King Talon was so surprised by his actions that he didn't immediately react.

"We cannot risk any adverse effects, Your Majesty. I will test it."

Desaree opened her mouth to protest, then immediately closed it.

Talon gritted his jaw. "No, Verath. I cannot ask this of you. Of any of you. It should be me."

"You aren't asking. I'm insisting." And then, before anyone could stop him, Verath popped off the cork and downed the entirety of the contents.

Desaree's eyes went wide with shock. This wasn't... He couldn't... What if something terrible happened to him?! She clenched her teeth, watching, waiting, just like everyone else. Holding her breath tightly in her chest.

Verath shrugged and handed the empty vial to Saffra. "Hmm..." He looked absolutely normal. "Tasteless."

"Perhaps I missed an ingredient." Saffra frowned, eyes glued to him. Not because it was tasteless, per se, but because nothing seemed to be happening.

Until…

Verath's head snapped in one direction, then the other. His neck bulged and he rotated it. When his gaze fell on her, she noticed the growing size of his pupils. Dilated until his eyes were all but black. She opened her mouth—

"You know, I think I'll go for a walk!" he decided, sounding rather excited. "Yes. That's exactly what I need. And I'm taking Des with me. Come, love. I need to get you out of here." He covered the distance between them in two giant steps.

She gaped at him.

"Gods above, I'm not going to hurt you. Come." He took her hand and pulled her away. She was too shocked to give more than just a squeak as she glanced over her shoulder towards the others with a *what-in-the-name-of-the-gods-is-happening?!* look.

A slow smile spread across King Talon's face. "Well, I think it's working," she heard him say before the corridor swallowed her up.

"Slow down," she hissed, pulling against Verath's grasp. He was walking so quickly she nearly had to jog.

Instead of doing what she asked, he swept her into his arms with more speed than she thought possible. She screeched in surprise. It was the most unladylike noise she'd ever made. He chuckled. The sound of it rumbling in his chest, reverberating through her.

"It's the brew, isn't it?" she whispered.

"I feel so…*alive.*"

"Gods," she hissed, which earned another chuckle. She expected him to put her down when they emerged from Claire's chambers. He didn't. "Where are you taking me?" she demanded.

"Outside." He marched her straight to King Talon's tower. The guards quickly stepped aside and the servants scattered.

"Leave us," he commanded, as if he were the king. He may as well have been because when she next looked, they were alone.

She didn't find her feet again until they stood on King Talon's large terraced balcony. Verath looked around, scowling. "No, this won't do." He sighed.

"Uhm. I thought we were going for a walk?" She wasn't sure how she should act around him when he was like this.

He swung his head around to her, pupils blown wide. Even in human form, he looked crazed, more dragon than man. Her heart began thumping wildly in her chest. She knew she shouldn't be afraid. She had never had reason to fear him, but this...this was not Verath.

"Come now, *Des*." Her name was a slow purr on his lips. A jolt shot through her, sending heat straight to her core. He held out his hand. When she didn't take it, he swept her into his arms and planted a heated kiss on her lips. She was so surprised by his quick movements that he'd already set her down and taken her hand, pulling her from the balcony before she realized what was happening.

He led her up several flights of stairs and through a trapdoor. She gasped. "But, this is the queen's garden. We...we can't be up here."

He growled. "The king won't know. And if he does, he won't care. Better here than out on the castle lawn."

"I do not understand..."

"You will in a moment." A wicked grin split his lips. It was followed by a moment of shock as she realized what he was up to.

"Oh. Oh, no..." She backed away from him.

He hesitated and a flash of something tender crossed his face. "I won't hurt you, Des. Come, I wish to fly, not walk. And I wish for you to join me."

"But I..." She shook her head. Even though her stomach was doing flips, even though she'd dreamed something like this might be offered, she was not his rider. She was not his mate. She would only ever be his lover.

"I'm going to transform," he said, walking towards her. "You may climb on my back or not. But if you don't..."

"If I don't?" She planted her feet and squared her shoulders, glaring up at him.

He threw his head back and laughed. Gods, that laugh. It sent tingles racing through her. Even if he wasn't in his right mind, she was still drawn to him. "If you *don't*, I'll snatch you up in my talons —my maiden prize." He brushed a finger along her jaw.

"You wouldn't dare," she hissed.

"Oh?" He arched an eyebrow. His eyes were still crazed. "Care to test that theory?" Without further hesitation, he moved away and transformed.

She watched, openmouthed, as red scales sprouted all over his skin. His body grew in size until a hulking beast of a dragon was crouched before her. She blinked, shaking her head. It almost didn't feel real. She knew he was a drengr, but he'd never been close to her in this form. It had been easy to forget there was a beast lurking within.

"I..." she croaked, backing away, barely enough awareness to keep from stepping in any of the flower beds.

Verath snarled. A plume of smoke engulfed her. She froze. When it cleared, the sound of talons clicking on the flagstones made her eyes go wide. He was really going to do this, he was really going to snatch her up if she didn't climb on his back!

He lifted his forearm to reach for her. She threw up her hands to placate him. "All right. All right. I'll do as you ask. Just...give me a moment. Please."

The effects of the brew were supposed to do this, she realized. They were supposed to overtake the host, make them energetic, excited, alive...erratic. Verath had never been one for impatience, but now he exhibited it in spades.

She sighed. There was nothing for it. As terrified as she was by the prospect of flying, especially without a harness, she steeled her nerves. Claire had done it. Gods, Claire had flown across the entire kingdom without a harness.

She stepped forward and let her head fall back, taking in Verath's enormous form. He snorted, impatient. Talons clawed against the flagstones. He wouldn't wait long.

"You could have at least explained how I'm supposed to do this," she snapped, hoisting her skirts in one hand and placing her other on his hide. It was as she expected, warm to the touch, almost scalding.

He lowered himself to the ground, not caring that he trampled several flower beds to do so. Doing the best she could, she hoisted herself up on his forearm and then attempted to climb up his back. She had to jump to reach the spikes along his neck. And it took several tries to grab one and then all her strength to wrench herself up and into position.

"Gods, how does Claire manage?" she gasped when she righted herself.

Verath hardly waited before he lifted his belly and stood. Her stomach lurched. The world below was much scarier from the back of a dragon. It didn't help that she was at the top of the castle, at its highest point. Now that she was on his back, she could see over the tower's walls.

Her stomach climbed into her throat. She took deep breaths to calm it. Verath took several steps and she yelped, holding on for dear life, careful not to skewer herself on his spikes. A roar split the heavens. Verath's head thrashed back and forth as if embracing the beast within, then he crouched and sprang.

She didn't bother clamping down on her scream as he surged into the sky. She was pressed down into the dip between his neck and shoulders, gripping so tightly with her thighs that her legs screamed, too. Everything was heavy for several moments, and then the weight was gone. She gasped as giant red wings stretched out to either side of her. They swept downward, sending them higher and higher. Verath roared again, clearly pleased.

She glanced down at the castle, just in time to see Talon and the others emerge from the tower's trap door. They gazed up at her with wide eyes.

A laugh bubbled up from her chest as she got over the initial fear. "Gods above!" she gasped as she looked at the world anew. Spectacular! Absolutely spectacular. Claire was right. Flying was... well, nothing really compared, did it? She giggled again and pressed herself against Verath, sucking up as much warmth as she could. If ever she was glad of her heavy skirts and the thick winter fabric of her gown, it was now.

Her insides swooped as he changed course, taking them on a

wide circuit above the city before he took them north. Not once did her smile slip. Not once did the butterflies tumbling about in her stomach settle.

An hour later, when Verath landed on a rocky outcropping that overlooked a vast grassy expanse, her nerves still hadn't abated. She caught the sight of grazers beyond and realized his intentions immediately. "Oh no."

He waited as she climbed down from his back, well, slid rather ungracefully, before he took to the skies and left her there. She wasn't sure where exactly they were on a map, other than in the middle of the wilderness. But she knew what he planned.

She watched, shivering in the cold, as he hunted. Here in the southernmost part of Dragonwall, they didn't get much snow and she was glad that today there wasn't any sign in the sky. Verath circled his prey. A drengr in form wasn't too different from their dragon cousins. They were still beasts, after all. This proved true as she watched him hunt with lethal precision—watched him settle on his prize and dive, jaws ready to strike.

"I do not think I will be able to eat for weeks," she muttered, her appetite all but spoiled as she observed the bloody spectacle. Verath landed three grazers before his appetite was satisfied. Then he came back for her.

"Well, at least you aren't a messy eater," she decided, trying to fracture some of the tension. He merely snorted in answer. There was no point in being angry with him until after the effects of the klizite wore off. She was sure he'd regret his decision to volunteer once the dragon's bane kicked in.

CHAPTER 21
TRAVELING TO ASHVALE

Claire ripped a warm roll in half, dipped it in honey, and plopped it into her mouth. She closed her eyes, savoring the taste. In the coming days, she would desperately miss fresh bread. Even though her upcoming trip into the forest wasn't technically a solo journey, any provisions brought wouldn't compare to what was before her.

The queen's table was lavish. Jade spared no expense for this luncheon. Fresh bread, sautéed vegetables, fruit salads, potatoes, and all manner of vegetarian dishes were spread before her. Taylynn and Feowen sat across from her. Beside her, Lord Marquin. Jade sat at the head, presiding over them as if she were holding court. "Have you decided how long you will be away this time?" she was saying. "I do hope you won't keep away for too long."

Claire swallowed another mouthful and washed it down with a gulp of crisp apple cider. "I believe a week, Your Majesty. Two days simply wasn't long enough. Time is running thin and I hate to be away from Kastali Dun longer than necessary."

"I see. So you *do* plan to return then?"

"Of—"

"She has made no such plans as of yet, Mother. Let us not forget her blood. The noble families have not yet met with her to discuss matters of the crown."

The queen shot Taylynn a scathing look. "Clearly she has no interest in that, do you dear?" Jade returned her attention to Claire.

"Uhm…" This was not how she'd hoped this would go. She almost shot Taylynn the same scathing glare.

"She can hardly have interest in something she knows little about," Taylynn continued. "Once she meets with the noble families and the council, she will better understand what her blood means and what it would mean to rule—"

"How *dare* you?!" Jade hissed, her composure shattering. "You would dare encourage her to depose me then, and you would speak of it here in front of me!"

"Peace, mother." Feowen's voice was calm. "We are all family here. I think what Taylynn *means*,"—he too shot his sister a scathing look—"is that Claire should understand her blood right entirely. I think we can all agree that she has no desire to take up rulership in Esterpine, especially given her desire to return to the capital, to return to the friends she has made there."

"Yes, exactly," Claire quickly added. She made a mental note to hug Feowen when next she had the chance. What would Koldis say about all this, were he here? A deep sigh slipped from her lips. "As it stands, Your Majesty, I am eager to return to the capital. Thus, I will be spending a week in the forest to hone my magical ability. I've already spoken to Lord Marquin about it, and he is in agreement that a week is reasonable."

"Indeed, Majesty."

"Very well, Lady Claire." Jade nodded, as if to clear the air and rid herself of the matter entirely.

Claire stole another glance at Taylynn. It was rare to see the princess wielding any sort of emotion, but this time, Taylynn's distaste was clear in her clenched jaw, flushed cheeks, and the frequent glares she paid her mother. If she wasn't mistaken, things between them had escalated since the blood stone incident.

Much of the remainder of the meal was spent in silence. She *did* manage to catch Feowen's gaze several times. He always offered an encouraging smile. So different was he to his sister. Almost a direct opposite, as she'd come to observe during her time here.

Most of her plans for tomorrow were complete. Koldis had already explained to their pairs what was happening. They would cover for his absence, if the need arose. Taylynn wouldn't be missed, as she was often gone more than she was present. All that was left was to survive the remaining afternoon and evening.

THE FOLLOWING morning she was up early and eating as much as she could stuff in. She drank gobs and gobs of water too, even though she knew her companions would bring supplies. The reminder of her previous adventure was still fresh.

"You have everything you need?" Koldis asked, motioning toward the small bag she'd packed, sitting in the main room.

"All packed," she confirmed.

"Good. We will give you enough time to depart before we sneak off after you. I'm to meet Taylynn by the southern gate. She wants you to travel south-east this time. I think she plans to take you all the way to Ashvale," he said.

"Ah-ha! So the two of you've been talking, then?" She lifted an eyebrow.

"Do I look as if I want to speak to her? No, we said nothing more than what was exchanged last night."

"*Riiiight.*" She didn't bother hiding her smirk. She'd seen Taylynn pull Koldis aside during dinner, seen the fire flashing in both pairs of eyes. But he was correct in that the conversation had been short.

"Just finish eating, would you? So we can get this damned trip over with." He stalked off before she could offer anything snide. She resorted to mimicking him under her breath. That, at least, lifted her mood and made her smile. He'd become so...dramatic.

There was nothing formal about her departure. No one besides

Lord Marquin and Koldis came to see her off. Aolis looked her over, as if inspecting her to make sure she hadn't snuck anything with her. She was entirely covered, which wasn't a stretch. Being an outsider, sprite blood or no, she explained away her conservative attire easily enough with the change of autumn to winter, even if the forest's climate was controlled through magic. Otherwise there'd have been snow on the ground.

"You will do well, I think." Lord Marquin offered a genuine smile. "Your mastery of the *Ednuar* has surpassed even my expectations."

"Shalaya, Kenya."

"Mekvelli an barah nin an morviah sinahaya." *May the peace of the forest be upon you.*

"Edah sinahaya, Kenya." *And upon you, Teacher.*

Blessings received, she turned to Koldis and gave him a big hug, whispering loud enough that Lord Marquin would hear her reluctant farewell.

"I'll see you when you get back," he said for good measure.

She nodded, departing along the southern path that would take her out of Esterpine. Daring a backward glance, she saw them both standing side by side, watching her until she rounded a bend and left them entirely.

As she walked, she hummed to herself, thinking about the various possibilities this journey would bring. Her biggest hope was in finding the staff. That would certainly speed things along. But if that happened, she'd have to stop off at Pelwynn's on the way back. She certainly couldn't waltz into Esterpine carrying a long lost relic. Not that she believed anyone would remember it. She wasn't even certain Jade had been alive when Queen Isabella had ruled. Jade was Isabella's niece, after all. And Jade's mother, Queen Ametrine had ruled for nearly fifteen thousand years, taking over when Isabella left the forest to take up rulership beside Eymar.

Gods! Living and ruling for that long. She couldn't even fathom it. Couldn't fathom what Pelwynn's life must be like with so many countless years stretched behind him. It felt like an age.

But time moved differently here somehow, among immortal beings. Some moments stood still, while others raced by. Sometimes it felt like the world was a speeding bullet train, flashing by so quickly, each window a different moment, each individual experience merely plucked from its moving cars—

"Enjoying your walk?"

Claire faltered, then blinked. "Jeanine?"

Jeanine smiled and jumped from the foliage, like she'd been—

"You were waiting for me, weren't you?" At this, Jeanine smiled. "Come to see me off, then?"

"Oh, more than that! I'm coming with you on this...*journey*."

"As am I," came the familiar voice of Feowen as he ducked out onto the path from behind Jeanine.

At that, she couldn't help but laugh. "And does Taylynn know?"

"Believe me," came another musical voice from behind them. "She knows and she isn't a mite happy about it." Taylynn strolled up, Koldis behind her, scowling at the princess's back.

"Well then," Claire said, hands on her hips, grinning. "I think we will make a merry little party, won't we?"

"I couldn't miss the opportunity to visit Ashvale again," Jeanine said.

"Ashvale?" Claire scowled. "So we really *are* going all the way to Ashvale? And how is it that Jeanine knows when I don't?"

"My brother might have pried the information from me." Taylynn offered Feowen a harmless glare.

Koldis harrumphed, annoyed. "At least *someone* is capable of prying information from you, Princess. I wasn't sure it was even possible."

Taylynn ignored him entirely.

"Well then..." Claire looked between them. "Shall we get going?" Koldis grinned at her, tossing her the small pack she'd made him bring. She caught it and slung it over her shoulder, setting off. "I do hope I'm going the right way," she called back to them.

"The forest will lead," was all Taylynn said as they set out. She supposed that would have to suffice.

THEY'D BEEN WALKING for hours when she heard the thunderous crash through the underbrush. It echoed and the entire forest went silent. Her first thought was of the darkness, of it seeking to claim her like it had before.

For most of their journey thus far, she'd kept her talking to a minimum, learning quickly that it was pointless to question Taylynn. The princess didn't appear interested in giving up any information at present. So she'd been content to listen to Jeanine and Feowen chat—mostly Feowen as he explained things about the forest.

"What was that?" she whispered, coming to a stop as the others came up behind her. Another loud crash sounded, and with it, a slithering. From the reaches of her memory, she recognized the sound. Her muscles went rigid.

"Peace, Lady Claire. It is only a *simeík*. It will not harm you."

Her shoulders relaxed. "Oh. Is that so?" At this, she threw Koldis a glare. He shrugged as if to say, *How were we supposed to know?* She remembered all too well the last time she'd encountered one of these creatures, she'd been absolutely terrified as Reyr pulled her into a hiding place to watch its passing, convinced it would kill them should it spot them.

"They are guardians of the forest," Taylynn said by way of explanation. "There aren't many of these ancient beings. They are the king tree's shepherds."

Another crash sounded and this time, the creature in question came into view. It looked exactly as she remembered. In fact, it might have even been the same one, with its skirt of roots that slithered, detaching and reattaching to the ground as it moved. It hesitated, spotting them—spotting Taylynn.

Taylynn stepped forward, greeting it in *Ednuar*. It held forth its hands as if in question, protecting a glowing orb of glittering greenish-blue light. "A soul," Taylynn said quietly, but loud enough for them to hear. "One of the reborn."

Taylynn lifted a hand to hover over the *simeík's* and whispered a few words. Claire strained to hear but couldn't discern what was said. The orb of light glowed a little brighter, as if recognizing the princess.

"Well, that's not something you see every day," Jeanine whispered.

Claire could only watch, mouth agape, as the root being bowed its head and then turned away from them, thundering off into the forest.

"Uhm..." Claire cleared her throat. "So it's true, then? Sprites are reborn into the forest. Do they all get shepherded somewhere like that one?"

"Only those who are truly worthy. All souls find a home here, but those who have the purest hearts—as deemed by our king tree—are specially honored to inhabit some of the wisest and oldest trees."

Behind her, Koldis grunted but said nothing.

"Wow..." she breathed. "So the trees...they really *are* alive. I'd thought I felt them before."

"Many are, yes. Though, they are not alive in the way that you think. But they do possess a sentience that lends awareness and connects them."

She was too awestruck to say much more as they once again began their journey, this time following after Taylynn as she strode forward and led them down the path they'd been following.

EVENING ARRIVED AT LAST. They stopped to make camp and sat around a fire of green flames, carefully constructed by Taylynn. They'd passed several creeks that had allowed them to refill their water supply frequently. From Taylynn's limited explanations, she gathered that the path had turned from south to south-east, taking them towards Ashvale.

"It will be a little over two days," Taylynn had explained when she'd asked.

"What do you hope to find there?"

"It is not what I hope to find, Lady Claire, but what I hope you might."

It was as close to an answer as she'd expected.

A loud, content sigh sounded beside her and she looked over, watching Koldis stretch his long limbs out as he leaned back against his pack. Nearby, she heard the singing of metal as Jeanine and Feowan sparred. She was surprised that Koldis hadn't suggested they do the same. Her skill with a sword had grown, and she'd gotten much better at channeling Cyrus. It had taken practice, but she found that without letting him take over entirely, she could relax her mind just enough to pluck techniques from his ancient soul memory. She did it more and more frequently.

"Hah!" A shout of triumph from Jeanine had her turning towards them. Taylynn sat nearby, legs crossed, eyes closed. She looked to be meditating, but Claire knew better. If she focused her own mind, clearing it and putting the blossoms at the front and back, she could see the telltale signs of white light surrounding Taylynn and branching away from her in strands. She wasn't sure what, exactly, the sprite princess was doing, but she had an inkling that Taylynn was communicating with the king tree somehow.

She glanced at Koldis and caught him watching Taylynn too, but as soon as he caught her, he looked away, closing his eyes as if to rest. Koldis and Taylynn hadn't spoken a single word the entire day. Perhaps the shield was determined to prove that there wasn't anything unfolding between them, but she didn't buy it.

In fact—

"Taylynn, do you think we might practice while we have some time?"

Taylynn's eyes snapped open. "A wise idea." She stood and came to sit before Claire. This got Koldis's attention. His eyes cracked open and she didn't miss the way they fixed upon the sprite princess.

"Shall we work on your focus with the earth elemental?" Taylynn asked. "I believe that's what you were struggling with when last I interrupted you with your tutor?"

"Yes, growing vines," she clarified. Pelwynn had suggested it.

At first it seemed like a mundane ability, to conjure green tendrils from the earth. But it wasn't. She remembered all too well the vines that had tried to snare her in the forest, to keep her in the clearing of blackness, to trap her.

"Vines have all sorts of uses," Taylynn said, as if sensing her thoughts. "They can be used to hold things in place, to construct bridges, act as ropes, snares, and more. Well then, show me how you've progressed."

Eager to please, well aware that she now had an audience, she crossed her legs and exhaled, closing her eyes and tightening her focus. Then she lifted her hands over the soil and began humming. She often started like this, wordless. It was a recommendation Pelwynn had offered, to center herself and find a tune. She didn't bother with words this time, putting the blossom in the back of her mind to quiet her nagging thoughts, and imagining the vines she wanted. Curling green tendrils broke from the soil. She didn't need to open her eyes to see them. Everything she pictured in her mind played out before her. Jeanine's small gasp was further evidence that her efforts were working.

She didn't allow the vines to shoot up too far, instead, strengthening their stems before allowing several runners to branch off. Then she allowed them to both grow and strengthen as they shot up above her, to tangle in the trees overhead. Only then did she stop her humming and open her eyes.

It was Koldis she found first—found him gazing at her with his lips parted. She hadn't shown him much of her progress over the past week and suspected that seeing her magic was entirely different from listening to her recount her small successes.

"Very good," Taylynn said. "Now, allow these to grow around our clearing. If you create enough runners, you can generate an entire weave around us, a small cocoon with us safely inside. Think of the creepers as the structure and allow them to thicken with the main shoots as the support."

She nodded, closing her eyes again to hum. And so she continued like this for a while, building and reinforcing each of the vines she created, until she hissed. Along her right forearm, she felt the familiar burn that signaled a new mark. She opened her eyes to survey her work. The thin tendrils she'd initially summoned had turned to a thick woven stock in the middle of the large hut she'd created all about them, sheltering them within. A cocoon of green with little leaves that filled in the sparse areas, blotting out the world beyond. Jeanine and Feowen were still standing behind Taylynn, swords in hand.

"Well, that's handy," Koldis said, smiling. His eyes sparkled with approval.

"It's more than *handy*, Drengr. An ability like this could save her life some day."

Koldis's jaw clenched. He looked like he was about to fight back, but Claire paid him a look that silenced any retort he might have made.

"*Shalaya*, Taylynn," she said. "That was instructive." Truthfully it was more sprite magic than she'd managed with the new techniques Pelwynn had taught her.

Remembering her arm, she pulled up her sleeve. Along the skin of her right inner forearm, vines twisted in a single woven strand from elbow to wrist, with leafy shoots that branched off. It was beautiful. Koldis scooted closer, taking her arm and brushing his finger over the marking.

"Very impressive," he praised. "I daresay, our king might not even recognize you when you return."

Something in those words left her beaming. It wasn't that she wanted to appear a stranger to Talon. Rather, she wanted to return to him strong. Strong and better than ever. She wanted to be a worthy queen, worthy of his love and his throne. And she had every intention of making that happen.

CHAPTER 22

FORT LEADER VOTE

Kastali Dun

Tamara leaned into Byron's scaled neck, keeping her eyes trained on the land below. They were searching. Byron's voice sounded in her mind intermittently as he called out for Verath.

"I will kill him if any harm has come to Desaree," she grumbled so that he'd hear.

"Peace, love. I am sure she is fine. He wouldn't let her come to harm, even drugged up as he was."

For nearly three days, Verath had been absolutely unreasonable, spending long stretches of time out flying. When he wasn't, he was even worse within the castle walls, striding about making ridiculous demands, operating at a productivity level impossible to keep up with. After his initial return, King Talon quickly realized it was better to send Verath off flying, to get him out of their way. Verath insisted on taking Desaree with him every time.

"I told Desaree to refuse his demands," she said, letting the telepathic thought stretch between them.

"I know, love. But she cares for him, worries over him. She doesn't want him out in the wilderness alone in his state."

She all but snorted. *"It isn't as if she can communicate with him when he's in form, and especially not when he's this unreasonable."*

It wasn't until last night, when Verath didn't return, that they'd grown worried. They had waited for hours in King Talon's tower beside the fire. It wasn't until Lady Saffra voiced the concerns they were all too afraid to put into words. "We do not know exactly when the klizite will wear off and the dragon's bane will kick in," she'd said. "The combination will all but paralyze him."

"How badly?" Tamara couldn't help asking.

"Think of a paralyzing giant snake bite, but worse. Obviously he's the first person we're testing this on, but I suspect his muscles will seize up and extreme lethargy will take over."

Her jaw had dropped open then. "What business did we have allowing him out to fly? He could fall from the sky and..."

"And harm Desaree," Saffra had said at last, leaving them sick with worry.

"He wouldn't listen to reason," Talon said by way of explanation, as if that had made their king's actions justifiable. "I'll go out and look for him."

"We will *all* go," Bryon countered, jumping to his feet.

And that's how they found themselves soaring over the vast grasslands as dawn brightened around them.

"Don't fret, Tam," Byron said, banking left. *"If we don't find them, the others will."*

"I promised Jocelyn and Saffra I would bring her back safely." Both women had been close to tears at remaining behind. *"And Claire. Gods. If anything happens to Desaree, Claire will—"*

"I know." Byron's calm helped, but only so much.

They flew for another two hours. Byron was ready to call for a break—more for her sake than his—when she saw a sparkle of red glinting far in the distance. Byron saw it at the same moment and let out a roar. A relieved laugh bubbled up in her chest when they grew closer and saw Desaree standing beside Verath's form, arms waving to flag them down.

She was alive.

Byron took them into a steep dive. They were on the ground in seconds. She was out of her harness and off Byron's back, racing towards Desaree. Their arms locked around each other. "Verath! He just...he..." Desaree began sobbing into her shoulder. "I didn't know what to do. We were flying and he...he..."

Tamara glanced at Verath's large glittering form. "He's breathing," she confirmed, trying to calm Desaree's frantic sobs. "He's alive." To her mate, she silently said, *"I'm going to kill that shield."*

"He started acting strange," Desaree managed to explain. Tamara snorted, as if Verath hadn't *already* been acting strange for days. "But...but I could tell it frightened him. I thought we were going to die, Tam. He went into a steep dive. I barely managed...I almost fell. When he put us on the ground, he didn't even land. It was more of stumbling and sliding. Then he just...he just..." Desaree burst into a fresh wave of tears. "We've been out here for *hours*. All night. I thought no one would..."

"Shhh...." She combed her fingers through Desaree's hair. "We're here now. It's all right. You're both safe."

A series of images and words raced through her mind. It was Bryon. He was alerting the others to their location and informing them that Verath was alive.

While she was comforting Desaree, Byron began circling Verath. He lifted his hands and began speaking, voice low as he crafted an incantation. She couldn't help but watch in fascination as Byron used magic to roll Verath into a more comfortable position, ensuring that his forearms and legs weren't resting at odd angles and that his tail was spread behind him. Nothing appeared broken.

She'd only just started her training with magic. After everything that had happened at Fort Squall, there'd been little opportunity until they were safely settled. She'd only just started learning the language and small words. She could summon bits of light and do simple things with hot and cold, move small objects, and the like. She certainly wasn't anywhere as skilled as Byron.

"There now, see?" she said, patting Desaree's hair. "Byron has him in a comfortable position now. He'll be all right."

"I'm so *angry* with him for volunteering," Desaree cried. "He could have been killed."

"Could have, but wasn't," Bryon said, striding over. He took Desaree's free hand and gave it a squeeze before turning his gaze to the skies. "The others should be here shortly."

"What are we going to do?" Desaree said, wiping her eyes on the back of her hand, sniffling. Tamara pulled a clean handkerchief free and handed it over.

"Well, there won't be any moving him in this form," Byron said. "Best we can do is let the poison run its course. We're only a few hours from the capital. We can get a couple of tents together—set up camp. Don't worry. You won't go through this alone." With that, he paid Tamara a quick, knowing glance, then stalked back over to Verath.

"I'll make sure the others bring plenty of refreshments," she added in quieter, soothing tones, "and warm clothes." She had only just realized Desaree was shivering. "Here, come rest against Verath. His warmth will keep the chill away." The tension in her shoulders began unknotting once she'd seen Desaree comfortably settled in the crook between Verath's forearm and his chest. Verath's eyes were closed, and his breaths steady. He may as well have been sleeping deeply, which made sense because he'd never answered any of Byron's telepathic calls.

She ground her teeth together then let out a long, calming breath.

HOURS LATER, tents were constructed to shield from the cold winter wind. A comfortable camp had been born. Much to her surprise, Bedelth had agreed to bring both Saffra and Jocelyn. She supposed that Claire, having flouted propriety, forged the way for others. She didn't miss that it was Bedelth who delivered them, not any of the *other* shields.

Jocelyn and Saffra ran to Desaree and the three of them hugged and broke into sobs as Desaree recounted her story all over again.

Saffra appeared not to notice the way Bedelth's eyes followed her through the camp after he'd transformed. He stood off to the side, arms crossed, a deep frown marring his features.

King Talon didn't stray far from Verath's side. Half the words out of his mouth were curses as he muttered under his breath. The others never strayed far either, but she was certain that King Talon felt entirely responsible for how things had turned out. He was furious enough that every question directed at him received a snapping answer. None of them dared bother with him after that.

Desaree and Jocelyn—being the sensible ones—quickly took charge of their camp, overseeing supplies as they were unpacked. Tamara jumped in when she noticed the spread of food before them. "I'd be happy to help with the dicing," she managed, a small smile at her lips as she recalled her first few days in Fort Squall.

"Nonsense," Jocelyn said, shooing her away. "Desaree and I can manage."

But she wouldn't take no for an answer. Soon enough she was dicing carrots, onions, and potatoes, wielding a knife as if she were born to it. The cookery had sent along a generous slab of meat as well, along with rolls and cake. It would be a merry meal.

Saffra kept busy, circling Verath, scribbling notes on the parchment she had clipped to a thin board. King Talon's Shields had erected a makeshift writing desk for her, complete with plenty of parchment and ink for her observations.

As the afternoon waned and the fire glowed brighter, everyone calmed and fell into a steady ease. The danger was over. Verath was safe. Now they could all relax and discuss the next phase of their plan.

It took nearly two days for Verath to wake, and another two before he was well enough to fly home. He managed to make it back to the castle before transforming and collapsing on the king's tower stones in the queen's garden. Jovari and Bedelth had to haul him to his chambers. Desaree had followed, fussing and giving orders for food to be brought immediately.

Tamara smiled, recalling the way Desaree had hovered and cared for him in his weakened state. It would be some days yet before he was back to his normal self. In the meantime, plans continued. Saffra set up nearly a hundred cauldrons in the cave beneath the keep. She began the process of brewing enough poison to fill Lake Plymlet. Tamara and Jocelyn helped for now. As soon as Verath was better, Desaree would join them.

Byron handled most of the matters pertaining to Fort Squall, which consisted of frequent meetings at Fort Kastali. She checked in with him often, letting her mind drift to his. It still thrilled her that he was a mere thought away, that she could step into his mind, or he hers, whenever the need arose.

Today, however, she set aside the tedious work in the cavern and flew with Byron over to Fort Kastali. Her chest was aflutter, her body jittery with nerves. She glanced at the landscape below, placing a hand on her stomach. *"You're sure this is a good idea?"* she asked, yet again.

"We cannot avoid it forever, my love."

He hadn't actually answered her question, but he was right. In truth, she had hoped to, even despite the tension building up to this moment. Perhaps it was best to get it over with.

Fort Squall needed to select permanent leaders. It was time for the dreaded vote. While the position often passed from father to son, a vote was always taken. There was a chance she and Byron wouldn't be selected by the majority. Votes were especially welcome in times like these, when a fort leader's son was young enough to have his authority questioned. Byron, after all, was still a boy in the eyes of many, especially those pairs who were verging towards five hundred and beyond.

She worried her lower lip. Byron didn't appear concerned. If only she could approach the matter with such nonchalance. Especially knowing there were other, equally suitable contenders. Alark and Brylee were the first high ranking pair that came to mind. Alark was a wingleader and had been very close with Davi. He was also some six hundred years of age—seasoned and experienced. Dagen and Sandra would also be a good choice, favorites among all, capable of leading the fort just as well as Emmy and Davi had.

"Peace, love. Let's not worry over the outcome."

But of course she was worried! Mainly because she wasn't even sure what she wanted. If they didn't win the vote, the succession of fort leadership in Byron's family would end. But if they did...

Gods above. No one would vote for her and Byron knowing she wasn't yet twenty. She had no business whatsoever leading a fort.

"There is more to leading than age and experience. We have advisors for that. Those older and wiser to guide us. If chosen, we would lead for many long years."

He was right, as usual. But her stomach lurched as he descended towards the fort's battlements. So she clamped down on her thoughts and dismounted from his back.

Fierran greeted them warmly, clapping Byron on the back and bowing formally to her with a "my lady" before escorting them into the darkened corridors of the fort. It was bustling, as always. This was what it was like to see a fort at full capacity. It's corridors thriving, rooms filled. They were greeted by all who passed. Some she recognized from her own fort, some she didn't.

"My lady," Amirah said, falling into step beside her. Amirah was Soren's Rider, and a wing second. She would be one of those present for the vote. "You look as if you're going to be sick," she added, voice low. "Can I get you some tea?"

Tamara pursed her lips and shook her head. "No, thank you. Having you beside me is strength enough." Amirah reached for her hand and squeezed. It was the nicest gesture the woman had ever given her. Then she rushed away to inform the others that they were on their way.

When they entered the conference room, it was packed. Most were wing leaders and seconds from Fort Squall, since they were the only ones permitted to partake in the vote. But since they also planned to discuss battle matters first and foremost, there were a few of Fort Kastali's leaders and seconds present. She also spotted Reyr in the corner, lounging against the wall with his knee bent and foot propped, grinning at her like a cat who'd caught a mouse. She offered him a shy smile in return.

After friendly introductions, Byron wasted no time in taking charge, bringing the room to order. She admired his ability to display authority. She still didn't have the courage to step up the way he often did. Most times, nothing more than a quiet squeak escaped her lips.

"Be patient, you will find your courage," was all Byron said as he continued speaking. "With the dwarg's pledge and word from our spies, we hope to depart as soon as the snow begins melting. We wouldn't dream of depriving anyone of their celebrations, so we leave two days after the spring equinox," she found him saying. It was just under three months away. That would give Saffra time to brew everything she needed, time to plan for their departure north. They couldn't just fly up as a large army. The dragons would see them coming. They'd have to travel on foot, in small groups, first by ship, and then cut across land.

"How is this possible?" someone gasped. She didn't recognize the voice—someone from Fort Kastali. "What solution have we reached for keeping Squall's End safe from dragon fire in light of an attack?"

Byron answered, "We have formulated a plan with King Talon that will see them entirely safe and allow us a formidable advantage. Only..."

"At risk of divulging too many secrets, we must keep this one tucked tightly beneath our wings—for now," she said, surprising even herself. She didn't let it show on her face. It must have been Byron's thoughts that she'd somehow plucked from his mind. "Very few people know, and we can only reveal what is pertinent. You will have to trust us—trust your king." Her gaze met Reyr's and he nodded. Byron's hand slipped into hers and offered a reassuring squeeze.

There were nods of acceptance and a few murmurs. She waited for someone to contradict her, to tell her she was too young to quiet their concerns, but no one spoke. Byron took advantage of the silence to plunge ahead, discussing a few more bits of strategy before it was time to move towards the dreaded vote.

For this, members of Fort Kastali departed. Reyr would oversee collecting the slips of parchment. As was custom, the doors were locked and they would not be disturbed until a decision was reached. Each pair was only allowed one vote, otherwise the room would have been twice as full. As it was, there were still a couple of riders in attendance, those likely to be voted for.

One at a time, each drengr went to the front table and cast a name on a slip of parchment that was folded and placed in a deep stone bowl. Reyr remained at the back of the room, allowing each voter complete privacy. When it was Byron's turn, she detached herself from his mind, not wanting to see the vote he cast. It felt... strange to vote for herself, even though she knew he was doing it. He believed they were a good fit and stood by it.

When all votes were cast by the thirty-four wing leaders and seconds in the room, Reyr went to the front of the room, settled in the chair behind the table, and began unfolding each sheet of parchment. He read each vote out loud, placing each in a respective pile.

"Dagen and Sandra. One," he said, reading the first. Her heart galloped forward. Byron reached for her hand. There weren't enough chairs, so they'd opted to stand against the wall while they waited. She didn't dare look at a single person in the room. She kept her eyes firmly fixed on Reyr.

"Dagen, Sandra," he said again. "Two." This time, her shoulders tightened. Another parchment was unfolded. "Byron, Tamara. One." A huge breath rushed out of her lungs, quiet enough, fortunately, to be heard by no one but her mate. "Alark, Brylee. One." Byron's hand gave her another squeeze.

This was too much. She wished more than ever she could flee the room. She shouldn't take it personally, each vote against them. And perhaps it was better this way. A unanimous vote would not feel earned. And yet...

"Byron, Tamara. Two." Reyr said, reading the next parchment. He continued like this. Nearly all votes were between the top three contending pairs. However, someone had thrown Soren and Amirah's name in. Surprising, given that Soren had only been a second, more recently moved to wing leader when his own died in the attack on Fort Squall.

Time moved at a snail's pace. At this point with the votes so well balanced, to reach majority, any pair that surpassed eleven would win. Reyr was approaching the bottom of the bowl. "Alark, Brylee. Eight." He took another. "Byron, Tamara. Nine." She had to work from keeping her tears back as they pulled ahead of a pair that had been alive so much longer. "Byron, Tamara. Ten." She was trembling now. Tied with Dagen and Sandra. She'd been keeping count. There were only two votes left. Reyr pulled the second to last. He hesitated. She couldn't breathe. "Byron, Tamara. Eleven." He carefully set the parchment down on the pile. If the last was Dagen and Sandra, it would be a tie, and a new one would be cast between the two contenders. Reyr pulled the final parchment, opened it, and said nothing. His eyes flicked up for the first time. His gaze locked on Byron's. Her stomach sank. "Byron, Tamara," he said. "Twelve votes."

She blinked. The room was silent. Then it erupted. Fists pounded against the table in excitement and respect, several of the occupants roared their congratulations. She simply stood mute, not quite believing. It wasn't until Byron took her waist, pulled her into his arms, and kissed her in front of the entire room that she realized it. They'd won. The fort had believed them capable of leading, and if the fort believed it, she needed to believe it too.

CHAPTER 23
ANSWERS IN ASHVALE

Ashvale

Claire wasn't sure what to expect of Ashvale, but not this. The sprite settlement was different from Esterpine in many ways. Where Esterpine was elegant with glittering sheets of shaped glass and crystal, Ashvale was quaint, with moss covered cottages. It looked like a place meant for forest nymphs. Mesmerized didn't begin to explain the way she felt walking down its streets. She trailed behind Princess Taylynn, who led them to a large three story cottage.

They'd arrived in the middle of the day, so the walkways were bustling. Those they passed stopped to watch. As soon as their onlookers realized who the prince and princess were, they swept into deep bows whispering in *Eldunar*. Some of their voices were too low, but she caught much of their respectful greetings.

Her feet ached from days of walking. She was tired, hungry, and wanted nothing more than a hot bath and soft bed. The cottage rising up before them looked as if it could offer that and more. Something warm and inviting—a direct opposite to the cold palace.

"This accommodation belongs to our family," Taylynn

explained, standing before the door. "We stay here whenever we come to visit." She ran her hand over the knob without speaking. The sound of a lock unlatching had Claire and Koldis glancing at each other. "We do not keep palace staff here, so our home is closed up while we are away." Without a backwards glance, Taylynn disappeared into its depths. Feowen led Jeanine in after her. By the time Claire and Koldis stepped through, Taylynn had the large entry room glowing with light.

"It's..." Claire trailed off, stepping away from the others to take it all in. She turned in a circle, eyes studying the ceiling, the stairs that led to the upper floors, and arched doorways leading to the other rooms. "It's magical."

"It feels more like home than the palace ever will," Feowen said, as if reading her thoughts. He casually removed his boots and plopped them on a set of shelves by the door. Following his lead, the rest of them did the same.

Every inch of the cottage was wood, and aside from the floor, every inch of wood was carved by an expert hand. Each arch was bordered with vines and flowers. Deep lines along the walls depicted murals across the stretches of plain wood. The banisters along the stairs were wrapped with gossamer fabrics that shimmered. Plush rugs underfoot were woven with vibrant purples and blues. Heavy drapes framed the windows, letting in the forest's glow from without.

"Now—" Taylynn turned. "Who would like a tour?" Her face held nothing of the stoic seriousness it usually did. The princess loved this place—it was written in her expression, in the relaxed posture of her shoulders.

Claire glanced at Koldis and noticed (with a measure of satisfaction) that he was transfixed by Taylynn's expression. "Koldis would *love* a tour, wouldn't you?" She elbowed him, which made him blink and glance down at her, only to frown. Caught in the act. "We both would," she added, grinning at Taylynn.

"Good. Follow me."

Little had changed between Taylynn and Koldis in the past couple of days. They'd settled for frosty politeness on the few occasions they spoke to each other. But she didn't miss the way Koldis's gaze followed her. And much to her delight, she even caught Taylynn frowning at him on the rare occasion he was preoccupied and didn't see her staring. A frown was better than nothing, she supposed.

They were led through a formal and then informal sitting room. Instead of sofas, they were filled with plush stuffed poufs. A cozy dining room was conveniently situated beside the cookery. It wasn't quite like any she'd seen in Dragonwall, or even Esterpine. While most sprites did their cooking out of doors, this one was clearly meant to break the trend. Or perhaps Ashvale was simply different from the rest of the world.

The cookery was outfitted with a water pump, sink, countertops of glossy wood, an iron stove, a giant fireplace, and a latticework of dried plants hanging from the ceiling. It looked more like a modern day kitchen than the old fashioned cookery she'd seen at the great keep. A huge table ran down the middle with plainly carved chairs—somewhere a family might gather informally for meals. A quick glimpse into the pantry showed that it was filled with all sorts of magically protected foodstuffs like cheese, eggs, flour and sugar, dried fruits, nuts, and the like.

Claire had asked early on—because she'd seen wooden furniture in Esterpine as well—why the sprites were okay with chopping down trees but not eating meat. The answer was simply that as long as it wasn't a tree with a living spirit, and the tree was willing to be of service, they had no qualms about utilizing what the forest provided. It was as the king tree intended. Here, that was very evident.

The bedrooms, of which there were six, were on the upper floors. Each had its own bathing chamber and plumbing, complements of sprite magic. There were even toilets—or as close to what she considered a toilet—which left her grinning in delight. These had a pull cord, something comparable to her own world, which released a catch in the bottom.

The top floor attic was her favorite place in the whole home. Because of the shape of the roof with its sloping eaves, it had a lower ceiling that tapered along the edges of the room. There were multiple windows along the long side where the roof sloped down, overlooking the single story cottages that filled Ashvale. There were two writing desks, more plush poufs for sitting, thick rugs, a fireplace at each end, book shelves, a wine cabinet, and a table with a half-finished puzzle stretched across it.

"It doesn't look much different from the homes in my world," she confessed, turning to take everything in. It looked lived in—well loved.

"Best room in the house," Feowen said, falling into one of the poufs. He was swallowed up by it. He reached over and dragged another beside it to kick up his feet before noticing that Jeanine was watching him with open curiosity. Sitting up straighter, he removed his feet and patted the vacated pouf to urge her over. She sank down beside him only to have him grin wickedly before throwing his feet onto her lap.

Claire watched, releasing her bottom lip when she realized she'd been biting it and staring.

"Let us take this time to freshen up and decompress from our journey," Taylynn said. "Then we can tour the city, make a few introductions, and eat our evening meal."

It was a plan none of them could argue with.

No one knew Claire in Ashvale—a relief in and of itself—so she had no qualms about donning a traditional spriten gown and showing off her markings during their tour. And what a tour it was! She instantly loved it more than Esterpine. Perhaps their quaint cottages were more her style than the elevated elegance of glass houses. Despite the difference in building structure, much of the city was designed similarly to Esterpine's layout, including the place where the evening meal was held. Sprites gathered in the large clearing at low tables on cushions. She took every opportunity to greet her tablemates and converse in *Eldunar*. Aside from their open looks of curiosity, they didn't act surprised by her ability to speak it. Perhaps to them she looked like a strange sprite—someone with far fewer markings, a lack of otherworldliness, and yet, still somehow spriten. They did, however, throw obvious glares at Koldis, who openly ignored the looks with feigned obliviousness that impressed her. She made an extra effort to translate most of what was said to him, so he wouldn't feel left out. She noticed Feowen did the same with Jeanine.

As the meal drew to a close, a female stood and drifted their way. She bowed and began speaking with Taylynn. They exchanged pleased greetings before she invited them to join her at her home tomorrow. Then she drifted away as gracefully as she'd come.

"Lixiss honors us," Taylynn mused, but something in her voice was pleased.

"What did her invitation mean?" Claire asked. Taylynn sat directly on her right. She kept her voice low so those further down wouldn't be privy to their discussion. While she'd caught most of what Lixiss and Taylynn had said, they'd spoken rapidly and some words hadn't been familiar.

"She has offered you the drink of enlightenment. It is sacred—reserved for our people alone." At this, Taylynn leaned around Claire and paid Koldis a pointed look, as if she expected him to ask for so much as a *sip* when it came time to drink it. He snorted and looked away, ignoring her.

"So it's...it's real then?" Claire asked. "I'd heard of it—of what Ashvale was famous for, but I wasn't sure..."

"It is absolutely real. Why do you think I orchestrated this trip."

Understanding dawned upon her. "You're hoping I'll get answers—answers the tree hasn't yet given you. Answers about the staff and how to find it."

"Hmm." Taylynn looked thoughtful. "So, Koldis wasn't inventing nonsense, then. Saffra *did* see Isabella's staff."

"She saw Isabella's staff crossed with Cyrus's sword. Together, I wielded them against Kane."

"And? What happened when you did?"

She frowned, chewing on the inside of her cheek. While the rest of the table continued its conversation, she noticed that her own companions were listening intently. "I blocked his magic somehow. But after that? Saffra doesn't know. The vision never had an end. I might not have survived. I don't...I don't know."

Taylynn sat up straighter. "I think the remainder of this conversation is better done behind closed doors. If you are finished, let us retreat."

They cleared their places and deposited everything at the communal collection before retreating back to the cottage. With an unspoken understanding, they shed their shoes and traipsed up to the attic. Feowen went to each fireplace and created the green flames she was so used to seeing. It was a welcome heat. Then they sank into a collection of poufs with satisfied sighs.

It was Taylynn who spoke first, breaking the comfortable silence. "Whenever I communicate with the tree, I rarely receive a direct explanation or answer. Most of what I get must be interpreted." She glanced at Feowen and Jeanine, perhaps wondering how much she ought to say. Claire held her breath, afraid to move. "I have always done the tree's bidding. Go here—do this. Go there—do that. But a handful of years ago, the commands became more predictable and possessed wider reaching consequences. It began with Lady Saffra. I was sent to her. She was only a child then, seven, eight perhaps. I do not know if she was always meant to be a seer, or if what I did made her such. I like to believe it was already in her blood, and my tampering left her stronger." Claire sucked in a breath, eyes going wide, but didn't say anything. "I gave her water from the spring at the base of the tree's roots. Simply drinking the water is not enough, but with the king tree's blessing, it became...more."

"Her visions of me..." At this, Claire could no longer keep quiet. "She started having visions of me at a young age. She never knew exactly what they meant."

Taylynn nodded. Her gaze was far away. "Our Tree has roots in this world, in all worlds, but in each, it is known by a different name. I am sure your people have plenty of names for their deities, Claire, but here, the tree is our supreme being. Or rather, what lies within it. The tree alone, its bark and branches, is simply a mani-festation. But with the thing inside, it is not merely a tree, but *the* tree. It demands balance, and so much has happened to upset the balance of this world. But it knew of you—oh yes—who you were, what you are, what role you must play. Of that much, I was certain. It was ready and waiting for you. When Cyrus came to the forest, it was *I* who pushed him towards the Kengr Gate and towards your world—"

"You—" Koldis exploded to his feet, face red with rage.

"Sit down, *Drengr*," Taylynn hissed. Her words were so forceful that Koldis's legs collapsed and he flopped back into his pouf, but his rage didn't abait. "I was not responsible for anything that happened to him beyond that. I did not kill him, if that is what you wish to accuse me of. Do not make an accusation you might regret." She exhaled, as if to calm herself. "What happened with the stones was...out of my control. The thing that called Cyrus here. A vision—I am told. It did not come from the king tree."

"It was from Kane," Claire said. "He manipulated Saffra to meet his own ends."

"Yes, that was my understanding too, although I knew little of it at the time. We could not deny the shield his due, nor the king his property. Kane's ambush, the vodar, all of it happened outside of our control—*my* control. But I knew. Yes. I knew when it happened what must be done." She shook her head. "'Send him through the gate,' said the tree. 'Guide his path.' And so I did. I followed him—not too far behind—into your world. With the power borrowed from the tree in this world and yours, I was able to push him towards you."

Goosebumps erupted across Claire's skin and she recalled something Pelwynn had mentioned when they first met. Of Taylynn's role in everything. Of her *meddling*. "You were the reason he fell into my corn field and not someone else's."

The princess nodded.

A low, draconic growl broke the silence. "He might have survived had you not sent him through the gate. We would have found him in the north, treated his wounds, brought him home."

"Yes." Taylynn's face fell. "And Claire? Would you have found her in the north, too?"

Koldis snapped his mouth shut. His shoulders fell. His eyes darted to Claire's and she held his gaze, a sudden sick feeling in her stomach. "He had to die so that I would come here," she whispered. "It was the only way. He... I think he knew that."

"Nothing Cyrus ever did was needless," Koldis said, resigned. The storm clouds did not leave his eyes. If anything, he hated Taylynn even more. "You've been manipulating us—all of us."

"That's my sister," Feowen muttered. He and Jeanine had been quiet.

"Yes...and no." Taylynn shook her head. "I learned long ago, one does not ignore the wishes of the tree. To do so is..." She swallowed and fell silent. Claire had a sudden thought of Queen Jade, of the things she knew of Jade's reign. How long had Jade been ignoring the tree? Did it even speak to her anymore?

"Taylynn's right, Koldis. It's not fair for you to blame her for any of this. I loved Cyrus and I knew him for a mere week. I can't begin to know what you felt..." Claire shook her head. "The world has been out of balance for a long time. But think of what it means that I am here. What it means for Talon. For the kingdom. And what it means for Dragonwall if it's true—that I'm the only one who can defeat Kane."

"We do not know that," he snapped. "*You* are the one that made the promise."

"An unbreakable promise?" Taylynn asked, sitting up straighter.

She nodded and told the sprite princess all about what she'd said in making her promise to avenge Cyrus's death, to eliminate Kane or die trying. Taylynn relaxed into her pouf. "That wasn't my doing, nor was Cyrus's gift. But the tree must have known that you and Cyrus would devise a way to cement your fate. Sometimes, all fate needs is a little push in the correct direction. Oftentimes, I am that push. And not just for you..." She sighed, suddenly looking much older than the twenty-some years she usually appeared. Positively ancient. "I'm tired," she said, coming to her feet. "Please excuse me. I shall retire for the night." A moment later, she was gone.

"Well, that was cheery," Feowen said, standing and moving over to the wine cabinet. "Anyone?" They all nodded, so he poured them each a goblet of spriten wine and passed them around. He and Jeanine retreated to the table to work on the puzzle.

Claire kept Koldis in her sights. He drained his goblet and set it on the floor beside him. She did the same. He was still disgruntled, she could tell. Instead of letting him stew, she stood and plopped down on his pouf. It was too small for two bodies, so she was all but in his lap. She put her arm around his shoulders and leaned her cheek on his head. "I'm sorry," she whispered, voice thick. "I hope I am a fair trade for Cyrus." Her heart wept knowing the cost—what Cyrus had paid so that she might come here.

You are more worthy than I will ever be, and more important, too, Cyrus mused. His words softened the guilt she felt. Softened the pain.

"Claire." Koldis didn't weep, but his eyes glittered as he turned his upper body and wrapped his arms around her, burying his face in against her collarbone. It felt like comforting a child. She knew how much he'd loved Cyrus, how Cyrus's death affected him more than some of the others.

"For what it's worth," she said against his hair, "Cyrus thinks I'm worthy."

A chuckle fell from his lips, muffled against her skin. "You are more than worthy. Cyrus lived a full life. I cannot say it was good nor bad. He experienced both at different times. But you? Yours is only just beginning."

She hesitated. "The journey is only ever the beginning, isn't it?" She pulled away and tilted his head up to gaze into his eyes, searching, before she kissed him on the forehead. "You should apologize to Taylynn."

At this, the innocence left his face and his jaw dropped, but she saw some of his playfulness return as she stood and went back to her pouf. "Why in the name of all the gods would I *ever* do that?" he all but growled.

"Oh, I don't know." She shrugged nonchalantly. "I think she's drowning in burdens. More than she lets on. Kind of like someone else we know?" She lifted a knowing eyebrow. "I think what you said hurt her more than she would ever show. Could be a good excuse to...you know...make conversation."

He leaned back casually. "She said she was tired. She's already sleeping by now."

"Right. An excuse to get away from *you*," she chided. "Which means that by showing up at her door, you'll be doing exactly what she tried to avoid."

His lips pulled up at the corners. He stretched and let out a loud yawn. "You know, I think I'll retire too." Standing, he gave Feowen and Jeanine a salute. She noticed the wicked gleam in Feowen's eyes but wasn't sure if Koldis saw it too. "Good night, all." With that, he too disappeared down the stairs.

"Well," she said, standing to look at the puzzle on the table. "If we hear shouting in a few minutes, I won't be surprised."

Jeanine laughed. "You'd better join us here for those next few minutes before you head down into the hallway."

"I think that's a good idea." She took a seat and set about looking for puzzle pieces to fit into place. It was a coastal landscape, with a deep sandy beach and a crescent half moon shape. There were ships on the horizon, and a vivid orange sunset.

"I've never seen the sea," Jeanine mused. "But I'd like to."

Feowen glanced at Jeanine, his eyes lingering on her expression as she fit a piece into the puzzle. He said nothing and they fell into companionable silence. Much to her disappointment, no sounds came from below. She wasn't sure if that was a good thing or not.

At last, she took her leave of Feowen and Jeanine, deciding that they might also want some time alone. Seeing the way they glanced at each other whenever they thought the other wasn't looking reminded her too much of Talon. It made her heart heavy with longing. All she could hope for were answers—answers to all the questions she had—so that she could hasten her return before her heart cracked open.

CHAPTER 24

DRINK OF ENLIGHTENMENT

Ashvale

Claire found Feowen, of all people, in the kitchen the next morning. He had a towel thrown over his shoulder and was pulling a loaf of bread from the giant brick oven. Jeanine wasn't there, so she had a rare opportunity to be alone with him. He set the loaf on a wooden board, grinned at her, and said, "Morning."

"Since when do royal princes bake bread?" she teased.

"Ach! My mother would have a fit if she could see me now. Baking is...servant stuff, apparently. But I enjoy it. It's one of the things I love most about coming here. Baking bread. There's something therapeutic about kneading dough, don't you think?"

She grinned. "I couldn't agree more." She drifted over to the pantry, looking over its contents. Her grin turned to a pleased smile. "There are oats! And...blueberries?" She turned and stared at him holding a large jar. There was also a selection of *other* fruits, but it was the blueberries that had her most excited. "How?"

He grunted, like she ought to have already known the answer. "It's all spelled to stay fresh. Not frozen, per se, but magic keeps it from decaying."

"I love sprite magic," she whispered, turning back to the pantry. She collected a handful of items, found a pot, and began making enough oatmeal for everyone. While she was stirring, Feowen stuck a slice of buttered cinnamon bread in her hand. She sighed as she bit into it. "Delicious! You really *can* bake." She paired a wink with her compliment.

He grinned and glanced away, perhaps flattered by her praise. "I hope Jeanine thinks so too," she heard him say in a low voice. As if summoned, the female warrior stepped into the kitchen dressed in her usual. Claire didn't miss the sword strapped to her waist. Taylynn and Koldis meandered in shortly thereafter. They both pretended the other didn't exist, but Claire didn't miss the increase in frowns Taylynn threw at Koldis whenever he was occupied. It was killing her—not knowing if Koldis had indeed gone down and apologized. Judging by the increased tension between them, *something* had happened.

They sat around the large table eating Claire's favorite— oatmeal with a handful of blueberries and brown sugar—along with slices of Fewoen's cinnamon bread. "This is heavenly," Jeanine said, looking at Feowen as if she'd discovered a new secret about him.

"Yes, yes," Taylynn tutted. "My brother always enjoys cooking and baking when he can squirm out from beneath my mother's grasp. And he's rather good at it, too." They all heartily agreed.

Afterward, they set out to meet Lixiss. Her cottage was at the edge of the city. She greeted them warmly when they arrived, saving Claire for last. "*Kevjahi*, Claire. Welcome to my home." She spread her arms wide. "Enter, enter."

The first thing Claire noticed was that Lixiss's home reminded her of Pelwynn's—filled with clutter. Some sprites fell prone to the same struggles humans did, like severe hoarding. Lixiss led them through to a kitchen. Her house was smaller than the royal cottage, only a single story like most of the others, but just as warm and inviting. They all crowded into the kitchen, and like the royal cottage, there was a large table in the center. They took seats around it.

Lixiss busied herself at the hearth where a small cauldron hung, bubbling. She was short for a sprite, but like all other sprites, her skin was pale and covered in markings. Her hair was jet black and hung down to her waist in thick sheets. Her gown, like most sprite gowns, was sheer, but more opaque over the areas she didn't want to show off.

"The drink of enlightenment is only brewed on special occasions, but I consider the arrival of Isabella's long lost descendent to be one of those occasions," she said, keeping her back to them. "Taylynn tells me you come in search of answers. I cannot promise the drink will bring you such, but it has been known to do so in the past. It is made from the bark of the ash tree. But not just any ash tree, an ash tree grown in *this* area that bears the soul of one of our own. It must *not* be taken without permission, or the brew is rendered useless."

Claire opened and closed her mouth before settling into a frown. The idea of consuming anything belonging to a living tree that housed a dead Sprite didn't necessarily sound appealing. But she supposed that for the magic to work, there had to be something semi-sinister about it. And what was more sinister than consuming the bark of a dead sprite, even if it was just the leftovers of the sprite's soul.

"Don't fret, the ash tree gave us permission for the brew. Normally we go through a full ceremony, invoking the king tree's permission for something like this, for seeking truth and answers, but Taylynn informed me that secrecy would be better. And where Taylynn is involved, so too is the king tree." She hesitated. "There are only a handful of us in Ashvale who know how to brew such a drink, and I pride myself on believing I'm the best at it. If answers are to be found, your best bet is through me." She busied herself about the kitchen gathering a goblet and a ladle as she began scooping some of the mud looking sludge into the goblet. Then she muttered a few words and what was leftover—there wasn't much —disappeared. "There now. It's a little hot but ready for consumption." She handed the goblet to Claire.

Claire looked down at it. Its viscous consistency didn't allow it to slosh so much as jiggle. She could only imagine how it tasted. Koldis leaned in to look over her shoulder. "And I'm just supposed to drink it? What will happen once I do? Does it start immediately? Am I going to pass out? Have visions?"

"You'll remain mostly coherent," Lixiss answered. "I would just be sitting when you drink it. Whatever happens afterward is the tree's doing. You'll see what it wants you to see, learn what it wants you to learn. Beyond that? It's different for everyone."

Claire nodded. "Well, bottoms up." She took the goblet and tilted it up, drinking down the sludge. It was a slow process. And she was right, it very much tasted like it looked, like mud—not that she knew how mud tasted. She might have known if she were still four.

She choked it down, trying not to let her roiling stomach show on her face. She couldn't help the sound that escaped when she polished it off. It was absolutely revolting.

"Well, I never said it would taste like strawberries." Lixiss's amused expression told her the sprite knew exactly how it tasted.

She hardly heard the female's words. The kitchen tilted on its axis. She slammed the goblet down on the table and grabbed the table's edge with both hands. It felt like she was on a ship, rocking back-and-forth. She closed her eyes, squeezing them tightly. Beside her, she heard Koldis come to his feet, felt his steady presence up against her back, his hands on her shoulders. He squeezed to let her know he was there, so she leaned back against him.

Everything stopped spinning and she opened her eyes, but what she saw was absolutely not what had been there a few seconds ago.

The forest was falling into twilight. It was the time just before full darkness set in, when the effervescent glow surrounding her would increase tenfold. The insects had already started their singing. The sounds of trickling water tickled her ears. A gentle breeze fluttered the leaves around her, caressing her skin.

She sighed with her whole body. It was peaceful, pure. Not that the forest wasn't generally peaceful. But this was a different kind of peace, one that told her that here, there wasn't the same sickness lurking.

But why *was* she here, and where was *here*, exactly? Had she strayed too far from Esterpine? Was this a quest Pelwynn had sent her on? Part of her lessons? She frowned, trying to remember what had brought her here.

"Come to me, child. Let me see you."

She tensed at the intrusion. The voice was neither male nor female. And it spoke to her mind the way dragon voices did. But it wasn't Koldis's voice. And he was the only drengr in the forest. At the thought of him, she felt a reassuring pressure on her shoulder, like he was here with her. But he wasn't, was he? She put her hand on her shoulder but felt nothing. A phantom memory of his touch, perhaps.

"Come. Come," the voice coaxed. She hesitated before following after it. *"There you are."* She came to an abrupt halt before a pool. It wasn't the babbling brook she thought it was. Instead, there were small falls that trickled out of it, feeding the forest. *"Ahh yes, the pool of eternity some call it. Life water—living water."*

She lifted her head—up, up, up—and gasped. "You...you're the king tree." She would have recognized the giant anywhere.

"I am many things in many places. And in many places to many people, I am many things. But here, yes. To you, I am a giant tree." The hairs on her skin stood on end. She blinked, then gasped, then blinked again, because now the tree was gone and in its place, the Crystal Palace loomed before her. The dirt paths around the palace were bustling. Those who saw her, nodded with polite recognition. Had she teleported? She blinked a few more times and the tree returned.

Blink—tree. *Blink*—palace. *Blink*—tree.

It was dizzying and her stomach lurched.

Another blink, and there was Jade standing before her in the throne room, pulling on a pair of silk gloves. "I must go and find Lady Claire," she said to someone out of sight.

Blink—the forest. She stood alone, looking at a path. Twigs snapping behind her had her whirling around. Her eyes widened.

"Lady Claire! Thank the tree. There you are." Jade's appearance had changed between one blink and the next. Her hair was coming undone. Her skin was dirt smudged. Her silk gloves were gone. But it was her voice that was most concerning.

"Your Majesty? Is everything all right?" She offered the queen a formal curtsy and glanced around. They were alone.

"I'm glad I found you. You must come with me. There is a sickness in the forest, Lady Claire and I have found its source. We must defeat it. Come with me and we will put a stop to it together."

"I..."

So Jade knew? She wanted to cleanse the forest, too? Claire had wondered, believing that perhaps only Taylynn and a select few others knew what festered. But if Jade knew, if Jade wanted to do something about it, then Claire would help her.

"You've found a way, then?"

"I have. Hurry, follow me." Jade didn't wait but slipped back into the dense foliage. Claire blinked after her. Perhaps the tree she'd seen had been a mere hallucination and this was the here-and-now of her real life.

She quickened her step to follow after Jade, filled with the jitters of anticipation. It was time to cleanse the forest. A measure of peace stole over her at the thought.

Blink. Bright white light replaced the dim effervescent glow of the forest. She stumbled and turned, taking in the openness. Cold bit into her face. A world covered in snow. Her breath caught in her chest, frigid air burning. Jade was gone. There, behind her was the marble dragon, its body covered in snow accumulation.

"What—?"

...was she doing here?

She'd seen it once, during her travels across the kingdom. Had touched its lifelike body only to be sucked into its mind. Reyr never could explain what had happened. To this day, she still believed Jovari and Koldis thought she was merely making a scene, being overly dramatic. But she was certain that whatever slept in the marble body had been hostile. Had even tried to kill her.

Blink. She saw an image of herself reaching out to touch it. A flashback of a memory?

Blink. The image was gone. The dragon opened its eyes. It *saw* her. She gasped and stepped back. *"I will have my revenge,"* it said. *"Free me from this prison. You have tortured me long enough. I have paid your price. Free me."*

She licked her lips. "I...I'm not Isabella."

Blink. Taylynn appeared beside her. "He shouldn't be impossible to wake." The dragon's eyes were closed now, as if she had only imagined them opening. "Come, let us go to him."

Instead of following, she turned in a wide circle, creating patterns in the snow. What was happening? Why was Taylynn here? And why in the name of the gods would Taylynn want to wake up a monster? This was a dream—it had to be.

"Are you coming?" Taylynn asked over her shoulder, lifting an eyebrow.

Blink. The world darkened again. Back in the forest. This time she stumbled and landed on her knees. Pain bit into her skin and reverberated up and down her legs. She was surrounded by more than just the forest. It was all darkness, cloying, stifling darkness. She hissed, trying to scramble away. "You cannot run from me, my dear. My bargain was sealed in blood. I will have you."

"Kane," she gasped, more of a cry. She froze in panic, tears of anger and fear filling her gaze—tears of betrayal. This had to be a dream. She blinked again, hoping that this would send her somewhere else. But no amount of blinking made him disappear from view. Behind him, a sheet of glass, or...water—she couldn't quite tell—made a wall. There was a dark cave beyond it.

Kane uttered a single word and pain seared through her, forcing her mouth open, forcing the scream that broke from her lips. Absolute agony. He laughed as she struggled to free herself from his invisible cage. She tried to speak, to sing, but nothing happened, and her wrists—they were already bound. So were her feet. That's why she'd stumbled. That's why she'd fallen to her knees. She'd been tricked—and yet, her mind was foggy. She couldn't quite make sense of anything she was seeing. Too many fragments—too many broken pieces.

Blink. Kane disappeared. A sob broke from her chest—doused in relief. The world was entirely white, except for the giant Tree before her. Had Kane done something? Struck her? Killed her?

Her breaths turned to ragged gasps. Giant roots wriggled like snakes, digging into the whiteness around her. Below them— somehow she could see below—was another world. A flash of a child's smiling face lit her mind—*her* smiling face. She was so innocent, so carefree in her laughter. She knew nothing of what would happen some day. What would happen when a mysterious drengr would fall into her cornfield and send her racing through a seemingly impossible world. Beneath the roots was her world.

She could see other worlds, like layers upon layers, all smashed together.

"If you are worthy, I will give you what you seek," came a disembodied voice. She lifted her attention from the nothingness floor and pinned the tree with her gaze. *"But first, there is something you must do. A balance that must be struck."*

Images began flashing before her eyes. Some of them were foreign, and others not. She saw Talon and her heart skipped—saw him dressed in black, standing at the base of the dais in his throne room, filled with people, as she beheld him on the day of their bonding ceremony. She saw them flying together in battle, Pelwynn's bow nocked with a phoenix feather. She saw Reyr, traipsing through the forest, determination written on his features. She saw the dragonstones, hidden around the kingdom in various flashes. She saw the other shields too. But mostly, she saw flashes of all the same things she'd just seen. Queen Jade, Kane, the sick forest, the marble dragon, and Princess Taylynn. The images flitted by faster and faster, jumbling into a confused mess. She blinked to clear her vision. Blinked again, and the scenes disappeared. Before her, stark against the white, laying on the tree's roots, was Isabella's staff. She gasped and jumped forward, reaching for it. The sprite markings along its length flared into life.

The world went dark.

She was tumbling, tumbling through the roots—through darkness. She jerked and felt herself slam into something soft and unyielding. Something familiar. There were hands on her shoulders. Her vision cleared. For a moment, all she remembered was the prize she'd seen, the prize she'd grabbed. But when she opened her eyes and looked down at her hands, they were empty and there was no staff.

CHAPTER 25
IMPOSSIBLE TRUTHS

Ashvale

Koldis held Claire's shoulders as she jerked in his grasp. Like the others, he could do nothing but watch as she babbled, gasped, and jerked against him. Whatever the drink had done, whatever it was showing her, happened within her own mind. He'd gathered snippets. Words. Jade's name, Kane's name, Isabella's name. Beyond that, he could not say. She jerked a final time and he knew it was over—felt her sigh of relief as she relaxed against him, opening and closing her hands.

He held her shoulders a moment longer, just to be sure she was all right, then sat back down. No one said a word. From the expression on Claire's face, he could see why. He had to bite his tongue to keep from speaking.

It was Lixiss who broke the silence. "Whatever you saw, girl, keep it to yourself. If the tree wanted the world to know, it would make it so." Claire's eyes darted around their group, as if only realizing they were there. Her gaze was conflicted, but she kept her lips pressed together.

"When the tree shows me things," Taylynn said, her voice hesitant, "they are often jumbled, frightening even, and make little sense. Sometimes they seem absolutely unbelievable. The tree provides food for thought but relies on *me* to make sense of it. You need time to digest. Time with your thoughts." A moment of silence and then, "We will take you back to the cottage and give you some space."

Koldis exhaled. He would never tell her, but Taylynn's words allowed him to relax. He half expected the sprite princess to begin questioning his queen, demanding answers in front of all of them. In truth, he was tempted to do it himself. Instead, Taylynn had done the opposite, despite her hungry expression.

"Yes, that sounds good." Claire got to her feet. He hovered. He couldn't help it. She wasn't moving as confidently as she usually did. He wanted to be close in case she needed an arm to lean on. Their goodbyes to Lixiss were hurried and brief. The sprite ushered them out with a knowing smile. Something told him she was unsurprised by Claire's behavior, had probably seen it before.

They settled Claire comfortably in the attic with a cup of tea in hand. Jeanine and Feowen announced that they were going for a *long* walk. A few moments later, Taylynn announced the same. Koldis knelt before Claire, putting his gaze level with hers. "Want to talk about it?" he asked.

She lifted an eyebrow. "You're fretting like a nursemaid, you know."

A bark of laughter exploded from his chest. "Can you blame me?"

She shrugged, sipping her tea. "I saw things. Lots of things. I *do* want to talk about it with you, but maybe after I've had some time to make sense of it."

"Perhaps talking about it would help make sense of it?"

"It might." Her eyes took on a faraway look. "And it might not. No. Taylynn was right. I should spend some time alone with my thoughts." She reached out to trace his jaw. The gesture took away some of the sting.

"I'll just...go have a walk myself, then." He hesitated at the door. "Please do not leave the cottage, Claire. You know I do not like leaving you unprotected and we are in an unfamiliar place."

"I won't leave," she said. "You have my word."

~

Taylynn sat with her legs crossed and eyes closed, a peaceful look upon her face. Somehow, he'd known where to find her. She was tucked just outside of Ashvale proper. He sat on the mossy ground beside her, facing the same direction.

"Come to irritate me, *Drengr?*"

Her words were nearly identical to last night's, except she substituted *irritate* for *accuse*. He had apologized after knocking on her door—and it had grated him to do so. Especially because someone like Taylynn would know if his apology wasn't genuine, which meant humbling himself more than he'd wanted. She'd merely narrowed her eyes, then shut the door in his face.

"As much as it pleases me to do so, *Sprite*, no. Irritating you is not my intention. Not at this moment."

She hummed and said nothing more. Silence stretched between them, so he closed his eyes, listening to the forest. He heard more than just the breeze through the trees and the chattering of insects. He knew exactly where each forest creature was located within close proximity to them. Normally, he tuned them out, and sometimes it was easier than others. Right now, it was almost impossible.

"Meditation is supposed to calm the spirit, Koldis, not agitate it."

He scoffed. "I can find no peace in my mind."

"What do you hear when you shut your eyes?" Her voice was low and curious.

"Life," he said, before he could stop himself. Then he cringed. He hadn't even told Claire. Why did Taylynn deserve to know?

"Yes, I can see how that would be agitating. It is like that for me too. Most of the time it is just too much." His eyes flew open and turned to study her. She didn't look as she often did. She looked small and hunched, curled in on herself. Her gaze was far away. "I never asked for this," she whispered.

Something inside of him broke open at her words—like calling to like. The urge to reach out and touch her was overpowering, but he clamped down on it. When she looked up at him, her eyes were old, deep wells of duty and overwhelming burden.

"Is there any way to make it stop?" he asked, without really explaining what ailed him.

She shook her head. He could never be sure what she did and didn't know. It was one of the things that rankled him. "You can accept it, live with it, but you cannot fight it. Have you ever gone swimming in the ocean?"

"I—" His brows pulled together. "I live by the coast. Of course I have."

She nodded. "I did once, too. It was…"

A huff of laughter fell from his lips. He couldn't help it. The thought of her swimming—and then something inside of him curled, scraping along the inside of his chest. Taylynn's lips turned up at the corners, suppressing a knowing response to his emotions. "Somehow the thought of a sprite princess in the ocean is as foreign as—"

"—a drengr in the forest. Which is why we can never be, Lord Koldis. That, among other things."

His lips parted. He blinked, trying to make sense of what she said. Was she *rejecting* him when he'd never attempted to court her? Not that he would. Gods! He didn't know his own true feelings, so how could she—?

"My point is, when you swim in the ocean, there are always strong currents looking to sweep you away. And they will if you don't fight them. But here, fighting does nothing more than exhaust the spirit. In your case, you must let the current guide you, take you where it will. Let it break over you and sweep you into its arms. Then and only then will you find peace with what you feel."

"That's…" He licked his lips and her eyes fixed on the motion. "That's your advice? Really? A bit obvious, don't you think?"

She shrugged and stood. But he wasn't ready for their conversation to end, so he jumped to his feet. She lingered, perhaps uncertain now that he matched her posture. Her throat bobbed.

"What do you think she saw today? Lady Claire?" There was a vulnerability in her voice that he seldom heard. Something about it elicited protective instincts he'd rather ignore. Not that she needed protecting.

He shook his head. "No idea. None whatsoever." He hesitated. "You and I aren't enemies, you know."

At this, she huffed. "No, you and I are something else entirely. Certainly not enemies, though it would be much easier that way, wouldn't you agree?" She took a single step back. Her gaze made him feel all too exposed. "Remember what I said about the currents, Koldis."

"No, wait." Without thinking, he reached for her. She looked down at their joined hands, watched him lace his fingers through hers—which made no sense whatsoever.

He frowned. He didn't have feelings for her—rather, he couldn't stand her. Why was he doing this? Why was he reluctant to let her go?

His gaze traced the look on her face, the impossible beauty of her narrow nose and pointed chin, the jumping pulse at her throat. Taylynn's expression changed when their eyes met. Pity? No. Not quite that. Sadness. Pools of it. "We cannot be, Koldis. I told you that." She gently pulled her hand from his and left him standing there, blinking after her.

In that moment as he watched her disappear, a deep and painful realization pounded against his chest, sucking the air straight from his lungs. No. It was impossible. The gods would never curse him in such a way. He huffed and shook his head. A strangled laugh fell from his lips. His disbelief was powerful enough to mimic denial. He was being ridiculous. All of this— ridiculous.

And yet...

"Taylynn, wait." He rushed after her, but she was already gone.

∿

Hours later, Koldis found everyone gathered in the attic. The path he'd taken hadn't been long, but he'd managed to slow his approach with each step as the severity of his reality crashed around him. He should have known—should have seen it. He'd been too distracted by his heightened abilities in the forest to think clearly.

His eyes found Taylynn the moment he entered, gracefully curled on a pouf with a book in hand. Her eyes were not even moving across the page as she stared at it, ignoring him. Feowen and Jeanine were sitting at the table working on their puzzle, chatting in quiet tones about their walk.

He drew himself up and barked, "Out, now. All of you. I would speak to Claire alone." There was no patience in his voice—no room for argument. There was a bloated pause, and then Feowen —damn him—snickered and took Jeanine's hand, leading her from the room. Taylynn was slower to rise. She paid him a look, no longer ignoring him, a look that contained a silent plea. He blinked and turned away, dismissing her.

Claire sat frowning up at him. When the door closed, he heaved a heavy sigh and all but fell into the pouf across from her, pinching the bridge of his nose. "Uhm. Did I miss something? What the hell was that for?" He didn't answer. "I would've expected that kind of a command from Talon, but not from you."

"Yes, yes…" he muttered.

"Koldis, what's going on?"

"You were right," he said, letting the words tumble from his mouth before he could stop them. Claire sat up straighter. "There is something going on between Taylynn and…and myself."

He rubbed his palms on his pant legs before clenching them, like he could squeeze the life out of a problem impossible to solve. A problem he never wanted. *"I never asked for this,"* she'd said. Because of course she hadn't been complaining about any kind of mutual ability they shared. It was because she didn't want *him*— didn't want the bond between them. And he didn't want her either. Did he?

"Koldis?"

"Hmm?"

"You were going to tell me what's going on."

"Oh. Right." He glanced around.

"Does it have anything to do with why you've been so weird since coming to the forest?"

"Of course not. Wait. Maybe."

She huffed. "You males are *impossible* sometimes. Why don't you just tell me. Start at the beginning, if you have to."

"That—I can do that."

So he did. He told her everything, from the moment he set foot in the forest and felt the thoughts, emotions, and feelings of the animals increase, to the rise in irritability he felt around Taylynn, to the way he couldn't stop thinking about her, looking at her, yearning for her.

"You've got a crush," Claire said, giggling. She immediately covered her mouth with both hands to stop the sound.

"I am not done," he drawled. "And no, it is not so simple as a childlike fantasy. Truthfully, I did not realize how *not-simple* it was until today." She lifted a brow. He relayed in great detail the encounters he'd had with Taylynn up until this afternoon. Claire's smile faded until it was replaced with shock. When he finished, the room was so silent he was able to hear laughter from the cookery below. Feowen and Jeanine, probably baking more bread. He wasn't sure if Taylynn had left. He hoped that she had.

"Koldis," Claire's voice was a choked whisper laced with panic. "You...you're sure? Absolutely sure? She hasn't touched your scales, so how could you possibly know?"

"No. No, she hasn't. And she never will," he decided, sitting straighter.

"No—"

"No, *what*, Claire?"

"No, you cannot just...just pretend this isn't happening. You can't just deny her—it. The bond."

"I can. Or have you forgotten what I am?"

"I..." The color drained from her face, leaving her cheeks pale.

"Talon would never—" She shook her head. "He'd never deny you this."

He snorted. "Just because both of *you* have found your happily ever after—"

"Hardly!" She threw up her hands. "If you think the easy part is over between Talon and me, you're wrong. I probably won't even live through this Kane thing."

"You think I am any better off?" he roared, jumping to his feet. Downstairs, everything went silent. He took a deep breath.

"Sit *down*," she hissed, clearly not impressed.

He plopped down—very improperly. "Apologies, my queen. I did not mean to lose my temper."

"Forgiven," she waved a hand to brush it away. "Koldis, I want to tell you what I know of Verath, because..." She shook her head. "But I can't. I made a promise, didn't I. Alright," she said, babbling on. "You came to me and told me this because *clearly* you're looking for advice. And apparently I'm your queen now, I suppose. I under-stand the severity of this, believe me, I do. It's not just your oath to Talon. You're a drengr and she's a sprite. Sprite royalty, to be more precise. She will rule once her mother—*if* her mother—dies. But it wouldn't be the first time, hmm? Queen Isabella and King Eymar—"

"Look where that got them—" he barked.

She paid him a look that had him snapping his mouth shut. There was more of Talon in her than she probably realized. Talon didn't tolerate interruptions either.

"You're right. Their love didn't get them far when their daughter decided to flee Kastali Dun and come to my world, some-thing I'm certain the king tree had a hand in. Branch in? Trees don't really have hands, do they." She covered her eyes for a moment, then rubbed her temples. "That damned tree has a hand in every-thing, doesn't it? Which makes me think...but never mind. The matter is this. There is a bond between you and Taylynn. You both can't stand each other, which, mind you, is something I *live* for. Enemies to lovers. Star-crossed-lovers. All that." He gaped at her. "I know, I know. She can't leave the forest because she's royalty and will probably rule some day. And you can't live in the forest because, well, you're a drengr. *And,* you're also one of Talon's shields. But..."

"But what?" He crossed his arms, smothering his rising amusement as he watched his queen do battle for him. She was rather cute when she tried to solve someone else's problems.

"*But* you both will live long lives. Think of it as a silver lining. If she were human, she'd be dead in another what, eighty years? Instead, she will live a long life, *you* will live a long life, and voila, you can both make each other happy in the limited time you get to spend together."

"You are jesting, no?"

She opened her mouth. "I'm being perfectly serious. Taylynn leaves the forest all the time. She even admitted it. You can visit each other, see each other here and there. Something tells me the two of you wouldn't want to spend all your time together anyway." She huffed at this last part.

He ground his teeth together. "You don't understand, Claire. If we—if we mated."

"The bond, yes I know."

"Isabella didn't live an immortal life once she tied herself to Eymar. Taylynn will take up *my* lifespan."

"Taylynn would be giving up immortality. So what? Isn't she already like, super old anyway? Maybe she wouldn't mind. As for the sprite throne. Her heir could rule, if the two of you have a—"

"Don't you *dare!*" He growled. He hadn't meant to sound so menacing, but if she dared mention what she was about to. She froze and shut her mouth. "You're impossible," he grumbled. "I hope you know that."

"I'm just saying..."

"Yes, I know *exactly* what you are *just saying.*" But the mere possibility left his insides flaming hot. This was too dangerous. He shook his head. "Regardless of your points, it would invalidate my oath."

She shrugged. "Who invented the oath thing, anyway? Seems

pretty outdated to me. Maybe you and Talon could work out some kind of agreement. It's not like you'd leave your king's side. Maybe take a little vacation here and there. Look, all I'm saying is, let's not rule anything out just yet. Okay?" There was so much hope in her eyes, so much warmth, that he fell silent. "We'll figure it out together, Koldis. All right?"

He swallowed. Even though she was his queen, he couldn't find the courage to make any promise of the kind. Taylynn wouldn't want him even if he did. And he? What did he want?

"As for the *other* thing—" A pillow smacked him in the face. He jerked back, flinging it away, eyes wide. "You should have told me you pig-headed-oaf. You should have told me about your ability. But instead, you thought I'd make a big deal out of it. Come on, look who you're talking to. Drengr voices in my head, remember?" She tapped her temple. "All the time."

He groaned, pinching the bridge of his nose. "Yes. I should have thought it through better. I suppose in that regard, we are not so different, you and I."

"Oh, we're plenty different. You're a pig-headed-oaf. And I? *I* am a queen." The grin on her face made up for the lack of teasing in her tone.

"Fine." He flung the pillow back at her. "Fine. Next time, I'll be more forthcoming."

"You'd better," she scoffed, stretching. Silence fell, and then— "I could do with a nap after the ordeal of this morning."

"Shall I escort you to your room, *my queen*?" He stood and held out his hand.

She eyed it a moment before she took it and let him pull her up. "Yes, I think that's a good idea." He did exactly that.

After he closed her door, he looked down the long hallway and stood silently, listening. He had no desire to venture out for another walk. The evening meal was still a few hours away. He had a lot of thinking to do. So instead, he went to his chamber and slipped inside.

He found Taylynn standing with her arms crossed, waiting for him. He swore under his breath. The princess dominated the center of his room. In her anger—for she was obviously furious—she looked about ten times taller than her usual height, which came to the center of his chest.

He gave her a toothy smile. "Well now, Princess, after such a pretty speech earlier, I hadn't expected to find you in my room so soon. Changed your mind, have you?" He kept his voice low.

"*Why* did you tell her?" Taylynn hissed, doing the same.

He sighed. "I don't see the problem. And forgive me, but did you listen at the door?"

"Of course I did," she snarled.

He crossed his arms. He wanted to be irritated—he did—but Taylynn's anger was so welcome, so satisfying, that he was too entertained to be upset. "That's rather rude, don't you think? I thought sprite princesses were supposed to be prim and proper. Hmm?" She opened her mouth to respond. "And anyway, Claire is my queen. My business is hers."

"Oh. Great." She tried to sound sarcastic, still keeping her voice low. "So if we were to...to..."

She was tongue tied, and he loved it.

"No, Princess." He strode across the room until he was looking down at her, until their bodies were all but touching. She had to tilt her head back to see his face. He expected her to step away, but she stood her ground. "If we were to do *anything*, that would stay between us. Mostly," he added, offering her a wicked grin. Her expression turned dumbfounded. "Look, I was merely seeking advice."

"You should not have told her."

"Why? Because she'd make it harder? Because she'd minimize the barriers that stand between us? Is that what you're afraid of?" Realization dawned on him. "You are, aren't you? Barriers are easy. They offer you an excuse to stay away from me. If she smashes through everything in my path, then all that remains is yours."

She stepped away from him, blinking. The sight of her retreat woke the dragon in him. He took a step forward, reclaiming the distance. "Taylynn..."

"No."

"Taylynn…" he said again, gentler this time, even if there was a rough, draconic edge to his voice. "We both hate each other, don't we? Even if we are not enemies. Not truly."

"No," she said again.

"Why are you here, Taylynn? Why are you in my room? To scold me?"

Instead of answering, she tried to step around him. He anticipated this and moved to block her path. He didn't touch her—wouldn't touch her. Not in his room without her permission, but he wasn't going to let her leave so easily. Not just yet.

"Stand down, *Drengr*."

"You came to *my* room. Not the other way around."

So they stood at an impasse, staring at each other, each breathing hard from frustration. He knew at that moment, knew with absolute certainty, that he wanted to claim her. That she was indeed his mate. She'd all but confirmed it. He didn't doubt that she knew. How she knew? That was a question he'd like answered.

He no longer doubted the inexplicable way he felt about her. Feelings that could only be explained by the existence of something deep and primal between them. He wanted to hate it, and yet, sparring with her felt too good. It made him feel alive and unruly and eager. Too eager.

He clenched his fists, trying to douse the fire coursing through his veins. Taylynn glanced down at the movement in his pants and looked back up at him, lifting a knowing eyebrow. Damn. He abruptly stepped aside. That alone had lost him the game. And yet, she didn't leave. Instead, she turned to him.

Now it was *her* turn to strike. He stood motionless as she lifted a hand and brushed her fingers along his jaw, a smirk on her pretty little face. Every place her skin touched his, heat followed. She stopped at his chin before dropping her hand. He clenched his teeth together. "You are rather handsome, aren't you?"

He opened his mouth to respond but she was already striding across the room. He quickly adjusted his pants while her back was to him. When she reached the door, she hesitated. "I do enjoy fighting with you, Koldis. You are a worthy opponent." Then she was through the door and he was left blinking, wondering if that had just happened or he'd merely imagined the entire thing.

CHAPTER 26

RETURNING TO ESTERPINE

Ashvale

Claire felt just as unclear about her *enlightenment* after a full night of sleep. If anything, more so. She really had no idea what she needed to do. Trust the king tree to be vague. Taylynn hadn't appeared surprised by any of this. But, it was an utter disappointment.

By the time they departed Ashvale, she fought to keep a scowl off her face.

Koldis walked beside her, a slight swagger to his step. After his big reveal, he'd been particularly sweet to Princess Taylynn. At first, she hadn't known what to make of it. He'd offered to take Taylynn's dishes after dinner, then fluffed a pouf for her beside the fire, and from there, had attended to her with the utmost care—all of which Taylynn scathingly refused. He'd even offered her the use of his arm when they set off for Esterpine.

"I am perfectly capable of managing on my own, *Drengr*," Taylynn had snapped, glaring at him. "I've been walking this forest since before you were born."

"Of course, Princess," he'd said. "As you wish."

"You're doing it on purpose, aren't you?" She kept her voice low. "Trying to irritate Taylynn."

"Just thought I'd remind her of our bond," he said, smug.

"Well, you're definitely getting under her skin."

Ashvale faded behind them, swallowed up by the forest. They found themselves traveling a path not unlike the one that had brought them. It would be a little over two days back to the spriten capital, which would put her back nearly a week after she'd left. She would certainly surprise everyone, waltzing in covered in more markings, which she'd carefully kept hidden before.

The first day passed in a blur. Koldis maintained his sickeningly sweet self. He offered Taylynn food from his own pack, offered to gather dried wood in her stead—for which Feowen created a roaring green fire—and he insisted she sleep on the fluffiest patch of moss when they located a clearing to make camp. She glared at him, ignored him, and yet, he still persisted. When they settled for the evening, Feowen and Jeanine practiced sparring while Taylynn coached Claire with magic. Koldis comfortably sat against a tree where he could watch.

The following day was much the same. With each step, she could feel Esterpine looming closer, like a beacon in her chest, thrumming to the same pace as her heart. Her forest tear pendant seemed to know too. She could feel it pulse against her skin.

"How do you think our king is managing in the capital?" Koldis asked, breaking the silence. The forest itself was anything but. There was the usual cacophony of chirping birds, buzzing insects, and rustling leaves. "Do you think they've found a way to reclaim Squall's End?"

"They would be careless to try," came Taylynn's sing-song voice from the back of the group. She'd fallen behind early that morning, allowing Claire and Koldis to lead—probably to put as much distance between them as possible. Between her and Koldis.

"Of course, Princess," Koldis answered, putting a hand over his heart and walking backwards for several paces to see her more clearly. To Claire, he added, "I certainly hope he doesn't exclude *me* from the battle."

"I should think not," she mused. "But who can say? He hasn't mentioned anything about it in his letters." However, Taylynn's statement had her thinking more deeply on the matter. King Talon was anything but careless.

"I hate not knowing how things stand," he said. "What is Kane up to these days? Has anything more happened in our absence?"

"You're not the only one. It bothers me too. Not knowing is hard. It's—" She faltered, then stopped. Around them, the forest had gone absolutely silent. Chills raced down her spine.

Behind her, the others stopped too.

"Taylynn?" she whispered.

"I sense it too," came the princess's answer. Taylynn pushed through Feowen and Jeanine to the front of their group where she surveyed the path ahead. Claire caught a brief glimpse of her frown.

"Is it the black—?"

"Quiet, Koldis."

"*Excuse me*, Princess. I apologize for wanting to know what—"

"I said, be *quiet*! Please." This time she glanced back at him and her worried expression silenced him. Claire linked her arm through Koldis's and they shared a long, silent look.

"We must proceed with caution. I cannot see the way ahead. It could be that the forest has directed us on a path that will take us through its sickness."

"It would certainly do that," Claire mused, remembering her own experience all too well. "But why?"

"In hopes that we might help heal it, of course. That is sometimes the case. Be on guard."

Koldis stiffened on Claire's arm. "Taylynn," he hissed. "Taylynn, it's a—"

A crash of the undergrowth nearby forced them into silence. A painful wail split the air. The sound of metal scraping against metal. Taylynn rounded on Koldis, a question on her face.

"—an animal," he finished. "Something large. I cannot say exactly what." He jerked his head to the right. "It's coming this way."

Taylynn gave him a brief nod. "The rest of you continue on down the path. I'll take care of it."

Claire hesitated. So did Koldis. Feowen and Jeanine stepped around them. "You heard my sister," Feowen said. "Probably not a good idea to disobey."

Koldis snorted. "Speak for yourself, Prince. As if I would leave my—"

"Koldis!" Taylynn snarled, cutting him off from the secret he was about to reveal.

He froze. His throat bobbed.

"Please," she added, her tone softening. She squared her shoulders, looking much taller than usual. "I am well equipped to deal with this. Carry on. I will catch up with you by nightfall. If not, continue on in the morning. You should reach Esterpine shortly thereafter. Claire and my brother can lead you there." She hesitated. "Please."

They shared a long look in the silence that followed. Some sort of silent communication with their eyes. At last, Koldis nodded, giving Claire's arm a tug. "Come, my queen. Let us continue on our path."

Claire looked over her shoulder once more to see Taylynn disappear from sight as the forest swallowed her whole. With each step, the distance increased. She strained to hear what might be happening behind them. The path had already disappeared, as if it had never been—as if Taylynn had never been.

Koldis was silent after that, his lips pressed into a thin line. They got thinner as the day progressed, when Taylynn didn't appear. Claire did her best to keep the mood light and pretended to ignore his tension. He wouldn't admit it for anything, that the loss of Taylynn's presence bothered him.

They stopped for the night, eating a rushed meal. Koldis wasn't in the mood to spar. He opted to pace around their small clearing. Every snapping twig left him jumpy.

Jeanine and Feowen were less concerned, matching their blades.

Taylynn knew the forest better than anyone. It was upon silent feet that she emerged, sneaking into the clearing to regard them as if she'd been there the whole time. The moment Koldis spotted her, his shoulders dropped, but he said nothing. Instead, he went over and sat against a tree with his arms crossed, brooding.

"It was a bear," Taylynn answered, meeting the question in their gazes. "Contaminated like the stag. I healed it and sent it on its way, but not after a fair bit of protesting on its part."

"I didn't think the creatures enjoyed being sick," Claire said.

"They don't, but the sickness has a way of infecting them. Never mind that now, she is fine. A sow. I do not think she had any cubs at the moment. All is well."

"You are unharmed?" Feowen asked, going to stand before her.

"I am fine. You worry too much, as usual."

Feowen nodded and went to sit by the fire.

Claire didn't miss the way Taylynn's eyes flicked to Koldis, who still hadn't said anything, before she too took a seat. Several minutes passed in silence before Koldis sighed, stood to rummage in his pack, and walked to Taylynn. "Here. You should eat." He handed her a cloth bundle, what was left of his rations. She took it without protest and set about eating, otherwise ignoring him. He came to sit beside Claire. She didn't miss the tension in the set of his jaw.

ESTERPINE LOOKED the same as it always did. Shortly before reaching the city, the others bid her goodbye. She needed to arrive alone, after all. She dallied, giving them enough time to get there before her.

She emerged between the city gate, wearing the same thing she'd left with. She traipsed through the streets with her head held high, straight to the palace. Queen Jade was lounging in the garden with a group of friends and noticed her from afar, just as she reached the palace stairs. Jade stood and rushed over, eyes searching, unable to see much beneath the conservative clothing.

"You have returned safely," the queen said, as if she expected anything otherwise. She leaned in and kissed her on each cheek, holding her arms. "I am glad to see you well, my dear. Your journey was a success, then? You look as if you are more sure of yourself." Her friends slowly gathered around them. Rather than reply, she allowed the queen her fussing—or the appearance thereof. "Ah yes, this looks like a new mark here." Jade tipped the edge of Claire's neckline down to reveal a glimpse of a mark she'd had before departing a week prior. "A definite success then, good. You must be tired. I will let you retire, but hope to see you at the meal tonight."

The queen's attendants murmured in agreement.

"Lady Claire," came Koldis's voice from the top of the palace stairs. She heaved a quiet sigh. He rapidly descended and scooped her up in his arms for a giant hug, successfully rescuing her. "It is good to see you home safely. Come, you must be tired." He ushered her away giving her little more than an opportunity to nod farewell to the queen and her attendants.

Back in her chambers, she went straight for a bath. Afterward, there were other pairs waiting eagerly. She greeted each by name, answered questions, and then slipped quietly out of the palace.

Her feet took her down a well worn path to a familiar cottage. The sight of it put a smile on her face. Or, perhaps, it was the sight of the stooped sprite tending his garden. "You are back, I see." He did not stand to greet her. "And did you find answers to the questions you seek?"

"Not really." She watched his back. "The king tree showed me plenty, but I'm not sure what to make of any of it. Perhaps you can—?"

"Not in the slightest, girl. *Varti yifah!* Keep your enlightenment to yourself," he snapped.

She huffed a laugh, then got on her knees beside Pelwynn to help. They worked in silence for over an hour. It felt good using her hands, allowing her mind to simply drift. She understood why he appreciated tending such a large and vibrant garden, continuously breathing life into the flowers and vines.

"We will resume our lessons tomorrow, I think," he said at last, coming to his feet.

"Yes, I think that is best." She stood and brushed off her hands. The evening was approaching and she wanted to change into something more revealing before dinner. The urge to show off her marks burned in her chest.

Pelwynn watched her, his eyes narrowing. "Your time here is nearly at an end, *Elam*. A few weeks, perhaps a month more. You are eager to return to the capital, yes?"

She was taken aback. "I...yes, I suppose. But only once I have learned all that I need to defeat Kane."

"Defeat Kane?! Silly child. There is no guarantee that you will gain all you need here in the forest." She opened her mouth— "I can teach you all I know of magic, yes. How it works. How it behaves. How to use it. The rest is up to you. Magic is a lifelong journey. You cannot simply learn and master it in a few months and call it done. Think of how boring life would be if you peaked now and spent the rest of your years stagnant."

She ground her teeth together. "I don't have a lifetime, *Kenya*. You know that."

"Yes. Yes. Well, begone. Think about what I have said. I will see you tomorrow." He shuffled back into his cottage and closed the door behind him, leaving her alone in the waning forest light. She really needed to find Isabella's staff.

CHAPTER 27

THE END OF THE ROAD

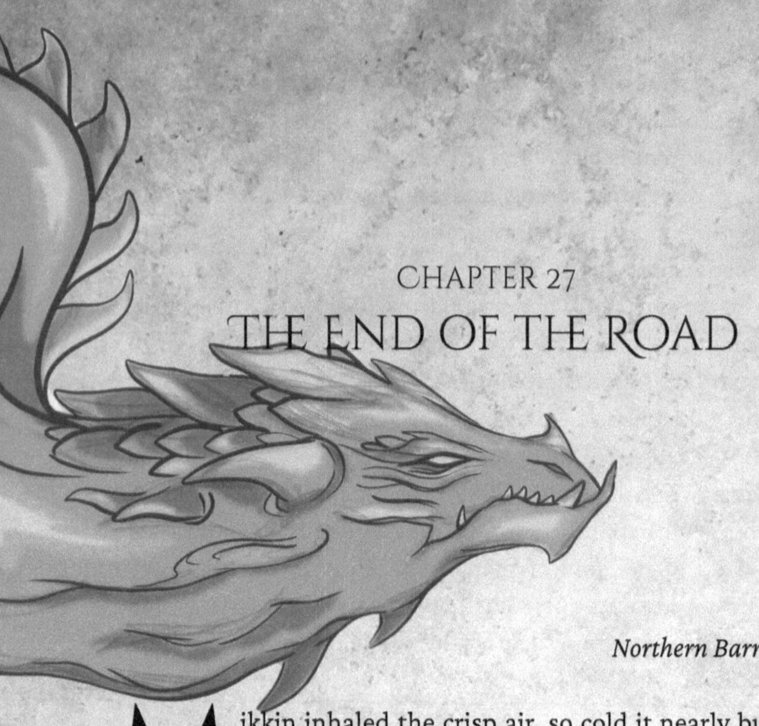

Northern Barrier Range

Mikkin inhaled the crisp air, so cold it nearly burned his lungs. It was colder in the open than down in the tunnels, made worse by the biting wind. Much worse. Here, winter was in full swing, the darkest day long since come and gone. In two months, spring would arrive, but until then, the world was covered in white. From their perch high up in the aviary of Bird's Nest, it was a view to behold.

"It is as we hoped!" Fik shouted over the wind, coming out of the mountain's carved shelter with a small cylinder in hand. "A message arrived ahead of us, from Lord Dubrael."

The dwarg wouldn't chance reading it aloud here, so they took a few more minutes soaking up the pale sunlight before departing back into darkness.

"I hate admitting that I'm relieved to be out of the wind," Jamie muttered. "But I'm sick of the dark." The lad had kept his spirits up along the journey, his curiosity and call for adventure battling his fear over losing his parents. He had no way to know if they'd died when the dragons swept across the north, burning and destroying whole settlements. He had reassured Jamie time and again that there was still a possibility they'd survived—but it was only a weak hope. Thousands of refugees had fled the remaining northern settlements, bound for Squall's End, all in hopes of seeking protection from the drengr. That was, of course, before Squall's End had been overtaken. Still, it was said that the dragons didn't harm the inhabitants there, that they merely held them captive. With the dwargs pledging to assist the king in reclaiming the city, he and Jamie had a better chance of seeing if Tynen and Mary had survived.

Here in the dim light, Fik was already unrolling the scroll. Beside him, Gro lifted a torch to read the script. "Dubrael has received word from the drengr king. Plans to reclaim Squall's End are underway. They have discovered a way to attack while protecting the citizens—"

"How?!" both Mikkin and Jamie blurted at the same time.

"It does not say. It appears the drengr king kept that a secret. Obvious reasons, methinks. The king plans to move his forces into position after the spring equinox."

"That's two months from now," Berbik chimed in.

"Aye," Fik confirmed. "But there's plenty to do until then."

"Is that all it says?" Jamie asked, peering over Fik's shoulder, as if it would help, since the lad couldn't read Dwargish.

"No, there's more. The forces and supplies we've pledged are to rendezvous with the king's armies along the coast, near Brezen. A delegation will meet us there. We are to arrive in staggered groups, multiple ships to disguise our arrival, giving the dragons and Squall's End a wide berth."

"We'll need ships then," Mikkin mused.

"Oh, aye. Lord Dubrael says that he has already started transporting armor and weapons for the drengr—" Fik sucked in a breath, his shock evident. "Dubrael has asked our allies to travel in secrecy, out of Kane's sight along the Shadow Road."

"The Shadow Road?" Mikkin's brow furrowed.

"A road that traverses the length of the Northern Barrier range in its shadow, but not on this side."

"He means to travel through Kalderland?" Jamie asked. "Why not move everything along the tunnels like we're traveling now?"

"It's the only way he can avoid moving through the cities that did not pledge," Mikkin said, realizing at once that Lord Dubrael was being smart about this. "Even though they're not enemies, they're not supporters either. Fauthiel and Tulian—they both refused to lend aid. Can we truly trust them? I'd say not. If Kane were to discover what we are doing, it might tip him off about the king's plans to reclaim the fort."

"Aye. Lord Dubrael says as much here," Fik added, tapping the parchment. "With the weight and size of drengr armor, it will take wagons upon wagons to transport. He plans to have forces and supplies assembled in Ice Port within one month's time. We have safe places there, secret places to hide while everything is assembled."

"And what are *we* to do in the meantime?" Jamie asked. They'd reached the end of the Great Stone Road. It didn't make sense for them to turn around when supplies would reach Ice Port in a month's time.

"We must hire ships, young Master Jamie," Fik said. "Lord Dubrael suggests somewhere between ten and twelve. It is mostly drengr armor we are transporting, with small forces from Safuil, Kisteg, Yberg, and Proaloth."

Each city could spare some one hundred warriors. It wasn't much, but the warriors wouldn't be much against dragons anyway. With some four hundred dwargs and armor to outfit a portion of King Talon's drengr, they'd need a lot of space to transport every-thing. There was no guarantee they'd find enough vessels.

"We will need to do all of this with secrecy," Mikkin said. "Which means it could take at least a month to find enough trusted captains willing to carry our cargo at the risk of Kane discovering us. If he does, he will send means to halt our support."

"It will be a challenge, aye, but one I do not think we are inca-pable of," Gro said, rubbing his hands together as if he welcomed it.

"How long until we reach Ice Port?"

"Four days, Master Mikkin," Fik said.

"Well then, I think we'd better get moving. What do you say, Unka?" The goblin had been quietly watching like the others, shifting from foot to foot.

"Aye. We move." Unka nodded, his eyes missing nothing. They'd have to keep a close watch of him once they reached the port city, more for the creature's safety than anything. Goblins weren't favored here or much of anywhere, really.

A FAINT GOLDEN light glowed at the far end of the tunnel. The western entry beckoned, calling them from the depths of the mountains, sloping up, up, up. They emerged into a torchlit atrium that left him blinking. A handful of dwargs milled about, attendants mostly, stopping to greet them, throwing strange looks at those in the party who were not dwargs.

Words were exchanged, few of which Mikkin understood. "They are recommending several inns," Berbik translated from beside him, keeping his voice low. "Fik tells them we plan to stay a short while here, taking in the sights before we return to Safuil. You have been claimed under Lord Dubrael's protection, so they will not harm the goblin," Berbik added. Mikkin exhaled, letting his shoulders relax, dropping his hand from the weapon at his side.

The atrium was similar to those in each of the dwargish cities. Uniquely carved stone, set in shapes with different types of rock patterns, showing off the might of the dwargish race. "Much of Ice Port is still owned and inhabited by the dwargs," Berbik said beside him. "You will find much of my people's work on display. Not just stone, either."

"What, then?" Jamie asked, keeping his voice low.

"You will see." Berbik grinned.

"Something tells me it has to do with the city's name," Mikkin postulated.

"Oh, aye." Berbik nodded.

Minutes later, they emerged from the large atrium onto a set of steps that spanned the length of the massive building. Mikkin blinked, letting his eyes adjust to the bright sunlight. His breath caught in his chest. "Ice sculptures," he whispered, glancing at Berbik who stood transfixed. Everyone in their party gazed at what lay before them.

The atrium's outer entry was set higher than most buildings, which sloped down towards the port and frozen sea beyond. Its plaza was filled with ice sculptures and snow. The buildings that surrounded it had sharply sloping roofs to deter snow buildup. What was most impressive, many of the yards boasted not greenery for decoration, but ice sculptures.

"We dwargs enjoy carving," Berbik explained. "It is a way to show off our skill."

"Ice Port," Jamie mused.

"Come," Fik said, lifting his voice for the entire party. "Let us find our inn and be warm!"

They made their way into the city. The dwarg homes were grand, most made of stacked stone bases with wooden or thatched roofs. Of course, you couldn't see any of *that* beneath the snow. Their yards had all manner of fountains and sculptures.

It was slow going, as they found themselves stopping frequently to point out carving after carving, each more beautiful than the last. A stallion, a bear, a maiden with a pitcher of water on her shoulder, a miniature forest with trees the height of a human. Mikkin eyed the forest with wonder, tempted to unlatch the gate and enter the garden. "Magnificent," he murmured, taking it in.

"Come along, Master Mikkin. There will be time aplenty to tour the city. Unless your hungry belly isn't in need of hot food?" Fik called.

Mikkin forced his feet into motion. Here, there were inns aplenty filled with common rooms, good food, good music, and merry company. That alone had him increasing his pace to keep up with the dwargs as they made their way through the streets. Bul and Moz took the lead, keeping their hands close to their weapons.

"I'd like a nice tankard of ale," Bur announced to no one in particular. "Perhaps two or three, and then a nap, and then some more ale."

"I'd be happy with some hot stew," Jamie mused.

"You'll have that and more, Master Jamie," Net announced. "There, that's where we will stay." Ahead of them, Mikkin spotted one inn that stood out among others. "Made to accommodate all sorts of folk, not just us smaller people. Your kind, too. Lots of seafaring folk come through here to transport wares."

"The Icicle," Mikkin said aloud as he read the sign. It swayed in the cold wind that caught between the tall buildings. As the name suggested, the entire building had hundreds of icicles dripping from it, frozen in place.

"Come lads, let's get out of this chill." Fik stomped his boots on the mat outside the door and the rest of them followed. The doorway wasn't grand or tall. Mikkin had to dip beneath it to enter, but the room beyond was spacious indeed. Vaulted ceilings towered over a room of tables and comfortable sagging sofas with a second floor landing hosting more tables. There were roaring fire-places at both ends of the room. Chandeliers of stone and candles cast everything in a warm glow, as did the fireplaces.

A group of minstrels were set up at the far end on a stage. They played stringed instruments, drums, a flute. It made for a merry backdrop of noise beyond the clank of cutlery, din of voices, and scraping of chairs. Laughter abounded, putting a smile on Mikkin's face.

"Haven't been here in some years," Fik announced. "But still looks the same as it always does." The dwarg led them to the bar, which was unique in its own right. It had two sections, one for shorter patrons and one for taller. There were a couple of barmaids present, including one dwargish female pouring out tankards of ale for a group of dwargs before her.

"You got rooms available, Mistress?" Fik asked, getting her attention.

"Oh, aye. Several for dwargs and a couple for your tall folk, too."

"Just one large, if it please you, Miss," Mikkin said. "The lad and I can share." Jamie might have been of age, but he didn't plan to grant him the freedom of his own room just yet. Never mind that they didn't have infinite funds. He'd promised Tynen to keep an eye on the lad and he intended to. Unka would also stay with them. He'd feel safer knowing they were in sight.

Coins were exchanged for keys and they trudged upstairs to drop off their belongings, wash up, and change into clothes befitting the establishment. A maid met them in the hallway to collect and launder their travel clothes for an extra steely. Then they met downstairs at a large booth in the corner that fit their party perfectly. The roaring fire brought warmth that thawed the chill in their bones.

Gro came over, sagging beneath a giant tray of drinks which were quickly passed around. Than and Net were engaged in a heated discussion about which of the maids were prettiest. Bur snorted at some of their comments but focused more on his drink. Fik and Berbik compared notes about the city, what they remembered, and so on. Berbik hadn't been here but once in his life, when he was much younger. Fik answered his questions. Was this still here? Was that still there? And so on. Mikkin merely let their talk wash over him, not focusing overmuch on any of it. He was too busy relaxing into his drink, letting his muscles loosen, basking in a successful journey.

The minstrels switched to a lively tune that had many around the common room clapping. The flute trilled. Feet stomped. Voices rose to be heard over the music. It was heaven. He couldn't help but think of how much Mardra would have enjoyed a place like this—

"All right, lads. Food." A barmaid dropped a large round tray filled with bowls topped to the brim with stew. Good stew, by the looks of it. Chunks of carrots and meat piled generously. And accompanying it were two large loaves of brown bread, steaming. Jamie, closest to the maid, began taking bowls off the tray and passing them down the table. She let him, paying the lad a shy grin before stealing a glance around the table. "You certainly make for an interesting bunch," she noted, her eyes falling on Unka before flicking away, as if pretending she hadn't noticed the goblin who stuck out like a sore thumb.

"Oh, aye," Mikkin said, holding her gaze in warning. "A merry band of friends at that." She nodded and picked up the empty tray. "Need anything else—you've but to ask."

She winked at Jamie before departing. Mikkin clapped a hand on the lad's shoulder. "She was rather pretty, I'd say."

"I—what? That wasn't..."

He laughed. It felt an age since he'd last laughed like this. "Just giving you a hard time, lad. You're welcome to eye anyone you wish." Jamie's face turned a deep shade of red. "We will be here quite some time, and I'm sure she's a nice gal."

Jamie opened and closed his mouth, looked down at his stew, then shoveled a spoonful in, silencing the matter. Mikkin just smirked before attacking the bread at the center of the table, using it to sop up the broth in his bowl.

Groans of pleasure erupted around the table as each of them tucked into their food. It was only the middle of the day, but the inn seemed a popular place to take a midday meal. He waited until his bowl was nearly finished before turning to more serious matters. "I take it the best place to purchase transport will be down by the docks?" He addressed the table as a whole, keeping his voice low enough. "But I'd wager that we don't want to go straight to the port master for such requests."

"Aye," Fik agreed. He finished scraping his bowl clean, letting the wooden spoon clack against its rim. "Better to treat with the ship captains on an individual basis."

"And how will we know which of those we can trust? I worry about them talking," Mikkin said, using one of the last slices of bread to soak up what was left in his bowl. His stomach was full and happy, and with that came a deep sleepiness that had him all but desperate to get upstairs to bed. An afternoon nap seemed a grand thing, but he had a feeling the day would melt away before one could be snatched.

"We can't know who to trust for certain, but I've a few notions," Fik said. "Gro and I have a few merchant friends. They have shipping lines, merchant vessels they've contracted. It's a start."

"But not today," Gro said, stretching, letting his hands come to rest on his belly. The other dwargs echoed his sentiments. "Today, we celebrate a journey well taken. The end of one road and beginning of another, eh?"

"I'll drink to that," Than growled, already well into his third. They all lifted their tankards, clanked them together, and drank deep.

Tables filled and then emptied, the ebb and flow of patrons coming and going throughout the day. Inns in big cities weren't simply for letting rooms; they were fine eating establishments and merry gathering places. As the afternoon wore on, a new group of traveling minstrels filtered in to join those already playing, letting some of them take breaks. They all seemed to know each other, laughing and sharing stories amidst their playing. Three of them were dwargs while the other four were human. One was a female who lent her voice to some of the songs. Patrons who wanted requests bribed them with coins, and every so often the younger drummer boy would circle the room with his cap looking for payment. Fik was quick to offer up coins. It would have been disrespectful not to, after the hours they'd eaten away listening to the music.

They didn't have the best view from their booth, but none of them wanted to move. Especially when Nera, the barmaid Jamie currently fancied, brought a tray of gooseberry pie slices over. Two hours after that, it was dinnertime and they ate again, thick slices of tender meat swimming in brown gravy with hearty servings of potatoes and carrots.

Soon enough, Mikkin was all but snoozing in the booth. His eyes fell closed, and he kept nodding off. "I think I'll fall asleep on my plate if I don't go upstairs," he announced. The others agreed. Dishes were cleared, quick plans made to meet here early in the morning, and he was on his feet, trudging up the stairs with Jamie and Unka following. He didn't even remember pulling off his boots before he was flat on his face in bed, asleep like the dead.

CHAPTER 28
NOBLE FAMILIES

Esterpine

Jeanine finished strapping her kingdom sword across her back as Feowen's knock sounded. His scowl, an expression she didn't often see, was visible through the glass. "Everything all right?" she asked, greeting him.

"It would be better if my sister wasn't such a busybody."

"What did she do now?"

In a perfect impersonation of his sister, he said, "'Our noble families wish to meet with Lady Claire. I need *you* to facilitate meetings whilst I am away, Brother.'"

She hid her smile. "She's gone again?"

"As of this morning, yes."

"So you're what, going to take Claire to make house calls?"

"Yes," he grumbled. "And you're going to help me."

"Oh?"

He stuffed his hands into the pockets of his pants. They ended just below the knee. He was barefoot, too, as usual. His markings swirled up his ankles and calves, disappearing. His tunic was sheer and sleeveless. He noticed the way her eyes traced his chest and the corner of his mouth turned up.

273

She clenched her jaw and brought her gaze to meet his. "What makes you so sure I'll agree to this...endeavor?"

"Oh, I have a few ideas. I believe my undeniable charm and wit make for good company. You and I spend plenty of time together as it is. I would hate to leave you alone while I parade her about. Wouldn't you?"

"You place a lot of importance on yourself."

His low chuckle made butterflies dance in her stomach. A dimple appeared on his left cheek. "I *am* a prince."

"Right! How could I have forgotten?!" She snorted and stepped away. He strode into her quarters, looking around as if he expected to find something amiss. Or perhaps he was looking to see if anything unusual stood out among the spriten furniture. Like the small pile of clothes she'd forgotten to put away, or the open book on her bedside table.

She cleared her throat. "So, when do we begin this...parade?"

He flashed her a grin. "I should think now is a fine time to start. She's at the sparring grounds with Koldis."

"Oh, you two on a first name basis?"

He shrugged. "I rather like him. I've never seen anyone get under my sister's skin quite like he does. Makes for good entertainment."

"Well, all right then. Lead the way."

They found a vantage point near the edge of the sparring ring and sat to watch. "I didn't realize she carried a sverak," Jeanine whispered, glancing at Feowen. He responded with a *hmm* but said nothing else. She didn't miss the way his gaze took in their movements, curiosity written on his features.

"She moves quite well," he murmured. "I hadn't expected that."

"She's been here long enough. You haven't seen her sparring yet?"

He looked offended. "Me. A prince. Remember?"

"You're just so busy and so important." She snorted. He bumped her shoulder with his. Her breath caught and she did her best to ignore it. They were friends. Nothing more. She was human. He was…immortal.

"She should have gone low and brought herself around to his left." She caught herself critiquing Claire's movements without realizing it. "Her motions are too heavy handed."

"Well bless the tree!" Feowen's eyes went wide with mock surprise. "To think, you have learned something from my efforts after all."

She rolled her eyes. "Perhaps Claire might learn a thing or two, too. She's good. Really good. But her movements are too much like the drengr. Too much strength and force. She's got a slight frame. And she's a sprite. She should move more like a cat not a bear—"

"Ha!" Claire shouted, interrupting their quiet murmurs, swiping her blade across Koldis's side, ripping through skin. Koldis answered with a smile, stepping back.

"Bear seems to be working pretty well for her," Feowen said, keeping his voice low.

"I can hear everything you're saying, *Prince*." Koldis whirled towards them. "I have superior hearing, in case you've forgotten. And if you're so keen, why don't you come and have a go?"

"With you, or Lady Claire?" he taunted, hoping Koldis would take the bait.

"I wouldn't be caught dead sparring with a spriten prince."

Feowen stood. "Very well then, how about sparring with a friend? Or even as my sister's—" He cut himself off, clearing his throat.

Koldis's expression went blank.

Claire's eyes narrowed. "You…you know?"

Feowen huffed. "I've known my sister for years immeasurable, Lady Claire. Longer than this shield has walked the earth. Longer than his parents, or even his parent's parents were alive. I know my sister." He hesitated. "Yes. I know exactly who and what he is to her." Feowen dusted off his pants, not that there was a speck of anything on them. "And speaking of my sister. I have come to collect you," he added. "Apparently you are to meet the noble families of Esterpine while my sister is away."

"What?" Claire said, right as Koldis said, "Away where?"

"Who knows where? She could be all the way in Ice Port for all I know or care."

"But you *do* care," Koldis said.

Feowen blew out a breath. "I try not to. A learned behavior, I can assure you. My sister is complicated, Koldis. Do not expect her to answer to anyone but the tree." He shoved his hands in his pockets and rocked back on his heels. Jeanine got to her feet to stand beside him.

"This must be the gods' way of cursing me," Koldis muttered, sheathing his sword. He turned to Claire, "Well, you heard them. You certainly don't need me for this." Then he stomped off.

Claire fought a smile. "Don't mind him. He's having a hard time coping with all of this."

"I should think so," Feowen chuckled. "It is my sister, after all. I can't cope, and I've known her for thousands of years. Though it never feels like that—not here, anyway." He glanced up at the trees. "Well then, shall we?"

"Uhm. I'd like to change first." Claire glanced down at herself. "And a bath, too. And what about Lord Marquin? I'm supposed to have lessons with him."

"Oh. Right. About that. Jade has learned of my sister's meddling and rather than forbid it—because that might reflect poorly—she's sending Aolis to tag along. We shall make a merry band, shall we not?"

Claire shrugged. "He's not that bad."

"Oh no. Of course not. Who said simpering was bad?"

JEANINE FOUND herself sitting stiffly beside Feowen in the living area of the noble house of Dorvyre. Orym Dorvyre was on the queen's council. His partner, Leenah, sat beside him. They had two children, both males grown, neither of whom were home. Claire sat beside Aolis Marquin, who'd drawn himself up with his shoulders back. Jeanine knew full well that Feowen couldn't stand the male. He'd muttered plenty about the queen's insistence on sending him along.

Claire looked stunning in her shimmering lavender gown, with her hair tied back and her swirling markings on display. She looked every bit Isabella's heir—not that Jeanine had seen any renditions of Isabella. According to Feowen, only verbal descriptions of the ancient sprite had been passed down. She'd been exiled and her face removed from any art that abounded in the forest world.

Jeanine fussed with a loose thread on her pants. No one paid her much attention. They were too busy discussing how overly honored the Dorvyres were at having Claire in their presence. Despite Isabella's tarnished reputation, royal blood was royal blood.

Lord Dorvyre was all smiles. "I do hope you plan to stay a few months more, now that you've adjusted to life here. Our family would love to have you join the celebrations for Spring Equinox."

"Oh yes," Leenah clapped her hands together. "Orym always hosts a grand ball in the queen's throne room. It's the party of the year."

"I...that sounds absolutely wonderful. I would love to attend, thank you. I cannot say how long I plan to stay, but if I am here, count me as your guest."

Jeanine blinked. She hadn't danced, truly danced, since she was a child, since her mother had enlisted her in dancing lessons. That was before leaving Lincastle for the middle of nowhere. Like all girls of elevated birth, she'd been instructed in dancing along with other polite society etiquette. She caught her mind wandering— caught herself imagining a ballroom floor of dancing couples, Feowen holding her against him, twirling about. She stifled the thought almost immediately, glancing around the room, glad no one noticed her heated cheeks.

"Splendid! Just splendid." Leenah beamed. "And I do hope you will come for tea again sometime. Any time, really. I would love for you to meet Rahlif and Tamnif."

Rahlif and Tamnif.

Jeanine had noticed a trend with sibling names. Like Taylynn and Feowen. They often ended in similar sounds. She wondered how the siblings felt about it. At the least, it helped bridge family associations.

"I would love to meet your sons," Claire said, smiling.

"Oh yes, you would like Rahlif especially. He serves in the queen's guard. Quite an honor."

"Is that so?" Claire's smile stayed put, rather forced if one had to guess.

Jeanine withheld her own smirk. She had a feeling that every parent in Esterpine was clamoring to fix their children up with Claire. Be it as friends or something more, Claire was in high demand now that word of her lineage had spread.

"Well," Feowen said, rubbing his hands on the knees of his pants. "We won't intrude on your hospitality any longer, Orym, Leenah. I promised the Persys family we would pay them a visit before the midday meal."

"Oh. I'm sure Ardith won't mind if you're late," Lord Dorvyre protested. "I'm sure our sons will return at any moment."

"Be that as it may," Feowen said, standing, "I appreciate punctuality."

Everyone else took this as their cue. Claire was the quickest to stand, following Feowen. She paid her thanks to their hosts, complementing their blend of tea, yet again, and then they were free, heading on to the next dwelling.

"Gods," Jeanine swore. She pulled off her boots and remaining clothing, following Feowen into the refreshing water of the pool he'd once shown her. Despite it being winter, she could absolutely get used to the climate here, controlled by magic. "Please tell me you don't need me to do that for the rest of the week. Two families are enough, right?"

Feowen was already in the shallows, bobbing around. His blue hair fanned out around him. She waded up beside him, fighting the urge to run her fingers through it. The water only came to her belly, so she crouched down until it came to her shoulders, letting her body rest weightlessly.

"My sister was explicit. She wants Claire to meet all of them, spend time with each of them. I think two per morning is plenty. I enjoy it about as much as you do. Claire has her secret lessons—whatever those are—in the afternoon. Taylynn expressly forbade me from interfering with those. So we must split them up day by day. Two down, six to go."

"There are eight in total, yes?"

"One noble family for each sitting on the council," he said, sending a torrent of water her way before dipping beneath the surface to swim. He'd brought her here regularly after their first exploration. Unlike the first time, she wasn't as nervous about dropping her clothes to swim. He pretended not to look at her nudity, but like most times, he looked whenever she wasn't paying attention. Her face no longer burned under his scrutiny. In fact, she rather liked it.

That was the frustrating thing. She liked him; he was beyond handsome and interesting in an otherworldly manner. She'd liked Jahl too, but more simply as a brother—until he'd left her for the capital. What she felt for Feowen was deeper than that. He had a way of making her insides curl when he grabbed her hand. Sometimes she imagined his kisses while drifting off to sleep at night, not that she'd ever admit it. He hadn't tried anything beyond hand holding, and plenty of sprites did that. She'd seen both sexes engage in the act. It had surprised her at first. Growing up as a child, she'd seen young girls holding hands out of friendship. She knew plenty of people like Jahl that wouldn't be caught dead holding another male's hand. And yet, she'd seen males and females alike do it here in the forest. It didn't have the same stigma it had outside this kingdom, and that made her heart heavy, because that meant Feowen wasn't doing it for any other reason than friendliness.

And yet...

She'd never seen him hold another's hand. He had male friends, she'd seen him with them. He'd never held hands with any of them—that she'd seen. He *had* held his sister's hand a few times, though. Ugh. Did he consider her akin to a sister, then? That made her stomach squirm.

"Heavy thoughts?" Feowen's voice made her flinch as he popped up from the water.

"Not really. Just...trying to get all of those simpering nobles out of my head."

"Hah!" Feowen grinned. "Yes, imagine living with them for several millennia."

"I can only imagine." She glanced around. "I think I shall try floating again," she decided. Feowen had been teaching her how to swim. Paddling was the first thing she had attempted. She was still trying to master the technique. But floating, that came more easily.

"Excellent. Remember, keep your lungs full and your body relaxed."

She wouldn't admit to him that she had ulterior motives. Namely, showing off her body. Since he seemed to enjoy gazing at her when she pretended not to notice.

She allowed her feet to lift, leaning back and filling her lungs. She relaxed and shut her eyes and let her arms span out to the sides. She felt herself breach the water and tried not to think too hard about what Feowen might be seeing, specifically, her bare breasts. Her eyes stayed tightly shut.

"Good, keep your breaths shallow." At the closeness of his voice, her breathing hitched and her hips began to sink. The flat of Feowen's hand connected with her lower back forcing a gasp from her lips. He gently pushed her hips back up.

Oh, gods! Oh gods oh gods oh gods. She dared not open her eyes now. He had never touched her during their lessons, at least, not when she was exposed like this.

"Shallow breaths," he said again, his voice turning low and raspy. "Keep your lungs full."

He didn't move his hand. Heat erupted everywhere, leaving her flushed. She squeezed her eyelids even tighter, knowing that if she opened them, she'd lose her nerve entirely and sink like a rock. In and out. In and out.

"There, very good." His hand didn't move. "Don't look now, but you're out of the shallows."

"What?!" she yelped. Her muscles tensed up, paired with an involuntary jerk of her hips, sending her low in the water.

"You're all right," Feowen said, taking hold of her arms, kicking to pull her back to the shelf that made up the shallows. "You mustn't panic. Remember?"

"Right. Well, if you hadn't steered me to the deeper side, I probably wouldn't have," she groused, embarrassed more than anything.

She looked at him and their eyes caught, silence stretching between them. His eyes dipped to her lips. She swallowed, afraid to move, to breathe.

"Jeanine..." Their eyes met again. His hands were still on her arms, she realized. Her heart galloped faster than horses' hooves. She pretended it was from her fright of deep water, but really, it was him. Always him.

She caught herself looking at his lips. They were slightly parted, always ready to tip into a smile. His face was close. She could easily make out the pattern of freckles on his cheeks, freckles that she'd grown fond of. Oh gods, she was still looking at his lips, wasn't she?

His hands tightened on her arms and he tilted his face slightly, bringing it closer to hers, giving her time to turn away. But she was frozen, all thought gone from her mind. He brushed his lips to hers, tentatively, gently. Sensation erupted across her skin and her breathing hitched. When she didn't pull away, he pushed his lips more firmly against hers. She closed her eyes, kissing him back, holding her breath because how could she breathe in a moment like this? Their kiss deepened. He moved his mouth over hers and she felt his tongue dart out in question. She copied his actions, moving her tongue out, against his. At the contact, she gasped.

A small noise came from the back of his throat. He released her as if he'd been stung, and backed away. A frown appeared on his face.

Her stomach flopped, eyes roving over his expression. "Did I...
did I do something wrong?"

"You...no." He took his hair in his hand and pulled it over his
shoulder. "I should not have done that. I apologize."

Her eyebrows drew together. Did he not like it? She opened her
mouth but could think of nothing to say. Fire flooded her cheeks.

"Shall we try floating again?" He'd turned away from her. She
wanted to see his face. To know what he was thinking.

"Uhm. Feowen?" He didn't turn so she sent a torrent of water
to douse him, anger overtaking embarrassment. "Feowen."

He rounded on her. "What was that—?"

She did it again, sending enough his way to give him a mouthful. He sputtered.

"*That* was for being an absolute idiot. You can't just kiss a girl
and freeze up like that. I've never been kissed before and even I
know it's rude. Gods. If I don't meet your standards, then you
shouldn't have bothered in the first place." She wasn't sure what
gave her the courage to speak to him like this. But...how dare he?! If
only she could swim and get away from him at this moment.
Instead, she began wading away from him, trying to keep her body
submerged, trying not to let her growing anger show.

"Jeanine, wait." He lunged across the remaining distance then
reached for her hand and pulled her back. Her foot slipped along
the rocky bottom and her body came flush to his. She gasped at the
contact but couldn't get away when his arms encircled her waist.
But...she didn't want to get away, did she?

"You are right. That was rather...rude of me. Let me set the
matter straight. My withdrawal has nothing to do with standards
met or unmet. It has everything to do with my being selfish. I know
how you feel about nudity." He glanced down. "I should not have
kissed you when you were feeling vulnerable."

Her mind turned to mush. She tried to think of something
reasonable to say. His body was firm against hers and she felt his
arousal pressed against her stomach. How was she supposed to
hold a conversation like this? All the same, she couldn't make her
arms work to push him away, either. So instead, she did something

her mother would have rolled over in her grave to see. She relaxed into him, offering him a sly smile. "I don't mind being nude around you, *Prince*."

His eyes smoldered. "I've cured you, then? I've cured you of your embarrassment? Bless the tree." She barked a laugh at his feigned relief. "Well then, if that's the case...may I kiss you again?"

She could do little more than nod as he brought his lips back to hers. This time, their kiss was fire and passion. Sensations flooded her body as his hands climbed up and down her back. The feel of him pressed against her. The way his leg went between hers to better hold her against him, pressing against her, making her gasp into his mouth.

She could have stayed that way forever. But it was Feowen who drew away at last, taking one of the hands she'd placed against his chest to kiss the inside of her palm. "If we stay out here much longer, we will turn to prunes and miss dinner."

Her brow furrowed. "But we've only been here an hour."

He huffed and lifted her wrinkled fingers to study them. "Nearly two, I think." Had they been kissing for that long? He glanced around before looking at her again. "You would like time to dress and walk back to the city, would you not?"

"Oh." She could think of nothing better to say. When he released her, cold water came between them and she suppressed a shiver. Wading back to the side, she found her clothes and dressed. Feowen had only managed his pants when she'd finished. But only because he'd been watching her. This time he didn't try to hide it.

"You're human," he said, shaking his head. "I never thought..."

A frown drew her eyebrows together. "Thought what?" She went to stand before him, closer than she'd ever dared when he was barely clothed. She could feel the warmth from his body. Before stopping herself, she lifted both hands and placed her palms on his bare chest, over the beautiful markings that swirled there. He glanced down, then away. "Thought what?" she prompted again.

He looked back at her, holding her gaze. "I never thought I'd have feelings like this for someone so..."

"So what?" An edge crept into her voice, one she couldn't keep hidden. What was he getting at?

"So different from myself," he said at last, putting his hands over hers, pressing them into his chest.

"Oh."

He snorted, his playful smile returning. "What did you think I was going to say? You know what? Never mind. Come along, or my mother will wonder why I'm late. It wouldn't be the first time you were to blame."

"Uhm, excuse me?" she said, donning an air of innocence. "Since when have I ever been to blame for *anything*?"

"I've been late to the evening meal plenty. Mostly because of you. Perfect excuse this time, do you not think?" He took her hand and kissed her palm again. Then he finished getting dressed before leading her back through the forest.

She traced her swollen lips with her fingers. She hoped to the gods that his mother wouldn't see them arrive, hand in hand. Especially when she realized his lips were just as swollen as hers.

CHAPTER 29
TAMING A CAT

Ice Port

Bennett watched the docks until Cat, hood pulled low over her head, disappeared into the crowd. Most were dwargs, but there were enough humans that he lost sight of her. He exhaled, the heavy sound lost to the icy breeze. It was done, she was gone. So why did he feel…uncertain?

They'd reached Ice Port that morning. Cat hadn't brought much for traveling, but she'd quickly packed up what she had, paid him the other half of what she owed, and disembarked. Still staring at the place she'd disappeared, he hefted the bag of coins in his hand, tossing it up, letting it clink back into his palm. The sound was muted in the din of noise from the harbor.

"Shall I ready the crew to depart, Captain?" Jonah came up beside him. They both wore heavy parkas lined in fur.

"What? Oh. No, not yet. Perhaps we might set foot on dry land for a day or two."

Perhaps Cat might change her mind, was what he didn't say.

"What happened to dumping her on the nearest iceberg and sailing away?" Jonah asked, a sardonic smile playing across his lips.

"You know the crew wouldn't allow it, even if I tried."

"Aye." Jonah hesitated. "They aren't happy to see her go. Hard to believe she's grown on them."

"And on *you*," Bennett pointed out. Jonah merely lifted an eyebrow, daring him to admit the same. Her ability to heal the crew, trade banter with lethal precision, and throw a punch—thanks to some training—had become useful indeed.

"Anyway," Bennett continued, "I'm tempted to see what she's up to. Get Tris. Have him tail her."

"You got it." Jonah moved off to give orders.

Bennett gave the dockyard a final glance before slipping below to count coins and divvy up his crew's pay. They'd spend it all in one place, likely, but it was theirs to spend as they wished.

"Jonah!" he called an hour later, summoning his first mate. Jonah's head popped in. "Tell the crew they can collect their pay. Draw straws. They're permitted to disembark once the remainder of their duties are seen to."

"Aye. Very good, Captain. They will be pleased."

"Did you already send Tris away?"

"Aye? Shouldn't I have?"

"That's fine. I'll find him later. Very good." He flicked his hand, dismissing Jonah.

One by one, his crew trickled in to collect their pay. A few asked if Cat would return. They were more pleased than ever by the increase in coin. When the matter was sorted, Jonah gave him the straw he'd pulled in his stead. Short. "The others have already scampered off," Jonah added, sounding apologetic. "If you'd rather, I can trade—"

"No matter, I can stay here tonight. Keep an eye on the rest of them for me, especially with the rumors we've heard about that sorcerer. Keep them away from the Osheans, should you see any. I don't want any serious injuries, either. Without Cat to heal them..."

"I understand."

Jonah shut the door and he returned to the paperwork on his desk. Docking business, mostly. But there were also several requests for his services, voyages that would take him south, even one that would take him across the Dragonfire Sea.

He didn't set foot on dry land until the following afternoon. Tris had reported little of note, that Cat had stayed up all night, gone from one inn to another buying a drink here and there, but mostly frugal with her coin. "It seems she's searching for information," Tris said. "Rumors, more specifically. Either way, it didn't sit well with me. She was asking about the Oshean ships."

"Did she see you?"

"Don't think so," Tris answered, proud.

Pleased with his efforts, Bennett paid him a steely and sent him off. That's how he found himself following Cat from one inn to another, halfway across the city. When she left *The Icicle*, he let her go, slipping over to the bar to have a seat next to the fellow she'd spoken with. A human, perhaps a decade older than himself, with a beard grown thick. The stranger bobbed his head in greeting, turning back to his drink, back to the young man beside him. And was that—

"I don't think I've seen a goblin in years." Bennett couldn't help himself. The stranger's head whipped around, a warning dancing in his eyes. "Meant no offense," he added, holding up his hands.

The barmaid slipped over and deposited a tankard in front of him. "Captain," she said. "Been a while. Figured you'd want your usual."

His eyes darted between the stranger and the maid before him. He flashed her a grin and slipped a coin into her hand. "You know me well, Kiki." He was almost surprised that he remembered her name, but then he recalled why that was, especially when her face blushed a deep red. She scampered away.

"You're a ship captain," the stranger said. "What sort of ship?"

"Who's asking?" he challenged, taking a sip.

"Name's Mikkin," the stranger said, holding out a hand.

He hesitated, taking it. "Call me Bennett—" A screech cut him off, followed by a string of loud curses. "Right on cue," he added, grinning wide. "She's never one to miss introductions." Mikkin's eyes widened at the sight of the bird that landed on his shoulder. "This here's Beaky. Beaky, this's Mikkin. And…"

"And Jamie," piped the young man beside them, eyes intent on the bird. "And Unka," Jamie added, introducing the goblin.

He barked a laugh. "Well met."

"*Well met. Well met,*" chorused Beaky.

"Off with you, you damned bird." He shooed her, but she pecked at him, so he grabbed a handful of nuts from the bowl on the bar, shelled them, and held open his palm. She ruffled her feathers proudly, then settled in to accept the offer.

"Smart bird," Mikkin mused.

"Oh aye. Smart pain in my arse," he said, finally shooing Beaky to the rafters. "Now, tell me 'bout that lass you were talking with shortly ago."

Mikkin's face darkened. "You know her?"

"Oh aye. Another pain in my arse. Far worse than that one," he pointed a thumb at Beaky.

"*Pain in my arse. Pain in my arse.*"

"Shut up, you damned bird!" he called up, but couldn't help the smile that pulled at his lips. "But to better answer your question, yes. I brought her here, against my better judgment. She wouldn't tell me why, and I'm fixing to find out."

"Well, you better find out soon. The questions she's asking…"

"And what would those be?"

Mikkin sighed. "I get the impression she's looking for…" He shook his head. "There's people around these parts you've got to worry about. Few can be trusted. How much do you know about the rising conflict here in Dragonwall? Politically speaking, I mean?"

"Enough. Though I wish I were ignorant of it."

"Then you've heard tell of a sorcerer? One responsible for the wild dragons taken up at Squall's End?"

"Aye."

Mikkin nodded. "I fear to know *why* she is asking after him, that lass of yours, why she's searching for him. Doesn't bode well with me. Said she heard rumors that he was here, wondered if we'd seen him, where he might be." Mikkin's fist clenched. "If I come to find that she's in league with him... I've half a mind to report her to the rest of my companions. She's going to get herself killed."

Benett's stomach dropped. "You're certain? Certain she's asking about Kane? Is he here? I heard rumors that he'd chartered Oshean ships to transport his beasts. I can't tell what is and isn't true anymore."

"Giant bats," Mikkin clarified. "Trust me, the less you know the better. You don't want to get wrapped up in anything that sorcerer has a hand in."

Bennett swore under his breath—it was worse than he'd expected. "I'm going to wring that girl's neck. Nothing good can come of this."

"Then you'd better stop her before her questions stir up the wrong folk." Mikkin nodded towards the door. "But before you do that, you didn't answer *my* question. You are a ship captain, no?"

"I am. What's it to you?"

"I might have need of your services, if you're up for hire?"

Bennett hesitated. The last services he'd granted in a tavern were to Cat, and look where that had landed him. Mikkin must have sensed his hesitation. "I'll be staying here a while. Something tells me I can trust you. And what I have to say will get your attention. At the least, agree to hear me out?" He waited for Bennet to nod. "Good. Then when you're done with your errand, come and find me."

Bennett sighed. "Beaky, we've got matters that require tending. Come." He stood. So did Mikkin. They shook hands. "I'll be back once this is sorted. Maybe not today, perhaps tomorrow. Until then, fair seas." He dipped his head and went out into the daylight.

CAT HISSED like a feral thing when he cornered her in an alley, grabbing her arm and pulling her through the snow. "What in the name of all gods do you think you're doing, *girl*?!" His voice was a low hiss. "Asking about Kane? Stirring folk up? Trying to get yourself killed?"

She wrenched her arm free of his grip, squaring her shoulders. "What I do is none of your concern, *Captain*. Your services are no longer needed. I thought I made that clear. You can,"—she made a motion with her fingers—"scamper off to whatever brothel you want."

He snorted. "I don't think so. Against my better judgment, I'll drag you kicking and screaming back to my ship if I find you are trying to track down the infamous sorcerer that Dragonwall *just so happens* to be at war with." His voice died to a whisper, as if speaking of Kane would summon bad luck upon them.

He clenched his jaw. Why did it matter?! What was it to him if this woman got herself killed? He took a deep drag of icy air, hoping it would bring him to his senses. He ought to walk away— ought to forget she existed. And yet...

Cat pressed her lips together; they were turning blue. It was freezing, even in his parka. She had to be cold wearing nothing more than a gown and cloak, neither of which were ideal for northern climes. "Come on, Cat. Put your claws away. Come with me out of the snow and let's talk somewhere warmer."

"I'm not going *anywhere* with you. Move out of my way." Arms crossed tightly to her body, expression hard, she made to step around him.

He sighed. "I'm not going to make this easy for you. I'll follow you from place to place, if I must."

"Then I'll report you for harassing me."

"To who?" He barked a laugh. "No one is going to trust a word you say against mine. I doubt you're known by many here, but I am. It'll be my word over yours." One of the merits of being a known and respected ship's captain was carrying a reputation. His spanned Dragonwall's coast and beyond. "Now, come along. I've letted a room not far from here. I'll buy you some food and we can talk by the fire. Just talk. Think of all the ways you can use your words to insult me. If that doesn't please you, I don't know what will." He flashed her a taunting smile, daring her.

"You think I don't know what you're up to? No. Let—"

"Problems here?"

Cat's words were silenced by the group of armored dwargs that filed into the opening of the narrow space. City guards. They spoke with a heavily accented common tongue.

"Master Dwargs." He turned to them, bowing. "None at all. My crew member is being difficult. But we were just on our way back to our inn." By law in any port, crew members were the responsibility of their ship's captain. It was a blessing and a curse.

He took Cat's hand without thinking, noticed her fingers were ice, as cold as her frozen heart, and pulled her back out into the street. The Dwargs stepped aside, eying them; they held their spears upright and offered nods as he led her away.

"I am not—"

"You *are*," he hissed before she could get a full sentence in. "As far as anyone here needs to know, you are part of my crew, you work for me. We're going. Otherwise I'll reject you as my crew, tell them why you're *really* here, who you're asking after, and let them decide what they want to do with you." He hesitated, turning to look her square in the face. His voice took on a threatening edge. "If I find out you're in league with him, I'll kill you myself. A captain has that authority over his own."

"Think whatever you want, *Captain*. I'm not part of your crew. My business is my own."

"You've made that clear. Much as I hate to admit it, I've decided you might not be in your right mind. So here I am, refusing to let you die doing something stupid." He laughed then, in disbelief, mostly at himself. She blinked at him.

Taking advantage of her surprise, he dragged her to the inn he'd purchased lodgings at.

She didn't fight him. Perhaps her shivering outweighed her desire to defy him. A blast of warmth swept around them. Rather than stopping in the common room, he dragged her all the way to his own spacious accommodation, calling out for food on the way. His wasn't just a bedroom. There was a sitting and dining area. A roaring fire greeted them. He flung her around and sent her sailing.

Watched as she tumbled onto the sofa. The set of her jaw was her only sign of suppressed rage.

"If you act like a child, I'll treat you like one." He towered over her, breathing heavily, trying not to let his anger muddle his thoughts. "Now, you're going to tell me exactly what this is about. And if I decide it's harmless stupidity, I might let you on your way. Otherwise, I'll tie you up—gag you if I have to—and carry you back to the *Lady Faith*. Maybe even throw you overboard if I find out you're a traitor."

She crossed her arms, shivering where she sat, but said nothing.

"I can play the silence game as long as you like, girl." She could have used magic, but she didn't. That had to count for something. He sighed and added, "The food will be here soon. Shall I have a bath ordered as well?"

"No," she croaked, glaring in his direction. The look was brief. He stared down at the back of her head as she watched the flames.

Tap. Tap. Tap. The sound of Beaky broke the tense moment. He strode for the window and let the bird in, watched Cat's minute jerk of surprise before she settled for indifference. Beaky landed on his shoulder, nuzzled his cheek, calming some of his ire, then took off to perch on the wardrobe. He removed his parka and settled on the sofa across from Cat, stretching his arms across the back. His tall frame was oversized for most furniture.

A knock sounded. "Enter," he barked. A serving maid scuttled into the room. "You can put it on the table," he told her, trying to offer a kind smile. She was gone a moment later. The smell of roast meat, potatoes, carrots, and bread filled the air. He almost, *almost* got up to eat. Then his eyes fell on Cat, still glaring at the fire, and he forced himself to remain motionless. Damn her if she made him eat cold food. But something was going on, and his instincts told him to wait it out, to hear her story.

She'd always struck him as a woman with a story to tell.

He wasn't sure how long they sat there. Five minutes? Ten? When her words finally came, she said, "He used me. I thought my magic was mine, but it's his. Payment for services rendered."

"His, who?"

"Kane's," she scoffed.

"So you *are* working with him?" He should have thrown her overboard—

"I'm not working with him," she said, sitting up straighter. "I'm no traitor."

"No? And yet, you have his magic. You're trying to find him."

"I..." Her throat bobbed. "I killed someone for him. That was the service rendered. I didn't put it together at the time, even though part of me knew when I used the poison."

His lips curled into a snarl. "Let me get this straight. You killed someone and in exchange, you were rewarded with magic. And now—I'm just guessing here—your treachery was discovered, which is why you're on the run. What I don't understand is, why are you looking for Kane? If you're not working for him, then why?"

"He did this!" she cried. "He created this. All of this is his fault. I wouldn't be here if he hadn't—" She huffed, cutting off her tirade. "My father. He...they..."

"I hope you understand you're making no sense whatsoever."

Her head whipped around, eyes piercing, smooth skin flushed with irritation. Even despite her cruel expression, she was beautiful, the gold streaks in her hair glowing in the firelight. "When I was a child," she said, "my father married a noble woman. We had nothing, came from nothing, a house in the Pauper District. He tricked her, made her think he was some well off merchant from another city. I wasn't sure where he got the finery, the jewels— well, I can put more of that together now. I've had plenty of time to think about it." Her expression tightened. "He did what he needed to, to make our lives better."

"How..." Bennett cleared his throat. "How old were you?"

"Not quite into my teens." She wrapped her cloak tightly around her shoulders, nestling into it. "He told me he loved her— this woman, this *Lady Kendall*. I believed it of course, and hated him for it. We were going to become a family, have titles, have a home far better than the shambles I'd grown up in. He told me I would have a sister—and wasn't that something to be excited about?!" Sarcasm rang in her voice. "I didn't *want* a sister. I didn't *want* a new mother. I wanted *my* mother. How could he so easily find someone new to love when my own mother had only just *died*—"

"How did she die?"

She huffed. "I don't know. How should I have known?" Frustration riddled her voice. "She was weak, coughing up blood for months. Then she just—" Her face turned hard, voice flat. "—just died."

Consumption, possibly. "I'm sorry," he said.

"Save your words, Captain. I don't need the sentiment."

"Fine. What happened after that?"

"My father married Lady Kendall." She shrugged. "It was exactly as he said it would be. I had a spoiled brat for a little sister. A girl who'd never gone without, never felt what it was like to be hungry, never wanted for anything, who wore frilly dresses, had all the doll houses in the world, had everything. Suddenly here I was, living in a nice home with glass windows." She barked a laugh. "Glass. Can you believe it? Not dried animal hide. I had beautiful gowns, too. Servants—until my father dismissed them when they got too nosy."

"Sounds like you made out rather well."

She snorted, turning her glittering eyes upon him. "Is that what you think?"

"Well?" He eyed her up and down. "I suppose you're going to tell me otherwise, so...keep talking." His food was getting cold, after all.

"It was Kane's doing. All of it. And my father's. But I don't know if my father really knew *what* he was doing. They said..." She shook her head. "They called him a nask. One of Kane's little puppet spies." Bennett's brows pulled together but he didn't dare stop her. "What does it matter anyway? I killed her—Lady Kendall."

She turned to stare into the fire.

"Because you hated her? Because she wasn't your mother?"

"No, moron." She exhaled, as if searching for some form of

calm. "It was made clear that Lady Kendall could rid herself of us at any moment. She was the bearer of the titles, the wealth. Without her, we were still nothing. My father sent me to a man in the city, a poisoner. I was given a bottle of…something. I knew it was bad, knew it would likely kill her. He didn't have to tell me what it was, and he didn't. I knew, and yet, in my head, I denied what I was doing. I put it in her tea, you see, just as instructed. One day she was fine, the next, a burning fever, and the next, dead. Her daughter was suspicious. I did what I had to, to ostracize her. I never claimed to be a good person."

Her sigh was deep and long. "After that, my father inherited the title, and no one could take it from him. He secured a prestigious position at court. A few years afterward, he secured an even more prestigious position when he became one of the king's trusted council. And surprise! While everything was going so well for him —all because of me, mind you, because I killed a woman to cata-pult his career—I discovered my magic. What a splendid notion indeed, that I might have a way of separating myself from him. Moving into the keep to train with the mages. I loved him, certainly. He was my father. But…" She shook her head. "It…that was the happiest day of my life, discovering that I had something, just *one* thing that was mine. Something I didn't have to fight to earn. Something that just came to me. The implications, what I might do, who I might become."

A long silence fell.

"Well?" she demanded.

"Well, what?"

"This is the part where you chastise me for my actions." She looked at him, waiting. Her face was hollow. All the hate usually present in her features was replaced with…nothing. His eyes swept over her, curled in on herself.

He sighed. "Come. Let's get some food. We both need to eat."

Sure, he had plenty more questions, but he was also starving. She didn't respond to his offer, merely stood and walked over to the table, her movements empty. He took a seat across from her and shoved a plate in her direction. She eyed it before lifting her utensils, taking each bite slowly, with little enthusiasm. He tucked into his own food.

"You were only a child when you did what you did," he said after a few mouthfuls.

She tutted. "Don't make excuses for me, Captain. I knew what I was doing."

"I'm not. You're an awful person with an unattractive attitude. A mere hour on my ship and I already wanted to toss you over the side. I would never make excuses for you. There. Is that what you wanted to hear?" She just blinked at him, not bothering to contradict a word. He shrugged. At least she wasn't denying it. "So, your magic. It wasn't of your own abilities, but something that came to you in exchange for poisoning your stepmother?"

"Yes. I... It..." She shook her head. "I don't want it anymore. It's not mine."

"Neither was the title your father stole, but you took it all the same." She flinched. It was such a small movement, he almost didn't see it. An expression flashed across her face, like she wanted to say something, but instead, she shoved another bite into her mouth. "Right. So, why Ice Port? You're here to confront Kane? To ask him why he was mean to you and your father? Why he brought such misfortunes upon you? Why he manipulated you? And then what? You're going to ask him to take it all back?"

"My magic is his," she hissed. "I don't want it."

"You *do* realize that Kane could easily kill you, or worse, manipulate you like he did your father."

"Who cares? The king was going to sentence me to death just like my father, or worse, lock me in the dungeon for the rest of my life."

"And you don't believe you deserve the punishment?"

There was a long pause and then, "I deserve it. But that doesn't mean I have to accept it."

"No, no of course not. It's much better to live with guilt, that is, if you're even capable of remorse," he said before holding his tongue in the bloated silence that followed. She didn't give him an answer, moving the food around on her plate. "Well," he said at last, "I suppose it's good to know you've got a thimble of goodness in you." She shot him a challenging glare. "You claim you aren't a traitor. There's that. But if you walk right up to Kane and he decides to turn you into one of his spies, that will make you just like your father, no?"

"I am *nothing* like my father," she snarled, the rage coming back into her face. "He did this. With Kane's help, they both did this."

"Right. If they hadn't? You'd still be living in a shithole, maybe working in a brothel, selling your body. Instead, you've got magic, probably not much wealth left to your name, considering you used most of what you had to broker a voyage here, but you're not bereft of everything. You're farther in life than you would've been, so why waste it? Way I see it, you don't have many options left."

"Your point?" She glared at him.

"My point is, *girl*, I've a proposition for you." Gods, she drove him up the wall. "Had you just answered my questions days ago, we could've saved ourselves this entire journey. As it stands, it's never too late for redemption. So, instead of throwing the opportunity away on Kane—because let's face it, no good will come of that—I propose something else. Join my crew, permanently. Use this magic you hate for something good. The crew will have you—I've no doubt of that. You've grown on them. You've learned to handle yourself well enough. It'll be good for them to have a female aboard, balance things out and all. I've need of a healer, a need I didn't realize until you came along—which is the only reason I'm willing to put up with your claws. And, against my better judgment, I'd rather not see you throw your life away."

"You cannot be serious." She had a way of looking down her nose at him.

He shifted in his seat. "I'm entirely serious. Or is the work too far above your ladyship's abilities?" She tutted at that. "Didn't think so. But don't think you'll be lounging around. Sailing's hard work. It has its merits, though. You'll have more freedom than you ever did at court. You'll see far more of the world on a ship than you would've, and certainly far more of it alive than dead at Kane's hands."

"Kane deserves—"

"He deserves a lot of things, girl. But you're not the one to mete out his punishment. Leave that to the king."

"I'm a fugitive. Wanted by the law."

He barked a laugh. "*That's* your best excuse? Gods. Half my crew are wanted for one thing or another. You'll gain clemency under me. You are no longer a citizen of Dragonwall, but a citizen of the sea, of *Lady Faith*, under my protection. That also means my word is law. And you'll have *me* to answer to. Understand?"

"I don't like you." She crossed her arms, leaning back into her chair. But he could tell she was thinking about it. Considering it. "I don't like sailing or the ocean," she added.

"I don't like *you* either. And I think you like sailing *and* the ocean more than you'll admit. I know for certain you like gambling with the crew, throwing a punch or two. Most of all, I know you enjoy healing 'em when they get into trouble."

She didn't answer. He scraped his plate clean, tearing off a few pieces of bread for Beaky, who swooped down and pecked them out of his hands. "But let's make one thing clear," he added. "If you crew on my ship, you'd better be getting used to Beaky."

She scoffed. "I've agreed to nothing."

He lifted a shoulder. "You ever been to Oshea?" Their eyes met, and he already knew the answer. "No? I didn't think so. In fact, I think the only places you've been are the salty ports I've stopped in along the way here. There's a lot more of the world than what I've shown you. Work hard, earn your bread, I'll pay you—"

"How much?"

He sighed. "Depends on the merchandise—on the job. But I'm fair about it. We're all paid fairly."

"Even you?"

"Even me."

Cat rolled her eyes, uncrossing her arms to pick at more of the food on her plate. He glanced out the window. It was already dark. "You can take the bed, I'll have the couch," he said at last.

She barked a laugh. "I hope you don't think I'm sleeping in here with you."

"Oh? Have you coin left to get a room for yourself? How fortunate." She didn't answer. "I'll give you this free pass tonight, girl, and possibly tomorrow, until you can get on your own two feet. But after you earn your first payment, you'll be expected to take care of yourself. Something tells me you won't have any problem with that."

She set her fork down and leaned back. Her lips were pressed in a thin line, her shoulders sagging. She didn't look at him, but instead, gazed out of the darkened window.

"I'm giving you a chance to use your magic for something that matters," he said at length. "Something other than yourself. A chance at redemption, though you can make of that what you will. I can't hold you accountable for a lifetime of bad actions; I'm not one to judge. But you can. The gods can. Your conscience can. You get to choose what you do next. So...?"

Her eyes met his, a brief flash of fierce determination in her gaze. "Fine. I'll do it. But I'm keeping my cabin."

"You'll have to take that up with Jonah. It's *his* cabin, and he's first mate."

"Then I'll be first mate."

"Oh, I don't think so. You've balls, girl, I'll give you that. But not enough to be first mate. That position's earned."

"But I'm a female. I'm not going to get naked in front of the crew. I require privacy."

"Oh, but I'm sure they'd love that—seeing you naked."

"Ugh! You're disgusting. I'll talk to Jonah, then. Perhaps he and I can come to an...arrangement."

"Right." He snorted. "Good luck there."

Her throat bobbed. "Are there no other cabins?"

"Just the two. We're a shipping vessel not a passenger ship. Unless you want to share mine?" He grinned. "No? Well then, I suppose..." He hesitated. She waited, something like hope on her face. Damn it all to hell. "We can get some lumber while we're here in port. Partition off a portion of the crew's area with another smaller cabin. It wouldn't be much, enough for a bunk, or a hammock, whichever you prefer, some shelves, a place you can treat your patients." His crew wouldn't let him hear the end of it. But he'd pass it off as part of the deal to bring her on permanently as healer. They wouldn't argue if that was the case.

"Done." She crossed her arms again, a look of triumph on her face, like she'd won some great game. But he was the true victor, wasn't he? Even if he didn't want to admit that to anyone, especially himself.

CHAPTER 30

A QUEEN IN THE FOREST

Esterpine

Claire watched the days melt into weeks. She thought she'd been busy before, but now her minutes slipped away like water through open fingers. It didn't help that Taylynn insisted she meet and spend time with *all* of Esterpine's noble families, of which there were eight.

Eight!

Socializing, sharing lunches, drinking tea. Most importantly, making friends. She wasn't stupid, she understood why this was important to the princess. She was gaining allies, people who would rally to her side if she ever needed them. After all, Dragonwall was technically at war, and she needed people who would support the rightful heir. She didn't tell any of them she never planned to rule in Esterpine—that she didn't plan to stick around for much longer.

Fortunately, it wasn't all tedious. She used this to her advantage, learning a great deal more about Esterpine's way of life, its governing body, and politics. Take the noble families, for example. Every thousand years, a vote was held to elect new council members. These acted as advisors to the queen. Sometimes the same members served for multiple terms, voted in repeatedly either by popularity or performance. Other times, they were voted out and replaced.

The noble families were those belonging to members of the council; they weren't noble simply because of long reaching lineages. This was a different way of thinking compared to what she was used to, compared to the way the drengr monarchy did things. Only the royal bloodline—her bloodline—was truly fixed. From the subtle undercurrents she sensed, there were several families unhappy with one specific facet of spriten politics: Queen Jade.

But that was for *them* to work out.

Her lessons with Pelwynn remained her sole priority. She was advancing with each element. Several days with Taylynn had boosted her abilities with earth. She was getting better at manipulating fire. Water felt more natural. Even air seemed eager to aid.

A sense of peace had settled within her, within both parts of her: the sprite part and the drengr part. She embraced it. But no matter how much she trained, one thing remained: She needed Isabella's staff.

"Your markings have multiplied," Pelwynn said one afternoon. It had been a little over a month since her return from Ashvale. "You'll need to take another trip into the forest, otherwise Lord Marquin will grow suspicious."

They sat in his garden pruning more flower bushes. It was an activity they did more and more frequently, especially after lessons. It helped her wind down.

"Lord Marquin is already suspicious," she said. "He wasn't prepared for the number of markings I returned with. But..." She shrugged. "He explained it away by my bloodline. Isabella's long lost heir and all that."

Pelwynn snorted. "As if blood has anything to do with it. You know how magic works. Aolis should too. Any bloodline can be strengthened to unparalleled levels."

She lifted a shoulder. "I'm not going to argue with him. But you're right, I suppose. I should send myself on another quest."

That evening, she returned to Esterpine to find a short note from Talon.

> *Claire,*
>
> *Missing you deeply. Cannot say much, only that I have a surprise for you. It should reach you before the equinox.*
>
> *Be safe.*
>
> *Yours,*
>
> *T*

SHE WAS equal parts vexed and excited.

Koldis rapped his knuckles on her crystalline doorway. "Anything of note?"

"No," she pouted, tucking the parchment away. "I'm going to take another trip into the forest."

"Oh?" His smile slipped from his face. "And when will you be leaving?"

"Tomorrow. I'll let everyone know tonight, during dinner."

He blew out a breath. "I'm not so sure that's a good idea. Something isn't right in the forest. Besides—"

"Besides, what?"

"You have marks aplenty." He crossed his arms, leaning against the wall. "There is no need for the forest."

"Oh. Right. I'm just supposed to magically get more marks without appearing to do anything and risk exposing Pel—" She snapped her mouth shut, glaring.

He stared at her. When it was clear she wouldn't expose Pelwynn's name, he said, "I suppose this isn't up for discussion?"

"Exactly so. And besides, it will help pass the time until Talon's surprise arrives."

"A surprise?" His eyes glinted. "What surprise?" The way he asked was telling. Talon had sent him a letter too.

"You know what it is, don't you?"

"No idea."

"I don't believe you."

He shrugged. "Not my problem."

"Koldis!"

"Claire."

They glared for several moments more, then his shoulders relaxed and his expression softened. "Why don't you just pretend to go into the forest, and instead, stay with your tutor? Going into the forest is dangerous and I cannot protect you. Unlike Taylynn, you have no idea how to...whatever it is she does to the trees."

"Cleanse them?"

"Oh. Is that what it is?" His voice was riddled with sarcasm.

"You know, you've been extra irritable ever since she disappeared. She didn't tell you that she was leaving, and you just can't get over it, can you?"

Taylynn had been gone for a month. Her absence put Koldis's temper on a short leash. He snorted. "Would you be happy with our king if he did that to you?"

"I—" She exhaled. "No, you're right. And he *has* done it before, though he had the wherewithal to leave me a note. But..."

"There are no buts, my queen."

"Ugh. Would you stop using that ridiculous title? I have a name, you know."

"Of course, my queen." He grinned, and the tension in the room broke.

She stood, and they went into the sitting room, getting comfortable on the sofa. She drew up her knees and rested them slightly against his thigh. "Taylynn will come around," she said, hoping to reassure him. "I'm sure of it."

"Perhaps." He leaned back, resting an arm over the back of the sofa, angling himself towards her.

She studied his face. "How are you feeling about it? The whole mate thing?"

"Truthfully, I really do not know. Taylynn frustrates me to the ends of the world—angers me, even—and yet, there's this fire burning deep in my chest."

"You're a dragon, there's always a fire burning *deep in your chest*." Her words were sardonic. He grabbed a throw pillow and shoved it in her face, making both of them laugh.

"It was quite a shock, you know," she said, after her laughter stopped, "discovering my bond with Talon."

"Yes, I've heard some of it from Bedelth."

"We hated each other, you remember? *Hated.* You saw how he treated me. Gods! He tied me to a torture device. You're the one who pulled me off it."

"Believe me, I remember."

"All that time spent hating each other, distrusting one another, and he was my mate." She shook her head, still overcome with disbelief.

"What happened when you touched his scales?" he asked. "I know it's private. I shouldn't—"

"No, it's...it's okay." She shrugged. "I had no idea what was happening when I touched him, no idea what it meant. Frankly, it was terrifying." She gazed at the crystalline wall, remembering the events as if they'd just happened. A strange bark of laughter burst from her lips. "You know, the funny thing is, I thought I'd been transported, that touching him had sent me to the lava fields in Hawaii."

"Hawaii?"

"It's a place in my world—beside the point. My point is, when it happened, I was so shocked that I fought it. I guess people see different things when they plunge into the minds of their mates. I saw a lava field, it's how I interpreted Talon's mind. Lots of black lava, rock formations, that sort of thing. But there were pools of it too, and when I stepped in one, I saw a memory of Taylynn telling him about our mate bond. I was..."

She sighed and shook her head. "I was *furious*. That he could hide something like that from me—information about both of us. We'd been getting closer, you see. Maybe it would have been different if he'd stayed the same—like he was before, brooding and distant and temperamental. But no. He was...changing. And in Brezen, we began spending time together, taking walks... *flirting*." Heat rushed to the surface of her skin. She hesitated, biting the inside of her cheek. "Sometimes I worry he only started spending time with me because Taylynn told him we were mates. That he wouldn't have bothered, wouldn't have wanted me if—"

"Oh, Claire." At this, Koldis reached out and tucked a strand of hair behind her ear, then took her hand in his, rubbing her knuckles with his thumb. "Talon would have wanted you regardless of the mate bond. You should have seen it from my eyes, the way you affected him in the throne room. Whenever you two are in the same room, breathing the same air, it does something to him."

"But...what if that is just the mate bond? Forcing him to feel something he wouldn't feel otherwise?"

Koldis shrugged. "Maybe it is. There will never be a way to know. From what I understand about mate bonds—and it's very little, given *my* lack of experience—a mate is someone the fates have decided you are equally suited for, someone of the same fierceness, of the same mind, of the same strength."

"Even if it often feels like we're two completely different people?"

"Even then." He huffed. "Look at Taylynn and myself. We couldn't be more different, eh?"

"True. All right. I didn't mean to digress. What I was going to say was, after I discovered Talon's deceit, I tried to run from him, to get as far away as possible. He chased me down. Actually, looking back on it, it was all rather romantic." She couldn't help but smile. "He fought for us when I was too angry to. He apologized. You and I both know how often he apologizes."

Koldis laughed. "Our king? Apologize? Undirfold must have frozen over."

"I know, right?"

They fell silent for a few moments. "Thank you," Koldis said at last. "That helped, I think. If you and King Talon can overcome the events that brought you together, then I have some hope for Taylynn and I. But—"

"But she will always be a sprite. Yes. I've considered that. Regardless, if the fates intended you to be mates, maybe they have something more planned."

"Perhaps you are right." He fell silent.

"I suppose it's time for dinner. The rest of our pairs are probably already there. Shall we?"

"Indeed." He stood, keeping her hand in his, and helped her to her feet.

She departed Esterpine the following morning. It hadn't taken much preparation, considering she wasn't supposed to bring anything. A couple of days wouldn't kill her.

She allowed herself to wander along whatever paths came her way. There would come a day when she'd miss this sort of thing, when life would become monotonous and she'd wish she was here beneath the trees. She recalled the way she'd missed the forest before, and reminded herself not to take it for granted.

She stopped often, to look at plants mostly. Plants enjoyed being caressed. She'd learned this working in Pelwynn's garden. They appreciated a kind word of encouragement or affection. Those were the sorts of plants that flourished.

It was mid morning when she came across unicorns. Her first instinct was to panic. She'd been overly observant of her surroundings, paying special attention to the sounds of the forest, always wondering not *if*, but *when* the forest's sickness would show itself. She'd not yet seen a sick unicorn, wasn't even sure it was possible, but if stags and bears could get sick, couldn't unicorns?

These weren't aggressive when she approached. She eyed them as she inched towards them, studying them. If Koldis were here with her, he'd probably know what they were thinking. Esterpine's unicorns were always friendly, always soliciting pets or asking for handouts during meals.

These did the same. The moment they noticed her they turned, coming to greet her with snorts and nuzzles against her palm. There were three. She laughed, petting and caressing their soft coats. "You're certainly beautiful, aren't you?"

They were snowy white, with piercing gold eyes. Their horns shimmered, but they were careful with them. The one in the back was the tallest, a male. He shimmied his way forward, growing impatient. When he reached her and thrust his snorting nose into her palm, she laughed and said, "Well, hello to you too! I would have gotten to you eventually." He simply snorted again and nudged her for more pets.

"I'm heading this way too, you know. Perhaps you'd like to walk with me?"

So they did. Two behind her and one at her side. Somehow the forest knew they were together, because the path widened enough for her to walk with her hand resting on the female's neck. They made slow progress until she reached a babbling creek where she took a nice long water break. She was growing hungry too, so she sang some berries into existence. She offered a few to the unicorns but they didn't show much interest.

The unicorns stayed with her most of the day. When evening approached and she made a fire the way Feowen and Taylynn had taught her, they took their leave. It was done without many words. She understood what they were telling her with their body language.

"Very well," she said, bidding them goodbye. "Perhaps our paths will cross again tomorrow."

They went back the way they'd come. She watched them until they were swallowed up, then sighed and leaned back against the tree. Sleeping upright wasn't comfortable, so she sang up a small hut of vines, grew a mossy bed, and fell into a fitful sleep. Her dreams woke her many times, full of the sick forest and crazed animals.

The next morning, she was craving bananas. They had them here in Dragonwall. Sprites used the word *asmah* to describe them, and she'd only had them here in the forest.

She sang the plant into existence and was rewarded with several clusters. She left them and took only enough to fill her belly before setting off again. She left her vine hut, too. The forest had a way of cleaning up natural things, and she certainly wouldn't destroy it, effectively killing the now-living vines. Perhaps other critters would use it as a home.

She trekked most of the morning deep in thought, wondering what she needed to do to find Isabella's staff. Taylynn assured her that it wasn't some relic hidden in Esterpine. If it were, Jade would have snatched it up years ago. It was in the forest somewhere, or protected by the king tree. In her vision, she'd seen it laying across the tree's roots. She hadn't missed that.

The forest went silent. She stilled and listened. The absence of sound had become a warning to her, signaling forest sickness and danger. She backed up and switched direction. It wasn't so early into her adventure that she needed to keep going. She could turn back and be in Esterpine by tomorrow evening. Two days away wasn't terrible, although she'd have to be a magical powerhouse to earn ten markings in two days alone in the forest.

A twig cracked behind her, sending her heart jumping. She spun around but saw nothing. She wished the unicorns hadn't left her. The forest looked healthy and alive, but there could be plenty of sick, wandering creatures. What would she do if she encountered any of them? Taylynn had not shared that information with her. Blood and magic—but beyond that, she'd be groping in the dark for a solution. A crash echoed into the stillness. Rooted in place, a figure appeared on the path ahead of her.

Her eyes went wide. "Queen Jade?" The queen rushed towards her. "Are—"

"Claire. Lady Claire. Thank the tree I've found you." Jade looked wild. Her hair was coming undone, a streak of dirt across her left cheek marred her usual pristine appearance. Her translucent gown had rips in the fabric.

"What happened?" she asked, distressed as she took in the woman's appearance. "Was it the forest?"

Jade was breathing loudly. She glanced over her shoulder. "I've found a way. A way to cure it."

Claire opened and closed her mouth. "Uhm...?"

"I had hoped to find...well, never mind. I will need your help. I cannot do it alone."

"Are you sure we should be here? I can return you to Esterpine. We can send someone—"

"No! No. We are here now. This must end. My forest is sick. I cannot allow it. But there is a way. I have found a way when my daughter could not. Come." Jade held out her hand, her face still wild.

The back of Claire's neck prickled. And yet...

"You're sure you've found a way? How?"

Jade hesitated, then sighed, shedding some of her wildness. "I must show you. Will you come?" Her voice had calmed.

Claire eyed her a moment longer, studying her outstretched hand. A memory flashed in her mind's eye. No, not a memory, per se. A scene from the drink of enlightenment. Coming across Jade in the forest. She'd seen this. The tree had shown it to her, this meeting, which meant she needed to do this. Would it earn her the staff?

She swallowed, aware of the wary prickling on her skin. She couldn't let her worry be the reason she turned her back on the forest. "Okay. Show me." Reaching out, she took Jade's hand and they set off along the only visible path forward.

CHAPTER 31

A SURPRISE VISIT

Esterpine

K oldis followed the sprite attendant who had summoned him. An urgent matter, he'd claimed. He couldn't think what might possibly be so urgent, unless it had something to do with Claire. The attendant had assured him that it didn't. He'd brought a couple of their own just in case—Rhywyth, Gradyr, Jorsid, and Madeleine—who'd been lounging in Claire's suite with him. They'd been playing cards when Haemar knocked and asked for his presence.

Ahead of him, the city's southern gate came into view. "Here, Lord Koldis." Haemar stepped aside and held forth a hand. Koldis blinked, his mouth dropping open. Then he let out a whooping laugh and lunged forward. Standing there with his arms crossed, lounging against the side of the gate's arch was a face he had not expected to see.

He swallowed up the space between them and hugged Reyr. Reyr laughed too, thumping him on the back. "Gods, it's good to see a familiar face after a week of travel."

Koldis eyed him. Reyr had a large travel pack on the ground.

"Has something happened? I wasn't expecting you. Our king is well?"

"Fine. It's all fine." Reyr waved a dismissive hand. "Nothing to be alarmed about."

"Then you must be the surprise Talon promised?"

"Indeed! I come with news, better said in person than on parchment." Reyr turned, taking a moment to greet the others.

To Haemar, Koldis said, "Why was he left standing here? He should have been brought straight to me."

"Apologies, Lord Koldis. Our queen is away and I was uncertain of how to proceed. He is welcome in Esterpine, of course. He may stay with you and your kind in that wing of the palace, if you wish." Koldis nodded. "Very well. I will leave you, then." The attendant slipped away.

"Come," Koldis said, grabbing Reyr's shoulder. "I'll get you settled. Tell me everything. How did you get here? How long are you staying?"

Reyr chuckled. "I convinced a couple of sprites at Ellia outpost to escort me. Apparently the request King Talon sent ahead of me either didn't reach the queen, or she didn't have time to respond and alert them. It took a bit of convincing on my part, for them to agree." He shrugged. "No matter. I'm here now."

"And your stay?"

"Until after the Spring Equinox." A generous stay, then. That was good. It would be wonderful to have him here. "There are things—" Reyr hesitated. "Things better said behind closed doors."

"Of course."

Reyr frowned. "Claire is not with you?"

"Gods, man, we aren't attached at the hip."

"She is your charge."

Koldis sighed. "She's away. She left, went into the forest yesterday morning."

Reyr stopped. "You let her—"

Koldis threw up his hands. "I didn't have much of a choice, Reyr. I'm sure she will explain it when she returns. She's become quite bossy, you know." His words did little to smooth the scowl on

Reyr's features. Finally, Reyr nodded and they continued to the palace, catching up on everything mundane.

When they entered the suite, the others lounging about roared with delight. Word spread, and soon all their pairs from Kastali Dun were crowded into the suite, some forty bodies. It was a tight squeeze, but everyone was eager to hear news from the capital.

"I had hoped to speak with Claire before everyone else," Reyr said. "But I can speak with her when she returns." He hesitated, glancing at Koldis. "She will be returning soon, will she not?"

Koldis shrugged. "She said a couple of days. So perhaps tomorrow or the day following." This brought another scowl to Reyr's face, but Koldis said, "Come, don't delay our suspense. Tell us."

Reyr cleared his throat. "We've found a way to defeat the dragons at Squall's End."

His words were met with whoops of excitement as he proceeded to tell everyone what was planned. "We intend to keep this information very secret so that it won't spread while we enact the plan. Given that you're all cut off from the rest of the world, we agreed that your knowing is safe enough. But I cannot give you exact details. That information has been restricted to a very select few. What I can tell you is, our forces will be departing under secrecy to rendezvous with the dwargs just after the spring equinox. By then, the snow around Squall's End will be melted. Until then, we cannot allow any word to reach the dragons."

"How will you keep a horde of traveling drengr hidden?" Amira asked.

"Most will fly up the coast from Kastali Dun in staggered groups. Some will travel with the cargo we plan to sail up to the rendezvous point. We are staggering the arrival, splitting groups, and staging everything at a safe distance from Squall's End west of Brezen. The key is to keep our groups separated, and once they're closer, they will remain in human form. We want nothing that looks suspicious."

Reyr continued to answer questions and fill in small details relaying everything he could.

"So...what is the secret solution you cannot speak of?" Koldis asked.

"Poison. But not like what you would think. We found a mixture of klizite and dragon's bane that will work in our favor." Rhywyth was in the middle of a question. Reyr paused to answer it.

It took a moment for Koldis to get over his initial shock. "Klizite is a drug. It—"

"Will delay the effects of the dragon's bane. We will put it in their water supply. It won't permanently harm them but it will make it impossible for them to fight. Make it easy for us to slaughter them."

Something in Koldis's gut twisted. This was war—he knew it was war. And yet...

"It isn't ideal, Koldis. I know. We all know," Reyr added. "But it was the only thing we could think of—Saffra's idea, actually."

"Saffra?!"

"They will burn everyone if we move against them, Koldis, Burn the whole gods damned city to the ground."

"I...I know. You're right, of course. So what brings you here, then? Surely not to simply tell us this plan?"

"Yes. And no. We weren't sure how long Claire would be. We thought you both should know we were mobilizing—departing Kastali Dun. We didn't want her to return to the keep and find all of us gone without knowing ahead of time what we planned. We thought it best..."

"Ah."

"We can talk more about it once we're alone."

Koldis agreed. It was a lot to digest. Especially when he knew there might be a chance he'd miss out on the attack, which left him feeling a little disappointed. The king would never allow Claire near a battle like that, even if the wild dragons were subdued.

NEARLY TWO HOURS LATER, Koldis and Reyr were finally alone. Most of the pairs had wandered off in small groups until Reyr sent the rest away. "The palace accommodations are certainly...unique," Reyr mused, walking around the central fireplace before finding his seat.

"Indeed. Quite different from the accommodations they put us in when we were here last."

Reyr barked a laugh. "If I recall correctly, when last we were here, you believed Claire had killed Cyrus and we were taking her to receive the king's justice."

Koldis huffed.

"Oh how things have changed. Sometimes I struggle to believe it, myself. Claire, our future queen."

"Future?" Koldis lifted an eyebrow. "She's already my queen, and she certainly acts like it."

"Oh, does she now?" Reyr smirked. "I would say I'm surprised but—"

A knock silenced him.

"Enter," Koldis called, then jumped to his feet when he saw who it was. "Taylynn?"

She glanced between them, then ignored him completely and said, "Lord Reyr?"

"Surprise." Reyr spread his arms wide, grinning. "You must be the sprite princess King Talon was on about."

"Was he really?" She lifted a brow in mock surprise. Reyr only grinned.

Koldis crossed his arms, taking her in. There were leaves in her white hair, not intentionally so. Her gown was intact, but she had a crazed look about her. He walked over. Caring nothing for Reyr's presence, took hold of her arms and studied her. "What's wrong?" She blinked, but didn't push him away. "Tell me," he urged, his voice quieter this time.

Her throat bobbed. "A bad feeling, that is all. I came to check on Claire."

He released her and plucked a leaf from her braid, twirling it in his fingers. "Claire isn't here," he said. "You would know that if you hadn't disappeared on—us."

"I do not answer to you, Koldis."

He sighed. "How long will we play this game, Taylynn?"

"For as long as necessary."

"I don't accept that."

"Well, you will—"

"Taylynn." A warning edge crept into his voice.

Her jaw snapped shut. She kept her gaze firmly fixed on his face, but he saw the emotions that passed over her features, one after another. Indecision, confusion, and if he wasn't mistaken, a small measure of vulnerability.

That alone drove him to do something he shouldn't have. He took her hand in his and kissed her palm, keeping his gaze locked on hers. Her eyes went wide. Small sparks of delight danced between his lips and her skin. "Tell me what is wrong," he said again. "Claire went into the forest for a couple of days. Is that what worries you?"

She shook her head. "No, what worries me is that my mother is missing."

"Missing?" He recalled what the sprite attendant had said.

Reyr came to stand beside them, arms crossed. "Haemar said something about the queen being away. That's why he didn't bring me into the city when I arrived."

Taylynn extracted her hand from Koldis's grip, but gently. "Something is wrong," she said, almost baffled.

Unease crept into his gut. "You think Claire is in danger?"

"I don't know," she said after a hesitation. For once, he had zero desire to bark a snide comment about her knowing everything. Especially once her arms wrapped around her stomach. "I don't always know everything," she added, as if reading his mind.

"What can we do to help?"

"If Claire is in danger, then she needs us," Reyr added, a firmness to his voice that brokered no argument. He frowned. "She's not answering my call."

"I wouldn't expect her to," Koldis muttered. He'd already tried to reach out after Reyr had arrived. He'd met nothing but a solid wall. "She often blocks me when she goes into the forest. Supposed to build character or whatever, some nonsense about doing everything on her own, or whatever it is these sprites believe." His words earned a glare from Taylynn.

"All right then," Reyr said. "We go find her."

"It isn't that easy, *Drengr*." Taylynn's ire wasn't directed at Koldis, and didn't that feel good? "You cannot just march through the forest and find her. It's a living, breathing thing, the forest. It changes moment by moment, rearranges itself, moves. A path that should take five minutes could take two days if the forest chooses it to. And believe me, for a drengr, it would certainly choose to. Furthermore, you'd be no help with whatever Claire might be facing."

Reyr opened his mouth—

Koldis put a steadying hand on his shoulder. "She's right. When it comes to the forest, we don't have anything to offer." He turned back to Taylynn. "What can we do?"

"*You* will stay here. If we are lucky, she will come back safely. I will go and search for her, or my mother, or both. See what I find."

Reyr twitched. "If you find her, will you keep my being here a secret?" he asked, like that was even important right now. "I'd like to surprise her myself—in person."

"As you wish. Assuming I find her. Perhaps I'll only find my mother." Something in her voice sounded less than pleased.

"Why do I get the impression that we cannot trust Jade," Reyr said, his brow furrowed.

"Because you can't," Taylynn snapped. She turned, but not before Koldis grabbed her hand again, halting her. She spun around to confront him, but her look of annoyance melted into something softer. She sighed, resigned.

"Promise me you will be careful," he said, kissing her palm again. It felt forbidden, that simple gesture. Intimate beyond belief. But she hadn't stopped him the first time, so he was being bold.

"I'll be careful," she said, her voice low. "Goodbye Koldis, Lord Reyr." She offered Reyr a quick bow of her head then extracted her hand and disappeared through the door.

Silence fell. A beat later, Reyr's throat cleared. Koldis tensed, waiting for the blow to land. And it did. "Care to tell me what that was about?"

He blew out a breath.

When he said nothing, Reyr added, "I find it hard to believe your stellar personality has captured the fancy of Dragonwall's sprite princess."

He barked a laugh and shoved his hands in his pockets, stalking back over to the sitting area, then opting for the dining table, which he leaned against to watch Reyr. "My stellar personality has won over plenty of females in my lifetime." Reyr laughed, which turned into a draconic rumble. But it was clear he wasn't accepting that answer. "All right, all right. Fine. We're mates."

Reyr blinked.

"I'm serious. Believe me, it isn't something I would joke about."

"She touched your scales? A bond was realized?"

He huffed. "Hardly. But she as good as confirmed it. What is more, I feel it in my soul."

Reyr opened and closed his mouth, then shook his head, expression unreadable. Except for his eyes, which were fraught with emotion before he squeezed them tightly shut. A brief moment of anguish transformed Reyr's features. It was only a second or two, then his eyes opened again and his face was blank.

"I am in deep trouble." Koldis said, his voice flat. "Believe me, I know."

"And Claire?"

"She knows. I told her as soon as I discovered it myself."

"And your *other* secret?"

He sighed. "She knows that too. She was angry with me, but it was short lived, dwarfed by the bigger elephant in the room."

"Right. So? What did she say?"

He snorted. "That I shouldn't ignore the bond. That I should find a way to be with Taylynn and still do my duty to the king."

A small smile pulled at Reyr's lips. "Good."

Koldis frowned. "You...agree with her?" He wouldn't have expected it. Reyr was always the honorable one of the bunch.

"I do. And I think if you asked him, our king would allow you to break your bond. I'm almost certain such a thing has happened in history, but kept quiet. Dragonwall's kings would not shout about it in the history texts." Reyr sighed, hesitating. "I don't think King Talon would be happy about it, though, losing you. He would probably convince you to continue serving him as a Shield despite your existing bond with Taylynn. Have you...?"

"We haven't sealed it. No. I'm not sure she even wants to—wants *me*." He clenched his teeth.

"It doesn't appear that she's rejected you," Reyr pointed out. The scene of him kissing her palm, of her not shying away, even when he did it in front of Reyr, came to mind. "Perhaps you are lucky," Reyr added. "A sprite princess who will one day rule, she would choose her kingdom over you, methinks. Which means you would never have to make the difficult choice between Talon and your mate in times of war."

"What makes you so certain?" he found himself asking, even though he knew Reyr was right. "Isabella chose Eymar over her queenship."

"Something tells me Taylynn is *not* Isabella."

He nodded. "She's devoted to her forest. You saw the leaves in her hair."

Reyr laughed. "I wasn't going to say anything but yes, I did. She's wild. Untamed."

"A lot like Claire, really."

Reyr hummed. "I can see the resemblance. They're distant cousins, after all. Are they not?"

"Yes, technically. Who would have guessed? Suppose that means if we do mate, Claire and I will be related."

And wasn't that something?

They fell quiet again. Reyr was pacing slowly around the chamber. "Is there really nothing we can do? This feeling of unease Princess Taylynn has, is it... Should we be concerned about it?"

"Yes, and also yes." Koldis stared at the wall, his eyes going unfocused. "If Claire is in danger, there's little we can do, short of traipsing through the forest and getting lost as we try to find her. Taylynn was right on that account. And if we *do*, or if we have a sprite accompany us, there's not much we can do to help her. Our magic is muted here. Believe me, I've noticed. Claire's? Not so much. She's changed, Reyr. Grown far more powerful. More mature. She's not the girl we found crying over Cyrus last summer."

Reyr's pacing faltered. "That's what we wanted though, is it not?"

"It is exactly what we wanted." Koldis felt a thread of pride course through him, pride at what Claire had accomplished, what she'd overcome, all the obstacles thrown her way. Gods, even when he'd made a idiot of himself, treated her badly, assuming she'd killed Cyrus, she'd overcome that too. Overcome him. Overcome King Talon and his wrath—

"Then perhaps she will be able to get herself out of whatever sticky situation she finds herself in."

Koldis could only nod. Images of the forest's blight flashed through his mind. Sick animals. Dead trees. Vines intent on trapping new victims.

And then, Queen Jade was there. Queen Jade and her growing distrust of Claire. Her growing worry that Claire might take her crown. It could be no coincidence that Jade disappeared after Claire went off into the forest. He only hoped Taylynn would find her in time to see that nothing awful happened.

CHAPTER 32

A TRADE

The Gable Forest

Claire insisted they stop to rest. Queen Jade had taken the lead and set a tireless pace, showing an amount of comfort and ease that could only come from thousands of years in this world. They'd walked for hours, enough that her feet were beginning to ache.

"We need a break."

"Right. Of course, of course," Jade said. "This is as good a place as any, I suppose. But..."

"But *what?*" Her nerves were frayed, otherwise she never would've addressed a monarch in this way. A slight breeze rustled the trees around them. She sighed, leaning into it, letting it cool her temper.

"There's a glade I know of, not far ahead. You would like it, I think. We should rest there." The queen appeared more subdued, at least, as she glanced down at herself and barked an uncharacteristic laugh. "I might even clean up a little. I admit, the forest often gets the better of me when I stay away from the palace too long."

Uncharacteristic. That was a good way to describe not just the queen's laugh but everything. This entire ordeal. Running into her.

321

Seeing her unkempt. Chasing after some cure Claire knew next to nothing about. But, if it meant cleansing the sickness...

"All right, fine," she agreed, sighing. "It's not far, is it?"

"No, no. Just a few minutes. I've been to this area many times." Jade pointed at a boulder formation partially hidden by forest growth. "When I was younger, much younger, I used to sit there with handfuls of berries and listen to the trees. It marks the trail leading to the glade."

"Lead on, then." Her stomach grumbled as she said it. Berries. She wouldn't mind a few when they stopped to rest. Fresh baked bread would be better, though. The craving for cinnamon rolls popped into her head. She almost groaned with hunger. She couldn't wait to eat herself silly when she returned to Kastali Dun. Meat pies. She'd go to the market and purchase a hundred of them—

"Can you hear it?" Jade asked. They hadn't quite walked for a quarter of an hour. But she did. She heard the falling of water. It always sounded so musical, so peaceful.

"I do. We're close?"

"Yes. Just...here." As Jade spoke, the trees thinned and opened to a small, rocky clearing with a quaint spring filled by a five foot waterfall. "We've got these all over the forest," the queen said. "There are several just outside of Esterpine. Have you found any of them yet?"

"No, actually. I haven't." She feasted her eyes, mesmerized. "May I?" She wasn't sure why she felt the need to ask. Perhaps because Jade was queen and this was her domain.

"Of course." The queen also stepped forward, going to the pool and dipping her fingers in. Claire did the same. It was cool. She washed her hands, face, neck, then drank deep. Jade let out a small laugh. "Always so refreshing. Well...take as long as you need, Lady Claire. I think I'll have a private break myself. Excuse me."

The queen padded away, disappearing into the foliage, leaving her there to splash more water on her hands. She sat back on her heels, surveying the sight before her, sighing deeply. This. *This* was why she loved the forest. Hidden gems that looked like they'd come straight out of a storybook. Out of a fantasy painting. She listened to the birds, watched a few swoop down and flutter in the water before taking off again.

She wasn't sure how long she sat like this, taking it all in. Five minutes? Perhaps more? The queen must have needed a long bathroom break. She suppressed a smile. Even queens needed their moments alone.

What would it be like being Talon's queen? Living with a male? Sharing his space? She certainly wasn't going to keep her suite if—when—they mated. She'd have a whole tower floor to herself in the king's tower. Her ladies in waiting would have their own rooms, and Desaree would preside over everything. This time, she smiled. Desaree would make a perfect head lady.

She hated that she didn't know how things were going in Kastali Dun with Des, with everyone, really. She felt as if the world was changing as much as she was, and she had no idea *how* it was changing outside the forest, no idea what direction it was taking. The sprites were so isolated. No wonder Taylynn snuck out as often as she did. Her hand drifted to the pendant around her neck. She zipped it along its chain.

Twigs cracked behind her, faint over the trickle of water. "Your Majesty?" She glanced over her shoulder. Nothing. The back of her neck prickled, but she pushed the unease away.

Where had the queen gone off to, anyway? This time, the hairs on her arms stood on end. She rubbed her hands over them, willing her nerves to calm. There were still birds singing, still insects chirping. This wasn't the silence that signaled impending sickness.

Sighing, she rose to her feet, looking over the beautiful spring once more, over the gentle waterfall. Another crack. Louder this time, just behind her, easily heard over the waterfall. She whirled around—gasped. The heavy branch came at her too quickly, colliding with her head. She had just a moment to cry out before everything went dark.

～

Drip...

Drip...

Drip...

Awareness stirred behind her eyelids.

Drip...

Something—a droplet—struck her forehead. It must be raining; she'd fallen asleep and it was raining. She'd been caught in the forest in the rain before, a couple of times. The forest's floor didn't see much rain. Most of its water came from the creeks and springs —from the magic of the king tree. But when it *did* rain, the canopy soaked up most of the moisture and let the excess droplets fall to the world below.

She groaned. Her mouth was dry and wouldn't close. She tried to swallow but couldn't. Her head throbbed. Had she slipped and fallen? Her eyes were closed. She squeezed them tightly to ease the pain in her head. Then she opened them and blinked. The ache receded. She tried to swallow again. There was something in her mouth, keeping her from closing it.

She blinked again, still not quite ready to move, still dazed. She was on the ground, looking up at the canopy. Like everywhere, leaves blotted the daylight from filtering through. The forest's effervescent glow told her it must be late afternoon.

It was quiet. Too quiet. Sickly quiet.

Drip. Another splash fell on her forehead. She blinked and this time, things came into focus. She gasped, sitting so abruptly her head swam and her temples throbbed, making her sway in place. Fear clawed its way down her spine as the hairs on the back of her neck prickled. The forest canopy wasn't green. A familiar sick, oily black substance dripped from the leaves. Dripped onto her—

"Well, my dear. You're awake, I see."

She whimpered against the gag in her mouth, turning, trying to scramble to her feet at the sound of the voice. *That* voice. She tripped and fell forward, her bound hands shooting out to catch her fall. She cried out and scrambled backwards, away from the red eyes gazing down at her.

Kane.

Her wrists were bound, ankles were bound, keeping her from standing. Another whimper came from deep in her chest. Her back collided with a wall of air. No, not air. A barrier. A cage. A set of glowing rocks were set in a perimeter around her, once black, but now red with molten heat.

"Koldis?" She shouted for him. *"Koldis?!"* Images flashed through her mind straight to him, pictures of where she was, of what was happening. But...there was no answer. He couldn't hear—

"There is no point struggling to break free," Kane said. "My barrier seals you in, keeps your magic confined inside."

Her magic?! Her breathing came in heavy drags, making her chest heave.

She collapsed and slid down the invisible wall. Little white stars popped against her vision. Kane was dressed in dark clothing, but his skin was as pale as a sheet of paper, stretched thin over his bones. He looked...*wrong*. Her heart hammered against her chest, hammered in warning at the sight of him—

"Kane, we had a deal."

Her head whipped around at the sound of Jade's voice. *"You?"* she cried. It came out muffled against her gag. The queen's appearance, standing there facing Kane, took all the fight out of her. Tears blurred her vision. How? *How* was this happening? Jade ignored her entirely, eyes focused on the intruder before them.

"Yes...yes. A deal is a deal. You give me Claire and I heal your sick forest. I haven't reneged."

"Well, then?"

Kane barked a laugh, his skin pulling away from his teeth. "You saw what I did earlier, *Your Majesty*," he mocked. "As I said, I will do that for every patch that requires my attention, but I certainly won't do it right this very second with you standing here. I do not answer to you. Go away, Sprite Queen. Go back to Esterpine and let me handle the blight." He hesitated, putting a hand over his heart. "You have my word."

"Your word," Jade said in a flat tone, eying him. Claire looked between them, blinking back her tears. "Very well." She glanced over at Claire and said, "It's a shame, really. But I must do what is best for my kingdom—for my forest. I am sure you can understand what it means to protect one's home. Sacrifices must be made. Goodbye, Lady Claire." She turned on her heel and disappeared into the undergrowth.

Hot tears leaked down her cheeks, soaking into her gag. She tried to call after Jade. Even if she knew she'd been betrayed, she tried to plead with her to come back, to rethink this.

"Now, now," Kane tsked. "No tears. I'm taking you away from here." He moved around the clearing, examining it. She was only vaguely aware of its sickness. The barrier wasn't just a cage, it protected her from the blight. Everything here was dead. Nothing made a sound. There was nothing *to* make a sound.

Her stomach dropped deeper at the sight of him. Kane. Here in the forest. And here she was, completely and absolutely alone against him.

No, not alone, Cyrus said. *Never alone. But you must get yourself out of this.*

How? She tugged against her bonds, taking advantage of Kane's back, trying to pull at the bindings around her ankles.

Cyrus didn't offer an immediate solution and that scared her even more. *You must find a way.*

She tried to speak but her gag stopped her. She needed a way to stall. Needed time to think. She wanted answers.

She climbed to her feet as best she could. Kane noticed her movements and stepped closer to the barrier where he regarded her silently, then he stepped right through it as if it were nothing. "Here, let me help you." He reached out and pulled her gag away, then walked right out of the barrier again. She blinked, looking between him and the glowing stones. She hesitated, then sprang forward, trying to do the same thing. Her body collided with the wall and it flung her backwards.

Kane laughed. "I don't think it works like that, my dear. But go ahead and keep trying. Now, was there something you wanted to say to me before we get going?" He hesitated, as if thoughtful. "I think you will like Shadowkeep. Appreciate its rugged beauty."

"You disgust me," she spat. She needed her magic, needed to figure out what she could use to get away from here, how she could break the barrier. She tried kicking the stones, tried throwing her body against the invisible wall, she even tried singing to call wind, fire, water, vines, anything and everything that she'd learned studying under Pelwynn, but her magic was indeed useless outside the cage.

Kane just stood there. Watching. Amused.

At last, she collapsed, exhausted from her efforts, exhausted from lack of food, mostly. Jade had waited until she'd gone nearly a day without food before pouncing. Waited for her to be weak. Waited for the opportune moment to sell her to Kane. All for what? To heal the forest?

Her mind raced over their previous interactions. Jade had said she'd found a solution—now she understood. *She* was the solution.

"Why is the forest sick?" She stalled.

Kane turned away and pulled something from his pocket. A vial. He uncorked it, said a few quiet words, and splashed its contents against a nearby tree.

She sagged. At least he was going to heal the forest like he'd agreed. At least, even if he took her away, there was that. Perhaps Jade was right, maybe selling her out to Kane was a sacrifice worthwhile in Jade's eyes. The queen wanted to do what was best for her kingdom. Even she could understand that.

Where the liquid touched the tree, a sheet appeared. It created a wall of shimmering substance that grew. Her eyes narrowed. The forest didn't change. The blackness didn't recede. Nothing was healed. Beyond the sheet, she saw a dimly lit rocky room. A cave.

"What is that?" she whispered, horrified. A vague image rested in her memories. She'd seen this before.

"It's a portal, of course." Kane stood before it, then ran his fingers through the sheet. Some of the liquid splashed to the ground.

She stared at it, eyes wide. A realization hit her square in the chest. "That's how you got into the forest the first time, when you attacked Cyrus."

"Oh, yes."

All this time! All this time she thought she'd be safe here and she'd overlooked that simple fact about Cyrus. "The sickness." She swallowed against her dry throat. "The sickness lets you in."

"More or less. I can only transport myself to patches like this, but once I'm inside a patch..." He spread his arms wide, leaving the rest unsaid. He could go where he pleased once he was here. "Now, I don't have all day. Shall we?" He stepped forward, eying her, as if perhaps trying to determine what might be the best way to move her.

She couldn't allow it. She couldn't!!

He had tried to kidnap her before. Tried and failed. She would not give in without a fight. She owed it to everyone who was counting on her. She owed it to Talon. Even if she was the one to defeat Kane, she certainly wasn't ready to do so now. She didn't even possess Isabella's staff.

"Why not kill me?" she said.

He tutted. "Why should I, when I can use you? Jade was ignorant. But not entirely ignorant. She understood your importance—your importance to *me*, anyway. Though, I must say, she vastly underestimated my honor." He snorted, finding this funny. "She thinks I can heal the forest. Unbelievable, isn't it?"

"You...you can't?" she said as the realization sank in.

"I can't. I know—I know." He clicked his tongue. "I tricked her, you see. Showed her what she wanted to see. I healed a small portion—that was easy enough. But where one place is healed, another will grow sick." He shrugged. "I made her some vague promises. But mostly, I lied. I'm quite good at lying." He walked around the stone barrier, examining it.

Of course he was good at lying.

"Then...you aren't the one who created the sickness?" Despite her rising panic, she couldn't help but ask.

"Hah! Me? I have better things to do. A certain drengr king to kill. Two more dragonstones to obtain. Wouldn't happen to know where those are, would you? After you stole them from me?" He hesitated a beat, then added, "No, Jade created the sickness all on her own, I assume. All by herself. The best part is, I do not think she realizes it's her fault. Imagine that."

"Oh, I can imagine," she said, bitterness coating her voice.

"Yes, certainly. I'm sure you've heard the rumors about her. I have. A queen whose time is long past. A queen who no longer hears the whisperings of her precious tree. A queen past her prime. Selfish. Power hungry. Greedy—even if she doesn't see things that way. I must say, I cannot fault her. I can even...relate to her. I'd hold fast my power, too." He hesitated, reaching out and plucking a dead leaf from a nearby branch. "I merely saw this for the opportunity it was, and here we are."

"You will never win," she said, sneering. "You will never beat Talon. You are *nothing*."

He rounded on her, anger transforming his features to downright frightening. She flinched, despite her protective barrier. "Now *that* wasn't very nice. I can see that breaking you will be difficult. But not impossible." He pointed at her, muttering something too quiet to hear.

And then it hit her—pain. Her body erupted with it and she screamed. It was unlike anything she'd ever felt, ripping through her. Worse than the vodar poison, so much worse. She collapsed to her hands and knees, gasping, trying to breathe. Her vision went dark at the edges.

"Lucky for me, this barrier doesn't keep *my* magic out," he drawled, but she barely heard him.

Another wave of agony tore through her, searing across her skin, straight into her bones. She screamed, pulling herself into a ball as the world disappeared, leaving nothing behind but the pain. She tried to push it down, but in those moments, it became her. Pure, unadulterated torture.

Something wet trickled from her nose. Blood.

Another wave followed, and another, blasting heat along her nerve endings until she was sobbing, arms pulled tightly around her legs. Sobbing and shaking.

I am here. Cyrus was a faint whisper in her mind.

"There now. There is no need to be disrespectful, hmm?" His words were far away. "Are you ready to apologize?"

"What?" she rasped.

"Apologize. Beg for my forgiveness." The pain had stopped, but it left echoes behind all over her body. "Well?"

"I have nothing to apologize for," she bit out.

"No? Very well then."

She screamed as another wave ripped through her, screamed and screamed until it stopped.

"And now? Are you ready to apologize *now*? To beg me to stop?" She could barely hear him over her sobbing. "Well?"

No. She...she couldn't. Wouldn't. She wouldn't give in. Wouldn't be reduced to begging.

He sighed. "I really don't have all day. But...well. A lesson is a lesson."

The onslaught picked up where it left off. She screamed until her voice was hoarse, until it even hurt to scream. And then she broke. A few words. That's all it would take for this to stop. So she said them. "I... I'm sorry. I'm sorry. Please. Please!" She spoke between quiet whimpers, unable to see through the blur of tears and the darkness that had overtaken her vision.

"There now." Everything melted away. Blissful, painless, nothingness. As if it had never happened. "Good girl." Kane stepped through the barrier. She heard his footsteps crunching the blackened leaves beside her, but she couldn't bring herself to move. He knelt and ran his hand down her cheek, wiping away her tears. The caress made her sick, twisting her stomach. But she couldn't seem to move, couldn't pull herself away after all that.

Then his fingers were in her hair, gripping tightly. Pain spread across her scalp as he lifted her head and forcefully turned her to look at him. "You have no idea what you've done," he hissed, his voice close to her ear. So close that she could feel his breath tickle her skin. She whimpered. "No idea the lengths I've gone to fix everything after your interference. I should peel the skin from your bones, flay you alive." He let out a heavy sigh. "Luckily for you, keeping you whole works better in my favor. Remember that today

I have been merciful." He released her and stood. His footsteps receded.

"Now, we must be going. We can certainly explore this again once we're home. I'll show you my library of poisons. I think you'll like that. And the spiders. It's a shame about the bats, really, but they will have their uses later."

She sniffed, trying to breathe. It was the only sound she managed. She couldn't speak. Couldn't think. Couldn't drag in enough air. *"Koldis, please!"* She knew he wouldn't hear her, and yet she couldn't help it.

"Get up."

She didn't move.

"I said—" A familiar wave of pain tore through her, ripping a fresh scream from her throat. She cried out for Talon this time, for each shield, knowing none of them would hear her. "—*get up!*" And then the pain vanished. But she knew that if she didn't stand up, he'd do it again. So she began to move, forcing herself even though her body trembled. Each motion was painfully slow. Once she was on her knees, she looked up at him, barely visible through her tearstained eyes.

"There now. That wasn't so hard, was it?" He made another circuit around the circle.

She had to do something. If she didn't fight with everything here and now, once he moved her to Shadowkeep, there would be no hope of ever escaping. No hope of getting out of his fortress alive.

"I'm going to move—" *Crack.* The sound of a snapping branch stopped him—made him hesitate. She hastily wiped her eyes and looked around. She'd heard it too.

Nothing moved.

Kane nodded, satisfied. "No more time to delay. Let's go." He bent to pick up one of the stones—

The world around her exploded into motion. Streaks of white crashed through the dead clearing. Streaks of...unicorns? A relieved sob fell from her chest. One charged straight for Kane, his horn lowered, flinging him backwards. He still held the burning red stone in his hand. She moved without thinking, barreling straight through the broken barrier.

Kane was fast, too.

He shouted a command and sent a spear of blackness right into the charging unicorn. A spear of death. The beautiful creature let out a wail, a scream so brutal, she stumbled and fell to her knees. His white body twisted and crashed to the ground, eyes glassing over in an instant. She cried out, crawling to his side.

He was dead.

"You *monster*!" she screamed, layering every ounce of hate she possessed into her voice. Fresh tears carved paths down her cheeks. The other two unicorns regrouped. She recognized them from before. They scattered, dodging the magic Kane threw at them.

"No," she whispered, climbing to her feet, stepping over the vines coming up around them. With good creatures in its midst, the blight sought to attack, to infect. It didn't touch Kane, but it came straight for the rest of them. For her.

"Go," she screamed at them, unable to bear another sacrifice. Vines sprang up, ensnaring their hooves. She acted on instinct, using what she'd learned from Pelwynn. With a flash of her arm and the focus of her mind, she sent tendrils of air to wrap around the vines and free the unicorns, pushing them to safety. She sent them far from the blight. They neighed in protest, but she wouldn't dare risk them.

"That was rather selfless. Also rather stupid," Kane said, circling her, ready to pounce. More vines threw themselves at her, wrapping around her ankles. Kane used the moment of distraction, his hands flashing through the air, an incant in his voice. She threw up a barrier of air against the black smoke that threatened to tangle around her. He growled, cutting through her air and throwing himself forward to grab her, to drag her through the watery sheet. She had drifted *perilously* close to it. She broke free of the vines right as his hand closed around her wrist. Right as the world disappeared into a flash of white.

CHAPTER 33

FROM STONE TO SCALE

The Gable Forest

Claire felt Kane's grasp around her wrist, biting into her skin, but she could see nothing. Her vision was seared by intense, white light, brighter than sunlight. A voice spoke. One that had her crying with relief.

The bright glare from Taylynn's magic dissipated, revealing the sprite princess in the middle of the clearing, her arms moving, wind ripping around her sending her hair wild, drawing dead leaves to her like a furious tornado.

Kane released Claire and stumbled back, cursing. He muttered incants as Taylynn moved against him, snakes of dark smoky magic curling around him as they battled.

"Protect us!" Taylynn shouted, keeping her focus on Kane.

There was no time to question it. She jumped into action, taking over to keep the torrent of air around them like a barrier. Taylynn's voice lifted over Kane's chanting. A nearby tree, blackened and dying, cracked. The sprite princess sent it straight for Kane. He lifted his arm and spoke a few words, blocking the attack. Taylynn moved faster, pulling more dead debris toward Kane, sending more magic to push him back. Kane had the same idea in mind, sometimes redirecting the path of flying objects towards them. It took all Claire's focus and concentration to keep the protective barrier of air roaring around them.

Over the roar, she could just make out Taylynn's shout, "Claire! We must get him through the portal, out of the forest!"

The portal. Right. She had to get him through the wall of water and destroy it.

Her barrier faltered for a moment.

"Stay focused!" Taylynn cried.

She dodged a stray wisp of Kane's magic. It ricocheted around the clearing. Heart thundering in her chest, she pulled more air, wrapping it around them. She didn't allow herself to think about all the pain Kane had caused her, about how she badly wanted to destroy him here and now. She especially didn't let herself think about what he had done to Cyrus.

You are not ready to take him on, Cyrus said, reading her deepest thoughts.

She did as Taylynn commanded. She stayed focused. Taking a deep breath, she kept the blossom at the back of her mind, then she did something she'd never done before. She partitioned the fore-front of her mind, leaving part of it focused on air's element. But only a segment of it. Then she focused on earth, summoning it.

But...

In a dead place like this, earth wouldn't answer. And yet, she felt a stirring, far, far away, whispering of life. Felt it respond to her.

She called up what she wanted, called up vines, growing them far from the clearing and bidding them come and help, to protect them. The words of her song formed in her mind without thought. Lifting her voice, she ensured that the forest would hear her. She flexed her hands on instinct, reaching, telling the vines exactly what she wanted. They obeyed willingly, eager to answer her call, to please. They would not refuse Isabella's heir—never.

Deep green appeared—a direct opposite to the blackened deadness around them. Creepers flung themselves into the blighted area behind Kane. They wrapped around him, around his ankles and then his legs before he noticed. They tugged. He gave a shout of surprise. The vines flung him, sending him backwards.

"Good!" Taylynn shouted. "Good!"

Gulping in breaths of air, she watched wide-eyed as Kane flew straight for the wall of water. Then he was through it, landing on the floor of his cave in a sprawled heap. He jumped to his feet, but not fast enough. Taylynn slashed her hand through the air, freezing the water into place. The ice shattered, splitting the silence with a resounding crack so loud it rang in her ears. Thousands of glittering fragments rained down onto the dead forest floor, turning to droplets once more, soaking into the blackened earth.

Silence returned. Claire blinked. Blinked again. Had they just...?

Exhausted, she put her hands on her knees, gulping in breaths of air. From the corner of her eye, the white shape of the dead unicorn lay unmoving. She wanted to go to him, to cry over his body. He'd sacrificed himself to save her when she couldn't save herself. Deep down, she couldn't help but wonder if his sacrifice had been worth her life—

The blighted forest wasn't done with them yet. A grating, metallic screech broke the silence. The forest rose up around them, sending an angry wail into the air. From everywhere, dead creepers flung outwards. Taylynn shouted something and waved her arm. "Come!" she screamed, pulling her away, nearly dragging her.

"But the unicorn," she shouted, trying to go to him. She couldn't bear the thought of giving his dead body over to the blight.

"We must leave him!"

A sob broke free of her chest, but she complied. She stumbled, trembling uncontrollably. Taylynn was all that kept her upright as they sprinted out of the blighted area, fleeing. They ran until they were surrounded by green again. Taylynn released her arm and she fell to her hands and knees, gasping, crying, too shocked to do anything else.

"We are safe, for now," Taylynn said, breathing hard. A comforting hand rubbed circles on her back. "Breathe, Claire. Deep breaths. There now."

In these few moments of quiet, everything came crashing down. She began sobbing in earnest. Her adrenaline dissipated, making her shoulders sag. "How...how did you...? Your mother. She—"

"Hush. Just breathe."

"I need to—" She tried to get up. Jade was out there somewhere, working her way back to Esterpine, back to where—

"Koldis! I have to—"

"No. Not yet." Taylynn's firm voice was a sharp command. "Do not tell Koldis what happened here. Not yet. That damned drengr will come charging straight into the forest, and it's not safe for him right now. If you must say anything, tell him I found you and that all is well."

She opened her mind. *"Koldis?"*

"Gods, Claire! There you are. What's wrong?"

"Nothing...nothing's wrong." It was one of the most difficult lies she'd ever told. *"Taylynn found me. I'm...I'm all right."*

"As long as you are safe."

"All is well," she said, hating the words.

"We cannot linger here," Taylynn said. Her voice felt far away, pulling her from the depths of her mind. "There is another matter that has come to my attention. Another thing that must be done. I will need your help. After that, we can address the crimes of my mother."

"You...you know?"

"I have surmised enough, but I'm sure you can fill in the missing details. When I found her absent from Esterpine, I knew something was wrong. I put the pieces together with a little help from the king tree."

"She betrayed me. Sold me to Kane—"

"I thought as much." Taylynn's lips pressed into a thin line.

"It was her all along. The sick forest. Her fault. Kane said it's because she's greedy, she won't step down."

Taylynn hugged herself, wrapping her arms around her stomach. Claire faltered, watching the transformation. The princess didn't look strong and powerful anymore. She looked like a girl whose mother had done something awful, whose faith in a woman who had once meant the world to her had been broken.

"I…I'm so sorry, Taylynn." Claire went to her then, pushing back her own tears to offer comfort. She felt Taylynn's sigh. "I'm so, so sorry." She wrapped her arms around the sprite princess, holding her close.

A dam broke.

Taylynn's body shook with silent sobs. Despite their troubled relationship fraught with hardships, despite what the queen had done, she was still Taylynn's mother. That betrayal would cut the princess deepest.

"What do we do?" she whispered, hiccuping.

"That is for the tree to decide," Taylynn managed between breaths.

When Taylynn calmed down, she sat down on the forest floor. The sprite princess joined her, shoulders sagging, eyes far away. They sat in silence for a long while. She tried to process what had happened, to catch her breath, to come to terms with everything.

"It's exhausting, sometimes," Taylynn said, letting out a bitter laugh. "All the time, actually. I understand why Isabella chose Eymar over this." She ran her hands through her hair, stopping at her braid, pulling out a few leaves and twigs. "I understand…" She heaved a sigh.

Claire swallowed. "Would you choose Koldis, if you could? If you weren't destined to rule here?"

"You have as much right to rule here as I do."

"Perhaps. But you didn't answer my question."

Taylynn picked at her sleeve. "I don't know," she whispered at last. "I'd like to know him better, at least. He seems…good." Taylynn lifted her eyes, a question written in them.

Claire held her gaze. "He is, unbelievably so. You are lucky to call him your mate."

Taylynn's throat bobbed. "It would hurt too much in the end, I think."

"Maybe." Claire shrugged. "But maybe that's what makes it worth it."

Taylynn didn't answer.

∼

Hours later after they'd traversed a wide swath of forest, Taylynn called up food for them and they took a much needed break. Her tears had long since dried, followed by numbness replacing the shock of what had happened. They'd been following a path that led them north. Taylynn hadn't given her much information. Did she ever? Some business for the king tree, but beyond that? Who knew.

She wanted to return to Esterpine. Wanted to see that Koldis was okay, that her pairs were safe. But, she also feared confronting Jade in light of what had happened.

Taylynn brushed her hair from her face and said, "We are leaving the forest, going north. We will be gone from Esterpine for...perhaps a week." Her words confirmed a sinking suspicion. "You may tell Koldis if you wish, but he does not need to know the details. Nothing beyond the duration of your absence."

She gave Taylynn her best *are-you-kidding-me?* look. Perhaps she had waited to tell her because she was sure Claire would protest, sure she'd turn straight around for Esterpine. But they'd already spent too long going in the opposite direction. And...was there much choice in the matter?

She reached out to Koldis and relayed what she could.

"What has she gotten you into now?" came his immediate response.

"I cannot say. You know Taylynn. But, I think this is important," she said, hoping he wouldn't talk her out of it.

"Very well. Be careful, my queen," came his response.

They set off again.

Taylynn assured her that the forest would speed their journey along. This was how she found herself at Riltar Outpost the following day, harnessing unicorns with Taylynn. The sprites loaded their saddlebags with provisions, equipped them with warm parkas, scarves, gloves, hats, and everything else they'd need. Then they were racing north.

She laughed the moment they were out from the cover of the trees. The world was white, heaped with mounds of snow. A magical winter wonderland. The cold that met them was a slap in the face.

Something in the form of another memory flashed through her mind, further solidifying her suspicions, but Taylynn was already far enough in front of her, racing into the growing darkness of evening. Too far for her to call out. Their winter gear was enchanted. She'd been in cold temperatures plenty; it snowed in Indiana, after all. She should have been shivering with cold after an hour or two, but she remained toasty, as if she sat beside the fire.

The unicorns traveled at an impossible pace. The landscape slid by in a blur. When they finally stopped to rest in the middle of the night, it was only to relieve themselves and have a quick bite from the provisions they'd been provided. "Unicorns can travel distances in hours that would take horses days," Taylynn explained. "Especially these." As she spoke, she rubbed the neck of her steed, Belanor. Claire's was Akkar, and he was such a hand-some boy. "Are you ready to continue?" Taylynn asked.

"That depends. Are you going to tell me where we're going?"

The sprite princess hesitated. "We are going to wake a thing that has not been awake for an age."

Her stomach swooped. "The marble dragon. I saw it in my vision—when I had the drink."

Taylynn's back was to her as she put her hands on her unicorn's harness, readying to mount. "I had wondered," was all she said before climbing up. And then they were off.

Claire did not sleep, not even in the saddle. They were going too fast. During one of their short breaks, Taylynn explained that if she fell off of a unicorn at these speeds, by the time she stood up, the unicorn would be miles away. Too far to cry out. They couldn't waste time backtracking or taking risks like that when she needed so badly to return and confront Jade.

They set a relentless pace as the morning took them deep into Kengr's territory. The path they cleaved through the fresh, untouched powder was forged by Taylynn, who used magic to make it easier for the unicorns to travel.

Even though she'd been here during late summer, it might as well have been a completely different place. Nothing was recognizable. Granted, she'd spent most of her time in the sky, looking down on the landscape from above. But Talon's shields had made camp in a few places along the way. Her mind went back to that time, when everything was so uncertain, when Jovari, Koldis, and Reyr mistrusted her. She thought of the camp they'd made the night when she'd been injured and it was Koldis's healing magic that kept her alive. The scar on her leg gave a twinge at the thought.

It was a little past midday when Taylynn drew them to a halt and they dismounted. The world was so glaringly white, so uniform and pristine, it was a wonder Taylynn managed to sort out their bearings. Wordlessly, Taylynn left the unicorns and beckoned her to follow, trudging ahead, blowing snow out of their path. The air was cold, each breath a frozen inhale. She kept her enchanted scarf up around her mouth and nose. Every exhale was a puff of condensation.

Taylynn stopped.

Claire's eyes narrowed. It was almost impossible to discern against the white landscape. The marble dragon. It looked exactly as she remembered it, except now it had piles of snow atop it.

"He shouldn't be impossible to wake," Taylynn said. Claire hesitated, blinking. It was strange, those words, hearing them for a second time. "Come, let us go to him."

A strangled laugh burst from her chest. Strange indeed.

She followed after Taylynn until they reached the beast. "You know, the last time I touched it, it tried to kill me."

"You shouldn't need to this time, so you need not worry." Taylynn made a circuit around the dragon.

"Now that we're here, can I ask *why*? Why do you want to do this? Why do you want to wake up a wild dragon when we've been fighting a war against them? When they've captured Fort Squall and hold the city?"

"Pale as snow his scales do gleam," Taylynn said to herself, her voice low. "But not forever." She exhaled through her nose. "Only blood can break these chains."

"You're not making any sense," Claire muttered, frowning. "You *never* make any sense."

Taylynn turned to her. "It is not what *I* want, Lady Claire—waking a dragon. Fright has spent an age paying for his crimes. Do you think he would behave differently if given a second chance?"

"You...you want him to fight for us?"

Taylynn shrugged. "Again, it's not what I want. But...yes. He was betrayed by the Ice Clan." The princess hesitated. "Soon, you will learn that my wants are immaterial. I merely—"

"Follow orders. I know."   Claire looked over Fright's body, recalled what had happened the last time she'd been here. "Surely he will be insane. All that time, trapped in stone."

"Aren't we all?" Taylynn shot her a grin. "Even just a little bit?" Claire snorted. "Well, anyway, we shall see. It would be a great feat, reversing Isabella's magic. But only blood can break these chains."

"So...you want to bleed on him?"

"Not *him*, Lady Claire. And not me. Blood—your blood. The blood of Isabella's direct line. I share her family's blood too, but not directly. *You* will wake him. And you will find no help from me on the matter."

Claire opened her mouth—

"Not because I wish to make things harder for you, but because I truly have no idea what magic will reverse this spell."

Claire hesitated. "And the king tree really wants this?"

"It was implied."

Claire walked around the beast, taking him in. She had to move snow out of her way to get anywhere. When she came full circuit, she frowned. "Surely you have some ideas?"

Taylynn sighed. "A few, I suppose. He was turned inert for his crimes, but his is a form from whence his ancestors originated. I believe that played a role in Isabella's magic. For example, turning a horse or a bear to stone would be much harder, because that is not the substance of those creatures."

"I see. And what if we wake him and he goes on a rampage? What if he's not repentant?"

"Well, that's why you will ask him before you sing your final words. But, I also have another idea for that." She walked forward and placed her hand over Fright's scales, right where his neck met his chest. "I think his heart might rest here? Deep, deep beneath." She closed her eyes and began humming.

Claire watched, wide-eyed as the stone around Taylynn's palm rippled. It spit out a small smooth chunk. She sucked in a breath as the area fell still again, as if the stone had never moved. "A...a dragonstone?"

"Not like those you are thinking of. This one will not have the power to work with the others—I don't believe. But it still has power. You can feel it humming. I think I might use it to control him, if necessary."

"I am not sure I follow."

Taylynn pocketed it, cleared some snow from the ground, rooted around in the dirt for a moment, and produced a rock dug from muddy soil. With her magic, she split the rock in two and handed Claire one half. "Watch." Humming, with no need to form words, Taylynn squeezed her half and it exploded into dust and rubble.

Claire gasped as the half in her hand mimicked the exact behavior.

"There," Taylynn said. "That is what I will do if he goes back on his word." She emptied the dust from her gloved palm and patted her pocket.

"Assuming he agrees to be a good boy in the first place," Claire muttered. She wouldn't admit she was impressed. Taylynn looked far too smug for that. It almost made her laugh.

Koldis and Taylynn were a perfect match.

"Now, have I answered enough of your questions?"

"Hardly. But let me see what I can do." She stepped forward and lifted her gloved hands, running them over Fright's body without actually touching him. She closed her eyes and thought about what she wanted to do. The short of it was, she would bring him back to life. It wasn't about creating new life, like the Asarlaí had done when they first made dragons. This one wasn't a shell. It already had a mind and soul dwelling within the stone.

In her mind, a flashback from her memories came to life. Fright was watching her, his eyes open, demanding she free him from his prison. "I am not Isabella," she whispered aloud, wondering if he would hear her despite her lack of touch. Then she stepped back and got to work.

First she began with her focus and mental intention, partitioning her mind with her blossom at the back. Her voice started deep in her chest, humming to form a tune. Then she began her song. The words came to her without thought, a natural extension of her desires, flowing forth on the tide of her voice.

> "Eskh kehv eah slahke, mi naqah aya astah."
> "Altah ana khir, yaella ana maha."
> "Eskh kehv eah slahke, mi naqah aya astah."
> "Mih mudah utah sah, aahma utah maruah utah jad."
> "Eskh kehv eah slahke, mi naqah aya astah."

THERE WASN'T QUITE a direct translation. But roughly, she said:

> *From stone to scale, I bid you wake.*
> *Undo the last, reverse the past.*
> *From stone to scale, I bid you wake.*
> *My blood is true, what's old is new.*
> *From stone to scale, I bid you wake.*

As she repeated the words, she felt an awareness stretching out towards her, awakening from slumber. She did not yelp or interrupt her song when she heard him, though she was tempted to. *"Will you free me?"* came his voice in her mind. Accompanying it was the force of his power. It took everything not to quake under his scrutiny. Beside her, a hand slipped into hers, squeezing.

"Will you give me your loyalty?" she returned. *"Will you fight for us?"*

"Will I have my revenge?"

"I cannot promise such."

There was a hesitation, and then—

"Why should I bend to your will?" His words were a heavy blow, breaking over her like an icy wind, but her mind did not falter. The hand in hers didn't let go. She pushed back, keeping her voice steady, letting the sound of her words rise higher. Despite the cold around her, sweat beaded upon her forehead.

"Any life is better than one of stone, Dragon."

"So it is," he huffed at last, submitting. The tidal force he brought ebbed and disappeared. *"Wake me, and I am yours."*

"Very well. I will hold you to your word."

There was no need to tell him about the fragment of stone missing from his body. No need to force him into submission. He would submit of his own will, or die for it.

She repeated the words of her song again, adding an additional stanza that encompassed Fright's agreement to serve, bundling his loyalty into his life force. The stone of his body rippled, turning to liquid. Eyelids opened, revealing a piercing blue gaze, a gaze that spoke of storms and power. Fright had once belonged to the Storm Clan, after all.

She brought her words to a close, tying off her song with the hum of her voice, transitioning it to a low creep, then ending it entirely. In response, Fright lifted his body from the ground, stretching his forearms and legs, and shook like a dog, freeing himself of snow. The movements were so unexpected that a laugh burst from her chest. He reminded her so much of an excited puppy, she couldn't help it. But she would not be fooled, this beast was nothing like a puppy, and had once done terrible things. Now he would be given the opportunity to atone.

"Welcome to the land of the living," came Taylynn's voice beside her.

She was shaking and only noticed when Taylynn removed her steadying hand. She trembled with mixed emotion, exhaustion, disbelief.

"I am glad to be alive," came the response, given to both her and Taylynn. *"But what would truly make me happy is to fly. Where might we go first? Preferably somewhere where I might rip my enemies to shreds. I long to use my claws, my teeth. Beyond that, I am at your service."*

Taylynn sighed and said aloud, "There will be no shredding enemies just yet. But you may fly, if you wish. Go, but don't go far. We travel south. See if you can keep up with our unicorns. They are quite fast."

"A challenge? I accept." With that, he launched into the sky, sending snow everywhere. From behind them, the unicorns snickered.

She watched him rise, higher, higher, higher, watched him circle them far above.

Taylynn turned to her. "What you just did, Claire..." The princess hesitated. "Well done. You should be proud of how far you have come."

Claire swallowed. "I...thank you."

"I believe there is another task that awaits you in the forest. A task I cannot help you with. It is time for you to seek out the king tree. You are ready."

Claire blinked. "What about you?"

"I have business of my own, with Fright. You and I will go south together, return the unicorns to the outpost. Then Fright and I will take a short trip. If all goes well, I will meet you back in Esterpine."

"And...your mother?" she asked. "I cannot just return and act like she did nothing wrong. She betrayed me, betrayed *us*. She—"

"You must deal with Jade as you see fit. I believe the king tree will have an opinion on the matter. One I'd rather not be around to hear—or see." She shook her head. "No, it is good that I must go away for a while. The time has come, and I do not think I can be there to witness it. Come now, let us return."

Unease crept into the pit of Claire's stomach, but she was too exhausted to fight it. Far above, Fright continued to circle, bellowing with delight. What must it be like, to live as stone for an age? To finally have the freedom to stretch one's wings?

Meekly, she followed Taylynn to their unicorns, mounted, and they set off into the snow. Deep down, she knew exactly what needed to be done about Jade, exactly what the tree would have her do, and she didn't look forward to it. So instead, she rested her face against Akkar's neck, nuzzling him, bracing herself for the inevitable. Bracing herself for what was to come.

CHAPTER 34
THE KING TREE

The Gable Forest

Claire found it harder than expected to bid Akkar goodbye. She rubbed his nose, fed him an apple, rubbed his nose some more, cooed at him, told him what a good boy he'd been. He snorted at the last part, humoring her need to baby him. Then he plodded over to the food trough set out by the sprites at the outpost.

She and Taylynn returned their winter weather gear, retreating to the shelter of the trees. The heavy drifts of snow stopped and green grass appeared. Fright remained out of sight in the sky. Taylynn had given him instructions to fly a little farther east along the tree line where she would meet him shortly.

"Remember," Taylynn said, adjusting Claire's braid and fussing over her, "your search for the tree will depend on your desire to find it."

Taylynn had already walked her through much of this. "What if it doesn't think I'm ready?"

"My answer is still the same. You are ready. Now, I will see you in Esterpine. Do not leave the forest until you and I have had another chance to talk."

She frowned. "Why would I—?

"Promise me, Claire."

"All right, I promise I will wait." She had no intention of running off just yet anyway. She didn't even have the staff. But something in the way Taylynn said it left her wondering what her visit with the tree might bring. She was beyond ready to return to Talon.

It was with a sigh of resignation that she bid Taylynn goodbye. They parted ways. She went south, following a path the forest set for her. As instructed, she kept her desires at the forefront of her mind. "When you are ready," she whispered to the tree, "I am here."

The hours stretched on. She wasn't empty-handed. She'd taken a small pack with provisions from the outpost. It wasn't as if she were on a magical quest anymore—not at this point.

She thought back over everything. It was no small feat, her *Ordeal* with a capital O, because it had been significant and she had grown a great deal through it. Changed a great deal. Not only was she hardened, there were fresh marks to show for both her fight against Kane and waking Fright. She hadn't removed her clothes, hadn't wanted to look at them just yet. But she was certain the markings would be noticeable.

For the first time in days, she allowed herself to think—to *really* think—of what Queen Jade had done. Being back in the forest, being away from Taylynn brought the queen's betrayal to the forefront. To her, sprites had always been pure beings, faultless, beautiful, ethereal, good. Jade had proven something to her. Something crucial. Even the most seemingly innocent person could be evil. And yet, Jade's intentions had been awful but understandable.

She frowned. Once she was Talon's queen, what lengths would she go to to save her kingdom? What would she do if the drengr were threatened and she had few options left? Her fists clenched at the thought. But the answer came just as easily. She squared her shoulders. Never—she would *never* betray an innocent for the sake of saving her people. It wasn't just the cost of life, it was the weight that would bear down upon her conscience. How could she live with herself? How did Jade expect to live with herself after handing Claire over to someone like Kane?

In a way, it was an act of war. Even if Jade didn't know Claire was Dragonwall's future queen, she was under Talon's protection. Kane was *Enemy Number One*. Jade had handed her over, knowing full well what Kane was and how he would use her, hurt her, possibly even kill her.

So...how was she to handle this treason? What was she to do?

It had crossed her mind plenty while Kane stood there torturning her, subjecting her to pain so great she'd wanted to die. It was during those moments her thoughts turned dark. Killing Jade for her betrayal, making her suffer, it felt satisfying while she screamed and sobbed.

But could she? Could she knowingly take a life? Even when that person was guilty beyond a doubt? Even if what they'd done was terrible?

She thought back to those first few weeks in Kastali Dun, when she'd given Talon two names. Two names that brought two deaths. Two names that belonged to traitors. Those deaths—she'd felt responsible for them. While she hadn't been the executioner swinging the axe, she *had* brought about their justice.

Could she do it again? Moreover, could she be the one to mete out that justice? Could she be judge and executioner? If she was the one to demand Jade's death, she ought to be the one to swing the sword. But...

Perhaps there was another way.

"There is always another way."

The stray thought brought her to a staggering halt. The forest had changed around her and she'd barely noticed. A vast awareness pressed in on her, sending chills down her spine. It was near. She took a few steps forward and pushed through vines that blocked the dirt path she'd been following. The pool she remembered from the drink of enlightenment materialized before her, framed in a spacious clearing. Opposite it, giant roots snaked into the ground at the base of a massive tree. Her head fell back to take it in. From its branches hung beautiful star shaped leaves and ripe round golden fruit.

"The fruit of life," it told her, reading the question in her mind. *"For all those who wish to travel beyond. For the weary."*

Final death. She remembered the shepherd ferrying a spriten soul through the forest. The desire to taste the fruit's flesh immediately evaporated. She swallowed, looking around. Blinking. The sight before her didn't disappear.

"So you have found me at last. Very few who do not wish to pass from this life ever do."

"Only the sprites' rightful queen, right?" she voiced aloud.

"Yes."

"But I do not wish to be queen of the forest."

"That is not a decision you are in a position to make. Not yet. But you will be, very soon."

Chills raced down her spine. "Queen Jade?" she couldn't help but ask as she gazed at the massive trunk before her.

"Yes. She has become a problem. When Isabella betrayed me—"

"Isabella betrayed you?" she asked in disbelief. She knew Isabella had been disgraced, exiled from the forest, from her people. But she always thought it was because of her choice to become Eymar's mate and forsake her crown.

There was a long silence. *"Yes. Isabella went against my will in a most destructive way."*

"How? Creating the drengr?"

"No. That was a task I charged her with. It became apparent that the drengr would bring balance to a race that was created from twisted magic. No, Isabella took the magical knowledge I gave her then twisted it to ensure their extinction." Claire's lips formed into an *oh*. *"Yes, you can imagine my anger. My...disappointment."*

"But...without the drengr, without the dragons, wouldn't the world go back to the way it was before the asarlaí?" It was an innocent enough question. After all, awakening the dragons was what sent the world spiraling out of balance in the first place.

"Yes, but at the cost of many innocent lives. To bring a race to extinction is to eliminate all those potential bright lights that might have

existed in the future. Going backwards is never the best path forwards. We learn to adapt."

"That's...you're right. I would never want Dragonwall to travel backwards."

"No, you certainly wouldn't. I believe you have all manner of forward-thinking ideas that will send this world racing towards a better future." She fidgeted, caught off guard by the tree's uncanny way of knowing her thoughts and desires. *"I know you, Claire, as I know all creatures and beings in all worlds. My roots are in every universe, in every stretch of every kingdom. But I am known by different names and different things in each of them. Here, I am simply the king tree."*

"But, you are neither male nor female," she blurted. "Why do they call you a king?"

A chuckle sounded in her mind. She blinked. *"Lady Claire, we have more pressing matters to address. We might talk for days, years, time immeasurable, if I allowed it. There are two things which must be discussed here and now. The first is the matter of Queen Jade. The second is this—"*

A flash of light caught her attention. There, at the base of the roots, was a wooden staff covered in markings. Her breath caught in her chest. She was rooted in place, almost afraid to touch it, afraid it was a trick.

"Yes, I have had it all along. I took it from Isabella when she failed to be the queen I once thought her to be. I have kept it safe for you."

She took a step forward and stopped. "Does this mean, if...if I take it, that I must become the sprite's next queen?"

"Is that what you want it to mean?"

She hesitated, even though she knew what she wanted. But, what if she said no? What if the tree was testing her? What if in saying no, it would retract the staff and she wouldn't get it to use against Kane. And then, she realized that in thinking about all of these things, the tree was probably reading her every thought.

She slammed on the brakes—forced her mind to go blank.

A chuckle rang out anyway, reverberating around the clearing, mixing with the sounds of the babbling water that departed from the spring. *"I will grant you time to think about your future. The staff is yours regardless of what you decide. It belonged to Isabella and her fore-mothers. It was never a precursor to ruling, it just so happened that her foremothers were rulers. Queen Jade's mother ruled successfully, even Queen Jade did, for a time. But nothing is forever, and a person must recognize when they have become unfit. Greed can be blinding."*

Claire nodded and stepped forward, closing her hand around the staff. It was cool to the touch, but the second her flesh came into contact with it, the markings ignited like turquoise fire, spreading down its lengths. The wind whirled around her, sending forest debris into a whirlpool, tangling in her hair.

The Tree's laughter rang out over the roar. *"It has bonded to you, Claire. Use it well, and with honor."*

The wind died down. She found herself nodding, unable to take her eyes from it. Until her thoughts drifted back to what she still needed to do. "What about Queen Jade?" she asked.

There was a long, long hesitation. *"I tried telling her many times that the time had come for her to find me, to partake of my fruit. But each time she set out to search for me, it was never with that intention. So I was forced to hide myself from her."*

"Then, is it her time to die? What if she won't come to you? What if she will never choose to eat the fruit?"

"That path is lost to her. Only those deserving may dwell for an eternity within my forest. No, Jade must well and truly die."

"She won't willingly die on her own. But...what about Isabella? Did you kill her?"

"I banished her from the forest forever."

Hope sparked in Claire's chest. "Then, can't we do the same with Jade?"

"You may. I will leave the decision up to you. Kill her, banish her. She is no longer welcome here. She betrayed what it is to be a sprite. She is the reason my forest is sick. She must go or die."

"And when she does, will everything heal?"

"Everything will heal." She heard the longing then, in the tree's voice. It was the first true emotion she'd discerned beyond amusement. The tree's desire to heal its forest ran deep.

She squared her shoulders, nodded. The staff was heavy in her hand. Regardless of what she decided, death or banishment, Jade wouldn't go quietly. She knew what the king tree expected of her. This was her responsibility. She was to be judge and executioner, just as she'd feared.

"You know what happens when she leaves, when you dethrone her?"

A lump formed in her throat. But all she could do was nod.

"Good. Then go, Lady Claire. But do not go forever. You will need my council many more times before the end. I expect you to find me again. Until then, the staff will guide you."

"I...I will," was all she could manage. Then she turned and left the clearing. A single blink later, and it was no longer at her back, as if it had never existed in the first place.

As she walked, she thought over what she would say. She must have run through the words a thousand, thousand times before she happened upon Pelwynn's cottage. An entire day had passed before it materialized. She was glad her path took her to Pelwynn first, and not straight into the city. As desperate as she was to reunite with Koldis, to see his face and feel his safe arms wrapped around her, she couldn't yet bear to tell him what had happened.

Moreover, she probably wouldn't have time to tell him anything before confronting Jade. Knowing that the inevitable was so close left her body clenched with anxiety. So it was with quiet relief that she found Pelwynn kneeling over his flowerbeds. He did not turn to acknowledge her. "You return to me changed, *Elam.*"

"Tahalya edah dea ana fanahs, Kenya." *Changed and yet the same, Teacher.*

Pelwynn continued to work without turning, so she took a calming breath and simply stood there waiting, watching, patient. How long until Pelwynn decided to find the tree? How long until he felt his debt was paid? Would it be when she pronounced her training complete and left him? Would he have any further reason to linger?

Years into the future, when she came back to visit the forest, would he be gone? That thought sent a pang of sadness through her. Of everyone she'd met here, he was her favorite. So different was he to the others, except perhaps Feowen.

At last, Pelwynn turned. His eyes darted to the staff before landing on her face. "You are more patient than you used to be."

She snorted. "I suppose I am. Or perhaps I've simply grown fond of you, old man."

The corners of his mouth twitched. "There is not much more I can teach you, *Elam*." He hesitated, his eyes darting back to the staff. "And it looks as though the tree knows this, too."

"There will always be something to learn, *Kenya*, especially from you."

"But I can no longer be your teacher." He brushed his hands on his pants and stood.

Her stomach dropped. "You...you will go to find the tree then?"

"Not yet. But you will be leaving soon. I can feel it, sense it in the breeze like whispers on the currents of change. Your time here is almost at an end." He hesitated. "Your gaze carries far more weight than it did when you left last week."

"It is heavier because of what I must do," she said. It came out as a whisper.

Pelwynn nodded, as if he understood what awaited her in Esterpine, but he didn't mention the matter. Instead, he said, "These months together have given me new life, *Elam*. Renewed purpose. I shall not depart yet. Not until I am certain the tree has no more need of me. But our training—there is nothing more I can teach you that you cannot teach yourself through life's experiences. Before you leave, come and see me. I have a gift for you."

Her throat was dry as she swallowed, but she nodded all the same, not allowing a single tear to well up in her eyes, even though the sadness threatening to overwhelm her wanted to break free. "I will," she promised before departing.

As the first glass houses of Esterpine materialized, she knew then that the time had come. Knew what she had to do. Knew who she had to confront. Squaring her shoulders, she walked into Esterpine.

CHAPTER 35

CONFRONTING JADE

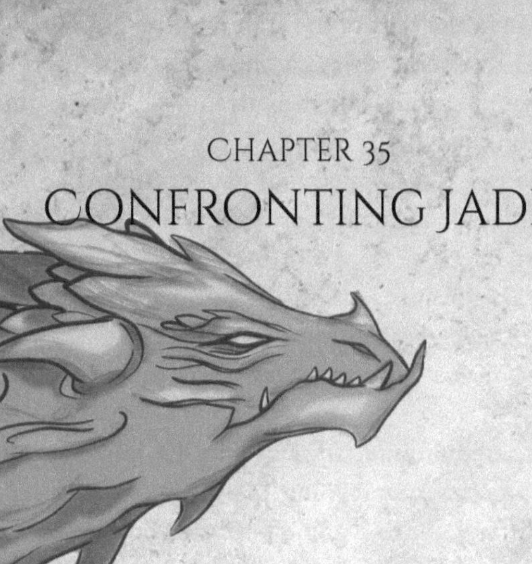

Esterpine

Claire reached Esterpine's center and the first thing she did was contact Koldis. *"You are safe?"* she asked. There was no telling if Jade had returned already, and if so, what she might have done believing Claire safely out of the picture.

"Of course...?" Her question had sparked Koldis's curiosity but instead he asked, *"Will you be returning soon? Is your business with Taylynn complete?"*

"I will, but there is something I must do first. And something I need you to do for me." She didn't tell him that she was already here, or what Jade had done, or what she intended. *"I need you and our forces from Kastali Dun to stay in your rooms—no questions asked. Seal yourselves in with whatever magic you can muster. Do not come out no matter what you hear. Not until I tell you otherwise. I will explain everything later."* Her words stretched into silence. *"Koldis, consider this an order from your queen."*

A hesitation and then—*"I do not like the sound of this, my queen."*
"Do it."
"All right. We will do as you ask, but you owe me an explanation."
"You will have it. Soon."

"Very well," he said at last.

She hesitated at the edge of Esterpine's square. Closing her eyes, she slammed the butt of the staff into the ground and sent a wave of power sweeping through the city. "Jade!" she shouted, letting her magnified voice ride the currents of power, summoning the queen to her.

The sprites in view stopped and gaped, turning in her direction. She sent the call again. Sent another wave so powerful nearby sprites staggered back.

"Claire?" came Koldis's voice. *"What's going on? Why is your voice sweeping through the palace?"*

"Not now. Do what I told you. Stay where you are until I tell you otherwise."

Sprites gathered around her, curious. She sent out pulse after pulse, calling for Jade, compelling the queen to answer. Feowen appeared, wide-eyed, with Jeanine beside him; they were holding hands. Again and again she sent waves, shouting for Jade. Whispers grew louder.

Feowen dropped Jeanine's hand and stepped forward. Everyone in the crowd looked at him. "Claire, what is—?"

"No! Stay back," she hissed. She lifted her staff and pointed it at him. A warning. He hesitated, eyes widening as he saw what she held. His throat bobbed. Jeanine grabbed his wrist and pulled him back beside her, giving her space.

She called once more for Jade, sending another wave of power out, and then the sprite queen appeared. Her only show of surprise was in her eyes. The rest of her face was hard and angry. "How dare you—?"

"Silence!" Claire's voice was a snap of power. The queen pressed her lips together. "You would dare ask me questions when you are the one who owes *me* answers? How dare *I*?! No, Jade, how dare *you*!"

Around them, the crowd had grown thick. She and Jade stood in its center with plenty of space. Jade's eyes flicked to her hand. "Where did you get that?" she demanded, taking a step before stopping.

"I earned it." She blew out a breath of air, shaking her head. "How could you do it? How could you think it would solve anything?"

"You speak nonsense." Jade lifted her chin. "Guards, Lady Claire has had a long day. Escort her into the palace, to her chambers. She needs rest." Behind her, the Queen's Guard materialized, clothed in elegant armor of starlight silver like the necklace around her neck.

"Oh, I don't think so. Stand down," she commanded, slamming her staff into the ground, using it to channel her intention as a wall of nearly translucent green created a barrier around them, sealing her in with the queen. The guards faltered, then stood with their hands on their weapons, eyes darting between her and the queen. "Jade, you will answer for your crimes against Dragonwall. You will tell your people what you have done, how you have wounded the forest over the years with your deaf ear and your blind eye. Go ahead. Tell them of your greed. Tell them why you must leave forever. Tell them why you must be exiled."

"How dare—?!"

"TELL THEM!" she roared, slamming the staff into the ground again, sending a jolt through Jade. Jade's eyes widened. She glanced at the staff. The red anger that had tinged her cheeks moments before faded and her face paled.

"What is she talking about, Mother?" Feowen asked from outside the barrier, his expression confused. "What crimes?" Jade glanced between them, her breaths coming faster, nose flaring. "What crimes, Mother?" Feowen repeated.

"Yes, tell him what you have done."

"I did it for the forest," Jade sneered, her face transforming from something that first looked so ethereal to something feral and vicious. "I did it to protect my kingdom. To protect all of you!" This last she shouted at everyone. "I did something a child like you could never do," she added, pinning Claire with her gaze. "A half-breed. You, with your tainted blood. You think you have rights here, as Isabella's surviving heir? Your blood flows with the abomination that shouldn't have existed. With drengr blood." She huffed.

"I should have known you would come here in hopes of stealing the throne. I should have seen it clearly the moment you first stepped foot here with the stones."

"You're right, I would never, *never*, hand an innocent person over to Kane. I would never bargain with a sorcerer to save my kingdom. Especially when that sorcerer is a liar. Did you really think he had the power to cleanse the forest? Are you really so naive?"

"We made a deal. I understood there was risk involved, but I would do it again, if it meant cleansing my world of his filth." Around her, gasps sounded.

"His filth? The blight is your doing! Kane could no more cleanse the forest than your daughter. Taylynn has been running herself ragged fighting the blight that your selfishness has brought. Kane tricked you. He used you and you were too blind to see it. Too desperate. You handed me over to him when all he had to do was make you a few enticing promises."

"Is this true, Mother?" Feowen looked cowed, utterly shocked. He glanced between the two of them.

Claire sighed, feeling so, so tired. "It's true. I wouldn't have gotten away were it not for Taylynn. Your mother found me alone in the forest, tricked me, took me straight to Kane and handed me over in exchange for false promises."

"He showed me what he could do—the promises were not false."

"They were! He tricked you and you fell for it. The only way to cleanse the forest is to cleanse it of *you*. And for that, you are banished. You must leave."

"I am *queen*. I decide what is best for my people. I welcomed you with open arms, and look how you have squandered my hospitality. I am going nowhere. You have no authority here."

"Mother—"

"No authority? My authority comes from the king tree. You should be relieved, considering what the tree truly intended for you. I picked the more humane of two options."

"The tree would never speak to you, a halfbreed—"

"The tree *did* speak to me. How do you think I got the staff?"

"Because you are a *thief*!"

She's trying to rile you on purpose, Cyrus pointed out.

She closed her eyes for the briefest of moments, willing herself to calm. Arguing would get her nowhere. Already the crowd was looking at Jade with expressions of horror and disbelief, but Jade hadn't noticed. She wasn't sure why, but she wanted to preserve what little dignity the sprite queen had left. "I think it might be best if you go quietly." She kept her voice low.

There was nothing more to be discussed. Nothing more to say, save the words of banishment that would formally bear down on Jade and force her to depart from her home. These were words she took no pleasure in giving. But she didn't allow herself to think about what it might be like, forced to go, forced to say goodbye to something she would never see again.

Thoughts like that dredged up too many of her own memories. Memories of saying goodbye to the farm, even though she thought she'd someday return. She never would. That was too hard to stomach.

"Queen Jade Siraye," she said, using the queen's full name. "I hereby—"

"No!" Jade screamed. The queen lunged, something shiny glinted in her hand. Claire's eyes widened, caught off guard. She sidestepped, trying to dodge the sudden attack. But Jade was faster. Thousands of years of training would always give her an edge, even with Cyrus living in her. Jade whirled around grabbed a handful of Claire's hair, wrenching her head backward, planting her dagger blade at Claire's neck. There was a prick of pain. A bead of blood trickled down her skin.

Claire froze, sudden fear biting into her. Jade tightened her fist, pulling hard. She smothered a whimper as pain shot across her scalp. It was nothing like the pain Kane had subjected her to.

"Drop the staff," Jade snarled in her ear. "Drop it or I will slice your neck clean open." Claire hesitated, then opened her hand and let the weapon fall. The loss of its presence was immediate. Her hand felt empty, cold. Her body—less powerful.

"Mother, *please*," Feowen shot forward, trying to push through the magical barrier that still stood in place. "Unhand her."

"Silence, Feowen." Jade barked a laugh. "My own son turned traitor. I always thought it was possible of Taylynn, but never you."

"Mother..." But Jade had already turned her attention away from him.

"This woman has attempted to take my throne. She is a traitor to our people, and as such, must suffer the consequences. But I am merciful. I will merely banish her, and spare her life." Whispers heightened around the crowd.

Claire's eyes were squeezed tightly shut against the pain along her scalp, but a tear freed itself. Not because of the hurt Jade was causing—or the implication of what the queen planned. Not because of the layer of broken skin beneath the blade where another trickle of blood was making its way down to her collarbone.

It was because of what she had to do next.

She dropped the barrier, letting her magic fall away around them. Jade's guards stepped forward, uncertain. "I've had enough of your charade," Jade hissed in her ear, pushing her forward. "If you so much as open your mouth to use magic, I will kill you." These words were spoken too quietly for the crowd to hear. "I thought to put you in your room but it seems I'll have to put you in chains instead, have you escorted directly out of this forest. I've had enough of your..."

But her mind was already blank, Jade's words far away, fading in the distance. Somewhere in the far reaches of her consciousness was a jasmine blossom. But closer at hand were her ties to one of the *Vahlim Eamtylla*. Earth. The pillar that supported all life. It didn't just grant life, it took life.

Another tear slid down her cheek. She heard voices, arguing, felt her body being forced forward, but that was far from her thoughts. Her eyes remained tightly shut as she fought this internal battle. There was another rough shove at her back. The blade at her neck pressed more firmly.

The word came to her—the one she needed. She didn't need to

speak it to use it. Pelwynn had taught her enough about the world, about sprite magic, about the connection between everything. *I will grant you permission this once*, came the answer to her unspoken question. It had been the tree's initial suggestion, after all. She was the one who'd hoped for a milder alternative. And it was the tree now, who granted permission to use the death word.

So she did.

Fialmaht. The word consumed her mind, her thoughts. She felt its weight on her chest, its power. Felt it rip through her. A thump sounded behind her, and the additional, smaller thump of a dagger hitting the mossy forest floor. She didn't look, didn't move. A sob broke from her chest, and then another. She couldn't bear it, couldn't bear to see what she'd just done.

You did what you had to, Cyrus said, but she ignored him. Had she really? Was it truly necessary?

Cries sounded around her. The distant sounds of chaos, like the dull roar of a muted tempest. When she opened her eyes and came back to herself, it was to find people rushing about. Jade had crumpled to the ground behind her. The dagger had fallen from her hand and her eyes were open and glassed over.

Feowen had Claire's shoulders in his hands, shaking her, speaking in her face. "Claire! Claire? Are you all right? Did you... never mind. I do not wish to know." He was glancing between the queen's prostrate body and Claire's tearstained face. He dropped his arms, then bent down. "Here," he said at last. "I believe this belongs to you." He handed her Isabella's staff—her staff, now. She felt an immediate calm rush over her, its wood sure and steady beneath her grip.

Around them, cries of surprise at the queen's sudden demise were traveling through the crowd. The queen's guards stood with their mouths open—uncertain of what to do. She was vaguely aware of Lord Marquin pushing his way towards them. When he saw the queen, he fell to his knees, but he did not cry. He simply gazed at the woman in shock. "I never...I...I..." He glanced up at Claire then. "Is it true? What you said? What she *did?*"

Claire gave him a single nod. His jaw clenched but he nodded in return, then put his hands on his knees and stood. She was vaguely aware of Aolis Marquin shouting orders as the queen's body was cleared away.

"The queen is dead," Feowen shouted into the gathered crowd. There had to be hundreds. "Dead by her own foul means and dishonorable choices. There is a new queen among us. Long live Queen Claire."

"What?" she gasped, staggering backwards, looking at Feowen with wide eyes. She ignored the new magic singing through her, surging over her at Feowen's declaration. Even though the king tree had hinted at it, she hadn't made her choice. Hadn't chosen this. But now it was too late. His words had brought about her rise to power. "No," she said, shaking her head. "No. That wasn't—"

"There must always be a queen, Claire."

"But—your sister."

"My sister is not here. Do you see her?" Feowen looked around and sighed. "Don't worry. It isn't permanent. You may abdicate the throne at any time, but until then, come. We must seal the magic before the forest is thrown out of balance again."

"I...don't understand."

"The forest was sick enough with my mother, and now she is gone. It needs all we can give it. It needs to heal. To repair the damage that was done. You are strong. You will fuel its healing. Isn't that what you want? To heal the blight?"

"He speaks true..." The voice echoed through her mind. She looked down at the staff in her hand, almost certain it acted as a conduit between her and the tree.

"Well?" Feowen prompted, waiting for her answer.

"I, yes, of course I want to heal the forest."

Feowen led her to the palace. Echos of "Long live Queen Claire" sounded through the crowd, but she barely heard any of it. Barely felt her feet moving—pulling her closer to something she didn't want. She was in too much shock, still trying to process what she'd just done.

She'd killed Jade.

When next she blinked, Feowen had already led her up the

Palace steps, Jeanine at their heels, and ushered her right onto Queen Jade's throne.

Her throne now, she supposed.

I don't want this, she tried to say, *I didn't plan this.* But the words caught in her throat. The forest needed to heal. If sitting on the throne, taking up queenship even for a day would fix things, so be it. Taylynn would return, and she would hand over the crown.

She would return to Talon, no matter what, even if it meant forsaking her birthright.

A crown was placed atop her head, but she didn't see it, didn't want to look at it.

"Claire?" The voice was distant in her mind, almost like the sound from a far-off memory. Koldis. *"Are we free to leave our chambers now? Will you tell me what is happening, my queen? We are worried."* A sob threatened to break free of her chest. His words, *my queen*, struck too close to home.

Sprites were filing in, as many as could squeeze into the space. Feowen had stepped down from the dais. But he gazed up at her with smug satisfaction, a look she wanted to wipe clean off his face.

Was his mother such a thorn in his side—in Taylynn's side—that he was already glad to have her on the throne? There was much she would give to see her own mother again. To be home, curled in her mother's arms, sobbing on her bed. To sit beside her on their porch swing sipping lemonade, listening to the drone of cicadas.

Or to be with Desaree, Jocelyn, and Saffra, nestled on the sofa in front of her fireplace, drinking wine and laughing about all their secret discoveries. Or to be in Talon's arms, sobbing. She wanted to be anywhere, *anywhere* but here.

But that is not what fate intended, Cyrus said. *You are here for a reason. You must use what you have, your influence, your power, to drive Dragonwall to a better future, just as the king tree said.*

She sighed. *You're right. I just wish the cost wasn't so high.*

Everything comes at a cost.

And now she felt the duty, the weight of the crown that Talon was forced to bear every single day. And she almost, *almost* regretted her decision to become his queen. Almost, but not quite.

Squaring her shoulders, she sat taller on her throne, willing her face to an expressionless mask.

"You may come down to the throne room," she told Koldis. *"And bring the others."*

She did not turn her gaze upward to see them descend through the hollow innards above. She kept her gaze faraway, her face set, the image of a perfect queen. The queen of a people so old, she couldn't fathom the stretch of years they held beyond her own.

She heard Koldis swear from the side of the crowd, where he'd stepped down off the stairs. She knew he'd seen her. The crowd parted, letting him through. But it was the sight of another beside him that finally broke through her frozen emotions. Her chest tightened. It took every measure of willpower to stay firmly seated on her throne as the crowd shifted enough so that all of her drengr escorts, their mates, and two shields could occupy the space at the base of the dais. Together as one, they placed fists over their hearts and went down on one knee, bowing their heads. But it was Koldis and Reyr alone who dared to lift their gaze from the floor. Their eyes locked.

Love like heat flooded her chest. "You may rise," she told them.

"My queen," Reyr said, a hand still resting over his heart, pride in his eyes. "I am glad to see that you are well. Glad to see you have settled into a position truly worthy of you. Worthy of your stout heart, steadfast courage, and quick mind."

This time, she allowed a sob to break free. Standing, she flung herself down the dais stairs and straight into Reyr's waiting arms. He lifted and spun her in a circle, laughing.

"How is it you're here?" she breathed into his shoulder. "Talon? He's okay?"

"He sends his regards," Reyr said, setting her back on her feet. "And he thought you might be heartened to see another familiar face."

"I'm so glad you're here." She hugged him again, then stepped back, glancing at Koldis. "Why didn't you tell me?" she demanded.

"And spoil the surprise? Come now, *Your Majesty*. You forget who you are talking to."

A laugh burst from her lips. How could she be mad at him? At either of them? When she was just so happy to have them beside her.

Around them, the crowd had begun filing out of the throne room, due in large part to Feowen shuffling them away. They'd had their moment to gawk. She wanted them out, wanted privacy. Soon enough, it was only those who had traveled with her from Kastali Dun, along with Jeanine and Feowen.

"You finally going to tell us what's going on?" Koldis asked, keeping his voice low. "I take it Taylynn's suspicions about her mother were correct?"

"It's a long story, but I'll tell you everything. Soon."

A brief silence fell, then Jeanine stepped forward, fist over her heart, and went down on one knee. "I beg, Your Majesty, that I be allowed to join your queen's guard as its first member."

She opened her mouth. "There will be no—"

"I think that's an excellent idea," Koldis and Feowen chimed in at once. They looked at each other, shared a smirk, then looked back at her.

"You think I should form a queen's guard? Even if I only plan to rule briefly?"

"I think it would be wise," Feowen said. "Our people will expect it—your people. They *are* your people, you know. My mother shouldn't have said those things about you being half blooded. Isabella's blood flows through your veins as powerfully as it would were you entirely spriten. You deserve a queen's guard. There will be many here who wish to serve. Many here who crave the honor."

"But I can't stay. I'm leaving. Sooner rather than later."

"So? My sister has ways we can travel out of the forest. I, for one, wouldn't mind seeing more of the world. Besides, something tells me all those who wish to serve will be of the same mind." He grinned. "And I'm sure our queen will grant us leave to venture home when we miss our trees."

"I...yes. I would never force anyone to serve me against their will."

"Good." Feowen nodded. His eyes flicked to Jeanine. "Then I too wish to submit my formal request to join your queen's guard."

"What?!" she shrieked, then covered her mouth with her hand. She knew exactly why he was asking, or at least, partly. He wouldn't let Jeanine leave the forest without him. Gathering her composure, she said, "Very well, Feowen. And how many guards do you suggest I take under my service?"

"Six, just like King Talon," were the words that echoed from Koldis and Reyr as Feowen said, "Eight. Six beyond myself and Jeanine."

She glanced between everyone. "It *would* be fun to one up my mate with more guards than he has," she decided, a smirk playing across her face. "Very well. Eight it is."

The rest of the day passed in a blur. She insisted on time alone with Koldis and Reyr so that she could tell them everything that had happened. Koldis was especially impatient with his demands about Taylynn. He wanted every detail, so she willed herself to be patient and answered every question.

During her retelling, they protested and growled in all the right places, especially when she told them about Kane and what he'd done to her. She minimized the pain so they wouldn't worry. When she came full circle and relived the confrontation with Jade, new tears spilled from her eyes. She hadn't wanted to kill the sprite queen.

"Why couldn't she just let me exile her?" she demanded. Her nerves were so frazzled it was impossible to control her emotions.

Reyr said, "It takes a great deal of power to let things go. Sometimes it's easier to fight. Knowing when to fight and when to let go shows true strength. Jade did what was easiest and she paid the price. Do not let it eat at you overmuch. Her choices were her own. You did the right thing in protecting yourself. She didn't leave you a choice."

His words followed her throughout the evening as everyone plied her with food and wine, crowding into her suite. Even

Feowen and Jeanine joined them. It helped to have so many supporters around her, friends and familiar faces. It brought her the comfort she needed—the comfort she would continue to need with each passing day.

There was still much to be discussed. Reyr hadn't told her the true reason for his visit. He'd brushed it off and promised they would discuss it in the morning. Perhaps it was better that way. She'd had enough for one day. It was with great relief that she finally dismissed herself and escaped to her room. When she was alone, she could do little more than tumble into bed and sink into an exhausted slumber.

CHAPTER 36
HEALER'S ORDERS

Dragonfire Sea

Bennett compressed his spyglass and slipped it back into his pocket. "All is well," he said, relaying the message he'd intercepted.

Salt code, it was called. A way for ships to communicate with small mirrors to catch the light. They could move the mirrors in short and long flashes that conveyed messages to nearby vessels. It would allow them to better coordinate their arrival along the coast in Celenore.

He stood on the rear deck, gazing out over the vast stretch of sea between *Lady Faith* and the other ships, scattered both ahead and behind them. They dared not travel too close together. They'd departed at different times from Ice Port, so as not to be suspicious. Each flew a small blue ribbon on the highest point of the mast as an identifier.

"How many are there so far?" Mikkin asked from beside him.

He glanced over before answering. "Nine. Just two more, and we'll be set to lift anchor."

Their negotiations had been brief. After settling on terms with Cat, he'd spent the next few days in discussion with Mikkin, coordinating between dwargs and a number of captains, all of whom he'd vouched for. To see Mikkin's relief was satisfying, knowing he'd done the man a favor in lending not only *his* ship, but his recommendations.

It wasn't out of pure generosity. He didn't do things out of the *goodness* of his heart. He had a crew, after all.

Still, once he had come to understand what Mikkin's purpose was, he couldn't refuse. Especially knowing Lord Dubrael would pay handsomely. And so his ship sat heavy in the water with ice metal once more, but not in its raw form like before. This was armor and weapons, safely stowed in the cargo hold.

Mikkin had insisted on traveling with him. He'd also insisted on bringing Jamie, Berbik, and that creepy little urchin, Unka. His was a merchant vessel. They hadn't balked in the slightest when he warned them they'd be sleeping in hammocks with the rest of the crew. "You'll be more comfortable on *Harper's Song*, with a cabin to yourself and some of the dwargish soldiers about you," he'd tried. But Mikkin had refused. Fortunately, he didn't mind Mikkin's company. Unka's however...the crew muttered plenty about the goblin.

Cat's head appeared on the stairs. Golden strands laced through her dark hair caught the light as she climbed the rest of the way up. Mikkin's eyes narrowed but he smartly said nothing. "Tris is fine," she offered in answer to Bennett's questioning gaze. "His ego was the only thing I couldn't mend." She crossed her arms and took up a stance a few paces away, staring out over the water.

"Thank the gods," he muttered, relieved. "Perhaps I'll keep him away from the rigging for a time." Tris had been up on the masts, reattaching ropes when he'd slipped. It wasn't common, but it happened to even the most experienced when they gambled with fate. Tris was apprenticing as a boatswain, which meant regular checking of the pulleys and rigging.

Few had seen him slip, but all had heard the awful impact. They'd carried him below, moaning and wailing, straight to Cat's cabin where they laid him on the patient work table. She'd somehow weaseled a larger accommodation out of him. Today, he was glad he'd given in to her demands. He'd seen Tris's body atop the worktable and thanked the gods she was part of his crew.

She'd shooed him away and set about mending Tris's spine and shoulder, both broken ,but not beyond repair. Were it not for her magic, Tris would have died. Of that he was certain. Tris wouldn't have been the first he'd lost to ship accidents. But perhaps with Cat around, there'd be few losses to worry over in the future.

"He'll be following you around all moon-eyed after this," Bennett mused.

"Not likely, if he wants to keep his eyes." There was no mercy in her tone.

"I take it he's resting now?"

"I told him that if he moves so much of a muscle from the table before you've been down to scold him, that I'll re-break his back myself."

Bennett winced. "That was...direct of you."

She shrugged. "I'm not here to play nice, Captain."

"No. I didn't think you were. I'll go down and see him now."

He made his way below, Cat following on his heels. Her cabin wasn't near his and Jonah's, having been partitioned from the large portion of the hull that housed all the rest of the crew. He tapped on the closed door to announce his entry, then stepped into the small room.

"Unka." His eyes fell on the green-skinned creature. "I didn't expect to find you here."

Unka hesitated. "Mistress said I was to keep watch," Unka supplied.

He glanced over his shoulder at Cat, narrowed his eyes in warning. She shrugged. "What? He wasn't occupied."

That wasn't what had surprised him, but he wouldn't be rude in voicing his thoughts before the creature, as much as he disliked and distrusted Unka. For Mikkin's sake, he was offering the benefit of the doubt.

Cat unceremoniously pushed past him into the cramped cabin. Rather than voice his protest in front of Tris, he followed after. Tris had his eyes planted on the ceiling. "I know what you're 'bout to say, Captain. I know I messed up."

"You could have been killed." Despite knowing it was an accident, that things like this happened from time to time, that Tris was one of the most sure-footed, well balanced, deft-handed of his crew, he still felt the need to say something.

"Suspect I would'a were it not for Mistress Cat."

Mistress. Was the whole crew using that damned title now? He held back a snort. "Yes, good thing we have Cat now. You've thanked her, I hope?"

Tris's throat bobbed. "More than once, sir."

"Good. And you feel well enough to rise?"

"Aye."

"Good, then get back to—"

"Tris will be taking the rest of the day off," Cat cut in.

He rounded on her, gaze narrowing. "Is that so?" His fist clenched. He took a deep breath. Tris would be dead, were it not for her. "I suppose it's for the best. Well then, perhaps you can keep Mikkin company up on the deck," he said as Tris sat up and swung his legs off the table.

"Yes, sir." Tris scampered out of the cabin, probably glad to be free of the rising tension.

"Unka, I would like a word with *Mistress* Cat."

"As you want, Captain." Unka edged around the table, keeping him in his sights, before slipping out of the cabin after Tris.

Bennet made sure the door was closed, then leaned back against it. Cat ignored him, setting about to tidy the cabin, like it suddenly required her attention. "I wasn't aware your position gave you authority over mine," he said, his voice low.

"You hired me to be ship's healer. In my *expert* opinion, I deemed it necessary that Tris rest for the remainder of the day."

"You healed him with magic."

"Right. But not his mental state."

"Since when do you care about anyone's mental state?"

She turned a saccharine smile on him. "Since you hired me to be your healer, Captain."

He inhaled, letting his deep breath fill his chest, long and slow, before letting it free. "Very well."

Her smile widened further. She closed the distance between them until her chest was nearly flush to his. She had to tilt her head back to look up into his eyes. "What is it about my orders, Captain, that unnerves you?" Her voice dripped with a taunting edge.

"Careful, girl." Somehow she'd discovered the power she held over him. Realized it before he could realize it himself. But he was still captain of this vessel. So he didn't move—couldn't move even if he wanted to. Instead, he changed tactics. "How are you finding your first sailing? Is there anything that I or my crew can do to make your stay in this cabin more comfortable?"

There. She wasn't expecting that. A crease appeared between her brows. "You're joking right?"

"Not a lick."

Her shoulders dropped. "I'm fine." She retreated across the cabin, fussing with the pillow and blanket that had been spread on the worktable for Tris. He crossed his arms, eyes narrowed as he watched her. "Was there something you needed?" she said at last, turning to face him again. Her voice feigned innocence but there was an edge to it.

"I don't buy your answer."

"I don't care."

He ran a hand over his ropes of hair, letting his head fall to rest against the door. "They like you, you know. The crew. You're falling in well with them."

"Again—don't care."

"Right." He studied her. She was dressed like the crew. He hadn't seen what she'd done with the dresses she'd brought, hadn't seen her wear anything feminine since that first trip ashore in Tortalia. While she dressed like them, unlike the crew, she cared for her wardrobe quite a bit more, keeping her clothes mended and smelling fresh.

He'd told her she'd have duties like the rest of them, and he hadn't been lying. She took watch up on deck, helped handle rigging, ropes, pulleys, and everything else the crew did. Took turns helping the cook at mealtimes, drew straws to remain on the ship when they took turns going ashore. And he hadn't seen her complain a single time, almost as if she was intent in spiting him.

He'd hoped it would be a harder transition for her. He didn't want to give her an easy time of it. Though, it didn't help when off-duty crew members saw her struggling with ropes and rushed over to either help, or take over entirely. He'd scolded Peter the first time he'd caught him at it. And then Emmon and Aaron. And then he realized he'd be doling out more punishments than he wanted to bother with if he continued down that path, so he turned a blind eye instead.

Gods.

"I *could* use a few ingredients for brewing," Cat said, breaking the silence. She stood with her back to him, like she didn't want to face him to ask.

"What sort of ingredients, and what sort of...brewing. Like, medicines?"

"Yes. Things simple magics won't cure." She turned to face him. Even on the other side of the cabin, they were only seven or eight strides apart. "Herbs, mostly. But also crimson mushrooms, horse nettle, hellrey root, shus bulbs..."

The cook kept only a minimal amount of herbs on hand—dried, at that. "We're at sea, girl. Where do you expect me to get crimson mushrooms and shus bulbs?"

"I don't know, Captain." She planted her hands on her hips. "Perhaps you should have asked me what I needed *before* we left port, if you really cared to know."

Heat rushed to his skin. He stalked across the room, reining in his temper before he said something he regretted. Instead, he planted his hands on the cabin wall, one on each side of her shoulders. "And perhaps you should have *told* me what you needed to be an adequate healer. This is your job, not mine."

She didn't so much as flinch. Instead, her eyes glittered and held his gaze. He glanced down at her lips before shoving away from the wall, away from the heat radiating off her body. "Make a list," he snapped, throwing the cabin door open. "I'll see what I can do."

"I'll do that," she snapped back. If she said anything more, he didn't know. The door slammed behind him and he stalked back above deck to the fresh air and the sea breeze, training his eyes on the sky where he found Beaky soaring around, catching the sun on her colorful feathers.

~

"WHEN I SAID *LIST*, I had something a bit more brief in mind." Bennett glanced over the length of parchment on the desk before him. Gods, it would cost a fortune too, half the items here. Cat had taken the seat across from him, not that he'd offered it to her.

She picked up his letter opener, using it as a nail pick. "You told me to make a list. You never said it had to be short."

"You really need all this?"

"Thomas has irritable bowls. Yerik's been complaining about joint pain. Cleto has headaches, Zama belches something horrible every time he eats, shall I go through all the rest of them? No? I didn't think so. Truly, you cannot possibly expect my magical incantations to heal every ailment the gods devised. Or do you? Then you're more ignorant than I thought. Most of these things require magical brews."

He bit down on his tongue, using the pain to think through what he said next. "If I had a steely for every time I wanted to throw you overboard, I'd be a rich man."

She huffed. "Oh, *I'm* sorry. Is this too much for you? Bit off more than you can chew with me? Rethinking your offer? Not quite the healer you signed up for—"

"Enough! Gods, enough. Spare me." They both sat glaring at each other, arms crossed. She'd be the death of him, this obstinate woman.

"If you're unhappy with my services, Captain, you're welcome to hire someone else."

He snorted. "We both know the crew'd mutiny if I did that, not that I have anyone else, lucky for you." He hesitated, glanced down at the lengthy list, read back over some of the items. "Some of these won't be easy to get. Expensive, too." She shrugged. "You do understand what sort of voyage we're on, don't you?"

"I'm not stupid."

He nodded. "We won't be stopping until we reach the coast of Celenore. And even then, that stop won't be more than wilderness. No big cities where we will be dropping anchor."

"And after that?"

"After that, we'll be on our way." At his words, she offered a stiff nod. A smile spread across his face. "Unless you'd like to stay after we unload our cargo? I'm told some of the king's own drengr will be rendezvousing with the dwargs to ensure their supplies and troops are delivered. Don't fancy seeing any of your old friends?"

"Very funny." For all her indifference, her skin had lost its fiery glow. She kept her eyes on the sharp point of the letter opener.

"You can stay on the ship," he said, his voice softening. "There will be no word of you onboard. You will be safe."

"Whatever." She stood, tossing the letter opener on the desk, letting her chair obnoxiously slide over the wood floor. She didn't bother to push it back into place. "Since it will be a while, I'll do what I can with the herbs Cook has on hand. But for everything else..." She gestured to the list.

He opened and closed his mouth, then said, "I'll see what I can do once we stop in the next port city. But that will be a couple of weeks from now."

"Fine." She hesitated at the door, her hand on the knob, her back to him. "For what it's worth," she said, voice dropping low, "your crew would never mutiny no matter what you decide about me. They adore you." With that, she opened the door and slipped out into the hall.

CHAPTER 37

PREPARING FOR EQUINOX

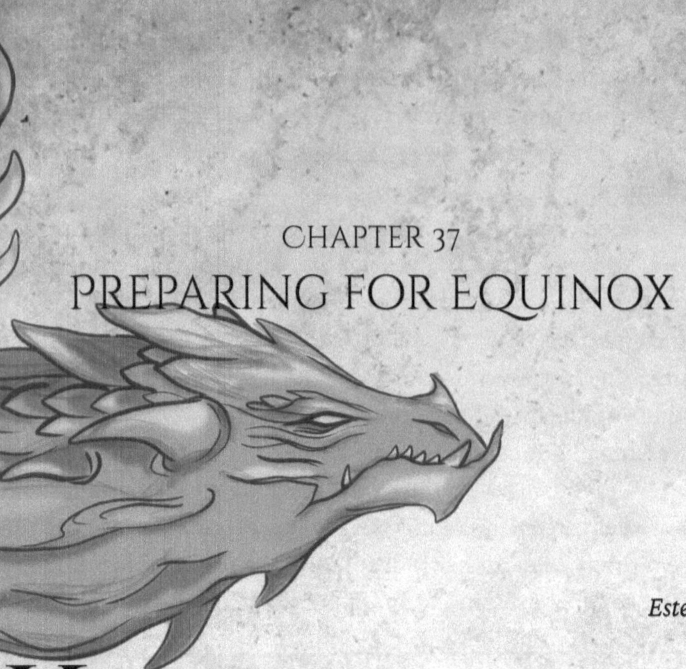

Esterpine

Koldis stood with his hands clasped behind him, watching Feowen parade sprites before Claire. She sat on her throne, reviewing potential candidates for her queen's guard. Most appeared eager for the opportunity.

Reyr stood on the other side of the dais. Nearly two weeks had passed since he'd arrived, informing them of Talon's plans. Claire had struggled with the idea but made it clear she would be joining them. Likely, King Talon would be furious to see her in danger, but she wasn't as vulnerable as she'd been before. Besides, she would have her queen's guard protecting her.

Besides Feowen and Jeanine, she needed six more. They must not simply be warriors, but also ambassadors. Individuals who would do credit to their race, bridging the gap between sprites and drengr. They had to be willing to say goodbye to their home for the duration of her life. It would be a blink compared to theirs, but it was still a prolonged sacrifice.

What was more, her future mating to King Talon would be an alliance. They'd discussed the implication of this over the past several days. As a sprite queen, she would tie their two races together, but instead of doing it as a disgraced, exiled queen, she'd be doing it as an honorable monarch. She'd battled the idea the moment Feowen had suggested it, because it meant she could not yet abdicate.

With Taylynn's helpful tricks, Claire's queen's guard could be away for long periods, so long as they carried some of the forest's essence. They would be given necklaces just like Claire's. Something to sustain them.

Speaking of Taylynn...

Koldis hadn't seen her for weeks, not since before everything went down. Claire assured him that she was fine, though she was tight lipped about whatever the sprite princess was up to. It irked him.

"I believe that's the last of them," Feowen said, which had him exhaling with relief. After nearly two weeks of formalities, he was board to tears. Claire's stomach gave a loud rumble which made Feowen grin. "Shall we discuss candidate choices over food?"

Gods, he couldn't wait for a proper meal—a proper hunt. Outside the forest, winter snows were already melting. The spring equinox was just two days away. Claire planned to stay for the celebrations; she wouldn't dare miss the ball. Their delay would still allow them time to travel to the king's war camp.

He was glad she'd chosen to stay a few days longer. Equinox was a holiday celebrated throughout the whole of Dragonwall, but especially sacred to the spriten culture. It was a time to rejoice in new growth and the promise of warmth to come.

Families would pull out their wire replicas of Kiaya, the goddess of seasons. They would venture outdoors into the springtime and take clippings of growing things, weaving them into the effigies. Some families had replicas of Kiaya so tall they skimmed their ceilings, while others were modest and small. But one thing was common to all: When the replicas were complete, each was uniquely covered head to toe with flora in the most beautiful ways. Gifts were then placed at Kiaya's feet for their friends and loved ones.

He had fond memories of his past equinox celebrations. This

would be Claire's first here in Dragonwall. The sprites would celebrate theirs differently, with replicas of the king tree. But there were enough similarities that he was confident she would get the full experience.

~

THE FOLLOWING MORNING, Claire's six new guards joined them for breakfast. It had been a discussion that lasted nearly all afternoon, but at last, she'd decided. Feowen had played the largest role in advising her. He and Reyr had given a few thoughts, too.

They sat at the large dining table in the palace's dining room. Like everything else, the table was made of crystal and groaning beneath the lavish spread. Warm breads, hard cheeses, fruit cobblers, herb potatoes, eggs, and porridge were just a few of the popular items before him. Claire hadn't wanted to move out of their suite, but she had taken to eating her meals in the palace rather than hiding away. She'd also insisted on inviting different families to join her for each.

She sat at the head of the table, making small talk about how they planned to build their effigy this afternoon. She'd been in good spirits all morning. Feowen and Jeanine sat on her right. Then there was Rahlif Dorvyre, Elyon Marquin—Aolis Marquin's daughter—and Filvro Holowyn. Reyr and Koldis sat on her left, followed by Gorded Cawyn, Aithlin Naeris, and Jassin Orythra. Of the existing noble families, only Rahlif, Elyon, and Gorded had been selected as guards. And of those three, only Rahlif had served previously as a queen's guard. Feowen assured them that he could be trusted. She'd done well to strike a healthy balance. Four females and four males. She'd been adamant about it.

"My mother had a large wire replica made for the equinox several thousand years back," Feowen was saying. "Unless you object, given our time constraints—"

"We will use it, of course. But...will it fit in our suite?"

Feowen snorted. "Not at all. It's for the throne room. But I've got a smaller one, it should fit nicely."

"Oh. I don't want to take yours, unless..." She hesitated, biting the inside of her cheek. "Would you and Jeanine like to spend the equinox with us tomorrow morning?"

Feowen and Jeanine shared a glance before he said, "We would be delighted."

"And the rest of you?" Claire asked, looking at her guards. "You are welcome to join us for tomorrow if you'd like, but I assume you wish to spend the holiday with your families?" There were a mix of uncertain expressions. "Well, whatever you decide, I support. Feel free to do both, but you are most welcome if you stop by."

Plans were made to venture out for the rest of the day gathering greenery for their effigy. The royal gardener often set aside clippings for the throne room tree. Unlike the personal trees, this one would stay on display a full week.

When the meal finished, Feowen stayed behind with Claire's guards, briefing them on their duties. They set out to gather clippings. All their pairs had wanted to join, so they made a large group as they meandered down the city's paths to its outskirts. Everyone else in Esterpine had the same notion in mind, so the city was crawling. Passersby bowed to their new queen.

They gathered clippings until their arms were laden with greenery. Then they returned to the palace, weaving them into the wire mesh of their king tree replica. A group was already hard at work on the giant tree beside the dais. Tomorrow afternoon, the throne room would be prepared for the ball. It was no wonder Claire was in such good spirits.

She laughed and chatted with everyone, a constant smile on her face. It was good to see her like this, and unfortunate that her mate was missing all the fun. Too soon, their duties would overburden them. A subtle thrill had taken him since coming to terms with their upcoming departure—that he would be joining his king.

Twice, Reyr had tried to talk Claire out of rendezvousing with Talon. And twice she'd stood her ground, insisting that she should be there with him. Koldis was certain the king had no desire to put his mate in danger, and yet, her argument was sound. Why shouldn't she take risks when the entire kingdom was taking risks?

There was nothing so special about her, other than the future task of defeating Kane. As to that argument, if she couldn't stand up in battle at Talon's side, how could she hope to defeat a sorcerer?

He didn't miss the subtle undercurrent of disappointment in her voice when she talked about her failure to beat Kane on her own. He almost knew what she was thinking. If she couldn't beat him now, alone, how would she manage in the future?

~

"THERE NOW! THAT LOOKS MORE FESTIVE," Claire declared. It was late into the evening. They were all stuffed from a marvelous feast held in the city proper. Claire clapped her hands together, positively glowing with delight. Through the effigy's woven branches, little glow lights glistened and twinkled. She'd used magic to create them.

"I know it isn't how these replicas are normally done," she added, biting her bottom lip, "but in my world we have Christmas trees—not replicas like this—actual pine trees, and we always string them with lights so they glow. Just like this." She turned to face Reyr first, seeking approval.

"I think it's lovely," Reyr said, perched on the sofa's arm. He'd scarcely taken his eyes off her. Reyr loved her, adored her, even—that was plain for everyone to see. And he fussed over her worse than any of the other shields. Like Claire, he'd done plenty of smiling once she'd returned from Kane's clutches.

"There's nothing wrong with taking some of your traditions and mixing them with what's done here. You are away from home, after all," Reyr added.

Her face flashed with brief sadness before she shrugged. "This is my home now, or at least, all of Dragonwall is. I love the forest—don't get me wrong—but I'm ready to return to where my true home is. To Talon—"

A knock cut her off. The door slowly opened. Their pairs had been coming and going all evening, but they had since retired for the night. Now It was just the three of them.

Koldis's heart skipped at the sight of Taylynn slipping inside. He stood straighter, pulling his shoulders back and immediately began cataloging her appearance. She looked well, certainly not like she'd spent weeks away in the forest. Her hair was freshly braided, several blossoms woven into the strands, and she wore a deep green gown that shimmered and displayed many of her markings. He couldn't help it as his gaze fell to the hidden areas. Areas he *shouldn't* have been eying.

As if sensing his gaze, hers snapped straight to him and held for several beats.

"Taylynn! You're back." Claire rushed over, embracing her. "What about you-know-who? Don't tell me you brought him—"

"No, no. He's safely hidden, with your tutor, actually."

Claire gave a snort. "Don't tell me you expect the two of them to get along."

Taylynn laughed, throwing her head back. Koldis couldn't help but watch with longing, wishing she'd laugh for *him*. "I hardly expected them to, but it was necessary. I could not miss the equinox. And I have news." She glanced around. "Lord Reyr, how do you fare?"

"Well, Princess. Quite well." He gave a bow of his head and added, "And you?"

"Well, indeed." She turned back to Claire, taking both her hands.

Koldis snorted. "I'm quite well too, but thanks for asking."

Taylynn turned a wicked grin in his direction but ignored the comment, instead leading Claire over to the sofa. Koldis went to sit beside Reyr, uncertainty growing in the pit of his stomach. He couldn't stop himself as he said, "Why do I get the feeling that whatever news you have isn't going to be good?"

Taylynn afforded him another glance, giving nothing away. He wanted to shoo everyone from the room, to grab her by the face and plant his lips on hers. To kiss her more fiercely than any female he'd ever kissed, so she would know she belonged to him. Only him.

Mine. Almost as soon as the possessive thought was there, he scowled and pushed it away. Gods. He really *was* in deep trouble.

"King Talon departs for battle soon," Taylynn said. That wasn't exactly news. They knew he'd begin moving his troops after the equinox. "But his plan will not work," Taylynn added. "Not entirely. Claire, you will be needed to protect the people."

"I..." Claire's throat bobbed. "I was already planning on going."

"Yes, I had a feeling. But you must listen. You will be needed in the city, to protect it from dragon fire. It will take merely a single dragon. One single beast who fails to succumb to the king's plans, to light the entire city on fire."

Koldis didn't ask *how* Taylynn knew exactly what the king's plans were. He knew he wouldn't get an answer even if he tried. Taylynn knew this information the same way she knew everything. And damned if it didn't frustrate him to no end.

"Yes, but surely—"

"There can be no risks, Claire."

Something in the set of Taylynn's jaw had him saying, "You've seen the battle, haven't you? You've seen something go wrong?"

Taylynn glanced at him, held his gaze, then closed her eyes and winced. "Yes. And without Claire, without her guards, many will *still* die."

"Without my—so we have to do something then, me *and* my guards?"

"You must protect the city, protect it from the fire. You can do that, yes? With the help of your guards? The magic you hold, paired with those who are sprites." She sighed, her eyes falling to the effigy in the corner of the room, as if seeing it for the first time. The corners of her lips pulled up. "I like what you've done with it," she said. Her smile broke free at last, transforming her face. "I think that's enough dark talk for tonight. It's the equinox, after all. Let us enjoy the change of season, the promise of what is to come. I would like..." She hesitated, glancing at Koldis. "I would like to spend the equinox with you tomorrow, if you would have me, Your Majesty."

Claire balked. "Uhm. Oh. Of course. And, as for the *Your Majesty*—"

"No, no." Taylynn put her hand on Claire's knee, squeezing. "Let us talk of those things after the holiday. We will discuss it in due time."

"Right." Claire swallowed. "What of the forest? Is it healed? I... you know what happened in your absence?"

"Indeed." Taylynn squared her shoulders. "You will be pleased to know I saw no signs of sickness on my journey here. None whatsoever."

Claire heaved a deep sigh. Everyone in the room did.

"Well. that's a relief," Koldis found himself saying. A knot deep in his chest unraveled. Taylynn merely nodded.

A beat of silence and then—"It's been a long day." Claire came to her feet. "I think I'll retire. Reyr?"

"Yes, I'm rather tired too. Goodnight, Princess." Reyr bowed to Taylynn.

Koldis cursed under his breath, but it was too late to say anything.

"Goodnight, all," Claire said, sweeping off to her room before any of them could respond. Reyr disappeared through the common room door leading out into the hallway.

Koldis cleared his throat, at a complete loss for words. Alone. He finally had her alone.

He expected her to flee. He held her gaze like a challenge, daring her to run. When the silence stretched on, he broke it at last. "Can I get you some wine?"

She rubbed a finger along the spine of the cushion beside her, glancing up at him. "I...yes, that would be nice."

He stood and poured them both crystal goblets before intentionally sitting down beside her, handing hers over. She didn't move. Instead, she sighed, as if resigned, and took his offering, leaning back against the cushions. "Where have you been for the past few weeks?" he asked.

"You know I cannot answer that." She took a sip.

His chest tightened. This wasn't what he wanted for them, this secrecy. He wanted...what *did* he want?

She glanced sidelong at him, then turned to face him, pulling her legs up and tucking her feet beneath her. He blinked, disguising his surprise, his *pleasure*, when she allowed her knees to rest against his thighs. He was afraid to say anything that might have her withdrawing.

"This will not be easy, Koldis. For either of us."

"I don't care," he whispered. But he *did* care. He cared about what would become of them, about what would happen if he broke his oath to King Talon, and most of all, he cared that by bonding with Taylynn, he was cutting her lifespan short.

"I've lived many thousands of years," she said, reading the expression plainly on his face. "My entire life has been in service to this world. To make it better, not just for my people, but for everyone. My whole life has been spent doing things my mother should have been doing, but was too blind to do. I had to act the queen when it was her responsibility. I should have already lived, ruled, and retired at this point. I am old, Koldis."

"By retire, I'm guessing you mean..."

"Yes." She looked away from him, her eyes falling to the effigy in the corner. It was covered artfully in every color of green and every shade of blossom. A beautiful rendition. "Maybe you've served long enough, Taylynn. Maybe it's time to do something for yourself, assuming..." He couldn't finish the sentence, couldn't face the reality that maybe things would be much easier if she *didn't* want him.

Her hand came out of nowhere, brushing back some of the hair that had fallen down across his forehead. He stopped breathing. "I know what I want," she whispered, looking at him, holding his gaze. His heart took off in a gallop, one so forceful he was sure she could hear it beating.

He hesitated. "You should do something for yourself, then. Perhaps it is time."

"My mother did many things for herself," she mused.

He tensed. "You cannot compare yourself to Jade. You cannot think that doing one single thing for yourself would mean becoming her."

"No...I suppose not, but perhaps that was how it started, once upon a time."

"And what of Claire? She's all but ready to pass her mantle over to you. To abdicate. Will you accept the crown?"

Taylynn hesitated, holding his gaze. "Should I?"

The question caught him off guard. He opened and closed his mouth, completely baffled. "You're asking me?"

"I am."

This was a test. He leaned deeper into the sofa, defeated. "Yes. You must. Unless there is another better suited. It must be you." And then, because he couldn't help it, he grinned and turned to her. "Does that mean I get to start calling you *my queen* instead of princess?" Her eyes widened a fraction. "Actually," he added. "Don't answer that."

He reached over and cupped the side of her neck, grazing his thumb along her jaw. Her eyes fluttered closed. He brought his head near hers, gave her time to pull away as his lips hovered so close to hers, but she didn't move. Everything around him disappeared.

He crushed his mouth to hers, enveloping her, still aware of the wine goblets they held. His lips moved over hers and she responded. A small sound came from the base of her throat. It had him begging entrance as he brushed his tongue over her mouth. She opened, breathing into him. This time he growled as fire erupted through him, pooling deep in his bones.

He wanted her. He wanted her tonight and he couldn't— couldn't have her. After what felt like an eternity of longing and merely an instant of bliss, he pulled away. They were both breath- less. "I would have you this moment," he said, his voice rough. "I would carry you off to my room and rut you until you screamed my name, except for my oath. Were it not for the bond that would seal us together," he breathed, hating his honor. Hating—only in this moment—that he'd made an oath so long ago.

She hesitated before speaking, "You would not be worthy of mating me if you had any less honor."

He snorted. "There's still plenty we can do without—"

"No." She held a finger to his lips, silencing him. "I will have you entirely or not at all, Koldis." His heart dropped at those words. He was so, so utterly lost to her. "Speak to your king. Gain his permission. If he allows us to be, then come and find me. Until then, I suppose we are resigned to kisses only."

He stared at her long enough that his heart calmed down. "You...you mean that. You would have me if King Talon gave his blessing?"

"I might regret it," she barked a laugh that had the corners of his mouth twisting up. When she saw his expression, her head fell back and she laughed in earnest. "You are too serious, *My Lord Shield*. Too serious indeed."

Him? Serious? Who *was* she?!

A single blink later, she'd abandoned her wine goblet and straddled him, capturing his mouth with hers, dragging her fingers through his hair, grinding her hips against his. Which meant she could feel his arousal well and true through the mere fabric separating them. "Wait, wait," he gasped, briefly downing his goblet so he could carelessly toss the empty thing away. It rolled to a stop somewhere on the other side of the room, but by that point, he'd already captured her lips again.

CHAPTER 38
EQUINOX SURPRISE

Esterpine

Claire woke, blinking up at the crystal ceiling. Her jaw popped as she yawned, but she didn't groan and roll over to go back to sleep, even if fatigue clouded her mind. Today was the spring equinox. She smiled at the thought of what sprites all over the city would soon discover.

There should have been heavy bags under her eyes. She'd stayed up nearly all night for a week. Even last night, when she'd snuck off to her room, she hadn't *really* gone to bed. She'd waited for Koldis and Taylynn before sneaking out.

She hadn't meant to see them through the crack in her door—okay, maybe she'd eavesdropped a little. Seeing them kiss had ripped something open inside her. She missed Talon like the sky missed stars when the sun rose, like the shore missed waves when the tide withdrew, like the mountains missed snow when warmer months arrived.

I am the queen, she said, laying there in bed. *I am the queen.* Words she'd spoken to herself more than a hundred times since Jade's death. A reminder, because there was work to be done. She owed her people this, this little thing, her presence during their most festive time of the year, time to let the forest heal, to regain the balance Jade had upset.

This was what it meant to rule. Making hard decisions. Putting her responsibilities above her wants. And it was only just the beginning.

Throwing her blankets back, she rose, made her bed, and lingered at her vanity, looking in the mirror. She'd matured, grown more otherworldly. She didn't look human anymore. A sliver of pain pierced her chest, for what she used to be. If her parents saw her now, would they recognize her?

She drew a shaky breath. Of course—of course they would. Those were the same green eyes looking back at her. The same golden hair woven into a thick braid down her back. She forced herself to smile. Yes—that was the same too.

But the markings covering her from head to toe, those were signs of the woman she'd become. There was still plenty of unmarked skin, but the luminescent tattoos were unmistakable. Even in the voluminous gowns of Kastali Dun, there would be no hiding what she'd become—who she was.

This time, she smiled in earnest.

After readying herself, she emerged into the common room. She'd heard everyone's voices before leaving her room. Hushed whispers of excitement. Almost as soon as she emerged, Feowen burst into the suite, his face glowing. "Was it you?" he breathed, looking right at her.

She stood motionless, dressed in a blush-pink gown that shimmered. She had Meira and Selphie to thank. Jade's handmaidens had insisted upon offering up their services once they'd found themselves without a queen. She'd first tried to decline, but upon seeing their bereft looks, she'd accepted. They'd spent two weeks preening, finding her new gowns, and weaving blossoms into her hair whenever she allowed them time to fuss over her. Mostly, she insisted on caring for herself—dressing herself.

They would never replace Desaree, and she wasn't sure she should bring them back with her. Wasn't sure how they would blend with the friends she already had. There it was: Yet another burden to carry, another decision to make.

To Feowen, she said, "I'm not sure what you're talking about." She did a good job of sounding innocent.

Like everyone in the room, Feowen was dressed formally, and for once, wasn't showing off a confident amount of skin. His tunic was a deep purple and wasn't translucent. His pants went all the way to his ankles. They were so black they swallowed the light. But they had shimmery thread embroidered along the hem.

The king's shields were dressed in velvet tunics of forest green and burgundy. Her pairs—who'd started filtering into the suite— were similarly attired in the formal styles of Kastali Dun. Everyone wanted to look their best today.

"What are you on about now?" Koldis asked from the sofa. He sat closest to the effigy. A brief glance revealed a heap of gifts at its base.

"What I'm *on* about," Feowen said, "is that there are star... things, glowing all over the city. All over the throne room. I've never seen anything like it."

"They're rather lovely," Jeanine said, pushing past Feowen to get through the doorway. Her gown was the same color as Feowen's tunic. Claire blinked, taking her in and suppressing a smile. This was the first time she'd seen Jeanine dressed so femininely. Despite her usual warrior getup, she looked breathtaking, proving that even warrior females could be soft and delicate.

"Star *things*?" Reyr asked, glancing between everyone.

"Star things," Taylynn confirmed, filing in after Jeanine. The suite's common room was packed. Seeing everyone here—her heart was full to bursting. Taylynn met her stare and offered a smile, like she already knew the secret because, didn't she know everyone's secrets?

Claire cleared her throat and glanced around the room. "Well, I for one would like to see these *star things* that are apparently all over my city. Shall we?"

Everyone filed out into the hall and down the stairs that wrapped around and around the central chamber of the palace. Far below sat the spriten throne, elevated upon its crystal dais. Beside it stood the giant replica of the king tree. But everywhere else, floating, bobbing, and glowing ethereally with shades of color, were the fruits of nearly one week's labor. Sleepless nights spent pushing her fingers to the limits.

She didn't look at the beautiful stars though. No, she watched the faces of everyone around her, especially Koldis and Reyr. Their expressions transformed, wide smiles softening hard lines. "Wow," Reyr breathed as they set foot on the floor of the throne room. "There are so many of them." Everyone's eyes turned upward, towards the shimmering stars that hovered some twenty feet above, turning slowly, bobbing as if floating in an ocean. "And, they're all over the city?" Reyr asked.

"Everywhere," Feowen answered. He hadn't taken his eyes off her, though, waiting. Their gazes met and she offered him a mischievous grin. "How'd you manage it?" he asked. "And...why?"

She shrugged.

"It was you?" Koldis asked, turning to her, his gaze darting over her face, as if seeing her for the first time.

"Try not to act so surprised," she told him.

A peal of laughter caught their attention. Taylynn stood, eyes glowing. "My mother would've never done something like this. It's perfect, Claire. *You're* perfect. Are you sure you don't wish to keep this position permanently?" The question was an innocent joke, but Claire didn't miss the way Taylynn's eyes flicked to Koldis and back.

"Definitely not," she said, pulling her shoulders back. "Absolutely not. One hundred percent positive. Ten out of ten, I do *not* wish to keep this position."

"How?" Koldis asked, looking at her. "How'd you manage this without us knowing?"

"Yes, I'd like to know that too," Feowen chimed in.

She glanced around before answering. Most of the other pairs had drifted around the throne room. Some had slipped outside. She led everyone out of the room to the stairs that spanned the palace entry. There, they had a perfect view of the magic before them.

Silence fell. And then—

"Well! Now I know what all that parchment was for," Reyr muttered.

"You knew about this?" Koldis rounded on him.

Reyr held up his hands. "I thought she had letters to write, you know, now that she's queen and all."

"No letters," she said simply. "But it did take some thought. With the equinox coming, I wanted to give my people something special, something different, but what? I used the parchment, copied the markings for each of the elements, air, earth, fire, and water—just like they appear on my skin. Copied them onto each sheet of parchment. Then I folded, and folded, and folded, star after star, all night for a week."

Years ago, she'd joined an after-school club for origami. Thank the gods it had come in handy here. While she could fold a number of shapes, stars seemed the most appropriate.

At the top of the stairs, they had a good view of the city proper. Everything that wasn't obscured by trees. Even through the trees, her stars could be seen floating, glowing with rainbows of colorful light, shimmering like prisms.

"But...there must be hundreds, thousands," Koldis said. "There's no way you could have folded that many."

"I didn't. I only managed a hundred or so." She lifted her hands in front of her, flexed her fingers. There was a reason she hadn't allowed anyone but her new handmaidens into her bedroom chamber, and even then, she'd managed to hide all the stars under her bed as they accumulated.

"You used magic to multiply them," Feowen mused, finally understanding.

"Yes, hundreds of times, but only after painting the elements onto each sheet and folding them up. I snuck outside late last night and sent them skyward using the markings for each element to encourage them to do what I wanted. Air—to make them float and send them on their way. Earth—to tie them down so they wouldn't drift up to the heavens. Fire—to give them light and make them glow..."

"And water?" Feowen asked.

"Oh…" A smile came to her lips. "That's my favorite part. Rain-drops refract light in the most beautiful ways."

"Ahh, that's how the light shimmers through each color," he said, nodding with approval. Koldis and Taylynn had drifted close together. She pretended not to notice the way his hand caressed the princess's back while they gazed upon the city.

She hadn't used the multiplication magic until *after* she'd sent her hundred skyward. Then she'd done exactly as Pelwyn had taught her during their first lessons together, partitioning her mind, imagining iterations of the stars. One hundred became two, became four, became eight, until there were thousands floating through the city. And she hadn't done it alone. Isabella's staff had been in her hand the whole time.

It tied her to the king tree, to its vast wealth of power. Not only had she heard the tree's voice a few times over the past couple of weeks, but she'd felt the surges of power when she performed magic. The staff was a conduit. And that gave her hope—hope that it would be enough to defeat Kane.

"That's…" Feowen turned to her, placing a hand over his heart. "Your Majesty, it's the most beautiful thing I've ever seen. A perfect, thoughtful equinox gift for all of us, for our people."

She bowed her head in acknowledgement.

In truth, she'd started drafting the idea the moment she'd woken up the morning after killing Jade. What might she give an ancient people who had everything they wanted, who could craft whatever they wanted with magic? And that's when the idea had slowly built, morphing into what it was now. Something beautiful to reign in a new era. Stars, a symbol of hope and new beginnings.

Sprites emerged from their dwellings, eyes lifted upward, looks of wonder on their faces. They pointed, *oohed* and *awed*, laughing with delight. A few joined hands and danced in circles, giggling.

"Well," she said, looking at everyone gathered. "Shall we go up and open gifts?"

She hadn't been expecting it, but she'd received so many that it took her all morning to unwrap them. Each of her pairs had gotten her little trinkets, and she treasured every one. But it was the gifts that had come from Kastali Dun, from Talon and his shields, from her closest friends, from Jeanine, Feowen, and Taylynn, that were the most special.

Of those, she opened the shields' gifts first. A beautiful silver ring with a sunset orange stone from Bedelth. A pair of teardrop earrings, ruby red, from Verath. A bracelet with lovely purple gems from Dallin (even though he wasn't oath sworn yet). A necklace with little sapphire flowers from Jovari. A coil of delicate gold chain that wrapped around her upper arm from Reyr. And a beautiful emerald green tiara made of spriten starlight silver from Koldis. At first, she'd been confused by their gifts, by the representation of color in each one, until she realized that this was their way of giving her a piece of them, a piece that she might carry with her always.

And that's when the tears started.

"Come now, Your Majesty," Reyr said, wrapping her in his arms. "Today is a day to be happy, to celebrate, not weep."

"I *am* happy!" she confessed into his shoulder, her voice muffled. "I'm so happy I'm weeping."

His only answer was a chuckle.

"I, for one," Koldis said, "am keen to see what King Talon has gifted you. Are you going to make us wait all morning?"

There were so many crammed into her suite that all of them were seated on the floor, elbow to elbow.

"All right, all right," she said, wiping her eyes with the back of her hand. "Hand them over, then."

Koldis dropped a couple of packages into her lap. She lifted the first one, ripping away the brown paper and blinked. She turned it over in her hand. A glass bottle with clear liquid and a gold inscription written in delicate font. "Essence of Talon," she read aloud without thinking. Then her eyes widened and a crazed laugh burst from her lips. "Oh my *gods*! I can't believe it. I can't believe he really did this!"

"Essence of...*what?*" both Koldis and Reyr said at once, weird expressions on their faces.

She popped open the cork and inhaled. A sigh fell from her chest. It wasn't perfect, but it was damn close. "Salt and smoke," she mused, dabbing a little on her wrists and her neck. "He found a perfumer and had it made for me."

"And why in the name of the gods would he think to do that?" Koldis grumbled. "I knew he was a shade cocky but *Essence of Talon*? Really?"

She barked a laugh. "It's a joke," she explained. "The night before I left, I told our king that I loved his scent. I told him that I wished I could bottle it up in a perfume or a candle. He remembered."

Gods, she missed him.

"All right, all right," Koldis grumbled, accepting her answer. He shot a glance at Taylynn and said more quietly. "I hope you don't expect me to make *you* a perfume now."

She couldn't help the bark of laughter that burst from her lips.

The other gift from Talon was larger than the first. It was also wrapped in brown paper. But she could already guess the contents before fully unwrapping it. The smell of sugar filled the room. As soon as the paper was gone, she feasted her eyes on all the brightly colored candies.

"Now *that* was my idea," Reyr said smugly. "But I let our king pick them out."

"From Flynn's Fine Sweets?"

"Where else?" His grin was infectious. She immediately tore into the bag and popped a toffee into her mouth, sighing. Then she passed the bag around, insisting that everyone should have one, or even two. It meant the entire bag would be gone in a few minutes, but she didn't care. She was too happy to care; she wanted everyone else to share in her happiness. Reyr's eyes narrowed, so perhaps *he* cared. She merely elbowed him and grinned wider.

From Jocelyn came a gorgeous embroidered shawl that depicted a black, iridescent dragon breathing fire. A perfect replica of Talon. She must have insisted that Talon transform just so that she could get his form correct. There was a leather-bound journal from Saffra with an inscription on the first page, so that she could record her life after coming to Dragonwall, tell a story that would last for thousands of years beyond her own. And from Desaree, a pocket book of miniature maps of all the territories in Dragonwall. Her eyes watered with the thoughtfulness of each.

Jeanine got her a pair of starlight silver bracers for archery, light as feathers. "I saw you eying them in the market last week," she explained.

And she was right. Claire had studied the beautiful stamped details, the sprite markings, and thought of all her time spent working with Pelwynn's bow. She'd wanted them immediately, but decided she'd get them later. "That was so observant of you. Thank you, Jeanine. I will cherish these."

Jeanine's gaze fell to the floor, but as soon as Feowen grabbed her hand, her shyness disappeared.

"I also got you something I saw you eying," Feowen announced, passing over his gift.

"You didn't," she gasped. Because she knew he'd seen her looking at spriten swords. The spriten market wasn't the same here as it was in Katali Dun, filled with merchants looking to make a living off of buying and selling. It was held once per week as a chance for artists, blacksmiths, and the like to show off their life's work. Art, weapons, clothing, sweet treats, all made by the one selling the goods.

The box was exactly the size of a sword, so it was no surprise when she lifted the lid and found a beautiful spriten blade sheathed within. The sheath was starlight silver, just like the blade, covered in Sprite markings. She lifted it from the box and pulled the blade free. It emitted a pure note of music that left her shivering with delight. "It will sing like all spriten blades?" she asked, hopeful.

"Indeed," Feowen said, grinning. "And when I told Delayn that I was getting it for *you*, he added the extra gems there on the scabbard, cross guard, and pommel. Said it needed to be fit for royalty before I could give it to you." Indeed, it had additional glittering gems of different colors embedded into the metal.

"There's nothing wrong with owning more than one sword, is

there?" she asked Reyr, hesitant, because she felt a little guilty. Cyrus's sword was beautiful, but it was *his* sword as much as it was hers. This one...it was all hers.

"Nothing wrong at all," Reyr answered, winking. "You are of two peoples, so it makes sense that you would have a sword to carry from each." She nodded, relieved.

Taylynn's gift came last. A delicate starlight silver ring, no stones, no adornments, just a few bands woven together. Simple, yet elegant. "I have imbued it with my own magic," she said, holding up her hand to show a matching band. "They are a pair. It means we will be able to sense one another. Should you ever be in danger, I will feel it. And vice versa. You will be able to find me no matter where in the world I am, and I will always be able to find you."

Claire opened and closed her mouth. Koldis looked stunned, and...jealous. "I... Thank you. It's perfect." She slipped it on her finger and smiled, holding it out. "What do you think?"

～

"I should like to wear my hair up tonight," she told Selphie. "To show off my marks." They were preparing for the ball, which had already started. But apparently as queen, she was expected to make a late entrance.

"Of course, Your Majesty," Selphie began twisting and pinning, pulling her locks into place. Beside her, Meira held a brush and gold glitter, to be dusted over her skin. Tonight, she'd sparkle as the brightest star.

Her gown was gold, a hybrid of styles to match the blood that flowed in her, both sprite and drengr. While it was made out of the fabric that all sprites wore, there were layers of skirts that trailed the ground, cascading around her, with a generous train. It would have to be pinned into place after her entrance or she'd never dance properly. In true sprite fashion, the upper half was revealing, almost immodestly so. Layers of fabric looped around her neck, plunging down to cover only her breasts before anchoring to the voluminous skirts. Most of her stomach was on display, including her bellybutton and her entire back. A narrow band of gold wrapped beneath her breasts around the circumference of her torso, crossing her back. It was set with white diamonds that glittered.

"I hope we did well, Your Majesty, to incorporate the fashion of Dragonwall's capital with our own." Selphie's voice was tentative.

"It's perfect," she told her. "Absolutely perfect."

"I'd like to see it some day—Dragonwall's capital," Meira ventured. "I've seen paintings, with dwellings stacked atop one another. A giant castle."

"It's a sight to see," Claire mused. "I was shocked the first time I laid eyes on it."

"Do you think...that is to say...if you ever return, that we might..."

"You wish to travel?" she asked, eyebrows lifting.

"I..." Meira and Selphie shared a look, something she couldn't quite read.

Perhaps it was better that she tell them now, rather than spring it on them later. She couldn't tell them everything—not yet. Not when she hadn't discussed the particulars with Taylynn. But...

She sighed. "After our celebrations here, I will depart the forest to travel. I will be taking my queen's guard with me."

Their eyes widened and they shared another look. "You will be riding to war, then?" Meira asked, squaring her shoulders. "You will need us, then. We will accompany you, to ensure you want for nothing along the road, and once you've reached the battle. We must keep you looking your best."

"That's not—I mean... I cannot ask that of you, to leave the forest." Never mind that she'd be putting them in danger. Even if they remained at camp and didn't actually partake in the brutalities of battle.

"It would be our honor to accompany and serve you, Your Majesty," Selphie said. "We are your handmaidens. It is our place."

But I have Desaree, she wanted to say. Even if queens in the past had a whole slew of ladies, she certainly wasn't at the point where she needed multiple people fussing over her. What was more, she wouldn't just be taking them to Fort Squall, it would be on to Kastali Dun. She'd no plans of a permanent return to the forest. Yet, she couldn't say anything without revealing that her position as their queen wasn't permanent.

She chewed on the inside of her cheek. "All right. You may accompany me."

To their credit, they wore their excitement quietly, with gentle smiles and glittering eyes.

"You've really never left the forest?" she asked after a few more minutes of their fussing.

"Our queen forbade it," Meira said. "Said it was impossible. But Princess Taylynn said, if we wished, that she would make it possible."

Her head whipped around, forcing Selphie to hold several pins in place. "Taylynn put you up to this?!"

"Well...no...yes...I mean to say..." They both shared yet another look.

"Well, if she did, then I very well couldn't deny you even if I wanted to. The princess always knows best." She almost snorted. Of course it was Taylynn's doing. What wasn't?

Selphie finished with her hair and held up an extra mirror so that she could see the back.

"It's a masterpiece," she admitted. "You've done well." But she missed Desaree's fussing and would have rather had her friend here, with her gentle hands and stimulating conversation.

"Thank you, Your Majesty." Selphie bowed.

They were both dressed in traditional spriten garb, as excited as she was to go down to the throne room. She looked them over, taking in their eager expressions. Like all sprites, they were ethereal and beautiful, with markings that swirled over their skin, though not as many as she'd earned in being here, she realized, keeping the thought to herself.

"There, you are ready." Meira finished a last dusting of gold on her exposed shoulders before they exited her private bedroom.

Only Koldis and Reyr waited. Both shields saw her and gaped.

"I don't think I've rendered either of you speechless in quite some time," she said, breezing past them, leaving them to blink after her. "Shall we go down to the ball?"

"At once, Your Majesty," Koldis managed to croak.

Her handmaidens both had escorts waiting just outside, so Koldis and Reyr took an arm each, sandwiching her in the middle. "You'd better not tell our king about this dress," Koldis growled.

"Thanks, Mom," she said, grinning up at him. "Any other nagging requests before we go down?"

He huffed. "I'm only saying that he'd be quite jealous. Knowing how you look tonight—not being able to enjoy your company."

She chuckled. "I'm not so sure he's the Jealous type. Well, perhaps he is, but he knows my heart belongs to him." She offered Koldis a wink.

"He does, indeed," Reyr said. She hadn't gotten much time with her favorite shield since his arrival. It had been one thing after another, meetings mostly. She leaned her head against Reyr's shoulder. "I'm glad you're here, by the way. I know I haven't had much time with you, nor the opportunity to tell you how happy I am that you made the trip here. But honestly, it may have been the best equinox gift I received."

"Better than *Essence of Talon?*" Reyr smirked, lifting his eyebrows. Koldis cleared his throat. "And anyway, King Talon and I both thought you'd appreciate seeing me. He was ready to come himself, but..."

"But he's the king and his people need him." She hesitated. "Has he missed me much? Has he been...okay?"

There was a long pause and then, "He's missed you, as I'm sure he's said in his letters. Between us, he's been more irritable than normal. Complains that he can't properly eat anymore. But I'm rather impressed by how well he's handled it."

"He won't have to miss me for much longer," she said.

"No, I dare say he won't."

The hallway ended just ahead, at the start of the staircase. She hesitated. Behind her, her handmaidens and their escorts also paused. In a few moments, she'd be on display for her people.

She'd be the queen they expected. There would be no peace, no quiet, no rest. Only formalities and expectations. *I am the queen,* she repeated for the umpteenth time, hoping this time she might believe it. Dragging in a deep, steadying breath, she said, "Well, shall we?"

"Yes. I think its time for your people to see their queen," Reyr answered.

Keeping both their arms locked in hers, she stepped out onto the stairs.

CHAPTER 39
EQUINOX BALL

Esterpine

Jeanine finished the final touches on her hair. She'd donned a silver gown for the ball; it shimmered with every movement. A tap on the glass door got her attention. She saw Feowen waiting outside, his attire matching hers. She faltered, then picked up her pace to admit him.

"Flowers?" She eyed the bouquet.

"For you, of course. I hear this is the sort of thing humans do?" He lifted a perfectly arched dark eyebrow.

"Yes, I suppose so. My father used to sneak out during spring and collect wildflowers for my mother." A pang of sadness tightened her chest. She pushed it away.

"Right. Have you a vase for them?" She eyed him a moment longer, then glanced around the dwelling. "Ah, this will do," he said, striding forward before she could stop him. He plucked a vase from one of the displays in the sitting area, muttered a few words in his language, effectively filling it with water before slipping the flowers in. He'd picked a variety, with bursts of color in every shade.

She watched, unable to tear her eyes from him. He wore the same black pants from earlier, but his silver tunic was nearly translucent. His luminescent markings flowed over the corded muscles along his back, shoulders, arms. Her mouth went dry. She swallowed.

"Jeanine?"

"Huh?"

"I said, where would you like them?"

"Oh." She cleared her throat. "On the table, please." She barely looked at the flowers, even though they were beautiful, unable to tear her eyes from him. He set the vase down and stalked over to her.

"You look ravishing," he said, pulling her into his arms. His eyes darted to her chest, to his equinox gift. A stunning necklace of starlight silver that glittered with white diamonds.

"Feowen!" she scolded, trying to push at him as he pressed her against him.

"What?"

"Everyone can see us."

Sprites made their way along walking paths to the palace where the Spring Equinox Ball was being held.

"So? Let them see." His mouth captured hers. She forgot her nerves as heat pooled low in her belly. His lips lingered, but at last, he pulled away. "I hope you will promise me the first dance of the evening? Actually, on second thought..." He hesitated. "Is it too much to ask that you reserve *every* dance for me?"

She tutted. "I'll see what I can do."

Feowen only smiled, taking her hand, leading her through the city. "These stars are truly something," he mused. They glittered in the growing darkness, light sparkling through various colors. It was enamoring.

"I can't believe Claire folded so many. My fingers would have fallen off."

Feowen barked a laugh. "I'd have kissed them better, you should know that."

"Since when did you get so sweet?" she teased.

He turned to her, eyes narrowed. "Perhaps when you became interesting?"

"But I have always been interesting, and that would imply that you've always been sweet. Mostly, you've just been annoying."

He dropped his jaw in mock surprise. "Me? Annoying?"

She grinned, ignoring the heat that flushed her cheeks. Instead of answering, she squeezed his hand. They had arrived.

The steps of the palace loomed before them. Couples milled about, sprites in their finest, laughing, some carrying crystal goblets brimming with wine.

"I think I'll need some of that," she found herself saying.

"And I think I can accommodate," Feowen answered, tugging her up the stairs. She huffed a laugh, letting him lead her.

Music, previously just a whisper, exploded all around her the moment they were through the doors leading to the throne room. Not only were her ears alight with sounds, her eyes feasted on the decadence of color. The throne room was bursting to the brim with greenery and growth. Boughs of heavy blossoms draped across trellises that had been constructed all around the perimeter. Within the center, the floor was kept empty for the myriad of dancing couples. Gowns of gauzy color fluttered around bodies spinning this way and that. Laughter echoed high up into the cavernous crystal.

She stood frozen, hand in Feowen's, taking everything in. Across the way, she spotted several of the villagers from Kaljah. They waved at her and she waved back. Feowen gave her a moment before pulling her aside. A server passed, tray full of crystal goblets. Feowen dropped her hand to grab two, passing one over.

A myriad of sweet flavors burst on her tongue. "Careful with that," Feowen warned. "Blossom wine is reserved for special occasions like this one. I imagine it's much stronger for humans. I won't mind carrying you out of here, but something tells me your dignity might."

The mix of flavors was indescribable. They blended and transformed, sticking to her tongue long after the liquid was swallowed.

At first, she thought it was fruity. Then it tasted floral. Then tart. "It's delicious," she breathed, taking a healthier sip this time, trying to pin down what she was tasting.

"Careful," Feowen warned again, lifting an eyebrow even though he was smiling.

A hush fell across the throne room. The music stopped. She hesitated, then found Feowen's gaze trained above, on the spiral stairs.

Her breath caught in her chest. "Wow," she breathed. "She looks like a goddess!"

Claire appeared on the landing, a shield on each arm. She descended the winding stairs. Her gown fanned out behind her, trailing in her wake. It wasn't until she was closer that Jeanine made out the exact cut of her gown. Her cheeks flushed at the amount of skin on display. While sprites had no qualms over such things, humans often did. But Claire showed no signs of discomfort. She wore her gown with pride, a radiant smile on her face, crown glittering atop her head.

The entire room went to one knee.

"Welcome, one and all. I am enamored by the display tonight. Our organizers have truly outdone themselves," Claire said. "Please, rise, enjoy."

This low, Jeanine couldn't quite see what was happening, but when those around her began to stand, she followed suit.

Claire stepped foot on the floor and the spriten musicians took that as their cue. They picked up their instruments and began playing again. Claire's escorts led her to the throne, where she sat to watch the festivities. "Will she sit there all night?" Jeanine asked Feowen.

"Only for a time. It's customary for the queen to preside over the festivities for a time. She'll dance later, I'm sure. I suppose I should request a dance...that is, if you can spare me?"

She grinned. "I'm not quite sure I can, but I suppose for our queen, one dance should be observed. You are her captain of the guard, after all."

"Very well, I will take your suggestion to heart." He placed a hand over his heart, mischief dancing in his eyes. "And anyway, speaking of dancing, shall we?"

He began pulling her towards the dance floor. "But..." She took another sip of her wine. "I haven't finished my—" A serving sprite appeared, this one male. He reached out with an empty tray. Draining the remainder of the sweet liquid, she gave a giggle, enjoying the warm rush through her blood, and set the goblet down. Feowen did the same before sweeping her out onto the floor.

It was a dizzying rush of bodies. Feowen held her firmly. She hiccuped, laughed at the immodest sound of it, then hiccuped again. Feowen only chuckled. All around her, the colors blurred to a swirl, vibrant and entrancing. Her gown swept out behind her. It was a wonder she didn't trip.

Beneath her skin, her blood rushed. Whatever the blossom wine was doing, she *loved* it. The fire in her chest made her feel bold. Like she could grab Feowen right here on the floor and kiss him in front of everyone.

"You probably could. I'm sure they wouldn't mind." His eyes smoldered, catching hers.

Her jaw dropped open. "I...I said that out loud?"

"You did."

Gods! How had she not realized?!

"It's the wine," Feowen said, chuckling.

"The—wait, I said that out loud too?"

"You did." He spun her around, catching them up in another procession of dancing couples.

"But, I don't..."

"I told you it was strong. You drained the whole goblet."

Her mouth opened and closed. Wait, had she? The whole goblet? Oh yes, she had. Just before setting it on the tray. But, it was *so good*! She already wanted another.

"I'm sure we can make that happen," Feowen said. Because she must have said *that* out loud, too. "I told you I wasn't sure how it would affect humans. But never mind. Let's dance a bit more, and then you can reward yourself."

She gave him a bold pout, which only made him grin wider.

They danced and danced. At one point, Feowen did get her another goblet of wine. She drank it quickly. After that, she didn't bother questioning his ability to read her thoughts. "I swear I was only thinking that," she said, when she accidentally commented on a kissing couple in the corner. Feowen merely laughed.

As the evening wore on, Claire abandoned her dais to dance. There was no absence of partners to be had. Her first was with Reyr and her second with Koldis. After that, Jeanine spotted Koldis with Princess Taylynn. In fact, he didn't much leave her arms the entire night. Claire, however, was passed from sprite to sprite. Some were nobles, others weren't. She didn't deny a single request, of which there were plenty.

Jeanine didn't envy the queen her responsibilities. How tedious they seemed. Her feet must have been killing her.

"They probably are," Feowen agreed. "And she's probably tired of all the formalities too." Feowen pulled her over to the dessert table. Jeanine's eyes went wide at the mini pies, tiny cakes, and frosted fruits. "I'm going to leave you here. Something tells me— you mostly, with your loud verbal thoughts—that you'll be plenty distracted by all these delectable bites while I ask our queen for a dance?"

Yes, she would be quite occupied here. Feowen laughed at that. Then he kissed her cheek and went in search of Claire. She grabbed a plate, filled with tasty bites, then stood off to the side to watch the dancing couples. A few villagers offered her greetings as they passed.

She watched Claire and Feowen spin about the floor. It was almost uncanny, the small similarities she saw in them now. Knowing they were cousins helped, but there were tiny markers. Like the similar shape of their noses, the mild angle of their eyes, the swoop of their jaws.

"She makes a fine queen, does she not?"

She jumped, almost spilling the contents from her plate. "Oh. Lord Reyr. Hello."

"Hello." His eyes traced Claire's movements. He retracted his gaze for a moment, spotted her plate piled high, and smiled. "That looks tasty." Quick as an adder, he plucked one of the mini pies.

Hey, that was hers. Not fair!

"Mine now," he said, mouth full, grinning while he chewed.

"Oh, gods. It seems the wine puts all my thoughts on full display."

"The blossom wine?" He lifted his brows. "Dangerous stuff. I'd recommend staying away from it."

But she'd already had two goblets!

"Well then, no wonder you're speaking every single thought that comes to mind. Did Feowen put you up to that?"

"No," she grumbled. He'd warned her, sure. But it had tasted so good.

"It is rather delicious. Already had three myself." Her jaw dropped. "I'm a drengr, remember?"

Oh, right.

A few minutes later, the song ended and Feowen reappeared, greeting Reyr, who took his leave, offering her a snickering grin before doing so. Great, she'd probably said something else embarrassing.

"Having fun?" Feowen asked.

"Too much, it seems." She picked the remaining treats off her plate before Feowen led her back onto the dance floor. They danced for hours, until the night waned, the music slowed, and the energy of the room calmed. That's how she found herself in Feowen's arms, her head resting on his chest as he gently rocked her to the lull of the music.

"I'm glad you'll be joining me when we leave," she whispered. The thought of leaving him behind was sad, but that hadn't stopped her from volunteering to be Claire's first guard.

"I'm glad, too. I like this thing between us...whatever it is. I like you, spending time with you. I haven't been this..."

"This, what?"

"Enamored. Not by anyone or anything for a long, long time."

His complement sent warmth trickling to her toes. She wouldn't have to say goodbye to him. Whatever was happening between them, it could carry on. Who knew what they would face when they reached Squall's End? But at least they would face it together.

"Together," Feowen confirmed. Then he tilted her chin up and kissed her, right there in front of the entire sprite kingdom.

CHAPTER 40

COMMISSIONING A BOW

Kastali Dun

Talon eyed the ships that would carry their precious cargo north. Carefully packed in padded crates, glass bottles of poison were carted onboard. There were more than a hundred, small enough to fit in carefully reinforced packs.

Saffra and Verath stood beside him.

"You have done well, Lady Saffra," he found himself saying. He was pleasantly impressed with her work, not because of her abilities, she was a woman of power after all, but because of her age, the number of years she had seen compared to the rest of them.

"Thank you, Your Majesty." Saffra appeared to grow taller beside him. She hadn't merely overseen the brewing of their most precious weapon. She'd worked with Mistress Rosanne, crafting cloaks for their operatives. Magical disguises that would help them mask their scent and blend with the terrain. It would be a dangerous job, reaching the lake undetected by the wild dragons. Dragons could scent humans, but they would especially recognize the scents of the drengr.

They'd chosen carefully, small groups of operatives who understood the risk, that it was worth taking. They would approach

Plymlet Lake from different directions. Getting them into position was the biggest challenge. The sooner they departed north, the sooner they could begin. They had only to finish loading the cargo.

Wings from Fort Squall and Fort Kastali had already departed, flying up along the coast. They would island hop once they reached the Scattered Islands. From there, they would travel through Celenore on foot, just to be safe. Once they reached the rendezvous point, they would safely oversee the offloading of the cargo.

"If everything is timed correctly," Verath said, "the dwargs should arrive shortly after these ships. We should have camp set up by then."

"Let us hope." His hand tightened around the parchment in his fist. Another update from Lord Dubrael. Over the past month, Dubrael had been hard at work, moving warriors and supplies west along the Northern Barrier Range, to ships they had contracted. Excitement skittered down his spine. He couldn't help his anticipation. Dragon armor made of ice metal. They hoped to avoid confrontation with Kane's dragons, but should their plan go awry, being protected would afford them the upper hand. He'd seen works of art depicting the great battles between dragons and drengr, long ago during the days of Rage. He'd seen the armor worn. Pieces of it resurfaced around the kingdom from time to time, even now. But most of the pieces had been scattered or lost. There were several full sets intact, erected in each of the forts as sculptures to remind the drengr of their history. The sets were precious relics, fifty thousand years old, too valuable to dismantle. Now, they would have many of their own.

The clanging of bells announced the new arrival of another ship. Talon blinked against the pale sunlight. With each day, the chill of winter had receded. Spring equinox had passed in a blink, and his efforts had turned entirely to plans of reclaiming Squall's End.

It hadn't been the equinox he'd hoped for. Selfishly, he'd hoped Claire would have returned, even though she'd only been gone a few months, even though he wanted her to remain in the forest, safely tucked away until they finished this task of reclaiming what belonged to the kingdom. Still, he felt the loneliness of her absence as everyone celebrated.

A small smile pulled at the corners of his mouth. What had she thought of his gift, he wondered? At the least, it would have reminded her of their time together that night, sharing the same bed, tangled together in each other's arms—

A throat cleared beside him. "I believe everything is in order," Saffra announced. He glanced at her. "If you have no further need of me—?"

"Yes, yes. That is all. Thank you, Lady Saffra. Verath can—"

"No, no. I am perfectly capable of escorting myself back to the keep, Your Majesty. Besides, I would prefer to be alone. I enjoy walking and could use the time to clear my head. All those days in the dark..."

He eyed her a moment longer. There was something more behind her desire, something he had an inkling hunch about, but wouldn't dare voice. He'd seen the way Bedelth hovered over her as of late. Seen the way she either pretended not to notice, or feigned obliviousness at the increase in Bedelth's attentions.

"Very well." He gave her a nod and turned back to the ships. It was a sort of therapy, watching the industry unfold before him. It wasn't merely their own ships being loaded. This was the busiest port in the kingdom.

Verath remained beside him, arms clasped behind his back. "Desaree is still insisting," he said. At that, Talon snorted. Verath continued, saying, "I've told her time and again. War is no place for a handmaiden. That she must remain here where she will be safe."

"Saffra has also insisted several times," he mused. "I simply cannot risk their safety. If anything happened to them Claire would—"

"Have a fit," Verath finished, interrupting. "I know. I told Desaree the same thing."

"And? What did she say?"

Verath chuckled. "That I vastly underestimated her ability to keep herself safe. That I was being unfair. That she had just as much right—if not more—to assemble on the sidelines as all the other servants we are taking. That without her and Jocelyn and Saffra, we wouldn't be flying into battle."

Talon nodded. "She's right on all counts."

"I will not risk her, Your Majesty. Not for all the world."

"I never said you should. But I do not think it is your choice to make. And…perhaps it will not be so dangerous as long as she remains within the safety of camp. After all, we are bringing hand-selected civilians to support with mundane tasks."

"Would you allow Claire to go?"

"No," he said after a long silence. "I wouldn't want to risk her. And yet…" He hesitated. It wasn't his decision to make. Claire didn't belong to him, just as Desaree didn't belong to Verath. Knowing that didn't suppress the nature of his beast. He sighed. "As a dominant predator, my drive to protect the ones I love is strong. But it will get me into trouble. It will get you into trouble, too, Verath."

"What are you implying?"

He shrugged. "I'm merely saying that we cannot control them."

Verath huffed and shook his head. "Your word is law, Talon. You say who goes and who stays. They are not needed—there is no need to risk them."

He knew that saying any more on the matter would only frustrate Verath. "What of Dallin? I assume he is still intent on joining us?"

Verath hesitated. "He is young, but…"

"But you like him."

"I do. He has impressed me, despite his age. He's got so much potential. Room to grow. I hate to say it but, perhaps I was wrong about him, wrong to want so badly to dissuade him from becoming a shield."

"How long should I wait before telling him the good news?"

Verath snorted. "If I had to say, at least until Claire returns. She will feel left out if you swear him to oath before that."

"Then we will treat this battle as his final test, see how he does?"

Verath nodded. "I'd say that's fair."

Their gazes returned to the activity on the docks. They stood side by side in comfortable silence for a time. With each passing minute, he felt himself relax a bit more.

The majority of their preparations were complete. A number of wings would remain behind to protect the city. He didn't anticipate trouble. His absence would not be widely broadcast. Court would continue under the watchful eye of the steward and council. No major decisions would be made. And hopefully, in a matter of weeks, this entire mess would be sorted.

"I can remain to oversee the rest of this," Verath said, nudging his shoulder. "I know you have other matters on your agenda."

He hesitated. "That's probably for the best. I'll see you back at the keep."

Taking several steps backwards, he turned and retreated through the market and up the city streets. Behind him, what remained of his castle guards trailed. He didn't need them, but brought them anyway. Mostly because Lady Saffra had accompanied them on their walk down. Half had returned with her.

Where he walked, people stopped to gape at him. Some with enough propriety to bow, others too shocked to realize what was proper before he strode past. He didn't care—was too deep in thought to care.

Taking a detour, he slipped down a wide street in the middle of the city. The sounds changed here. There was still the normal hum of voices, creaking wagons and carts, and distant sound of bells, but there was also the loud clang of industry. A number of black-smith and carpentry shops lined this part of the city.

Perhaps it was too soon for this. He was taking a gamble. And yet, he couldn't help his eagerness.

"Wait for me here," he said to his guards. They nodded, turning their watchful gazes to the street and its surrounding buildings.

He stepped off the muddy thoroughfare, through a soggy storage yard and into a large workshop. There he found the bowyer, a man of middling age, bent over a workbench with a small paintbrush in hand. The smell of wood was overwhelming here; it was everywhere, different types, pieces cut to ideal widths and lengths that would soon be carved and honed into weapons.

"Your Majesty!" The man jumped from his stool, shooing away the apprentice who'd been hauling an armful of supplies into the room. The bowyer wiped his hands on his leather apron, smoothed back his hair, and offered a nervous smile and bow. "It is an honor."

"No need for formalities, Langdon. I'm here to talk business."

"Right. Of course. Is it a bow you're wanting?" Langdon's eyes darted around the shop, never once landing on the king in his midst.

Talon cleared his throat. "I'd like to commission one, yes. Your work is the finest in the city. This won't be ordinary—I need exceptional craftsmanship. A bonding ceremony bow...for a friend." He slipped his hands into his pockets. He knew of no drengr in the world who would trust a friend to commission a bow like this, but, well, he couldn't exactly say it was for his mate.

Too soon! his mind screamed. He hadn't received Claire's final answer yet. He wanted her to choose him—hoped beyond hope that she would. The letters they'd exchanged recently had further bolstered his confidence. She missed him as he missed her. She planned to return to him when she accomplished what she set out to do. And yet, to act as though he already had an answer could only work negatively against him, tempting the fates to deal him a different hand, just for being so confident.

"Right, right," Langdon said, oblivious to his internal struggle. "It should be a magnificent piece, then. What thoughts have you? Let's sketch up some ideas." Langdon pulled out a chair, several sheets of parchment, and a stick of graphite.

He had plenty of ideas, had allowed his mind ample time to run away with itself over the past weeks, months. It was the only thing that kept him sane in her absence, pretending their future was certain, allowing himself to assume it was.

Stifling his doubt, pushing it down deep where it wouldn't taunt him, he grabbed the chair and flipped it around backwards.

Langdon waited for him to sit, and then took up his stool and the stick of graphite. Together, they began plotting.

CHAPTER 41

SNEAKING AWAY

Kastali Dun

Desaree glanced around the corner, keeping to the shadows of the apothecary shop. She motioned the others forward. They sprinted across the lane, careful to keep their cloaks drawn tight over the baggage they carried. Breathless, her heart hammered in her chest. "I think we're clear," she whispered. "That was the last of the city guard."

The docks loomed up before them. It wasn't quite dark. The evening meal would be held soon. But that also meant they were perilously close to missing their chance.

"Hurry," Saffra hissed, rushing them along as their feet slapped the wooden slats. A vast maze of walkways jutting out over the water stretched before them. "Look for *Boundless*. It's the largest of the six and doesn't leave until sundown." They rushed to Dock Nine, where most of the ships had already been loaded earlier today. Even though the day was drawing to an end, there was a flurry of activity all around them. Orders were being issued and several of the ships were already pulling out.

"There!" Jocelyn cried, pointing. They raced forward, dodging bodies still finishing the final preparations.

Their plan hinged on the captain of the Boundless remembering who Saffra was—how important she was.

They stopped before the giant vessel, its sleek hull was several body lengths from the dock, connected by gangplanks at the front and rear. The deck towered over them, nearly too high to see. But there was a rush of activity aboard.

"Follow my lead," Saffra said, leading them up and onto the deck.

It took several minutes for anyone to notice them. A crew member halted and said, "Pardon, ladies, but ya can't be here. We're settin' off in a moment—no, Telek, not there. Put them below! Anyhow, the time to say goodbye to yer lads was earlier—no, Rory, secure that first—"

"We're not here to say goodbye," Saffra said, interrupting as she dropped her hood. She stood nearly as tall as the man before them. "I'm here for Captain Kett. I have business with him." She glanced around. "Ah. There he is." Without waiting for permission, she led them up a flight of stairs to the rear deck.

Desaree glanced around then placed a hand over her stomach to calm it. The deck beneath them was in constant motion, even here. She glanced around, looking over everything. Her eyes couldn't find a place to land. There was too much activity.

"Lady Saffra," Captain Kett said, stepping forward. This deck stood taller than the rest of the ship, offering a magnificent view. "Is everything a'right? Did the king send you? Has there been a change in plans?"

"Yes, and no, Captain. As you know, the cargo on these ships is *very* precious. And as was mentioned, we three were the ones who engineered it." Saffra's voice didn't falter. "The king decided it best that we accompany it, just to make sure nothing goes awry. If anything were to happen…"

Captain Kett frowned and scratched his beard, eyeing them. Desaree's heart skipped, but she was careful—*oh so careful*—not to fidget. They were *meant* to be here. They had just as much right as the servants. She'd gladly perform physical labor. She was no stranger to it, after all.

"Beg your pardon, my lady, but…"

"I've got the order here, Captain, from the king." Saffra produced a sealed letter. The king's seal.

"Huh," the captain said as he took it. He scrutinized the seal before breaking it to read the contents. Each moment felt like a lifetime. How long did it take to read a few lines, anyway?

A flurry of butterflies blossomed in her stomach.

The captain nodded and slipped the parchment into his vest. "Very well then. The king's word cannot be questioned." He surveyed them. "Which one of you's Desaree and which is Jocelyn?" They introduced themselves before he led them below. "Best you not associate too much with the crew. They're too bawdy for the likes of your ladyships. I'll not have ya tainted by their association. You'll have to share this cabin, as I didn't have anything extra prepared. You'll come on deck if you need to, but stay outta the way. I got places for you to sit up top, if you need. But rather you stay down here if it can be helped." He eyed them warily. "Come find me if you need anything. Me—not the other crew, mind."

With that, he shut them in the tiny cabin with four bunks. It would do just fine. They waited until they didn't hear anything more. Then a collective sigh broke the silence.

"It was too easy," Jocelyn whispered, tossing her things on the nearest bunk. Desaree eyed the other three beds before picking the one just above her. She unclipped and pulled away her cloak before climbing up.

"Here—" Saffra was already busy rummaging through her belongings. She handed each of them a ball of sticky, tacky, amber colored candy. But it wasn't candy and it tasted horrible. "It will keep you from getting seasick. Captain Kett is right, the less we can spend above deck, the better. I don't want it coming out that we forged the letter. He'd be forced to turn around. It would delay plans. I don't want to be the reason this whole thing goes belly up."

Desaree nodded, swallowing the mass in her mouth and grimacing. She'd been too nervous to pay much attention to the nausea rolling through her, but now that they were alone, she was glad Saffra had thought beyond getting them on board. Still, her mouth tasted like she'd grabbed a handful of leaves from the nearest tree and shoved them in.

"I hope you didn't expect it to taste like sugar," Saffra drawled, noticing the look on their faces.

Desaree shrugged, then sighed, leaning back against the wall, already, the effects were calming the roiling feeling in the pit of her stomach. "We did it," she mused. "I almost don't believe it."

Saffra snorted. "You're welcome. And if anything goes wrong—"

"I know. I know. It was my idea." Desaree shrugged. "But you cannot deny that you don't want this as badly as I do. Everyone expects us to sit back and let others do all the work. Gods, even the servants were given the opportunity to come along and help."

"You know as well as I that it's because of who we are," Saffra said.

Desaree snorted. "Right. We're *ladies*. But what about Claire? She's a lady too, but Talon wouldn't lock her in an ivory tower, would he? The rest of us are supposed to what, sit at home embroidering cushions all day—?"

"There's nothing wrong with embroidering cushions!" came the muffled voice from below.

"That's not my point, Jocelyn. There's more to being a lady than flouncing around in pretty gowns all day." She hadn't always believed that. It was Claire who'd made her realize it.

"Indeed," Saffra tisked, still standing in the middle of the small cabin, watching both of them. "Except if I recall, Des, you're the one who insists on the pretty gowns in the first place."

"Well, there's a time and place for every sort of attire." Desaree crossed her arms, staring Saffra down.

Saffra shrugged. "All I'm saying is, this was entirely *your* idea, Desaree. For the record. In case anyone ever asks. Because...they probably wouldn't believe it unless you were the one to admit it."

Saffra had a point. She was usually the daring one. After all, she had magic and that meant options.

Desaree grinned, relishing in the foreign thrill shooting

through her veins. This was so unlike her, but— "I'll gladly be your villain."

The sounds around them changed. Saffra held up a hand and they listened. More shouts filtered down to them—orders being issued. "It's just the command to sail," Saffra said, letting out a breath. "We made it in time. It's done."

The three of them settled in as the ship made its way out of the port.

A ROAR SPLIT the air and Desaree jumped. They were sitting on the floor of their small cabin, playing cards. The night had passed uneventfully, except for the times that they needed to relieve themselves. There were no toilets on a ship like this. Most of the crew were fine with hanging over the edge, the notion of which had been appalling. So a bucket was located and that was that. The morning had seen them in the small cook's space eating biscuits and jam. After that, they'd passed the time in their cabin with the deck of cards.

Now they all sat frozen, eyes locked together, listening.

"Was that...?" Jocelyn's throat bobbed.

"Stay here, I'll go above." Saffra jumped to her feet.

"Oh, I think we will *all* go above," Desaree decided, not wanting to miss a thing, especially if this was what she thought it was. Or rather, *who*. Her stomach twisted into knots.

They raced for the stairs. The hall was dim and they held their arms out, steadying themselves as they made their way. The roll of the ship made them lurch from side to side.

She'd left a letter on Verath's bookshelf, knowing full well that he'd miss her at dinner. She hadn't been sure how long it would take him to spot the parchment, but hoped they would be well on their way.

They reached the deck and the ship lurched with impact. Heavily booted feet struck wood as a ruby colored dragon transformed. The three of them cowered in the doorway, shadowed to avoid notice.

Verath towered over the rest of the crew. His muscles bunched beneath a white tunic as he stalked across the deck, his head turning this way and that. The crew gawked. There were other ships in the vicinity, all keeping a wide berth.

"Where is she?!" The roar made her flinch. "I can smell her on this ship. Where is she?"

The captain was already racing across the deck. "My lord?"

Verath rounded on him, voice raised. She saw his eyes then— even at this distance—flashing with anger and...worry. "Lady Desaree. She was here. Her scent is all over this ship, I can smell it." He turned in a circle, as if expecting to see her assembled with the crew.

She backed deeper into the shadows. Behind her, Jocelyn and Saffra did the same, peering over her shoulder. Her throat was dry, too dry.

"Of course, my lord," Captain Kett said. "Of course. I'll have her summoned from—"

Verath moved quickly. Had she blinked, she would have missed it. The captain was pinned between Verath's forearm and the nearest mast. His crew stood motionless, eyes wide. They didn't dare interfere. "*Why* did you allow her aboard this ship? Your orders were to carry cargo, not a human female."

Desaree opened her mouth, not quite sure what to do. Meanwhile, the captain fumbled with his vest pocket, all but begging Verath to take the parchment bearing the king's seal. Verath dropped his arm and looked it over while Captain Kett sagged in relief. The moment was short lived. Verath bared his teeth, pinning the captain once more, a hand firmly pressed to the man's chest. "This is a forgery," he hissed, waving the slip of parchment in the captain's face.

"I think you'd diffuse the situation," Jocelyn hissed.

"Me?"

Saffra snorted. "Who else?"

"I'm not leaving this ship with him," Desaree said.

"Then go out and tell him so, but for the gods' sake, put poor Captain Kett out of his misery. The man's quaking. It's Verath, remember? He frightens everyone almost as much as King Talon does."

Desaree'd forgotten that bit—

"Operating under a forged letter from the king is illegal. I ought to have you—"

"Verath, *enough!*" Desaree stepped out into the sunlight. She wasn't dressed the way she usually was. Instead, she'd donned a pair of trousers and a roomy tunic that hung nearly to her knees, belted tightly around her waist to show off her generous curves. It ended at the elbows where she'd rolled the sleeves, showing off her forearms.

"Desaree..." Verath took her in, blinking. She noticed the way his shoulders relaxed at the sight of her. "What have you done?" The letter crumpled as he closed his fist around it. But he'd shifted his focus from the captain, who now sagged up against the mast.

She strode over to them. "Captain? I apologize for this mix up. You may return to your work after Lord Verath apologizes for handling you so inappropriately."

"I will do no such—"

"You will!" she seethed, rounding on him. "You will, or you'll have me to contend with."

"I already have you to contend with," he bit out, his scaly beast resurfacing.

"Well," she said, crossing her arms, lifting her chin, "then you'll have *more* of me to contend with. Apologize—now. You are *not* acting as a shield ought."

He flinched, glanced between her and the captain, hesitated, then bowed to the captain. "Forgive me, sir. The lady is right. I ought not to have handled you so forcefully before understanding the...situation." At this, his eyes darted to Desaree and narrowed with accusation. But he stood anyway and said, "I hope we can lay this matter to rest."

"Of—of course, my lord. No need to fret." But the captain still gazed at them with wide eyes, his fear not quite gone.

"We tricked Captain Kett into letting us aboard," Desaree explained. "As you can imagine, we are perfectly capable of such things." She squared her shoulders, as if proving her point—that she was perfectly capable of taking matters into her own hands should the need arise. "None of this is in any way his fault." Verath looked as if he desperately wished to argue that point but he smartly kept his mouth closed. "Now then, for the record, we knew exactly what we were doing when we forged that letter. I take full responsibility. I snuck into the king's study—it was my doing. All of it." She would leave Jocelyn and Saffra out of it. "When we arrive at the battle camp, I will submit myself to King Talon's justice."

"When we arrive at...?" He barked a laugh. "You're not arriving anywhere. I'm taking you back to the capital."

"No. You're not." She planted her feet, crossed her arms. "I'm staying on this ship. You will take me nowhere without my consent. Not unless you wish to do something you will dearly regret..." She loved him, gods, she did. But if he did this, if he took this away, made this decision *for* her, against her will...

She wasn't sure there'd be any coming back from something like that. He must have seen exactly what she was thinking, written plainly on her features. He swore under his breath then glanced over at the shadowy stairwell. An agitated hand combed through his head of dark hair, hair that she had only just recently trimmed for him, and yet, it seemed to have grown nearly a handspan in only a couple of weeks.

"You need another haircut," she said, sighing.

"Is that so?" His voice was flat. His eyes took on a far away look, but only briefly. He was talking to King Talon, telling him what had just happened. She knew it without him saying a word. His eyes always did that when he was using his mind.

"I'm not going back, Verath. We're going to the camp. If it's safe enough for servants, it's safe enough for us. You can fly back to Kastali Dun and tell our king what I've done, and that I'll submit myself to his justice once I'm there."

"Fly back to Kastali Dun?" He huffed out an angry sound. "I'm not going anywhere. You think I'm going to let you stay here alone?"

"Saffra and Jocelyn are with me, as you well know." As if on cue, the two women stepped out of the shadows, but only just.

"Be that as it may, I'm not leaving any of you here *unchaperoned.*"

"I'm not a child, Verath—none of us are. Saffra is plenty capable of using magic, should it come to it, which it won't, because Captain Kett can manage his crew just fine. I don't need a chaperone."

Gods. She wanted to smack him. Was he really implying that the crew would be dishonorable? Especially knowing full well who they were and what the consequences for such behavior would be? It was an insult to the crew—to everyone onboard the ship.

A muscle in his jaw ticked. "I'm not leaving."

She snorted. "Fine. Then if you're staying, you'll have to find somewhere else to bunk. No one wants you around with *that* attitude." Huffing, she turned on her heel and marched off, back down into the shadowed stairwell. She didn't look back, even though she knew she'd see him gaping.

"He's been standing on the deck for two days," Saffra announced, shutting the door to their cabin. "You're going to have to face him sooner or later."

Desaree sat on her bunk. She tucked her feet up and rested her chin on her knees, letting her eyes go unfocused. Saffra was right. She couldn't ignore Verath for the duration of their voyage. She thought perhaps after the spectacle on deck, that he'd come looking for her, that he'd insist on discussing what she'd done, but he hadn't. Instead, he'd given her space to cool off. Space to think.

Two days was plenty of time for thinking.

While she didn't regret her decision to leave Kastali Dun, she did feel guilty about hiding this from him. She'd even considered how she would feel if their roles were reversed. If Verath had snuck around and disappeared without telling her. That alone left her stomach knotted.

So fine, yes, she'd made a mistake. But, given the chance, she would do it again if Verath insisted on trapping her. Still, she didn't want a relationship of secrets—didn't want either of them to feel forced to hide things.

A deep sigh exploded from her chest. "I suppose I should go talk to him."

"I think that would be wise," Saffra agreed, taking a seat beside Jocelyn on the bottom bunk. She swung her legs over and dropped to the floor, leaving the cabin. They'd stayed mostly below deck. The captain had been extremely accommodating, especially once Verath was on board. Likely he was terrified that anything short of exemplary behavior would get him eaten alive by Verath's scaly red dragon.

It was an overcast day, but even still, the brightness on deck took a moment of getting used to. She locked eyes on him. His back was to her, standing at the prow, his legs shoulder-width apart, arms clasped behind his back. His dark hair rustled in the sea breeze. She watched for him for a moment, admiring the bulk of his muscle. In the time they'd been together, despite their intimate moments, she'd never grown tired of the sight of him. In fact, with each passing day, her appreciation of him grew.

As if he sensed her, he glanced over his shoulder. Their eyes met. He held her gaze for a moment, and even from here, she could see the way his eyes calmed at the sight of her. He turned forward again. It wasn't a dismissal, per se, but more of an invitation.

She crossed the deck to stand beside him. "Have...have you been standing out here for two days?" was all she could manage. He grunted in response, keeping his gaze forward. Well, then. "Verath, I...I'm—"

"You do not owe me an apology, Des." His voice was soft.

Her mouth snapped shut. But, wasn't he furious with her for deceiving him?

"It was my own actions that steered you here, that made you feel the need to do this behind my back, to run away because you felt you had no other choice." He sighed and his shoulders dropped.

"I..." She cleared her throat. "I shouldn't have kept it from you. But...you are correct. I felt I had no other option."

"Des..." He turned to face her, taking one of her hands in his. "A war camp is a hard place, the kind of place I would spare you from. There's little privacy to be had, certainly no bathing chambers, the food isn't ideal—for you humans, that is. It's busy. Messy, even. Exposed to the elements. And dangerous, should the dragons discover it." His gaze searched hers. "It isn't a place willingly endured. War camps serve a purpose. The people within them serve a purpose—"

"And you're saying I have no reason to be there? I have no purpose to serve—"

"That is not—"

"No, it is! It's exactly what you are saying. And you are right to say it. I have no purpose in going," she finished, her voice taking on a desperate edge. "When Claire was here, I had a purpose. Caring for her brought me joy. It gave me a reason to wake each morning. Something to occupy my time. But when she left..." She inhaled. "There are only so many times I can tidy her chambers, only so many gowns I can commission on her behalf while she's away, only so many..." She shook her head, letting her frustration out. "You are right. This was..."

She turned on her heel to leave, but Verath didn't relinquish her hand. "Desaree..." Shivers raced down her skin. "I like to think your purpose is to bring me joy, but that is a selfish notion. I know you, I know your capacity to care. You take pride in helping others, in giving yourself. It's why you took Claire under your wing when she arrived, why you mother-hen her so much. Your capacity to care for others, to do thankless work without complaint, has always drawn me to you. Our war camp will be lucky to have you. We will find something for you when we arrive. There are meals to be prepared, tents to be constructed and maintained, and so much more." He bent and kissed her forehead. "I should have been more observant. I should have listened to what you were feeling, why you felt this need to join us. I was selfish and...distracted. Forgive me."

She exhaled, hesitating, then threw her arms around his waist, burying her head in his chest. "Thank you," she breathed, pushing into him. His arms tightened around her and he kissed the top of her head.

"You will still have the king to contend with. He didn't sound happy to discover your deceit. Especially that you snuck in and used his seal for forgery."

She stilled. Yes, there was that to think of. Was he truly so angry? She supposed he was. He'd become less frightening as of late. "What...what did he have to say?"

"He has agreed that you will not be punished for treason, which would be a most unforgiving death. Mainly because your treasonous actions were not made directly against the crown for nefarious purposes." Her skin chilled. She swallowed. "However he has reminded me that such behavior still warrants punishment." His words were heavy. "He mentioned something off-hand about digging latrines. I suppose we will find out when we arrive."

A bark of nervous laughter burst from her chest, leaving her lighter than she'd been in days. Perhaps she hadn't realized how heavy this deceit was weighing on her. "I will accept whatever punishment King Talon metes out," she said, looking up at him. The corner of his lips twitched. "Will you kiss me now?" she added.

That brought a smile to his face. "That depends, will you allow me into your cabin?"

She fought to keep her expression calm. "There is only one bunk left. Top bunk. Though I'm not sure your hulking form will fit in it."

"I am sure I'll make do." With that, he leaned down and captured her lips, moving over them with a hunger she'd missed. When he pulled away, she was left breathless. Never mind that they were in broad daylight. Never mind that half the crew was gaping at them. "Ignore them," he said, as if reading her mind. So she did, taking his hand and leading him below deck.

CHAPTER 42
PARTING WAYS

The Gable Forest

Claire had never traveled as a queen. Had never realized what it entailed, or how much coordination was involved. Everyone had an opinion, like when exactly they should depart, what provisions ought to be brought, how many gowns would be needed to keep her looking queenly. It was a wonder they'd made it out of Esterpine, traversing the western path that would take them towards Fort Squall.

A week had passed since the Equinox Ball—a night she wouldn't soon forget. There'd been dancing into the early hours of dawn, tables groaning with sweet treats and savory bites, and ethereal music that felt like pure magic. She'd laughed until her face hurt and danced until her feet ached.

While it didn't compare to the ball held in Kastali Dun, simply because of Talon's absence, it had been splendid in its own right. Her body ached for Talon, for his nearness and his touch. She missed their banter, their secret looks, that feeling of sharing something between just them, something no one else could fathom. The feeling of being a team. Gods, she even missed her ability to speak telepathically.

She was closer than ever to having him back. Each step through the forest was one step nearer to him. She was giddy with anticipation, eager to the point of bursting. There was an undercurrent of fear too; she'd changed in the past few months. What would he think of her new marks? As a drengr, would he find her off-putting? Would he miss the girl she was?

"So...what's with the bow? Was it a solstice gift?" Reyr's shoulder bumped into hers.

"Oh, hello." She hadn't noticed him falling into step beside her. "It was a gift."

"From?"

"My tutor. He thought it might serve me better than sitting stagnate in his cottage."

Her mind swept back to their parting, to Pelwynn hunched over his flowerbeds. She'd been heartbroken to say goodbye. Heartbroken by the thought that he might not be there when—if—she ever returned. But the moment he'd seen the look on her face, he'd scolded her and told her to quit acting like he was already gone. That was when he'd led her into his cottage, offered her the most priceless thing in his possession.

"I see," Reyr said. "You will receive a bow during your bonding ceremony too, you know."

"I...right." She'd considered that. The bonding ceremony bow —the bow every drengr gifted his mate. Talon's gift would be special for obvious reasons. But Pelwynn's bow held sentimental value, too. It had been the missing piece that allowed her magic to blossom. "I suppose I can frame my tutor's bow on the wall and keep just the arrows to use with the one Talon will give me."

"What's so special about the arrows?" Reyr eyed her quiver. She offered him a sly smile—

"Hey you two, Taylynn suggests we pause for respite in the glade up ahead." Koldis had fallen back into line with them. "That is...if it is all right with *Her Majesty*."

"Enough, Koldis." She sighed. He'd been laying it on thick as of late. "And yes, fine with me. I could use a rest."

They'd been walking for hours—a procession of nearly fifty-five bodies making their way through the forest. Not only were there twenty pairs, she'd brought her handmaidens, her eight guards, Taylynn, and two shields. Trailing behind them was a delegation of unicorns, thanks to Taylynn. "You're a queen now. You'll need to arrive at King Talon's war camp in style," was all she'd said.

Once they reached the edge of the forest, their delegation would split up. Her pairs would take to the skies by night and travel on foot by day, just in case. The rest of them would travel by unicorn. Much to her shields' dismay, the unicorns would travel faster and they would soon outpace them. When Taylynn had first broken the news, both Koldis and Reyr had protested, insisting they would also travel by unicorn. Taylynn nixed that idea, making clear that no unicorn would agree to carry a drengr when the drengr could transport themselves.

Taylynn had also provided beautiful cloaks hemmed with gold beading for everyone traveling with the unicorns, granting them a magical disguise. The unicorns had their own ways of cloaking their presence. Once they arrived at the war camp, the unicorns would have the option to return to the forest.

She slowed until the unicorns caught up with her. Placing her hand on a nearby female's neck, they walked side-by-side. The female snickered and tossed her head leading her to the glen where the others were resting.

She caught a flash of black in her periphery and her heart jumped. Taylynn had assured them that the forest was cured. Still, old habits and all that—

Another flash of black made her twitch. She could have ignored it, but instead, she moved away from the other unicorns. There were fifteen in total. Not all of them would carry people. A few already carried packs.

She crept forward, preparing to call up a protective bubble of air. The black shape materialized into a black unicorn. It watched her with dark eyes.

Her chest swelled.

"You're Tourmaline, aren't you?" she whispered.

"*I am.*"

She startled. "You can speak in my mind?"

"*If I wish.*"

She took a tentative step forward and held out an open hand. Tourmaline bowed his head, giving her permission. A nervous laugh burst from her lips when she ran her fingers over his sleek coat.

"*You travel west, to the battle brewing along the coast?*"

"I...how did you know?"

"*It is my business to know many things. I am lord of the unicorns, after all.*"

"You are?" She hadn't even known there was such a thing.

"*I am.*"

"How old are you?"

"*Old enough to remember the tree when it was lonely in this place we now call home. I would like to join you on this journey. Will you have me, Queen?*"

"I... Yes. It is not my place to deny you. I would be honored, but I cannot promise your safety. You are sure?"

"*As sure the seasons pass, as the sun rises and the moon sets, as the tides wax and wane.*"

She gave a nod. "Very well, then. Would you like to come and meet the rest of my companions? Or will you keep your distance until we are out of the trees?"

There was a long hesitation and then, "*I will keep my distance, for now.*"

She nodded, giving Tourmaline a final pet before retreating back to their group.

~

It took several days to reach the borders of the spriten kingdom. Taylynn took Claire's arm and slowed their pace, allowing the unicorns to pass. "I cannot go with you to the war camp," Taylynn said. "Fright and I have more pressing matters."

"What matters—?"

Taylynn held a finger to her lips. "Do not ask."

She swallowed. "I do not want to be queen, Taylynn. Are you sure there is no way I can abdicate before I leave? I cannot return to Talon as a spriten queen."

The princess sighed. "You must—"

"No."

"Claire, you *must*. We talked about this. To unite our two peoples, you must be queen when the two of you complete the bonding ceremony. A spriten queen united with a drengr king. It must be so. I am certain."

"And then what? How can I be a good leader for the spriten people when I am away so much of the time?"

"Our people have endured for an age—longer still. We will continue to. For us, you will be gone for a mere blink. But eventually you will return with your mate, and you will deliver the throne to me." Claire's shoulders fell, defeated. "I know it is not the answer you wanted, but the support of my people—*our* people—will count for more if you fight beside Dragonwall's king. One united front."

"They aren't here now. They aren't here for the battle of Squall's End."

"But they are. *You* will be there, and your guards. You are all that is needed."

"And you are confident that I will change the tide?"

"It is not my confidence that matters," Taylynn said.

"*It is mine.*" The king tree's words whispered through the trees.

They had fallen farther behind, so they picked up the pace until they were even with the last of the unicorns. "I suppose Tourmaline was your idea too," she hedged, glancing at Taylynn.

"Hah! No. Believe it or not."

"Will he survive outside of the forest? Will the others? They don't have living water to carry like the others."

"Unicorns do not need it. Their magic is of a different kind. They have not grown reliant upon the forces here to survive. But if they wish to return at any time, they are free to come back."

She nodded in agreement. "They will be treated with the utmost honor while they are with me. I would never keep them against their will. Would never keep any of my delegation against their will."

"Good. I suppose this is goodbye, then."

"Wait, right now? You're not going to say goodbye to Koldis?"

A wicked smile spread across the princess's lips. "I already have."

"Oh. And...when will I see you again?"

Taylynn took her hand and squeezed. "Perhaps sooner than you expect. Never forget what you are, Claire—who you are. You are the balance long sought, the weapon much needed, and the force that will bring a sorcerer to his end. Farewell, cousin." Taylynn dropped her hand, then disappeared into the forest.

When she caught up with everyone, Koldis gave her a searching look. *"She's gone then?"* he asked.

"She's gone."

He offered a brief nod before returning to his conversation with Feowen. If the prince knew his sister had departed, he offered no sign. Likely, he was beyond used to seeing Taylynn come and go.

The trees thinned, all but disappearing. She gasped when she recognized the outside world. Her previous steps out of the forest had been far north, in the dead of winter. But here, the snow lay in patches and grass was growing. No, not just grass, fields of wildflowers!

She laughed, which caught everyone's attention. Her smile faded. This was where they would say goodbye. It was daylight still, nighttime still hours away. None of the drengr could take to the skies until then.

Koldis was the first to wrap her in his arms, lifting her off the ground. "Well," he said, "when next we meet, it will be on the eve of battle. I suspect you will arrive a few days before us."

"I know you'll be tempted to warn Talon that I'm coming," she said, "but I must insist that you don't. It was my choice to assist. He should hear it from me."

Koldis and Reyr shared a look. "As you wish, Your Majesty." Koldis merely lifted his brow, like she was up to some kind of mischief.

She hugged Reyr next, burying her face in his neck. "Thank you for visiting," she said, her voice muffled.

"Any time."

"Take care of Koldis and our pairs," she added. "Don't get caught. We can't risk the dragons seeing you."

"We'll be careful," he assured her.

She went to each pair, offering a farewell. She'd grown rather fond of them, and after all, this wasn't goodbye. She'd see them in a few days.

She was just hugging Madeleine when a gasp sounded behind her. She whirled around.

"Tourmaline," Feowen whispered from nearby.

She gave Madeleine a final nod before stepping away, walking over to the unicorn. "So, you decided to join us after all. I had begun to wonder." She lifted a hand and let him sniff her.

"I am true to my word. Are you ready?"

"Yes," she said, speaking aloud. "Though I'm no expert at riding without a saddle."

"I'll keep my hooves light. When you are ready, Queen." He lowered himself. She blinked. Whispers erupted behind her, the sprites especially. She glanced over and caught Feowen's wide eyes before climbing upon Tourmaline's back. She balanced her quarterstaff in front of her, took his mane in the other hand, and gripped his body with her thighs. He stood.

"Well?" she said to those who'd be traveling with her. "Shall we see if we can race the rest of our companions to camp?"

Her words spurred a flurry of activity. Both parties bid each other rushed farewells and her entourage mounted up. Feowen took the lead while the rest of them formed around her.

She shared one final glance with Koldis and Reyr, her goodbye riding in her eyes. They offered nods. "Keep her safe," Reyr said to Feowen, his final parting words. The prince bowed his head, keeping a hand over his heart. Tourmaline lurched beneath her and she tightened her grip. With a breathy huff, they were off, their surroundings a sudden blur, racing into the late afternoon light, chasing the sun towards the horizon.

CHAPTER 43

ARRIVING AT CAMP

Celenore

Claire kept her cloak firmly drawn. Tourmaline was a bulk of muscle, racing over the landscape. He'd taken the lead, allowing the other unicorns to fan out around him. Their journey had been nothing short of a blur, literally, as the landscape slid by. Trees, rolling hills, rocky outcroppings, creeks, and even swift rivers, barely discernible. There and gone, in just a few blinks.

One thing was unmistakable. Spring was out in full force; it was the prettiest she'd ever seen Dragonwall. A wealth of green was returning to the land. There were fields of wildflowers in shades of purple, pink, yellow, and orange. Birds flirting for mates. Animals waking from a long slumber.

Part of her wanted to slow down and take it all in, this beautiful kingdom that was nearly hers, with nothing but a technicality separating her. She'd been careful to pick the prettiest places to stop. She refused to show up on the eve of battle exhausted. Besides, Talon's forces would be slow in reaching the rendezvous point, and even then, they'd need time to set up camp.

"Your Majesty, we should stop at that rocky formation there." Feowen came up beside Tourmaline.

"You know, I already told you—"

"—to call you Claire. Yes, Cousin, I'm well aware." The corner of his mouth tipped up. "But for now, with your position being so new, I rather enjoy using the title."

She sighed. "Yes, fine. Let's rest for a bit. I want to consult our map. We should be getting close?"

"I believe so. Let's stop and take a look."

Jagged rocks jutted up all over the landscape, peppered randomly in clusters as if a giant had ground up massive chunks and tossed them out like dice. The hills and grass were a vivid green, dotted with wispy pink wildflowers. She kept an eye on her handmaidens and guards while she and Feowen consulted the map he'd brought. She had her own handbook from Desaree, but it was tucked away.

Feowen pulled a starscope from his pocket. She'd been enamored by the device yesterday, expressing her surprise. Day or night, indoors or out, the scope allowed its user to see a perfect mapping of the stars overhead.

Feowen placed it to his eye, turning his gaze skyward. He alternated between glancing down at his map and looking skyward. "Here." He put his finger on the map. "We're somewhere here."

Close. They were so close to where Talon ought to be. Her stomach somersaulted. "But that means..."

"That we should arrive in the next few hours." He grinned at her. "Ready to reunite with your king?" His eyes glittered with mischief.

"More than ready."

Selphie and Meira insisted on preparing her. The gown they surprised her with was similar to her ballgown, a hybrid with long layers of silver gauzy skirts and a bodice that looked like armor, pieced together with rigid starlight silver boning and panels of translucent silver cloth. Only her breasts were hidden by multiple layers. The rest of her chest and arms were protected by a single layer, putting her glowing marks on full display.

Her spriten sword was belted at her waist with a belt that had been painted silver. Cyrus's sword was strapped to her back with another silver belt, opposite her bow and quiver of *yirnik* arrows.

"Your hair should go up," Meira said, fussing over her. "To display your marks."

She didn't argue.

"I hope you won't mind," Selphie added, producing a black drawstring pouch. "We also had this made for you."

She stilled. "What is it?"

Selphie handed it to her. When she removed the starlight tiara inside, she gasped. The metalwork was exquisite, with woven bands that twined like calligraphic flourishes, coming to a point in the center. A cluster of white diamonds bracketed a glittering black, iridescent jewel.

"It's black seledonix. Very rare. Found only in the Gable Forest."

She blinked, at a loss for words. It was black like Talon's scales. It sparkled like them too. Her handmaidens wouldn't have known to use a stone like this without input. Talon's Shields hadn't so much as breathed a word of it to her. She wished they were here, so she could hug them.

"A queen of two kingdoms," Selphie mused.

"How much do you know?" she asked, eyeing them.

"Enough to know where your heart lies. We are happy for you, Your Majesty. You will make King Talon a good match. But we will keep your secret, you needn't fear."

She blew out a breath and nodded.

"Here—" Meira reached for the tiara before placing it upon her head. A perfect fit. It came to a point over her forehead. She could feel the jewel there, sitting against her skin. Meira produced a small mirror.

"It hardly looks like me," she said, taking in the coiffure of blonde hair piled atop her head, the tiara sitting perfectly. She looked exactly like a spriten queen. A shiver raced across her skin.

"Are you ready, Your Majesty?" Selphie folded the discarded clothing and stuffed them into a travel pack.

"I'm ready," she said, and squared her shoulders.

~

Talon's camp came into view in the distance, little white tents dotting the landscape. "Let's slow down," she said to Tourmaline. "I would like to give them plenty of warning."

"As you wish."

She held up a hand to slow her companions' pace to a gentle trot. Warning shouts rose up. Several wooden watchtowers had been constructed, making their approach discernible. She narrowed her eyes, studying the flurry of activity.

"They've spotted us," Feowen said from beside her.

Butterflies filled her stomach. Somewhere in that mass of tents was Talon. Her mate.

It took everything to stay calm. She wanted to throw off her cloak, discard her tiara, and jump from Tourmaline's back to race through the tents.

Her mind was a fortress, sealed tight. Not so much as a single stray thought came through. Her abilities had strengthened.

People filed out to the edge of camp. She could make out faces now. The gathering crowd began to cry out in surprise. "The sprite queen! The sprite queen has come!"

Did they realize *which* sprite queen?

The crowd split, parting like a wave. She blinked, and he was there, striding into view. Her breath stilled.

"Stop." A gentle tug of Tourmaline's mane and he halted. She sat frozen, her eyes tracing Talon's every scar from beneath her hood. Tracing his straight nose, his high cheekbones, his strong jaw. He was exactly as she remembered, his tall frame topping even the shields beside him, with broad shoulders and corded muscle. His sverak was strapped to his back, along with two baldrics of knives along his chest. A simple crown of gold was atop his head, fighting with his messy black hair.

His silver eyes locked on her; she swore she saw sparks dancing within.

He stood motionless. She couldn't move, either. A sob bubbled up in her chest and she forced it down. She didn't make a sound as—

"All hail the spriten queen!" Feowen's voice broke the silence. She flinched.

Talon's expression faltered, crumbled, then smoothed into something unreadable. It was such a rapid flurry of emotions, there and gone, she might have missed it if she'd blinked.

Her heart sank like a stone. She knew immediately the mistake she'd made, one she needed to rectify. *I'm not really their queen,* she wanted to shout. *This is just temporary!* But she *was* their queen, and there were appearances to maintain. Especially with nearly the entire camp assembled.

She lifted her hood, revealing her face, her tiara. Gasps echoed through the onlookers. Several curses also caught her attention. They sounded a lot like Bedelth, Jovari, and Verath. She didn't dare look at the shields. Instead, she swung her leg over Tourmaline and landed gracefully on her feet. Then she took a deep breath. Her right hand held tightly to Isabella's quarterstaff. It was the only thing keeping her calm. Her queen's guard also dismounted and formed ranks.

She turned away from Tourmaline and advanced, keeping her chin held high. Each step closer to Talon unraveled the tense knot strangling her. He didn't bother hiding the absolute look of betrayal at the sight of her. She'd chosen the sprites over him, chosen a queenship over their mate bond. That's what it looked like, anyway.

"Your Majesty," he said. His voice sent shivers racing across her skin. He bowed low—so low. She was certain he'd never bowed like this for anyone else in his entire life. His eyes traced every inch of her body, devouring. When he stood again, his expression had changed once more. Now there was only a frown of determination and drawn eyebrows.

"King Talon," she said, offering barely a bow.

She half expected him to demand, here and now, what she was doing here. This had never been the plan. She wanted to tell him everything. To tell him how she felt, to tell him how much she'd missed him. She wanted to throw herself into his arms. To wrap her body around him—

Her eyes dipped to his lips. He noticed the action and his gaze darkened, little gold flecks smoldering among silver pools. She broke their stare.

"Bedelth, Jovari, Verath," she said by way of greeting, acknowledging them at last. A few months ago, they'd have taken her into their arms, hugging her. Now they regarded her with silent shock, uncertain how to respond. Opting for formality, they each bowed and placed hands over their hearts.

"Shall we walk?" Talon held out an arm. She blinked. The gesture was so...casual. So simple. And yet, it spoke of something deeper between them. It brought so many memories. She forced her eyes to remain clear of the tears threatening to pool up.

"I would like that, yes." She stepped forward and linked her hand through his elbow.

"The rest of you can clear off," Bedelth grumbled, letting his deep baritone penetrate the hundreds of onlookers.

She and Talon remained motionless, staring at each other as everyone around them began moving away. The rest of the world seemed to fall away with them.

"Shall I...have someone tend to the unicorns?" She was vaguely aware of Jovari speaking with Prince Feowen.

"We will see to them shortly," came Feowen's reply. "Once our queen has been settled."

The crowd cleared and Talon led her away from the camp. When it was obvious that her queen's guard had no intention of abandoning her, Talon's shields took that as their invitation to follow. With a quick motion, Feowen stepped forward and took her staff.

Silence descended. The longer it stretched, the more she was at a loss for words. She'd rehearsed this speech over and over and yet, now she remembered none of what she wanted to say. Months spent apart. She couldn't think of a way to begin telling him all that had happened.

It was Talon who broke the silence. "Where are Koldis and

Reyr? Where are my other pairs?" His voice was stiff, like he wasn't sure where to start. The battle playing out on his face was obvious. A male so often in control of his expression was allowing it to crumble. She could read him plainly now. He wanted to respect her decision—the decision he *believed* she had made.

"Koldis, Reyr and *our* pairs are on their way. I felt it best they travel by night and keep on foot by day to avoid detection. Reyr and Koldis agreed, as did my captain of the guard."

"Your captain of the guard," he repeated, his voice flat. "Prince Feowen."

"Correct."

"So...you have made your choice then."

She stopped, the motion abrupt, and turned to face him. "And if I have? What would you say to me?"

He dropped her arm and stared at her—just stared. Then he blew out a breath and his shoulders sagged. "I would say..." His voice wavered. "I would say that I want you to be happy, Claire. That I respect your choice—respect *you*. If this queenship is truly what you want?" His eyes darted to her forehead, to her tiara. "It wasn't...this was not what I expected."

"And what *did* you expect?"

"That if you hadn't chosen me, it would have been for your family. So that you might someday return to them. But instead you..." He shook his head, motioning with his hand to her markings. *See how you've changed?* the gesture said. *See how spriten you've become?*

Worry seeped into her. "Talon..." She reached up and freed a lock of hair that curled around his crown. His eyes closed at her touch. "Talon, look at me." His eyes flew open. "You are the *only* thing I want in this world, and all others. I would choose you over everything—I do choose you."

His eyebrows pulled together, and then understanding transformed his expression. He blinked, his surprise evident. He glanced over his shoulder to where their guards stood and then took a step closer. "Claire..." Her name was desperation on his lips.

A quiet sob broke free of her chest. She couldn't hold her

emotions back any longer. To hell with her queenship. To hell with her composure. She flung herself at him, crushing her mouth against his. He caught her up, wrapped himself around her, holding her, kissing her back. There was nothing gentle about their mouths as he took her. A growl started deep in his chest, resonating. It rumbled through her, straight to her bones. His arms tightened with a fierce possessiveness that felt more dragon than human. She was almost certain he wouldn't release her, not now, not ever.

They broke for air, gasping. His chest heaved against hers, but he didn't let her go. Instead, he turned his head, looked at her queen's guard, her handmaidens, looked at his shields—

"You're all dismissed," he commanded. It came out as more of a growl. Several of her guards, Rahlif and Gorded in particular, looked stunned to be receiving orders from someone other than their queen.

"It's..." She cleared her throat, pushing at Talon to let her down so she could stand on two feet. He did no such thing. "It's all right," she managed to get out through her breathlessness. "You should all go and get settled. Verath? See that they have adequate...tents— near ours."

"Of course, Your Majesty," Verath gave a little bow of his head. She didn't miss the smile that curved his lips. He hesitated. "Also, I think..." His eyes flicked to Talon, who gave a tiny nod. "When the two of you have—erm—finished, there's a few people who would be glad to see you." Verath bowed again, then turned on his heel, leading the others away.

She knew immediately of whom he spoke. The air whooshed out of her. "They came? Here? To the camp?"

"They did, but not without trouble," he said, lowering her to the ground. "Desaree specifically," he added.

"*Desaree?*" she squeaked.

He sighed. "I never took your handmaiden for a rule breaker. Something tells me she picked that up from you."

"Oh, no," she whispered. "What...what did she do?"

Talon sighed. Some of his happiness was replaced by wary fatigue. "She forged a letter—used my seal."

"She did *not!*" Her jaw dropped, mostly to hide the snicker of amusement that threatened to break free. "*My* Desaree? We *are* talking of the same person, yes?" Talon only nodded. "Why? Just so that she could be here?"

"You have very loyal friends. As I understand it, she wanted to help in our efforts beyond what was done to brew the poison. But... her reasons weren't good enough to avoid punishment."

Claire's stomach squirmed. Forgery was treason in Dragonwall. And using the king's seal...

She tried to keep her worry at bay. She knew exactly how severe Talon could be. But, Desaree had broken the law. And yet, she felt responsible for her handmaiden, even if Desaree's decisions were her own.

"You know," she said, "I probably would have done the same thing—snuck in and used your seal if it meant getting what I wanted, even if my reasons weren't necessarily sound."

Talon barked a laugh. "Yes, I know. I thought of you immediately when Verath informed me of what happened. They took a ship, you know, to get here. Snuck aboard." Her jaw dropped. "Verath stayed with them—not to worry. It did not affect our plans. I have other shields. Besides, I don't need fussing over. I'd have rather he stayed with them, just in case." Talon's eyes searched her face. Then he said, voice soft, "Nothing has ever stopped you from doing what you want when you put your mind to it, but something tells me you would have used a bit more logic than Desaree."

"Oh, really?" she challenged, not quite so sure. "And allowed you to leave me behind while you marched off to war? Flew off, whatever."

"Desaree is human, Claire, she has no magic."

"I...I know. I'm just saying." She sighed. "I left the keep to help the villagers in Celenore, remember? I expressly disobeyed you when I was not supposed to, putting myself in danger."

"You had three of my shields with you, protecting you. It is not a fair argument."

"I snuck into your tower and stole one of the queen's gowns for Saffra that night of the ball."

"Also, not the same." A smile pulled at his lips, like he was waiting for her to name each transgression, each bit of rule breaking since coming to Dragonwall.

Oops.

"I listened in on a bunch of your private conversations before you knew about my telepathic ability."

"Sorry, but you'll have to try harder than that."

"I defied you in the throne room the first day we ever met, even though you were a king and I was a nobody."

"Claire," he said, his scars softening, "you were *never* a nobody—"

"Oh, wait, I've got a good one," she said. "I snuck through the garden door and into the city, that day I was angry with you. I got myself kidnapped. Now *that* was a stupid decision. One I made based on pure emotion. One that put me in danger when I knew I wasn't supposed to leave the keep without guards. A rule you set in stone. Isn't a king's rule law?" This time, a wicked smile formed on her lips, because she knew she had him.

"You clever little fox," he growled, tightening his arms around her.

"And you didn't even punish me for it—but, I'm not saying you shouldn't punish Desaree."

"I already did."

"Right, like I said. I'm not saying you shouldn't. I guess I'm just saying...none of us is perfect. We all let our emotions guide us from time to time, even if it's in the wrong direction."

He huffed. "Yes, I seem to recall a certain king who strapped you to a torture device when his emotions got the better of him."

"There. See? So...what was her punishment?" Somehow, even though she feared what he might say, she knew she could trust him. He wouldn't cause Desaree physical harm, even if treason was a severe punishment in Dragonwall. Perhaps he was too blinded, and it shouldn't have made her feel all warm and fuzzy, but it kind of did. Maybe their mate bond had changed the lens through which he regarded his kingdom.

"Let's just say Desaree's got blisters from digging. And I didn't allow Lady Saffra to heal them."

"Blisters?" Her jaw dropped. "You had her digging latrines, didn't you?!" The image of Desaree on shovel duty flashed through her mind. And yet, she didn't laugh, because Desaree had never been one to shy away from work. Something told her that her friend bore the punishment nobly.

Talon shrugged. "Verath requested I go easy on her, and while I agreed, Verath's idea of easy was not my idea of easy. Like me, he's rather besotted. Something I can understand. Perhaps that's made me soft." He hesitated. "Has that made me soft?" There was a genuine question in his eyes. Talon, of all people. A king people were terrified of, was worried about being *too* soft?

She tutted. "There's nothing wrong with being a little soft, Talon. As long as you are hard where it counts." She wanted to make so much more of that statement than she did, but she kept her mouth firmly shut.

He kept an arm about her, kept her pressed against him. The rest of their entourage had long since moved off. She reached for his face again, memorizing the feel of his scars beneath her fingers, kissing him hungrily, cementing the taste of him in her memory for all of eternity.

A laugh bubbled up from her chest. Oh, gods! To be here with him in his arms! "I missed you so much," she whispered, not caring about the sob that broke free with her words. Then she buried her face in the crook of his neck, hugging him to her.

"I missed you more," he said into her hair, nuzzling her and inhaling deeply. "You smell like a sprite." She pictured his nose wrinkling at the declaration. A bark of laughter fell from her lips. It was all she could manage as she pressed herself against him.

"And for the record, Desaree isn't the only one in trouble. You've got some explaining to do, love." He kept his voice low. "But we can get to that later. For now, I just want to enjoy you all to myself. I ought to be furious that you're here. Instead, I'm irrevocably happy to see you." With that, he took her hand and pulled her away. "Oh, and in case you've forgotten, you owe me many more walks, and by my calculations, even more kisses."

She giggled. "The latter of which I will happily repay in full before we return to camp."

Their fingers threaded together before they disappeared far enough from camp to avoid prying eyes. There, she eagerly made good on her promise. So many kisses that by the end, she couldn't have counted them even if she'd wanted to.

CHAPTER 44
TIME IN THE TENT

Celenore

Claire took in the expressions of everyone at the table in Talon's command tent. From shocked to downright horrified. Jovari's mouth opened and closed like a fish. Desaree had tears leaking down her cheeks, her bandaged hands resting on the table. Saffra sat baffled, eyes wide, with her mouth gaping. But it was Talon's expression that captured her attention. The rage in his eyes, the way his body tensed with fury, the way his jaw flexed.

"I'm all right," she assured them. Except, her voice cracked. "Really. I promise. No lasting harm done." That wasn't exactly true. But she didn't want them to worry. Didn't want—

"He *tortured* you," Talon hissed, baring his teeth. "He subjected you to unbearable pain, and I wasn't there to—"

"Talon, it was my ordeal to—"

"No!" His palm slammed against the table, making it shudder. "All of you—*out*." His skin began to ripple as a few black scales sprouted. "*Out!*"

She came to her feet. "No, stay. Everyone stay. Talon, control yourself. I'm not finished."

Talon looked as if he wanted to argue. He took a deep breath, and then another. His skin stopped rippling and the scales disappeared. She wanted to climb into his lap, to wrap her arms around him. Wanted to kiss away his fear, his guilt. But he was Dragonwall's king, and she was now a queen. She would not afford him leniency. These were times of war. She wanted to get through everything she had to say, to tell it once, and be done with it. Only then could she begin to put it behind her.

Talon sighed his acceptance. She reclaimed her seat and recounted the rest of her story, glad that she finished with the bits about the spring equinox. "Thank you for your gift, by the way," she said to Talon, holding his gaze. He blew out a breath and his features softened. "I'm sorry I didn't have the foresight to send something in return."

"You owe me no gifts. Choosing me, my kingdom, the title that comes with it—that was the only gift I have ever wanted."

Her throat closed up. She could barely manage a nod before turning to the others. "I loved your gifts—all of them. They are special to me." A few of them glanced down at the table as silence fell.

Feowen cleared his throat and said, "My sister will take up queenship over our people when the time comes. The Tree would like to see a union of both races. A union between the sprites and the drengr. Only then will Claire pass the mantle. It will herald a new era and show a united front against Kane. Once your ceremony is complete and your bond sealed, you will travel to the forest where Claire will abdicate. The crown will pass to Taylynn."

Claire nodded along.

"If that is the case," Talon said, "then we will begin planning the ceremony immediately. Claire has enough pressure on her shoulders. She doesn't need more. She doesn't need to rule the sprites."

"Talon." She sighed and reached for his hand, giving it a firm squeeze. He wrapped his fingers around hers. "We have more pressing matters at the moment. We're here to reclaim Squall's End, not plan a bonding ceremony."

He looked as if he wanted to argue, but gave a curt nod instead. "Once we've seen to that, of course."

She hesitated. "Koldis, Reyr, and the others should be here in a few days. Have the dwargs arrived yet? What of our plans and progress? Where do we stand? It looks as though you've only just set up camp."

"We have. The dwargs should reach the coast tonight, if they haven't already. Bedelth will depart with a small group. He was preparing to leave when you arrived."

She smiled at Bedelth. "I'm glad I caught you beforehand."

"As am I, Your Majesty."

She almost corrected him. *Almost.* But instead, she took a deep breath. Talon's shields never called Talon by his first name, except perhaps when they were outside formal settings. Plus, they'd known him for hundreds of years. Why would they do so for her?

"We've already sent our operatives out on foot. It will be approximately a week before they reach Lake Plymlet. We sent them in smaller groups, disguised as travelers. Their packs carry the poison. They were forced to travel light. Very little in the way of provisions."

"And then three days after that, we expect to see the results?"

"Correct. That is when we will reclaim Squall's End and the fort."

She glanced at Byron and Tamara. They sat at the opposite end of the table. Tamara caught her gaze and held it. She'd matured since their last encounter. Then again, they'd both changed. Had there been any other choice?

She cleared her throat and said, "We cannot pin all our hopes on the current plan. As much as I wanted to come here simply to see everyone, Taylynn sent me for a reason." Talon snorted. "While your plan with the klixite and dragon's bane appears sound, we cannot rely on it. Taylynn has foreseen this. We were sent, myself and my queen's guard, to infiltrate and protect the people in the city, ensuring they come to no harm. Continue with your preparations and consider us a safeguard—"

"No. Absolutely not." Talon's hand tensed in hers. It was a

command, one given with the expectation of being followed. "We will not risk you."

"Talon, this is not up for discussion," she said. "My guards and I are perfectly capable of protecting the city's people from dragon fire. It would take but a single dragon to destroy thousands. We cannot let that happen."

He held her gaze and the rest of the tent fell away. What was it about him that captivated her? His intensity. That's what it was. Pure intensity. While others in his kingdom wanted to look anywhere *but* their king, she couldn't tear her eyes from him. "Fine," he snapped. "We'll discuss the particulars later."

"No, we will discuss them now. And you won't change my mind. I am not the same girl who left Kastali Dun because yes, you are right, *that* girl could not be risked. *That* girl was not capable of what *this* girl is." At her words, a fierce wind ripped through the camp, hissing through the tent. It was so strong, so powerful, it snuffed out all the flames in the braziers. Its roar drowned out the world, even as cries of confusion and fear rose up outside, throughout the camp. Talon's eyes widened and his body tensed, ready to spring forward and meet some unknown enemy. The tent was cast into darkness.

As quickly as it came, it disappeared. With a single thought, the source of their light returned, flames in the braziers, but now they burned green.

Talon stared at her—just stared. The others around the table did too. Feowen chuckled, as if he'd been waiting for something like this. Then Bedelth began to laugh, his deep draconic rumble breaking the tension. "Not the same girl, indeed," he said. He stood and placed a hand over his heart. "Well, my queen, if you have no further need of me, I should be going. With nightfall upon us, we must fly fast to reach the rendezvous point with the dwargs. Dallin?"

The young drengr twitched then rose to his feet, also offering a bow.

"Of course." She looked between them. "I will not delay you

any longer. Fly safely, Bedelth, Dallin. May the wind be strong beneath your wings."

"And yours, Your Majesty." They both turned to King Talon, bowing before disappearing through the tent flaps.

Saffra watched Bedelth go, a strange look on her face, but said nothing. They'd had absolutely no time or privacy to catch up. When she and Talon had returned to the command tent, everyone was already waiting. Talon had simply walked her to her place and pulled out a chair. In truth, she'd almost been glad. What little energy she'd arrived with had fled in the quiet moments she'd spent with him. Either that, or he'd simply kissed it from her. Likely the latter.

She sighed, giving in to the exhaustion that dragged at her. The journey here had been tiring but not as much as the thought of what was to come. That alone threatened to overwhelm her.

"You need rest," Talon mused, as if reading her mind. "May I dismiss everyone now, *Your Majesty*?" His eyes sparkled, but otherwise, he kept his expression blank. She almost laughed.

"Yes, I believe we may conclude for the night."

"Well?" Talon said. "You heard her. Her Majesty needs her rest. You can all catch up with her in the morning." She caught the undercurrent of his meaning, as did the others.

She offered Desaree, Jocelyn, Saffra, and Tamara a warm smile by way of an apology. They stood, nonetheless. Desaree hesitated though, perhaps wanting to stay, to fret over her. But Saffra whispered something in Desaree's ear and ushered her away.

She blew out a breath and slumped in her chair.

Gods, was she being a horrible friend? She felt like it. And yet, she was so utterly exhausted. If she allowed herself time with them, she'd want to hear all their stories, and her body couldn't take another moment of excited conversation.

"Shall I summon your handmaidens," Feowen asked, hovering near the tent flaps. Selphie and Meira, he meant.

"No, Prince," the king growled. "*I* will take care of my queen. I assure you, I am perfectly capable." Feowen hesitated then nodded, offering her a final glance before he disappeared. Suddenly, they were absolutely and completely alone.

Talon poked his head out of the tent and said something to the guards. She heard retreating footsteps; he'd sent them away. She frowned, but didn't question it.

"Come, my queen." His gaze heated. He took her hand and helped her from the chair, leading her to a cordoned off sleeping area. There wasn't a cot, but the floor was piled with furs and pillows. She wanted to collapse. "I know your handmaidens probably do this sort of thing *for* you," Talon teased, "but, may I?" There was a need in his gaze, a hunger that pierced straight to her heart. She nodded, staring at the furs longingly. Her eyelids were heavy, and she strained to keep them open.

Talon set about undoing the straps that held her spriten blade and sverak in place, carefully setting them off to the side, but not before he hummed with interest at the spriten blade. He busied himself with the buttons along the back of her gown. As his fingers worked, she noticed that her belongings had already been brought in, including Pelwynn's bow and arrows, which leaned against the tent wall. "I've a nightgown in my bags," she managed, with little energy to add much else.

"Mmm." His fingers brushed her shoulders and her gown fell away, leaving her completely bared to him. Cold air kissed her skin, pebbling her nipples. She almost groaned when his fingers traced some of the marks along her back. "Beautiful," he murmured. Then his hands found her shoulders and his lips found the back of her neck where he kissed her.

She sighed and leaned into him. So good—it felt *so good* to be here in his arms, to have his hands on her. *Only* her. To claim his attention when it was demanded by so many. And yet, he'd always been this way with her, entirely focused as if no one else, nothing else but her, existed.

He's mine, she reminded herself. *Entirely mine.*

A tiny bit of her exhaustion melted away, especially when she felt the generous length of his arousal pressed against her back. "Why am I naked when you're not?" she huffed, teasing.

"A fine point, *Your Majesty*. Shall I undress for you?" He spoke the honorific with fondness, as if he couldn't wait for her to be *his* queen, even if it grated him that she'd been made a queen of the sprites, first.

She turned to stare at him. "Well, I assume you don't plan on sleeping in *that*, do you?"

He barked a laugh and scrubbed a hand over the scars on his face. "Truthfully? I hadn't planned on sleeping at all. There are matters that—"

"I should have guessed! Absolutely not, Talon. Tonight, you are mine. Only mine."

She saw the shiver her words brought. His hands dropped to his sides. He made a sound in the back of his throat that sent tingles straight down to her toes. While they couldn't *seal* their bond until the ceremony—as much as she was plenty fine with sealing it here and now—they could still share a bed.

"You're right, of course. Tonight I will try for some sleep," he amended. Sleep? She hoped he'd try for *other* things too, because if he didn't, she certainly would. Wicked thoughts flooded her mind. A second later, she was decided.

"That's good to hear," she said, inching forward. "May I?" The itch to touch him was driving her mad. She wanted to put her hands on him—everywhere. She wanted to see what her attention would do to him. Wanted to watch him lose control—though, perhaps not entirely, since she didn't want his dragon form bursting free and destroying their command tent.

He gave a tiny nod. She began undoing the straps and belt that held his weapons. Each of her movements was slow. She kept his gaze as she lifted his tunic over his body. She pulled at the ties on his pants and let them fall to the ground. He stepped out. She looked at him then, studying him like she'd done that day they'd gone swimming. Only this time, she was less furtive about it. Instead, she allowed her eyes to drop, feeling her cheeks heat at the sight of him bared before her.

"Do you like what you see, *my queen*? Am I worthy?" His voice was husky, and yet, there was an edge of uncertainty. She wanted to say yes, except she couldn't form a single word. He stepped forward, lifting a questioning hand. She nodded, giving him permission to touch her, only just realizing he'd left the tiara in place and she'd left his crown, too. Two rulers, come together.

He ran his fingers down her chest before circling her nipple with his thumb. Her core blazed to life and a gasp fell from her lips. His eyes darted up, sparks dancing in his sliver depths. She saw the hunger in his expression. Here in the dim light of a single brazier, it danced with a ferocity to match the desperate beast lurking beneath his skin. His other hand went lower, tracing over her stomach, alternating between his fingertips and his knuckles. She was nearly trembling beneath his touch, so very aware of every sensation, but she held still, afraid that if she moved even a centimeter, he'd stop. Lower still his torturous hand crept while the other continued to stroke her breast, to trace frustrating circles, overwhelming her with a growing need.

His gaze stayed fixed on her face, devouring each of the emotions playing out over her features. And then his hand went lower still and her lips parted. She couldn't stop her desperate gasp when his fingers brushed between her legs, confirming that she was just as aroused as he was. "Claire," he growled. "Tell me to stop." He brushed his fingers over her again and she quivered. But she wouldn't—*couldn't* stop. She was aching for this, for him.

So he didn't.

His face crumpled when he pushed a finger inside her, teasing her. That expression did something to her heart. Something beyond the pure pleasure of it, beyond the desperation that left her quivering.

This scarred and broken king had never believed she would want him. Now, as she allowed him to touch the most sacred place on her body, his face illustrated his wonder. Eyes bright and engaged, lips parted, brows knitted. Somehow, despite everything they'd been through, Talon *still* couldn't fathom where his hands were.

It broke something open inside of her, even as he slipped his finger out and pushed it back in. She gasped, reaching out to cling to his broad shoulders. "You are worthy of me, Talon. You are worthy," she whispered, digging her fingers into the muscle bunched beneath her grip.

A dragon's growl rumbled. "You are mine," he said, putting a king's force behind the words. He removed his finger, wrapped both hands around her waist, and pulled her against him. Their mouths crushed together, lips hungry and far from gentle. She wanted that. She wanted his strength, his ferocity.

She twisted her fingers in his hair, pulling hard. Everywhere their bodies touched, heat sizzled between them, making her core flutter, making her toes curl in the rug beneath her feet. His hands went to her thighs and he hoisted her up. She anchored her legs around him. They both gasped then at the feel of their bodies aligned. His chest rumbled, purring.

Finally, he removed their crowns, gently setting them aside, and laid her on the bedding. It felt more like a nest than anything. A nest for a dragon, and she, his prize.

She put her hands on his chest and gave him a small push. He broke their kiss, breathing hard, eyes darting over her face. "Too much?" he asked, concern lacing his voice.

"No." If anything, it was not enough. But she wasn't here to please herself. Not tonight. "You've had your turn. Now it's mine."

At first, he just gazed at her. She gave him another firm push, indicating that he should lie down. He did, watching her with a hooded gaze, devouring her. But there was something else there too, a nervousness she'd never witnessed in him.

She would break him of it. She would show him he had nothing to fear from her.

"Very well my queen," he said, his voice a low dare, "do your worst."

"I plan to," she answered, looming over him, enjoying the feel of his gaze as he devoured her body. She began placing kisses at his neck, simple, butterfly light caresses. He groaned, a hand reaching for her hair, tangling in it. Her core heated from the sound. Gods, he was already this responsive and she hadn't even moved lower yet. She looked up at him, a question in her eyes. He'd one arm propped beneath his head, angling it to better see her. She licked her lips and his eyes darted there immediately. "You will tell me to stop if...if it's too much—?"

"I would never tell you to stop. Touch me *anywhere*."

"Oh, good." A smirk crossed her face. "I plan to. Everywhere, in fact."

He swore under his breath. "I don't deserve you," he croaked at last.

She huffed, leaning down to plant another kiss on his chest, atop one of the scars. "No, you're right. You deserve so much more than even I can give. But I will give you everything, nonetheless." She caught his gaze, his look of utter disbelief. She didn't wait for him to argue. Instead, she began kissing each scar on his chest and then his stomach, until he was growling beneath her, until his bulk of muscle flexed repeatedly, until he was whispering curses beneath his breath. Slowly, ever so slowly, losing control.

What did it take, she wondered, to bring a king to his knees?

This time, she nipped at his skin. He swore again, and twitched against her, tightening his fingers in her hair, rubbing circles against her scalp. She knew exactly where she was going, what she planned to do, but she feared it would be too much for him, that he might stop her even if he claimed he wouldn't.

Sinking lower still, she kissed his muscles, nipped at his skin, letting her hands brace on his thighs as she knelt between his legs. The hair on his skin was coarse. There weren't any scars here that she could see.

When he was thoroughly worked up, she took him in hand, gripping him firmly. His hips bucked. "Gods, Claire," he rasped. That brought her eyes to his and a grin to her lips. But she held him tightly, hard enough to tell him he wasn't going anywhere. Not now. Not at this point.

Her mouth watered. What would he taste like, this dragon of hers? His eyes didn't leave her as she took him into her mouth. He bucked again and groaned, devouring the sight of her through heavy lids. There was so much playing out on his face. Disbelief, wonder, pleasure. This. This was exactly what brought a king to his knees—*this* king, at least. The most powerful king Dragonwall had ever seen.

He was hard as iron, and just as unyielding. Gods, he was delicious. A long groan rumbled from his chest and she felt him tense before his hips flexed again and again, his control breaking. Nothing—*nothing* in the world had ever come close to this kind of power. To this kind of satisfaction. Every single motion she made brought the best kind of progress. So close, she had him *so close.*

Until he toppled right over the edge of the cliff she'd brought him to, dragon wings unfurled, ready to sweep out and catch his plummeting body. There in their nest, she brought Dragonwall's king to his knees. "Claire," he rasped. "I'm... *Gods!*" he roared. She kept her eyes on his. On the pleasure etched into his features. That alone transformed his face into something more beautiful than she'd ever seen. Never—never had she witnessed an expression like this on him.

Slowing his fall, she didn't stop. Not yet. She continued until he was panting, chest heaving. Only then did she pull away, satisfied in a way she could have never imagined.

"I SHOULDN'T HAVE BEEN SO selfish," Talon growled as he rubbed lazy circles along her skin. Tracing her marks. He liked tracing them with his fingertips the way she liked tracing his scars. She was sprawled across his chest, completely exhausted but in the best way. They were still naked, covered in furs and buried in the bedding on the floor. She hadn't let him play with her after she'd finished with him. Her exhaustion had well and truly caught up with her.

But it was more than that.

She wanted Talon to understand that she'd done this for *him.*

Done it without asking anything in return. Especially after seeing the way his mask had cracked when she'd first arrived in his camp, believing she'd chosen the sprites over him. She needed him to understand what he meant to her. Beyond words, this was the way she wanted to prove that. It seemed he now understood.

"There was nothing selfish about it," she murmured against his skin. "Tonight was for you. Besides, I got exactly what I wanted."

"Hmm. What was that?"

"Pleasure. Pleasure at seeing you undone before me, my king. Pleasure at pleasing you before myself. Pleasure at worshiping you."

His breath hitched. "Claire—"

"Hush." She lifted a hand and placed her fingers against his lips, resting her chin on his chest to look at him. "Believe me, there will be plenty more opportunities for you to have your way with me."

"You're *impossible*," he huffed, dragging her up his body until their lips aligned. "Utterly impossible. And frustrating. Maddeningly so. But you're also brave, and kind, and strong. You're beautiful, inside and out. You're powerful. You're...everything. You will make a good queen. You *do* make a good queen."

Tears pricked her eyes. "Thank you, Talon." Her throat closed up.

"While you were gone..." he sighed, his gaze darting between hers. "It was..."

She waited. Opening up was something Talon was never good at. But she knew what he was trying to say.

"It was hard for me too," she whispered, settling back on his chest. "Extremely hard. I missed you all the time. I worried for you."

She felt his exhale against her cheek. "I do not know if I can do it again. Ever."

She hesitated, knowing what she *wanted* to say. That they wouldn't have to. But she couldn't promise that. Nothing about their future was certain. Instead, she settled on, "When we are together, we will always make the most of it." That, at least, she could guarantee.

"We will, indeed. Now...sleep, my queen." His arms tightened around her. She closed her eyes, breathing in the scent of him. Smoke and salt and everything Talon. It was the last thought on her mind before she drifted off, the smile on her lips never quite leaving.

CHAPTER 45
A NEW VOYAGE

Celenore's Coast

Bennett stepped out of the rowboat, glancing over his shoulder to the ship behind him. *Lady Faith* bobbed just beyond the shallows, her crew busy unloading cargo into rowboats. As promised, he'd instructed Cat to remain aboard below deck. He'd remain true to his word—wouldn't mention anything about her presence. Besides, if she encountered anyone who knew her, he didn't want to enact any of his rights to keep her on as crew. Things were simply easier this way. Yes, perhaps he'd become a little selfish. She *was* a good healer. Then again, anyone with a shred of magic was better than what he'd had before.

The other ships weighed anchor along the coast, too. Dwargs had already begun disembarking, doing much the same as his crew. They were far enough from Squall's End that the dragons wouldn't notice them. Hopefully the darkness helped with that, should any of the beasts happen to fly their way.

Mikkin was beside him, along with a few other dwargs. Jamie and Unka were busy helping with the cargo. His boots squished in the sand, making walking harder. He strode forward, approaching the small crowd that had gathered on the beach. "I'll find you later," Mikkin said, branching off to oversee their efforts. He grunted, watching him disappear.

A darker skinned drengr peeled away from the main group, coming straight for him. "You must be Captain Bennett. We've met. Not sure if you remember?"

"Ahh, yes, Lord Bedelth. Pleased to see you again." They grasped forearms. Beaky chose that moment to fly overhead, circle around, then land on his shoulder.

Bedelth nodded, his eyes darting to the bird. His lips tipped up at the corners. "Didn't expect you here, but can't say I'm surprised. Heard you were one of the best merchant captains in Dragonwall. After the delivery of that ice metal, I didn't doubt it."

He lifted his chin, but opted for modesty. "Rumors are rumors. I let my actions speak for themselves."

"Certainly. And what of this?" Bedelth asked. "No problems?"

"Everything went without issue. Took some time getting loaded and out of the port. But smooth sailing after that. As you can see, we've got our vessels unloading now. I was told some of your drengr might help with that. Most of it's being rowed to shore. Could take all night."

Bedelth nodded, his eyes darting over the activity. "I anticipated as much. The armor?"

"You'll have to speak with Lord Dubrael's folk about that," Bennett said. "But I understand there's a fair amount. How do you plan to get it to camp?"

"Camp's not far. We can transport it under the cover of darkness." Bedelth hesitated. "You'll be taking your leave after this? What are your plans next?"

He lifted a shoulder. He had a few ideas, but none that he wanted to voice to the king's right hand. Shields were the innermost circle of Dragonwall's hierarchy. They looked out for their king and their kingdom. His affairs weren't much their concern. "Perhaps we'll see where the seas take me."

To a busy port, first and foremost, since he owed Cat a bunch of ingredients for her work.

Bedelth nodded. "If that's the case, I've a request, if you'd like to hear it. Could be dangerous."

He lifted his brows. "Oh? Danger always has a way of finding me, whether I want it or not. But...you've got my attention."

"There's been talk of Kane visiting Oshea. You heard that?"

"Kane, huh?" He gave nothing away. "And if I have?"

"You are from Oshea, are you not?" At this, Bennett's eyes narrowed. "It's your hair, Captain, your accent, your skin, the shape of your features. Don't worry, I haven't spent my time tracking down information on you. A lucky guess is all."

"Right. Well then, what exactly are you asking?"

Bedelth rubbed the back of his neck, then motioned him away from the others. He followed, until they were out of earshot. The activity on the beach had already increased as more and more rowboats arrived, unloading. "What's the likelihood you might nip across the Dragonfire Sea? Pay Oshea a visit?"

He rubbled the stubble along his chin. "I don't often travel that way. Try to avoid it when I can. I guess it depends on the pay and the need."

"Right. The need is great. As for the pay, I'll pay in advance, half now, half when you return. We want to know why Kane's been traveling there. What he's got up his sleeve. I'd imagine you can get some of the folks there to talk? Sailors are a chatty sort, are they not?"

He grunted. "When you get 'em drunk enough. Yes. How much you talking?" Bedelth removed a bag of coins, handed it over, allowing Bennett to heft it. "A fair bit, then?"

"Aye. A fair bit. This is important to our king. You can be discreet, yes?"

"Quite." He hesitated. Was he really going to accept this so easily? He hadn't quite charted their next path beyond getting supplies for Cat. He figured he'd just see what work needed doing, what cargo needed shipping. But this...

It was good pay. Possible danger. But danger that would take him out of Dragonwall for a time. And wasn't that a good thing? He had a feeling that the events taking place in the kingdom were about to get dicy. So yes, maybe this would be a good thing.

"I accept," he decided, pocketing the bag of coins.

"Good." Bedelth hesitated. "What?"

"Might have to make a few stops for supplies first. Got a...well, never mind."

"Your business is your own. We've got matters of our own here —Fort Squall, namely. It will take you a couple of months, I'm sure, before you find answers. Return to Kastali Dun when you've gathered some intel. I'll see that the king pays you the rest of what you're owed. In the meantime, that should be enough for the journey, for your crew, and bribes, to boot."

"More than enough," he answered, his mind already running through preparations.

"Excellent. Well, then." Bedelth backed up several steps. He saluted him with two fingers, then turned on his heel, not bothering with goodbyes. Bennett watched him go, squishing awkwardly through the sand. Was there a way to trudge through sand with dignity? Not usually. A grin stretched across his features. There had to be several hundred gold coins in that bag. Enough dragons to make this journey well worthwhile.

THE SUNRISE across the coast was vibrant and peaceful. They'd managed to unload everything. Some of the ships were already departing. The dwargs had formed ranks and would be marching their way to camp on foot, as would the drengr who'd come to help with the cargo. Wagons were loaded up, horses hitched. It would be a slow transport, a couple of days to arrive at camp. But that wasn't Bennett's problem.

He stood on the beach facing Mikkin, Jamie, Unka, and the dwarg, Berbik. "Well, I suppose this is goodbye for now," he said, taking Mikkin's shoulder.

"You sure you won't stay? Sail up the coast and meet us closer to camp? Would be fun to share in the glory of battle."

He grunted. "I face enough battles at sea. No, thank you. Glory's all yours."

"Figured you'd say that. Had to ask anyway."

Bennett nodded, then he eyed Mikkin a moment longer. "I really hope you find what you're looking for. I hope you regain some of what you lost in the days to come."

"Thank you."

"Form up!" came the call from farther up the beach.

"*Form up! Form up!*" came the resulting cry, high above. Damned bird.

"Well, I guess that's our signal," Mikkin said.

He released the man's shoulder, then clasped hands with Jamie. "You'll take good care of him, I hope."

"Of course, Captain. He's become like family to me now." Jamie's eyes glossed over.

Bennett nodded. "Perhaps you'll find your parents in Squall's End, lad. I sure hope so."

"Me too," Jamie said.

He looked at Unka and gave the goblin a curt bow. "Hope things go all right for you, Unka." He still didn't trust the creature, but Cat had taken a liking to him, had even asked if he'd stay on as crew—without seeking her captain's permission, no less—but Unka had declined. He had family waiting for him in Pavv.

"Thank you, Captain. Tell mistress I will miss her."

He nodded, turning to Berbik. "Farewell, Master dwarg. I wish you all the best."

"Thank you, Captain," Berbik said with his guttural accent.

He gave them all a final bow, then turned and left, retreating to the remaining rowboat waiting to take him back to *Lady Faith*. It was a quick trip, and soon he was on the deck of his ship where he waited and watched. Watched as the procession of supplies and dwargs wound its way up the beach, past the bluffs, and out of sight.

"Well," Jonah said, coming to stand beside him. "Another journey, another job complete. You still interested in heading to port.

We could stop in The Scattered Islands. I'm sure there'll be plenty of supplies for Cat."

"That there will, my friend. That there will." He turned to Jonah, removed the bag of gold from his pocket, and handed it over.

Jonah's eyes went wide. He pulled loose the drawstring. Then his jaw dropped. "But...there must be...?"

"Probably a couple hundred. I'll need to go below and count them."

"But...what for?"

"Our next job, of course. Scattered Islands first, but after that, we sail for Oshea."

"Osh—" Jonah cut himself off to swear under his breath.

"Yes, indeed. We've got a long road ahead of us. I'll tell you about it below. Ready the crew to depart, get everything in order, then come to my cabin."

"Aye, aye, Captain. At once."

Jonah began shouting orders. Bennett took only a moment to see his crew burst to life, then strode across the deck and slipped below. He found Cat sitting at his desk when he entered his cabin. Her jaw was tense.

"Everything went well?" she asked. That she cared so much surprised him.

"It did, indeed." He tossed the bag of coins on his desk. Her eyes locked on it, mouth going slack. "Yes, that is exactly what you think it is. Coin. Plenty of it."

"But..." Her hand darted out to grab it. He used it as an excuse to touch her, snatching her wrist, forcing her to release the bag. "I was only going to *look*," she complained.

"Mmm-hmm." He brushed a thumb over her pulse absent-mindedly before releasing her. "I'll count them in a moment. Came from Lord Bedelth. We've got our next assignment." Her shrewd gaze darted over his face. "After we get your supplies, we set sail for Oshea. I told you I'd show you the world, Kitty Cat. Did I not?"

This time, she didn't bother scratching him with her claws. Instead, her lips parted in surprise. "Oshea?" she repeated.

"Indeed. Oshea. We've been charged with gathering intel. I'm wondering how *you* might play into that. A pretty girl like you? You wouldn't happen to be good at coercing information from people, would you?" He already knew the answer.

"What's in it for me?" she asked, leaning back, crossing her arms. He allowed his eyes to dart down to the bag of coins, pointedly. "Fine," she said. "Done. What else?"

"Oh, that'll be all for now."

A wicked smile took form on her lips. "Something tells me I'm going to enjoy this."

"I certainly hope so," he said, barking a laugh. "Now, get gone. I have gold to count. And no, I don't need your help doing it. Go."

Reluctantly, she scooted her chair back and stood. At the door, she paused and looked over her shoulder, a wicked gleam in her eyes. "I look forward to working with you, Captain." And damned if he didn't believe it. He couldn't help his chuckle as she slipped out and closed the door behind her.

CHAPTER 46
FLYING

Claire circled the camp with her ladies, her guards falling in behind. Gods, how the hell had she acquired such a ridiculously large entourage? Okay, she knew exactly how. Now, she truly felt like a queen, not that she wanted to. But there was no more avoiding it.

Desaree walked at her side, picking at her hands. "Stop that," she scolded. "Don't break the blisters until they're ready." Des dropped her hands, hiding them in the folds of her skirt. "I can put more bandages on, if it will help deter you," she added.

"You're a queen now." Des tutted. "You don't need to bandage my hands."

"I'd be bandaging them as your friend, not your queen, and I wouldn't *have* to, had you not been so foolish."

Desaree's face fell. "I already said I was sorry," she mumbled.

Claire sighed. "Yes, I know. I'm just...in a mood."

"She wasn't the only one who broke the rules," Saffra said from just behind them, where she and Jocelyn walked. "She just happened to be the one who took the blame for it."

"Well, isn't that noble?" Claire said, shooting Saffra a harmless glare over her shoulder.

Saffra shrugged. "It *was* her idea."

"Will you lot just behave?" Jocelyn tisked. "Now, tell us, Claire, what has you so irritated?"

"It's her time of the month," Des answered for her, not loud enough for anyone beyond their immediate party to hear. Her sprite handmaidens, who walked just behind Saffra and Jocelyn, had already given her plenty of cloth, having anticipated that her period was coming. "It started last night," Des continued, "so I imagine she's irritated about it because it means she and a certain *someone* can't have any fun together."

"That's not why I'm irritated," she grumbled. Okay, it was just a bit, but it was the mild cramps, back pain, and simply the hormonal flux that accompanied. Mostly the last part, which left her moody. After all, she had things she could take for the pain, but it didn't feel awful enough to ingest anything.

She'd known it was coming—was several days late, as it was. What irritated her was that it didn't wait a few days more. She'd only just returned to Talon, and now this? Ugh.

The morning after she'd arrived, after she and Talon had shared their romantic night together, she woke refreshed, but to an empty bed. Talon had already been up before dawn. "*Talon?*" She had opened her mind to him, searching.

"*I'm here, love,*" came his answer. "*I didn't want to wake you. There's breakfast on the table, and a gaggle of women lurking outside the tent, waiting for you to wake.*"

That had been motivation enough to dress and slip out. What transpired was a joyous reunion filled with hugging and tears. Desaree, Jocelyn, Saffra, and Tamara had updated her on everything she'd missed. They'd sat for hours, until breakfast stretched into the midday meal. That was when her spriten handmaidens had come looking for her. She'd introduced everyone, and much to her delight, they hit it off right away.

She'd worried that Desaree might feel...threatened? Like her job was at risk. But there was none of that.

The rest of the day had passed in a blur. There were plenty of preparations to keep them busy. And apparently, Desaree wasn't off the hook. She worked with Jocelyn in the cook's tent, helping prepare meals that were delivered to various tents.

During that time, Claire and Tamara stole bits of time together, or she and Saffra, depending on what their obligations were. Sometimes Tamara was busy with Byron, overseeing fort matters. Other times, Saffra was off utilizing her mage powers to assist with ailments, tent construction, and anything else that required a magical touch. The dwargs would be returning with Bedelth soon and they'd need more sleeping arrangements.

Now, here they were, the second morning after her return. They finally had some time together, except for Tamara, who was off working with Byron. They used this time to circle the camp, getting fresh air and a moment of quiet reprieve before more of their duties started.

"If I had to guess," Saffra said, "our king was probably so busy last night he didn't even sleep. Regardless of Claire's...lady time."

She exhaled. "Yes, you guessed correctly." They passed a group of drengr who spotted her and bowed. She didn't miss the way their eyes lingered over her markings, over the guards trailing behind. It was important that everyone see her and realize she wasn't some mythical being. That sprites didn't simply hide away in their forest all the time. She bowed her head in acknowledgement, then offered a warm smile. That brought a few hesitant smiles in return.

"It's not that I expect Talon in my bed," she said after they passed. "I understand his responsibilities better than I care to. It's just...he can't go nonstop and never rest. It's important that he takes care of himself—mentally, you know?" She hesitated, then snorted. "What am I thinking? I doubt Talon has ever really taken time for his mental health."

"You would know better than us," Desaree said. "Perhaps you should insist he take some time for himself. What sort of thing makes him happy? Besides you, obviously."

"Flying," she said without thought. "He loves flying. Des—

that's genius. Yes, I'll insist he and I go flying this evening, after it gets dark. I'll have to change into something a bit more...utilitarian," she added, glancing over her shoulder at her handmaidens. "Perhaps what I wore on our journey?"

"*Neem, Ayas Drollaya,*" Selphie said, a gleam to her eyes. Switching to the common tongue, she added, "We have already had the garments cleaned and tended."

"We will get you ready after the evening meal," Meira added, looking pleased by the prospect.

The rest of the day passed in another blur.

"Have you finished with Byron yet?"

They'd eaten and Talon had rushed off to more obligations. Meira and Selphie had helped her out of her queenly gown and into her traveling clothes, but even these were embellished to look worthy of her title. Since the last time she'd worn them, Selphie had added silver threads and beads, obtained from gods only knew where, to make everything look good. They had also insisted on doing her hair up in an elegant chignon with her tiara. She wished Des could have helped, but Des was back to her duties in the cook's tent.

"*I'm just about finished,*" came Talon's reply.

"*Good, then we're going flying.*"

"*We are?*"

"*We are. Whatever you have next, postpone it an hour or two. I know everyone has a right to your time, but you also have a right to your sanity. So we're taking a break. If you won't sleep, the least you can do is give yourself a few hours here and there.*"

"*Very well,* Your Majesty. *If you're issuing a command, I had better follow it.*"

She smiled, turning to her handmaidens. "Thank you, both of you. I'll be with Talon for the rest of the evening. Feel free to..."

"To?" Selphie lifted a brow.

"Well," she huffed a laugh. "I suppose there's not much to do here, is there?"

"I shall embroider more of your gowns, and perhaps add a few more beads," Meira announced.

"Oh, yes, perhaps the green one," Selphie added. The two of them clasped hands, putting their heads together as if they were making the most secretive plans, and walked off. She blinked after them. Were they...? She'd not noticed before, but now that she looked closer...

She knew sprites held hands, but these two seemed more intimate than that.

A smile touched her lips as she exited the tent in search of Talon. She didn't have to go far to find him. He was already striding towards her. "My queen," he bowed, the gesture elegant and far too unnecessary.

She turned to her queen's guard, who'd been posted outside the tent waiting for her. Her eyes caught on Jeanine and they shared a grin before she dismissed them for the night.

They brandished their fists over their chests, bowing in unison before disbanding.

"Quite the show," Talon said, eyeing them as they went. "A bit formal for your tastes, no?"

"Oh, be quiet. Come on. I've been dying for some fresh air. And the stars are out tonight."

"Yes, let's go." He led her out of the camp.

A thrill settled deep in her bones. The intimacy of what was to come left her giddy. It felt like ages since she'd shared Talon's mind. Now he would finally see everything that had happened over the past few months. And she knew with certainty he planned to comb through it. That meant she could no longer hide exactly what had happened with Kane, even though she'd toned down the details when she'd told him. Now he'd know just how much pain she'd been in.

She swallowed the lump in her throat. Okay, maybe this hadn't been the best idea after all? This was supposed to calm him, and if he saw everything from the forest, it would likely agitate him. But, they'd be here sooner or later.

Transforming, Talon's scales sprouted and his body grew. She watched, ignoring the tears that welled in her eyes. Seeing him again like this overwhelmed her in so many ways. "Have I told you recently how magnificent you are?" At her words, a pleased hum rumbled his chest. "I've often wondered if it's in a dragon's nature to be vain. What do you think? If so, I ought to pepper you with more compliments for the rest of the night—perhaps the rest of forever? Just for your ego, you know? Because I wouldn't want a vain creature such as yourself to be deprived."

He huffed. A puff of smoke left his nostrils. *"Just get on my back already,"* he said, bombarding her mind with the loud command.

She couldn't delay any longer. She did as he said, settling into the crook where his neck met his shoulders. As soon as her hands touched his scales, their minds melded. A sense of rightness passed over her. A sense of completeness that had her sighing into him.

He didn't wait, crouching and leaping from the ground. An undignified squeal of delight burst from her. It had been ages since they'd flown together. She hadn't realized exactly how much she missed it until now.

"I missed it too," Talon said. He banked, making a sharp turn to take them south, away from their camp, and away from possible prying wild dragons that might be lurking in the northern skies.

Talon's mind was filled with fatigue. She noticed it immediately, slipping in, running mental fingers over the dark formations that made up the lava fields of his psyche. He purred in response as she caressed his thoughts. Soon, he was doing the same to her, easing her emotions.

"May I look over your memories of the past few months?" He asked.

The fact that he asked left her warm. *"They are yours to browse,"* she said. *"We are mates. You need not ask. Not ever."*

She had nothing to hide from him and never wanted to. He hesitated, then accepted. There were so many things that didn't require words. Most of what they thought could be conveyed in emotions and feelings. The mind was a strange place.

She saw him flicking through everything. Felt his rage when he experienced her pain at Kane's hands, felt his relief when Taylynn appeared. Then she felt his pride, when he saw the way her magic had grown. He continued to pick through everything, up through the moments where she confronted Jade, took her throne, and celebrated the equinox. *"The stars were a nice touch,"* he said. *"Taylynn is right. You make a splendid queen."*

She beamed at his praise.

The only thing she kept to herself was Koldis. His mate bond with Taylynn wasn't her secret to tell. She locked it in a box and when Talon brushed past it, he didn't stop to ask. He respected her enough to know that if it was hidden, there was a reason for that.

There was no need to talk about the events of the past few months, or what he'd seen. Everything that he wanted to say was conveyed in his thoughts and hers. Emotions and feelings passed between them like firecrackers, lighting up their mind in bouts of sparks. What would take hours lasted minutes, and minutes, seconds. It was such a delightful way to communicate. The best part was, there was never fear of miscommunication. There was no hiding what they felt, what they meant to convey. No misinterpreting the other's words.

Minutes stretched into an hour, and then two, as Talon carried them in a wide circuit south of camp. She felt his body and mind relax with every sweep of his wings. Felt her joy rise with his. This was where he loved to be. And having her with him only made it better.

There was no predicting what the future held, but one thing was certain. As long as Talon had wings, there was a place the two of them could come together, a place void of obligations and responsibilities. Here in the sky, they could always be free. They could always belong to only each other.

CHAPTER 47
THE KING'S SUPPORT

Koldis studied his king as they walked through the camp. "Forgive me, Your Majesty, but matehood looks good on you."

His words made King Talon falter. Then a bark of a laugh burst from the king's lips—such a rare thing, laughter from his king. "It's *that* obvious?"

"Well, you're not scowling as deeply as usual, so there's that. And you look rather pleased with yourself. Much less grumbling, too. Oh, and you're not snapping at everyone. I take it Claire's appearance here in camp was well received?"

"Better received than *yours,* if you don't stop questioning me about it," Talon growled. But there wasn't hostility in his voice.

"Hah! I knew it. She certainly has enough charm to conquer even the hardest of hearts."

"Careful, Koldis, you're on thin enough ice as it is."

A nervous laugh escaped his lips. He held up his hands. "Only teasing, my king. No harm intended."

They passed several drengr as they made their way out of camp, to the fields beyond. After a tedious journey, they'd arrived only a few hours prior. It had been a relief to see Claire in the command tent, even if Talon had been nowhere in sight. The king had been occupied up until now.

"Come, tell me of Esterpine," Talon said. "Claire has shown me all that transpired, but something tells me *your* perspective will offer additional insight."

He hesitated, bracing himself. "I suppose it might."

He set about relaying everything that had happened, from the moment they set foot in the spriten city, to when they had departed. He even let a few hints slip about Taylynn, though nothing that would directly allude to their bond. He wanted to discuss that separately. And only after the hammer blow that was coming—

"You truly believe there was nothing you could have done to protect Claire against Kane, to protect *your queen* from him?" Talon said, an edge creeping into his voice that left him flinching. There it was. Exactly what he'd been waiting for. "I sent you to *guard* her, Koldis, to protect her."

He stopped walking and swallowed. His shoulders fell when he faced his king and saw the expression there. The disappointment. "I take full responsibility, Your Majesty. You sent me in your stead, and I failed to protect her. I cannot even bring myself to think of what might have—"

"Well, I can!" Talon said, losing control of his stoic demeanor. "I can and I *have*. Every moment since she has returned. Every time I see her and think of what might have happened if he'd succeeded. If he'd taken her to Shadowkeep. Nothing, and I mean *nothing* would have stopped me from flying north, from abandoning my post to save her. Nothing would have stopped me from—" He cut himself short and cursed under his breath.

Shame washed over Koldis. His skin burned. He hung his head and quietly said, "I am sorry, Talon. I have failed you." He rubbed his neck, trying to palm the tense muscles that bunched with the strain of his failure.

The king sighed, studying him. "I saw it clear enough in her mind. She would not permit you to accompany her into the forest. I understand how stubborn she is. How headstrong. I should not be angry with you, and yet, I cannot be angry with her either. But I *need* to be angry—at something, at someone."

"You have every right to be angry with me."

"No. I..." Talon shook his head. "As hard as it is, I am doing what I can to let it go." He huffed a laugh. "She even told me—she told me that if I tried to blame you, or if I didn't forgive you, I would have *her* to answer to. She protects you, Koldis. Your queen loves and protects you." Talon shook his head as if he couldn't quite believe it. Truthfully, neither could Koldis. To have Claire's love...

"None of us deserve her," Talon added. "Least of all me. But...I am trying. I am *trying* to be worthy of her."

Warmth blossomed in Koldis's chest. He placed his hand on Talon's arm. "You are worthy of her, more than you think. And if it helps you feel better..." He trailed off. Was this the right time? What if this was the *only* time? What if they didn't get another chance? Impending battle had a way of making everything feel more imminent. Had a way of making a person reveal things they might never say out loud.

"What is it?" Talon's brows pulled together.

He opened and closed his mouth. "Taylynn," he said at last.

A look of wary mistrust crossed Talon's face. "What about her?"

"I...I only meant that I am beginning to see what it feels like to feel unworthy of one's mate."

Talon gazed blankly at him, then his eyes widened. He took a step back, pulling his arm free from Koldis's grip. "You...she...*her?*"

Something defensive flared up in his chest but he pushed it down, keeping his voice calm as he said, "You do not approve, my king?" He arched a brow in challenge.

A crazed laugh fell from Talon's lips. But his king was putting the pieces together. Putting the clues in order. Clues that Koldis had dropped in his retelling. The mentions of her, of their randomly crossing paths, of her advice to him. Talon scrubbed a hand over his face. "Do you care for her?"

"She's my mate, Talon." Answer enough, wasn't it? Or...was it?

"Answer the question."

"I...yes. I didn't want to. I hated her at first, and she...I think she felt the same. But that changed. Now I want her more than I have ever wanted anything." He flexed his fingers at his sides.

Talon nodded, studying him with a gaze that left his skin itching. A shrewd gaze. A king's gaze. Then the rarest thing happened. A genuine smile, filled with warmth, stretched across Talon's lips, pulling at his scars. Before he could breathe a sigh of relief, Talon pulled him into a tight embrace and clapped him on the back. "Gods. What is the world coming to? First Claire and now this? Taylynn? Next we know, Jovari will come running with a mate on his arm, and Bedelth..." The king pulled away and held him at arm's length, happiness dancing in his silver gaze.

Koldis could only gaze back at Talon and blink. "You're not... but...my oath. How do I...what do I...?"

Talon clapped him on the shoulder. "A year ago, my answer would be different than it is today. I suppose we both have Claire to thank for that."

"And..." He swallowed. "What *is* your answer?"

"Take her. Take her as your mate, if you wish. But don't *for the gods* think I'm letting you out of your oath to serve me, to advise me, to be by my side when I need you. You're still my shield. We still have a fort to reclaim." That thought alone had them both sobering. "And then there's the matter of her queenship."

The elation he felt rising in his chest was quickly swallowed up. "I have no idea what to do about that." He ran a hand through his hair. Perhaps his king might have some advice.

As if reading his mind, Talon huffed and shook his head. "Let's get through one thing at a time, Koldis. Apparently, it's either my mate or yours, and I'll be damned if I jeopardize Dragonwall's future by allowing Claire to be queen of the sprites a moment longer than necessary. She's got enough on her plate with Kane—"

"I know. I know." He held up his hands, calming his king. "I would never ask that. Taylynn will be queen. She and I have already discussed it. While it's not ideal, we will make the most of the time we have together while we can. She's old, Talon. She's accepted that my lifespan will supersede hers. That when and if we mate, she'll only live as long as I do."

"And she's okay with that?"

Koldis shrugged. "As far as I know."

A smile twitched on Talon's lips. "Perhaps there will be a baby Taylynn that might take over for—"

"Don't you dare!" he growled, heat, anger...and yet, a smidge of desire taking root within him. "You might be my king but nothing will keep me from taking you to the ground if you so much as *utter* another word."

He couldn't let the thought take root. Couldn't bear to think about a child with Taylynn when so much was still uncertain. That way would breed disappointment.

They held each other's gazes, breathing hard, before they both burst into laughter. It felt good. So good to be able to laugh in spite of everything happening. Here and now there were no titles, they were simply friends.

He hooked his arm around Talon's neck. "Come, let us continue our walk while we commiserate over all the ways we have been entirely and utterly ensnared by our mates." He dragged them both forward.

And they had, hadn't they? Been entirely and utterly ensnared by their mates? It was a sobering thought, and yet, a hopeful one. It meant that no matter what happened, when it was time to take Squall's End, they had mates who cared for them, perhaps even loved them. Things in the days to come would be difficult. A true test to their abilities. But they would face those things nonetheless, and fight for a peaceful world free of Kane and his manipulation. A world where they could be with the mates they loved and cherish their bonds. A world where they could truly be happy.

ALSO BY MELISSA MITCHELL

The Dragonwall Series

Talon the Black

Reyr the Gold

Verath the Red

The Lady Witch Series

Wielder's Prize

Wielder's Bond

Wielder's Might

Witch's Ruin

Royals of Dragonwall Series

For the Crown

Stand Alone Titles

Blood and Ballet

Acknowledgements

With the suspension of my Dragonwall Series, getting this book to publication was a long time coming. So I would first like to thank all my loyal readers who have been desperate to get this in their hands. Your patience means the world to me. It's finally here. I can hardly believe it myself.

To my husband for being so supportive of my writing endeavors. Continuing to cheer me on and share in my excitement as my writing career blossoms. Thank you for everything!

To the many folks who helped make this book a reality. Jeanine Croft for her wonderful case laminate design, Kateryna Vitkovska for the beautiful illustrations, Ashley Jürgens for the lovely map, and Katrina Cozens for thorough edits.

To my Wattpad readers for sticking with me through the years. I know this book is a favorite, and I hope I did it justice. You guys give me so much fuel with all your comments and support. I loved reading your thoughts during the development of this book. Thank you!

Finally, to you, the reader. Thank you for picking this one up. If you're still here, then I guess I'm doing something "write"! Hehe. Get it!

ABOUT THE AUTHOR

Melissa Mitchell is a physics Ph.D. by day and fantasy writer by night. She is a California transplant, who moved to Georgia with her husband and dogs to chase her engineering career in illumination design. Aside from her love of tea, wine, desserts, and writing, she loves reading, ice skating, playing piano, baking, and bullet journaling (in no particular order).

Visit her online at: authormelissamitchell.com

instagram.com/melissa.nicole.mitchell